SONGS
FOR THE
BUTCHER'S
DAUGHTER

SONGS
FOR THE
BUTCHER'S
DAUGHTER

PETER
MANSEAU

SIMON &
SCHUSTER

London · New York · Sydney · Toronto

A CBS COMPANY

First published in the United States of America by Free Press,
a division of Simon & Schuster, Inc, 2008
First published in Great Britain by Simon & Schuster UK Ltd, 2008
A CBS COMPANY

1 3 5 7 9 10 8 6 4 2

Simon & Schuster UK Ltd
1st Floor
222 Gray's Inn Road
London WC1X 8HB

Simon & Schuster Australia
Sydney

A CIP catalogue record for this book
is available from the British Library

ISBN: 978-1-8473-7313-7

Printed in the UK by CPI Mackays, Chatham ME5 8TD

נאָך אַ מאַנוסקריפּט, און נאָך אַ מאַנוסקריפּט,
געוויקלט, געבנדן, פֿאַרקניפּט—
אותיות אין אותיות פֿאַרליבט.

a manuscript, and another manuscript,
entwined, bound together, wrapping each other—
letters and more letters, in love.

—*from "The God of Israel" by A. Leyeles*

TRANSLATOR'S NOTE

THE COLLABORATION BETWEEN ITSIK MALpesh and myself is perhaps one of the more unlikely literary associations in recent memory. At the time of our first meeting, in the fall of 1996, he was already a nonagenarian, and I was just twenty-one years old. He was a Russian Jew reared in an era when the czar's days were numbered; I was a Catholic boy from Boston born at the end of the Nixon administration. Having endured seventy tumultuous years in the United States, Malpesh had experienced far more of this nation's history than I had, yet he nonetheless considered me the authority on our common culture, about which he was voraciously inquisitive. A five-minute conversation with Malpesh might include questions concerning public access television, North American birds, desktop publishing software, and subscription rates for *Sports Illustrated,* all delivered in a well-practiced English still thick with the Yiddish he preferred.

During one visit, he quizzed me on the price of season tickets to Camden Yards, assuming I would have an answer readily at hand.

"Mr. Malpesh, how could I possibly know that?" I asked.

Before responding he studied me with troubled eyes, as if at his age stating the obvious was almost too much to bear.

"Because you were born in this language," he said.

In describing the circumstances through which our improbable partnership came about, it might be useful at the outset to provide some background. Certainly this will exceed the boundaries that most readers expect in a translator's note, and to those who object I must first apologize and then agree: Yes, the work of Itsik Malpesh can and should be read on its own. As both historical document and the life's work of a singular man, it deserves scrutiny on its own merits. In the chapters that follow I have rendered Malpesh's manuscripts as fully and faithfully as I have been able, making them available for the first time to the wider public. Malpesh's story hardly requires elaboration. "It is what it is," as he liked to say. (Or more colorfully: "The rest is commentary, and commentary is shit.") Purists may feel free to skip this translator's note, as well as the others, wherever they appear.

That said, it bears mentioning that Malpesh was a peculiar fellow who made peculiar choices. In fact, the notion of *choice* (religious, linguistic, sexual, cultural), and its lack, was so central to his work that I believe the particulars of who Malpesh *chose* to be his translator (however limited his options may have been) might shed some light on the man himself. And so, admitting that this statement implies a wishful hubris that the poet himself would appreciate, I must insist that Malpesh's story begins with me.

THOUGH IT WAS STILL six months before I would meet him, our connection began during the summer after my last semester of college in western Massachusetts. It was at this time that I took a job with an unusual organization. I wish it could be said that my employment resulted from careful consideration of many lucrative offers, but the more common truth is that I had borrowed my way through school and, newly graduated, found myself suddenly burdened with debt.

I had been a religion major, with a focus on scriptural languages, and upon receiving my degree felt qualified to do—nothing. Early on, I'd considered attending seminary after graduation, but in the course of my studies with the religion faculty I had somehow lost my faith. Worse, I started to wonder if I'd ever truly had it.

And so I looked for work. Hoping to apply what few market-able skills I'd acquired in school, I used my undergraduate's He-brew to check into options in Israel. I was eager to travel, open to adventure, but as a non-Jew, I found that my possible motives were a cause for concern. In more than one interview I was asked a question that I would eventually hear word for word from Malpesh himself: Are you some sort of missionary? To my prospective em-ployers I tried to explain that if I was to convert anyone it would only be to a nebulous, wishy-washy agnosticism, but this honest answer did not earn me many callbacks.

I had no better luck finding a position closer to home. My de-gree was from a public university in a state overrun by Ivy League graduates. Assessing the competition I might come up against for jobs in Boston, a counselor at the university career center advised me to look into the telemarketing field.

It was with mounting desperation that I turned to the local want ads one day and discovered that the Jewish Cultural Organi-zation, a small nonprofit located just down the road from my uni-versity, was looking for help. They needed someone to sort books in their warehouse; the only requirement was knowledge of the Hebrew alphabet. When I applied, no one asked if I was a mission-ary, but neither did they ask if I was a Jew. Because I was available immediately, I was offered the job.

The next week, I saw right away the reason they were in such a rush to fill the position. The primary mission of the JCO was collecting books; they received donations of used Judaica from all over the world. Walking into the warehouse, I realized they had succeeded themselves nearly into submission. Boxes of books blocked the entrance and tow-ered over the windows, keeping out all natural light. And, I was told, more books were arriving every day. Hundreds of them. It would be my responsibility to unpack the boxes and get the place in order.

It was not quite what I'd expected. I'd been boning up on my He-brew, supposing that increased facility with the language would help me catalog or otherwise familiarize myself with a warehouse full of Jewish books. I had told myself the work might be not so different from graduate school, which interested me as a potential religion scholar but remained beyond my financial reach. Working with books all day, I imagined, could be a way of continuing my education while getting a paycheck.

As I discovered my first day on the job, however, the books weren't in Hebrew. They were in Yiddish, a language that has about as much in common with its ancient cousin as English does with Latin. Sharing an alphabet and a small common vocabulary, Hebrew and Yiddish appear identical to the untrained eye, but they are entirely distinct. My job, I realized, was to organize books I could not understand.

Standing among miles of gray metal shelves, I saw that the books in my charge might as well have been cartons of cigarettes or bars of soap. I'd become a warehouse clerk, nothing more.

Nevertheless it was a job. And if the work was sometimes tedious—open boxes, sort books, shelve books—it did allow a fair amount of autonomy. The cultural organization's business offices, where most of its twenty or so employees worked, were located in another building across town, which meant that, day after day, I was mostly on my own.

And yet I soon realized I was not on my own at all. I was surrounded by boxes of stories. Opening them, I never knew what I would find. There would be books, of course: some in excellent condition, others worth less than the postage that had brought them. But that wasn't all. Hiding under layers of cardboard and packing tape, cushioned with rolled-up grocery bags, there were also mezuzahs and yarmulkes, tefillin and prayer shawls, kiddush cups and Seder plates. One morning I discovered a tiny plastic bar mitzvah boy, the kind that might stand atop a kosher cake. I found all manner of discarded religious items, the presence of which suggested that their owners had either died or given up on God.

Judging from the age of the books with which this spiritual bric-a-brac usually arrived—most had been printed in the 1920s and '30s, the years of Malpesh's prime—both possibilities seemed likely.

Before long, I got a sense of the kinds of people whose books were dropped on the warehouse's doorstep each day. They were, as Malpesh once described his contemporaries, "bastards of history, New World spawn of the Old World's dotage, lovers of ghosts, bards of forgotten tongues." And I began to like them.

It took longer to get a sense of the books themselves. To find each volume its proper place in the collection, I only had to read the first few letters of its title. Beyond that, what was contained between the covers, or who had created it, didn't matter much as far as the operations of the warehouse were concerned.

One grasps for meaning in the face of monotony, however. As I picked books from boxes hour after hour, I attempted to pronounce the names of their authors. Some, I would later learn, were the great masters of Yiddish literature: I. L. Peretz, Chaim Grade, Mendele Mocher Sforim. Once or twice I must have handled *Lider fun der shoykhets tochter*, the one published work of Malpesh himself. Yet I knew nothing of him then, nor of his peers. Their names were only sounds in a foreign tongue; the books they adorned seemed impenetrable.

But then I set my mind to it. Each day I spent a couple of hours opening boxes and finding the right places for the books in the maze of shelves. The rest of my time I devoted to puzzling over what was inside their covers.

By the month's end, while I had unpacked far fewer boxes than my employer hoped I would, I'd begun to learn the language.

Thereafter, making sense of the books in my care became for me an obsessive preoccupation; not least of all because, as I learned to read, I was learning also about a culture immensely appealing to a fallen Catholic like myself. For if Yiddish writers had one thing in common, I discovered, it was the kind of passionate irreligiosity that can only

5

be found among those who'd been born, raised, and sickened by spiritual tradition. In a poem by Malpesh's contemporary Jacob Glatshteyn, a line struck me as few ever have: *The God of my unbelief is magnificent.*

Like so much of what I would find in the warehouse's holdings, these words spoke to me as if they'd come from a catechism for those whom faith had failed.

DESPITE MALPESH'S LIFELONG INTEREST in the process of translation, he often lamented the fact that rendering his poems and stories in another tongue might transform not just his work, but his soul. "When a writer becomes unreadable to himself," he wrote, "who is to say that he remains who he was? Where is the evidence? His words are like a donkey born to a dog."

He never gave a thought, however, at least not one he recorded or shared with me, to the inevitable change that occurs not just in the writer who is translated, but in the one who translates him as well.

There is more to tell about how I came to be the translator of Itsik Malpesh, and about the great joke of the fates this arrangement would come to seem. If he had not thought I was something other than what I am when we met, would he have shown his work to me at all? Did the fact that I was hiding who I was influence my understanding of the life—and crimes—I discovered in his writings? And if it influenced my understanding, has it also influenced my translation? How could it not?

These questions will have to wait, however. Let us turn now to the writings themselves, and to the day I first encountered them.

Not long after first learning his name, I found myself standing in the third-floor Baltimore apartment that Itsik Malpesh had occupied for fifty years. For the duration of this initial visit, he sat all but ignoring me, peering out his kitchen window. A neighboring building was scheduled for demolition, and he—a small man in a cardigan sweater, wearing glasses, as he described them, "as thick as toilet lids"—sat by the window waiting to watch the show.

He pulled himself away just long enough to shuffle to a closet and retrieve a stack of hardback accounting ledgers. When he dropped them before me, I saw that their pages were filled not with numbers but meticulous Yiddish script. Twenty-two notebooks, each labeled with a letter of the Hebrew alphabet, they amounted to a handwritten encyclopedia of his days.

Now that I have read them all, I know the many ways in which the tale of Malpesh's life resonates with the events that led me to his door: a failed love affair, lies of faith, threat of scandal, and, most important, the promise of deliverance through the translation of words.

That day, though, sitting in a nonagenarian's kitchen, watching him gaze out over a demolition site to pass the time, who would have guessed that a life so full had been withstood by the frail frame enveloped by his sweater's tattered wool? Who could have imagined that the eyes behind those toilet-lid lenses had seen so much?

"Here you will find the untold story of the greatest Yiddish poet in America," Malpesh said as I examined his notebooks.

I had not been a reader of the language very long at that point, but I'd read enough to wonder at his boast.

"That's saying quite a lot," I said. "How do you think your contemporaries would have responded to such a claim?"

Malpesh sat down once again, pulled his chair closer to the window, and watched the machinery in the lot below. For what seemed an endless moment he said nothing, and I wondered if he had heard me.

"To be the greatest," he said finally, "one needs only to be the last."

The Memoirs of Itsik Malpesh

alef

IT'S A LONG WAY FROM KISHINEV TO BALTI-more. Separating the place of the beginning of my life from that of its likely end, the sea of history sent waves that threatened always to pull me down. How did I survive? I floated on a raft of words.

My first were those of the *mamaloshn*, the sweet kitchen Yiddish my mother used to soothe my cries. These were words like wooden spoons, feeding hot soup on the coldest days, cracking down on the pot when little hands reached to taste too soon. Before long, my earliest words were joined by the *loshn kodesh*, the holy tongue of Scripture. When, in my most distant memory, my father wrapped me in his prayer shawl and carried me to the synagogue to hear the language of prayer spoken, it was as though I was the holy scroll itself, carried in the arms of the righteous to lead the Simchat Torah parade. Father was not particularly pious and became less so through the years, but nonetheless he was a good Jew, said kaddish for his mother when she died, and was pleased to send his only son to the religious school where I learned to write my letters.

Such letters! The flexibility of the twenty-two letters of the *alef-beys* impresses me even now. With them I could write my name two ways, one as I heard it spoken each day in Yiddish—*yud tsadek yud kof*—and again as it was given in the Torah's Hebrew—*yud tsadek khet kof*—like the son of Abraham our patriarch. There is only a slight difference between Itsik and Isaac, but still it was a marvel to me to be one boy with two names—one for the streets, one for the shul—as if who I was depended always on the walls around me.

And that was only the beginning of what I would learn from the differences between my first two tongues. Look at the way the same four letters in the *loshn kodesh* find new life and meaning in the vernacular:

alef yud vav beys

In Hebrew, this spells Job, the name of the saintly, tortured, righteous man from the Teachings of the Prophets. In Yiddish, if we take this word and reverse the *vav* and the *yud*, it becomes simply *oyb*, "if."

You see how language itself explains the mysteries of man? Only in the relation of one tongue to another do we understand that God treats the life of each creature as a question; a walking, breathing "if." The rabbis would have us believe the Holy One sits in heaven with nothing to do but look down upon His world and wonder about this or that soul that happens to catch His eye. What questions He must ask Himself: *If I slaughter this one's children, will he still pray? If I wreck this one's body with boils, will he still sing that I am just?* What do we do if God puts such questions before us? To some, that is the true challenge of living: Who will we be if we become another Job? Will we bear our suffering as he did?

Ach, such thoughts are for the philosopher. The poet meanwhile is a heretic and a pragmatist by nature. Personally, if God in his mystery chooses to treat me as he treated poor Job, I'll tell him to stick a fig in his ass.

But I leap ahead of myself. Forgive me, my pen reaches always for the closing lines. It hates the start of things, the first marks on the virgin page. Yet before I explain what I have made of the world and what the world has made of me, I must tell you how I came to be.

* * *

9

IF IT IS TRUE what my mother told me, I was born in the scarred city of Kishinev on a Sunday in April, late one evening when white feathers filled the sky like a springtime snowfall. Kishinev was part of the Russian Empire then; before and since it has known nearly as many nationalities as have we poor Jews. Always another boot on its neck—Ottoman, Russian, Romanian—the city lay with its face in the gutter of the swampy river Bic, which never cared who among the goyim called himself czar.

According to my mother, my birth fell on the Russians' Easter of that year, 1903. (When in my boyhood I asked why my birthday was not Easter every year, she explained that the Christian holy day was a moveable feast, while the anniversary of my arrival was as fixed as a grave.) At the time, the family Malpesh—my mother, my father, my sisters, and my grandmother—was living in the center of Kishinev, near Chuflinskii Square, down the block from the market on Aleksandrov Street. My father was a cabinetmaker by trade, but before I was born he'd become manager of the city's goose down factory and now earned a comfortable living. My mother no longer needed to work but on a regular schedule gave assistance to the Christians next door. Her two daughters were old enough to look after themselves, and the mother in the neighbor's house was bedridden and had no girl children to care for her, so several times each week Mama went with baked goods to feed the invalid and her four sons. That is how it was in the community the family Malpesh lived in then: Jews living on the same street as Christians, with young ones of each running in and out of all the houses. Even in my boyhood, after the violence, the Christian children came to our door for pastries.

Kishinev was half Jewish, the other half made up equally of Russians and Moldovans. The Russians ran the local government, placed in power by the czar. They hoped to Russify the Moldovans, a rough people who were the natural inhabitants of the province of Bessarabia, of which our city was capital. Each of these groups believed they comprised a full half of the overall population, which accounted for what my father called the Christian mathematics of the Bessarabian census bureau: Fifty thousand Jews in a city of 100,000, and we were regarded as a troublesome minority.

Nevertheless, the family lived well. This perhaps bears explanation, as many Jews in Kishinev did not live at all well at the time. How could they? Endless regulations guarded against their prosperity. Jews were not permitted to live beyond the city's boundaries, and so most clustered together within a few squalid streets; they were not permitted to vote in the local elections that determined the governance of the city in which they were forced to live; their choice of employment was restricted by various ethnically affiliated trade guilds. Even those Jews who did find some success seemed to the rest to be interested only in currying favor with the authorities. Generally speaking, our lives were circumscribed by the ancient prejudices of the Christian population. That our numbers were on the rise while theirs were declining did not indicate to our neighbors that we were the future and hope of Kishinev, but rather that we were its threat and would soon be its doom.

How then did the family Malpesh rise above such conditions? As my mother told me, it happened like this: Five years previous, having just begun his employment at the local goose-down-gathering operation, Father awoke with a start one night, shaken by a terrible dream. In his sleep he had seen an entire flock of white birds with snapped necks, their blue tongues lolling out of beaks as black as ink, all impaled on giant spikes attached to mechanized wheels. The birds hung upside down, each with two webbed feet pointed to the sky like the hands of surrender. As the coal engine fire raged, a machine squealed to life and the carcasses inched forward toward a faceless man with blood in his beard.

My youngest sister, Freidl, later told me that Father said the shadowy figure in his dream looked "like hell's *shoykhet*," and she swore she would never forget the description. She was all of five years old but had once seen Moishe Bimko, one of Kishinev's kosher slaughterers, perform his work in the shed behind the synagogue. Six foot five and broad as a cow—even for a butcher, Moishe was a fright to behold. The man who served his role in Gehenna was too awful to imagine.

Grandmother shrieked when she heard Father's dream, convinced it was the product of a hex. "Some old witch has caught you with her evil eye," she said. He was not a superstitious man, but hearing his mother's reaction, he admitted the nightmare had rattled him. For days Grandmother pestered her son. "You must go see the rabbi. He will tell you what the vision means."

Mama disagreed. "The rabbi is the mayor's lackey," she said. "He will tell you the birds' two feet mean you should pay your taxes twice."

She suggested that instead of running to the synagogue, he should describe the image of the moving birds to Mr. Bemkin, who was the owner of the goose down operation. Father was reluctant; he wasn't proud of his job and found all affiliation with Bemkin's down company distasteful. He'd sought employment there only because a new law forbade hiring cabinetmakers who were not members of the Bessarabian Carpenters' Guild, and membership was denied to Jews. At the down operation he worked not with his hammer and planes but with a shovel, cleaning up the mountains of shit that were the byproduct of large-scale slaughter.

Yet to pacify my mother, Father agreed. He first made drawings of all he could remember from his nightmare: the engine, the wheels, the conveyor belt, and the curved metal spikes that held the geese in place.

When Mr. Bemkin examined these sketches, he saw the potential immediately. He was a Christian but also a shrewd businessman who valued the possibility of increased revenue over the particulars of religious affiliation. Father's "goose machine," he said, was very much like innovations that had guaranteed the fortunes of the large down operations in Odessa. But who in Kishinev, he wondered, could build such a thing?

Father volunteered to try. Through considerable elaboration upon his initial sketches, he finally hit upon a great idea: the use of five iron spikes to affix each goose to the workings of the machine. Four of the five spikes merely pinched the fowl beneath the wings, two on each side, keeping them positioned on the conveyor belt more with the threat of being pierced than by actual penetration. An additional spike, lowered from above, was intended only to be used when a bird could be kept still no other way. The spike would stab through the goose's neck, pinning it to the belt and allowing its blood to drain into the gutter that ran the length of the machine. By this design, many of the geese would survive the process and so could continue to produce down for another plucking cycle; only those birds that slowed production would be killed.

The machine was an immediate success. Within six months Mama had packed the family's rented rooms in the Jewish quarter, and they had moved to a two-level home near Chuflinskii Square with a view of the famous merry-go-round from the second story window.

For Father, it would be impossible to exaggerate the change of status this afforded him. Teams of Russian and Moldovan laborers now worked for him at the factory, and he proudly told my mother how closely they listened to him. When he demanded they pick up the pace to meet a rush order—"Pluck with pluck, my pluckers!" he'd cheer— workers who had harassed him as a shit-shoveling Jew months before now sped up or slowed down upon his command. It was almost as if they weren't Russians or Moldovans but extensions of his will.

In truth, it was hard for Father to take note of them as anything but parts of the great machine, or perhaps of a hungry animal. Yes, that was it: like the organs of some goose-eating golem. How else to explain the common feeling among the workers that they toiled deep in the gullet of a beast? With so much blood draining, the air in the factory hung thick with a meaty haze, and the farting squawks made by the punctured geese sounded—and stank—like the digestion of rotted flesh.

When the occasional worker spoke up against these conditions or the obvious cruelty suffered by the birds, Father was quick to say that he had nothing against either his geese or his workers. It was simply a matter of supply and demand. The demand for bedding required an ever larger supply of feathers; the end justified the means.

"In fact," he proposed, "given that one-quarter of Kishinev sleeps on Bemkin down every night and only, say, one one-thousandth of one-quarter of the city works here on the factory floor, I would say that we come out rather ahead. It's simple mathematics: If you add the suffering of the workers to the suffering of the plucked geese and then divide this total suffering by the pleasure derived from sleeping on Bemkin down plus the pleasure of those unplucked geese who enjoy life all the more knowing the fate they have avoided, it seems clear that our work here is for the common good."

Once the workers learned they could not approach their manager without coming away fully perplexed, Father's control of the factory seemed complete. He loved to watch both men and machine hum with activity each morning, nearly oblivious to the loss of avian life that was lubricating the whole endeavor.

As the birds moved through the processing room, it was each man's job to deplume a single section—left wing, right wing, upper breast, lower breast—so that by the time a goose had passed through a gauntlet of eight pluckers it was picked to the skin. Formerly a single bird would have taken half an hour to clean; now it was five minutes. And because each worker no longer left his stool whenever he finished a bird—a process that by tradition had involved the enjoyment of several cigarettes on the short walk to the fresh goose pile—even more time was saved. This last was accomplished by the positioning of a single man at the start of the disassembly line. There he sat all day long, pinning goose after goose with the sharp iron spikes. Under the old system this spiker had been the slowest plucker of the bunch, a portly fellow who broke a sweat with the slightest exertion. Now the workers no longer paused to brag or argue over who had plucked best; they worked as a unit, toward a single goal.

As the only man who knew how all the parts fit together, Father walked among his workers and assessed their labor: "Left Wing, pick it up! Right Thigh, you're leaving too much on the skin! Neck-and-Head, *do you need this job?*"

Under his supervision the storehouse filled with feathers, and Mr. Bemkin paid Father well for his service. Of course, as Mama liked to point out, it was not just their own family who benefited. Father found a way to deliver geese with overly rigid down to Moishe Bimko for the feeding of the synagogue's indigent. And the price of bedding dropped so significantly as a result of his invention that Father made it possible for even the poorest of Jews to have a comfortable night's sleep. Years later I'd meet men all over my new country, from Baltimore to Brooklyn, who sang my father's praises for his pillows and featherbeds. For a few blissful years, all of Kishinev slept on his dreams.

So it was that I was conceived one warm *shabbos* night, the first bird of the Malpesh flock to begin life's endless migration from the comfort of a downy nest. From the factory Father brought Mama a mattress stuffed plump as a New Year's challah, and for his effort she let him share it from the feast of Shavuot through summer's end.

For me that was when the trouble started. The trouble for the rest of Kishinev came soon thereafter. I do not mean to suggest that it was the first sign of my impending arrival that started it, but who could argue that the months before a child is born is a time when anything seems possible?

WHAT HAPPENED WAS THIS: A long day's journey north, in the little town of Dubossary, it was said that a body had been found. This was not unusual. Kishinev was a modern city, with sidewalks, streetcars, and factories such as the one my father managed. But Dubossary, though not very far away, remained rough country. The peasants there plowed rocky earth in the heat or the cold, as they had for centuries, and scarcely ate enough to stay alive. By local custom, the dead found in the fields were buried where they lay.

In Kishinev, when such sad findings were reported in the daily *Bessarabets*, they were read with the same interest as would have been given to accounts of the czar's bowel movements. Better in the Dubossary fields, the people of Kishinev liked to say, than on the merry-go-round in Chuflinskii Square.

This body, however, had caused some alarm. From the moment of its discovery by a vagrant great-grandson of serfs who'd stepped off the road to relieve himself, it was evident that this was a death for which someone would answer. First of all, it was only a boy, a youth of about fourteen, my eldest sister Beylah's age. He'd been stabbed several times and had bruises about his face and neck. Furthermore, the boy was a Christian. Word spread that he was last seen alive accompanying his grandparents to the Orthodox liturgy.

Who is to say where lies grow best? In the dark, like a mold? In the bright light, like a flower? In Dubossary they were growing everywhere. They took root in the marketplace, where they were tended by merchants. They were cultivated in the chapels, where they were harvested by priests. The boy had been killed, the rabble whispered, by Jews. The Jews needed his blood, the ancient tale went, to sweeten their matzo and thicken their wine; they needed his blood for their Passover feast.

Of course! Who else, O wise men of Dubossary? Who but the Jews would kill a boy and leave him on the roadside for a Christian peasant to piss on? Who but the Jews would be so stealthy in their motives yet so careless in their execution? Who but the Jews would build their own gallows, tie their own nooses, and hire the hangmen to stretch their necks? All these years later, it remains baffling to me that Jews know this same lie has been told for a thousand years, while Christians hear it each time as a revelation. That we should be judged and murdered by such imbeciles is sorely vexing. With a Cossack's boot on his neck, a Moldovan dirt farmer would strain himself to ask who was the Jew that knocked him down.

But such is the world. And such was our corner of it in those days that provisions traveled with difficulty over our rattling roads, but words moved like fire. Through the next three months, as I grew in my mother's womb, the lies of Dubossary impregnated our city and likewise grew, waiting for the day when they might burst forth with wailing and blood.

DURING THE PREPARATION time for Passover, Mama busied herself sweeping crumbs from the cupboards. She took all those foods the family could not eat during the days of unleavened bread and brought them to the Christian neighbors, who accepted her charity gratefully. Mama fed a flour-thickened soup to the invalid woman in her bed and inquired in a sideways fashion if she had heard any news lately, or if one of her sons had read to her from that day's *Bessarabets*.

"The newspaper says," Mama told her, "that a group of Jewish chemists have invented a new method of making wine without grapes." She studied the woman's face even as she put the spoon to her sickly lips, watching for a reaction that might betray hidden sympathies. Seeing none, she went further, as though exploring a wound. "The newspaper says this new wine is as red as blood," Mama continued, "but the Jews keep their recipe a secret. Have you ever heard such a thing?"

"All I have heard is nonsense," the Christian woman said. "There may be some unpleasantness in the countryside, but not here. Kishinev is a modern city." She strained to lift her hand and used it to pat my mother's cheek. "Look at us, two citizens talking over the news without fear of reprisal," she said in a calming tone. "For how many years have you been caring for us in this way? Four years? Five? As long as we have been neighbors. If this is so, then surely the world is not as wicked as you suppose."

Mama wanted to believe her, especially now that she was so close to the day of bringing an infant into the world. Her doctor had told her it might be early May, and she prayed for the tension in the city to pass before then. In the meantime, reading the mood of the goyim became a pastime as constant as divining the weather. When Father returned home from the factory each day, he'd catalog the peculiar looks he received as he made his way through town. He knew that every Christian who tipped his hat and bid him, "Good day, Mr. Manager," had some opinion about the boy whom the Jews had killed.

In such an atmosphere, it seemed as if Passover that year would be a somber affair, though it began without incident. Father's brother, his wife, and their son Zishe came from the Jewish Quarter to fill our large table, and together the family Malpesh sang the ancient songs of captivity and liberation.

I was by far the youngest at the table, but I was yet in my mother's womb, and so the four questions fell to my cousin, Zishe. Fate determined I would never meet this boy, yet I feel as though I can hear it now as if it were a memory: *How is this night different from all the others?* His words came haltingly, as he was too early in his studies to understand their meaning.

As the Seder progressed, Mama perceived the dark mood around the table. Her two girls, usually so attentive, sulked in their seats, not even smiling when they were called upon to drop spots of wine on their plates in commemoration of Egypt's plagues. In years past this had been a time of merriment among the children. Despite the seriousness of the subject matter, they rarely had the opportunity to openly and righteously play with their food.

Yet this night was indeed different from all the others, for it was then, after placing the last drop, signifying the plague by which God had slain the firstborn sons of Egypt, that my oldest sister Beylah, fourteen and brazen, dared to mention the fear that stalked

Kishinev's streets. Surely what she hoped to say was this: *Father, I'm confused by what is happening. We have a lovely home and we're happy here. Mama cares for the Christians next door, and I believe one of the boys there thinks I'm pretty. And yet when I step outside I feel cold looks from every window on the street. Could you please explain this for me?*

But this is not what she said. Perhaps poets and children know best how elusive our fine language can be. Like a poem that will not fall into form, a child's thoughts are often jumbled, stubborn, unappealing in expression despite their purest intent. How else can one explain why, sitting at the Seder table with her family in a time of great anxiety, my oldest sister Beylah would ask, "Is it true what the Russian girls are saying, that a boy in Dubossary was murdered by Jews? That Jews took his blood for their cooking?"

Father's face flashed red in his beard. He was not a man given to outbursts, but on this occasion he shouted. "How could you say such a thing! A disgrace!"

The other children erupted with related questions, finally giving voice to all they had endured at the hands of their Christian peers, hardships and slanders that, until then, they had hidden from their parents' notice. A full family brawl might have ensued had not Father's brother taken control. Uncle Leib was a quiet man with a gentle air and a perpetually earnest tone. The children often found him distant, but now he spoke directly to their concerns.

"Little Beylah, don't be ashamed for asking," he said. "What the Russian girls have told you they have heard from their parents, who heard it from their parents before them. It is a very old lie which some persist in telling about our people. An outrageous falsehood. Do you understand what I say?"

"Yes," Beylah said, "but—"

"What 'but'? From babyhood you have helped your mama make the matzo, yes? Did you help her this year?"

"Yes."

"And did you add blood to the batter?"

Beylah looked away and said softly, "No."

"And have you ever seen anyone add blood to matzo batter?"

"No," Beylah said again. She studied her empty plate, not willing to meet her uncle's serious eyes. It was still early in the Seder, so by then her plate held only those watery symbols of the plague, the ten red wine drops she had placed there. She put a finger in the violet liquid and used it to paint the plate with spirals and flowers. Years later she would tell me that she felt as though she was being spoken to as if she were still a little girl, not a young woman of fourteen. She wanted to lash out in response to this indignity, so she gathered up all her courage and peevishness.

"But I've never seen anyone make our wine," she said, "and the Russian girls say things about that, too. Why shouldn't we believe them?"

Uncle Leib was about to continue, but Father held up his hand. The children braced for another showing of his temper, but he had regained his composure while his patient brother spoke. He now sensed that beneath her bluster his daughter wasn't searching for answers, only reassurance. What she wanted was some suggestion that, whatever her Russian playmates said, the family Malpesh could still control its destiny. That Jews could still live as they pleased.

With the whole family waiting to hear what wisdom he would convey, Father winked at Mama and asked in full voice, "Mama, would you please pass the Christian blood?"

Beylah looked up in shock. Uncle Leib's eyes narrowed to slits of confusion.

"Yes, of course, Father," Mama said and grinned. "A nice big glass of Christian blood. I've been reading in the *Bessarabets* that it is very nutritious!"

Her daughters could not believe their ears but giggled at the absurdity despite themselves. Across the table, Leib, too, got the joke. He laughed heartily—"Yes, more Christian blood for me as well!"—and at the sound of their earnest uncle joining the gag, the children felt free to burst.

"Some for me, Mama." Beylah laughed. "Pour some blood for me!"

Cousin Zishe reached for his father's glass and took a big gulp.

Freidl sang, "I want Christian blood! More Christian blood!"

At this Mama tsked-tsked, "No, no, baby. Maybe when you're older," and the family laughed together as it hadn't in months.

Not everyone was amused, however. Grandmother had remained silent through Beylah's troublemaking, but now slapped the table with such force that the candles shook until they flickered out. "Shah! Stop! Someone will hear you!"

"Who will hear us?" Father laughed.

"The Christians," Grandmother hissed. "They are always looking for an excuse! Better for us all if the murdered child had been Jewish!"

"Ach, Mother, please," Father said. "I am the manager of the largest goose down factory in the province. I am the inventor of the goose-moving machine that has put feathers in every bed in Kishinev! Am I not safe in my own house?"

"Shah!"

"Is the Malpesh family not permitted—"

"Shah!"

"—to have some holiday fun around its own table!"

"Shah!"

"More Christian blood for everyone!" Father cheered.

Grandmother stood abruptly, knocking the table as she made for the stairs. Her plate crashed into her knife and her knife stabbed against her glass, and before anyone could reach it, the fine crystal goblet toppled forward and met the Seder plate with a smash. A red stain spread across the tablecloth like a rising tide.

Father tried for levity once more, forcing a final chuckle as he called after her, "Pity! All that blood will go to waste!"

But the horror on Grandmother's face coupled with the sight of the broken glass told the children that the joke wasn't funny anymore.

The Memoirs of Itsik Malpesh

beys

THE LAST DAY OF PASSOVER FELL ON A Sunday, the Christians' Easter. After the morning liturgies had been offered by Kishinev's priests, hundreds of churchgoers left their various houses of worship and convened in Chuflinskii Square. Much to their surprise and disappointment, they discovered that the major attraction that had lured them there that afternoon would not be in operation that day.

Several weeks before, foreseeing trouble in the rumors from Dubossary, an official from the Bessarabia Ministry of the Interior had contacted the owner of the carousel and suggested that it would be in the community's best interest if such excitements were not made available on the holiday. The fear was that idle crowds might grow restless and dangerous while waiting in line.

Given the number of carousel enthusiasts who indeed had gathered, this very well might have proven to be the case. However, not a thought had been given to how such a crowd might react upon finding not a queue but a wrought-iron fence surrounding the site of their planned diversion. No announcement had been made as to the reason for the carousel's closing. No bill had been posted begging pardon for the inconvenience. And so the crowd, left to ponder why their beloved carousel should be closed on the happiest day of the year, came to one conclusion. The Jews.

In every corner of Chuflinskii Square the loiterers now spoke of those mysterious people who comprised half of the town. *First they killed Christ. Now they've closed the carousel. Is there no end to their perfidy?*

With the scriptures of their Holy Week still ringing in their heads, the Christian mob began heckling Jews who had also come in hope of riding the carousel. One among them was the *shoykhet*, Moishe Bimko, who just then was approaching the crowd. He walked like a giant beside his young daughter, Sasha, his massive shoulders stooped to reach her hand with his own until they came to the wrought-iron gate.

No one dared approach so imposing a figure, but one boy at the edge of the jeering crowd launched a boiled egg, painted bright red for the holiday, into the air. Moishe saw it coming but had no idea what it was until it knocked off his hat and left dry shell and yolk in his hair. When his face flashed angrily at the boy—who, Moishe saw, was no older than his daughter—several Christian men rose from their seats on the steps around the square. They stood watching him like uncertain hunters, unable to decide whether to taunt the bear or run from it.

Moishe lifted his daughter into the crook of his arm and walked quickly away. Big as he was, he was at heart a gentle man and wanted no trouble. Yet the choice was not his to make. The Christians moved with him, creating a wall four deep wherever he turned. Then he saw they were not alone. A pious little Jew in a long coat held his hat on his head as a pack of boys ran forward to yank his beard. Moishe recognized him from the synagogue as the clockmaker, Sholem Rolnik. Across the square two teenage girls stood huddled together holding hands and weeping while young men, who in other circumstances might have offered whistles and compliments, now pulled at their skirts and spit in their hair. A Christian woman in a blue dress stepped forward to chastise the boys, but her words were ignored as the girls were pried apart and pulled separately into the crowd.

There were other Jews, too: perhaps two dozen by Moishe's count. But what was that number compared to the hundreds of Christians now flooding into the square? The Russians and Moldovans had come to enjoy their holiday and found this other spectacle instead. While it must be noted that some left in disgust at the sacrilege of their holiest day turned into a lawless carnival, far more remained for that most dangerous of human intentions: to see what would happen.

And what happened was this: though it began as small groups of friends and families laughing and drinking the sweet Easter wine that was the specialty of the Moldovan vineyards, in minutes the crowd in Chuflinskii Square had grown into a circling mob of hecklers, their faces so contorted with rage and glee that they resembled the beasts of the carousel. To a casual onlooker it must have seemed like the opening of a jubilant street fair. Moishe even heard music. Somewhere in the crowd an accordion sprang to life with a tune familiar to everyone—"Tumbalalaika," a song claimed equally by Christian and Jew. Then a voice joined in, singing in Russian. Moishe knew the lyrics well:

> *A young lad is thinking, thinking all night*
> *Would it be wrong, or would it be right,*
> *Should he declare his love, if he should choose,*
> *Would she accept, or would she refuse?*

The chorus was the same in any language, and the crowd seemed to sway to its cadence: "*Tumbala, tumbala, tumbalalaika . . . ,*" the voice sang, "*Tumbala, tumbala, tumbalalaika . . .*" It was a man's low rumble, reminiscent of a circus ringmaster, loud enough to be heard anywhere in the square. As the song continued, the circle of Christians drew nearer to Moishe, and he hugged Sasha tightly to his chest. When anyone ventured too close, he raised his butcher's fist into the air and watched as the approachers set their sights on easier prey.

Ten feet from where he stood, Moishe could see Sholem Rolnik flat on the ground, his black hat crushed under the heel of a churchgoer's freshly shined shoe. A gang of boys made a game of helping him up, then shoving him back into the dirt again.

Somewhere in the distance, yet closer than before, Moishe could still hear the singing. It was a riddle song—a young man testing the worthiness of his intended with a series of questions:

> Maiden, we'll be married when your answers I hear:
> What can burn without fuel for many a year?
> What can cry out forever without shedding a tear?
> And what can make life happy, without any fear?

Finally, Moishe made his way with Sasha still in his arms toward the bank of storefronts on the other side of the square. When carried this way, Sasha often made a game of wearing her father's beard first as wig, then as a scarf, then as a curtain. She played even as Moishe tightened his grip around her while passing through the edge of the crowd. He remembered that the dry goods merchant Yankev Hofshteyn had his shop nearby. Maybe he could leave her in the care of Mrs. Hofshteyn while he went back to help Sholem Rolnik and the two teenage girls, who were now nowhere in sight. But when he got there, just inside the doorway, he found the dry goods merchant bent over a stack of forty-pound flour sacks, stabbed and bleeding. A layer of white dust covered every surface around him. The store was filling with smoke, billowing out from the rear storage room like a steam engine. Of Mrs. Hofshteyn there was no sign; only a torn bit of floral fabric and the broken chain of a woman's necklace on the floor behind the shopkeeper's counter.

Moishe rushed back outside and saw that the sky was dark, even though it was the middle of the day. Smoke was pouring from the doorways and windows of other Jewish-owned storefronts. It was a sight that should have been accompanied by distressed citizens rushing about, notifying the authorities and forming bucket brigades. Yet Moishe saw bystanders standing around doing nothing, as if they were blind to the events unfolding around them. Three doors down from Hofshteyn's shop, an outdoor café remained open for business.

A Russian family was sitting in suits and dresses at a table with white china cups. Moishe stared with bafflement at the accordion player, offering them holiday entertainment with a grin that begged a gratuity.

How could they sit there tapping their toes and sipping coffee within shouting distance of a murder scene? he thought. But then he realized that the horde of spectators was hiding the crimes in progress, and it was possible to sit at the café and be unaware that a riot was under way.

Unless, of course, you were a Jew, in which case the reality of the situation was as obvious as the riddle song's solution, as the accordion player now sang:

> Boy, why ask questions when the answers are clear:
> It's love that burns without fuel for many a year.
> It's love that cries without shedding a tear.
> It's love that makes life happy without any fear.

There were more verses to "Tumbalalaika," but the singing came to an end when a block of young men, breaking from the crowd, careened along the storefronts, where a gaggle of Jews had gathered for safety. The café tables emptied. The accordion player pocketed his tips.

"Beat the Yids!" the mob yelled. "Beat the Yids!"

They came at him from all sides. Stones pelted his shoulders as Sasha shrieked, burying her face against Moishe's neck. A kick from behind him buckled his knees. A wooden club swung in their direction and missed, smashing instead through the window of Hofshteyn's store, raining shards of glass all around them.

When dew drops of blood landed on Moishe's hand, he had to study them for a moment before he realized the blood was not his own. An instant later, he saw the gash on Sasha's forehead and felt faint. He pushed his lips against her ear and told her it was about to get dark. Moishe then opened his coat, wrapped her inside, and charged at a small knot of men smoking cigarettes and throwing blocks of broken brick. The sight of the butcher roaring wild-eyed in their direction caused them to part like a biblical sea.

Once free of the square, Moishe stopped at the nearest Jewish home he could think of and banged on the door.

When Freidl answered and saw the kosher butcher standing there with blood in his beard, she thought it must be hell's *shoykhet* come to see her at last, straight from Father's dream.

Freidl's screams could not be silenced even as Moishe opened his coat and revealed Sasha huddled there, clinging to his neck like a cat chased up a tree. A moment later, Mama appeared at the doorway. She pulled the butcher and his daughter into the house and bolted the door behind them.

Inside, Mama bent over Sasha, wiping her face with a cool cloth and cooing in her ear. When Freidl saw the gash that stretched across the smaller girl's forehead, her screeching turned to tears. Even Father winced upon seeing it.

"That will leave a nasty scar," he said.

"If she survives the night!" Grandmother howled behind him.

"No, no," Mama said to Sasha. "Don't you listen to that. It's only a scrape and will be healed by morning."

While the women tended to the injured girl, Moishe took Father aside. "The Christians are burning buildings and beating Jews in the street," he said.

"What?" Father asked. "Where?"

"It began in the square, by the gates of the carousel. And it seems to be spreading."

Mama overheard them and stood at attention, holding an iodine-soaked wad of cotton between herself and Sasha as if it were the Christians' sacrament. "What is it, Abram?" she demanded. "What's going on?"

"A bit of Easter mischief, that's all."

Moishe shook his head. "No, Manager Malpesh. A pogrom is what it is."

"I don't believe it," Father said. "Not in Kishinev. We are a modern city."

"Tell that to *them*," Moishe replied, then turned to Mama. "Please keep Sasha here. I must guard the synagogue and my butchering shed."

With that, the butcher crossed the room, lifted his daughter so that they tangled like braids, and planted a kiss on her cheek.

"Be good for Mrs. Malpesh," he said. "Do you see her belly and know what that means?"

"She's going to have a baby," Sasha said, with a toddler's voice so self-assured that Mama looked at her in wonder.

"Yes, she's going to have a baby," Moishe repeated. "And that means you need to be a brave little girl. Do you understand?"

Sasha looked at her father, then at my mother, and nodded again.

"I know you do," Moishe said, and put her gently down on the floor. Speaking again to Mama and Father, he added, "Her mother is at home, at 41 Pushkin Street. If for some reason . . ." He put his big hand lightly on top of Sasha's head, then he turned and walked out the door.

After he had gone, Mama continued to dress Sasha's wound while everyone else ran upstairs to have a look at Chuflinskii Square from the second-story window.

At first what they saw seemed hopeful: the mob was dispersing. But then Father noticed how quickly the crowd was breaking apart, how groups of eight or ten men were running in different directions. Some hefted clubs, some bricks. Others carried what appeared from that distance to be sausage links, but Father supposed these must be ropes.

Grandmother moaned. She had not spoken of their Seder argument since it occurred, but now she cried out—"I told you what your jokes would bring!"—and she squeezed her son's arm as if she could see him slipping away.

Father shook loose of her grip and said, "The factory. I must make sure it's secure." He dashed down the stairs and met Mama at the door.

"Don't go, Abram," she pleaded. "It's not your responsibility today. Let the Christian owner worry about this Christian trouble."

"If they attack the factory, it will be because a Jew is its manager," Father said before lurching out the door. "Besides, it is Bemkin's holiday."

"Holiday?" my mother repeated after him. Immediately, she was convinced this would be the last word she would hear from her husband, and it rang in her ears like a death knell.

Mama ran to the second floor and then, through the window, she watched Father make his way down Aleksandrov Street in the direction of the factory. Seeing the fervor with which he sprinted past the merry-go-round, she decided that the last word he would hear from her would be, "*Fool!*" She pushed open the window and shouted it so loudly that it seemed to take up all the air in the sky. When the last of it had dissipated, she fell away from the window in a swoon.

Beylah grabbed Mama by the arm to keep her from crashing to the floor, but she hadn't lost consciousness, only her balance. Taking her firstborn by the hand, Mama breathed in deeply and told her what she knew to be the unfortunate truth.

"It is time," she said.

"No, it's too soon," Beylah replied. "Not until next month."

"A woman knows," my mother insisted.

AT THE DOWN FACTORY it was worse than Father had feared. When he tried to prevent the mob from dismantling his mechanized bird-mover, they held him down and stuffed feathers in his mouth until he struggled to breathe. But he fought his way free, even as they rained blows on his back and neck. Then they kicked him out the door, and he ran.

The streets of Kishinev were quiet just then, and Father reveled for a moment in the delusion that he might be entirely alone. That God had chosen this precise instant to empty the world seemed like wisdom worthy of the divine. His fantasy ended when he ran by the Old

Market area and saw Kirov, the Christian baker, outside the bakery door. With a paint can and brush Kirov had made a large white cross on the entrance to his shop. Inside the window, among yesterday's rolls, he displayed an icon of the Virgin. As Father left the Old Market, he saw that other Christians had followed suit. The unbroken glass of their windows caught the slanting light as the sun dropped lower in the west. The only other pedestrians were officers of the Kishinev police force, keeping order on this abandoned Christian block even as the smoke from adjacent neighborhoods curled into the sky.

At the mouth of Asia Street, Father saw a mob gathering in front of the synagogue. The rabbi stood on the sidewalk warning, "I know the counselors! I know the mayor!" but the crowd paid him no mind. Rocks and debris flew toward the yellowed windows. Several young men approached the gaping wounds like flag bearers with six-foot-long sticks topped with burning strips of cloth. The arsonists paused only when Moishe Bimko appeared in the doorway with his cleaver. Emboldened by the sight, other Jews gathered shovels and rods and ran to his side.

Father rushed on as the mobs clashed. He skirted the top of the Jewish Quarter, where it seemed a gang of Moldovans had just arrived. With axes and garden hoes they smashed every window they could reach, flung stones through those they could not, and charged inside the houses, chasing their residents into the street. One band of looters apparently took perverse pleasure in locating the bedding in each ransacked home and cutting it to tatters. They forced pillows and mattresses through the windows sharp with broken glass. As evening approached, a cool spring wind came in from the south, and ten thousand feathers fluttered through the streets in the breeze.

All through Kishinev, goose down cushioned the sidewalks. In Chuflinskii Square the carousel horses grew wings. The white crosses painted on Christian businesses in the Old Marketplace blurred in the falling plumage. On Aleksandrov Street, just as my mother, grandmother, sister Freidl, and Sasha the *shoykhet*'s daughter were barricading the entrance to the second-story bedroom, feathers blew in a gust against the window.

Mama was in the full throes of labor by then. In the moments of rest between contractions, she moved in and out of delirium. The sun was setting when she looked up from her bed and saw the sky filled with specks of white drifting to the street below. It looked so pretty in the fading light. Calling Freidl and Sasha to her side, Mama said, "Look, girls. Snow."

Father arrived at the Malpesh stoop just as Beylah peeked through the window.

"Open the door, Beylah. Quickly!" he called up to her. Beylah ran down the stairs and threw open the door. "Where is Mama?" he said as soon as he was inside.

"Upstairs with Grandmother and Freidl and the butcher's daughter. The baby is coming!"

"No, it can't be. The doctor said next month. She's just nervous."

Years later my sister told me that the cry that came from upstairs at the moment of my father's incredulous reaction seemed sent purposely to silence him. Beylah had a child of her own by the time we spoke of this, and she took pleasure in the notion of a laboring woman correcting a man's doubts.

"Perhaps you're right," Father said and ran toward the stairs. "Shutter the windows, and stay away from the door!"

On the second floor Father tried the bedroom door but found it immovable. He peered through the keyhole and saw not his wife but his mother, sitting in a rocking chair beside the bed, flipping madly through the pages of her prayer book. He could barely hear her over Mama's cries.

"I know there is a prayer for this situation," Grandmother said, and she turned the pages so quickly that it seemed they would tear.

"Open the door!" Father called.

Freidl answered, "We can't, Papa. Mama moved the bureau in

31

front of it, and Grandmother won't help me move it back. And the butcher's girl is too small!"

"I am *not* too small!" a little voice said. Through the keyhole Father saw Sasha stretching to reach the doorknob. Her little hand blocked the keyhole for a moment before she lost balance and toppled to the floor.

"I told you you were too small!" Freidl cheered.

"Minah!" Father called to my mother. "They're rampaging in the streets. We must hide here until it's over. Please, you need to do your best to keep quiet."

Mama cried out again, half-cursing my father, half-thanking God for his safe return. "Would you keep quiet if you were passing a goose through your nose holes?" Once she had caught her breath, she sighed with relief, then called out, as if to the ceiling, "This child has a very large head!"

Father wished he could lean in close and whisper in her hair, to spare the children what he must now say. Instead, he shouted through its wood planks and hoped that in the confusion, the words would only find her ears, "Minah, if they find us, we will die."

"For that I am certain there is a prayer!" Grandmother said. Before she could resume her manic page-flipping, Mama snatched the book from her mother-in-law's hands, slid its spine between her lips, and bit down on the soft leather covers as if the prayer book were a piece of meat.

Then Father heard a commotion and ran back down the stairs. He found the door kicked in, the divan overturned. The carpet was mottled with goose feathers blown in from the street. Four men in the corner were holding Beylah against the wall. Father would later say he did not recognize them, but when the attackers turned, they seemed to know him right away.

"Manager Malpesh!" one of them teased. "Does this goose belong to you?"

"Shall we pluck her for you?" another said. He grabbed Beylah by the hair and began yanking it out in bunches of five or ten strands.

"Do I pluck with pluck? Do we fill pillows fast enough for all the sleeping Jews?"

They started ripping her dress.

"Right Thigh, *faster!*"

"Left Breast, *do you need this job?*"

Father charged forward to free her, but two of the men picked him up as if he weighed no more than a bird. They tied his arms with a curtain sash and dropped him to the floor, then returned their attentions to my sister.

"Hold on there, men. You've got it all wrong." A fat man's voice boomed into the room. Father turned and recognized the same man who sat in Bemkin's factory all day, running birds through the great machine. Standing in the doorway, he was taller now than he had ever seemed on his stool, and he had blood in his beard. "She needs a spike before the plucking begins."

"No!" Father shouted as the man walked by.

The fat man was sweating as he fumbled with his belt, and stopped only when a shriek unlike any they had heard that day rang through the house. In the second-story bedroom, Mama had bitten clean through Grandmother's prayer book and now had nothing left to stifle her screams.

"Manager Malpesh has been holding out," one of the men said. "More daughters upstairs!"

Like the single-minded machine they had become on the factory floor, the feather pluckers moved as a body toward the stairs. Once they had gone, Beylah stooped to untie Father and helped him to his feet.

They ran up after the men, just as the bedroom door was forced open.

What they saw inside was this: my mother with her legs spread open, my little head just beginning to poke out into the world.

My grandmother and sister froze as the men entered, bracing themselves for the worst, perhaps for the end.

Only little Sasha Bimko dared to move. Who knows why? Was she as fearless as her father, even then? Was she eager to prove she was not too small to be useful? Most likely she was simply too young to know better. She crossed the room and stood between the bed and the door, then raised a tiny fist against the intruders.

In her exertions Mama was unmoved by the presence of the attackers, but she could see their faces clearly, noting how they ogled the spectacle for an instant, and then refused to look. Whenever she would later tell me of these events she would insist that the men stopped in their tracks and, in our house at least, did no more damage that day.

"They stood as if stricken by God," she said to me, "because at the sight of Sasha Bimko's fist they were astonished, and at the sight of your birth they were ashamed."

Our neighbors came at the sound of my newborn cries. If they had heard any of the earlier screams that shook the windows of our house (and how could they have not?), they did not admit it. Two of the Christian boys held their mother by the elbows to steady her, but as they moved through our wrecked rooms she seemed to gather strength. The next week a doctor and a priest each examined her and declared her recovery to be an Easter miracle.

The Passover miracles of that year were less impressive. Cousin Zishe was thrown from a window, but Uncle Leib survived his wounds. Moishe Bimko was found dead in his butchering shed, among the sharp-feathered geese he'd intended to slaughter. Widow Bimko took Sasha and headed . . . east? West? My mother told me a different direction each time she told me the tale.

"The details are difficult to recall," she would tell me. "But never forget this: Nothing that happened on the day of your birth matters as much as the fact that you came into the world. You will hear many stories about the circumstances, but I prefer to remember that God chose a dark day to make a spark called Itsik. Tell me, what does the length of the night matter when a candle is lit?"

Later that year, after the streets had been swept and the bodies counted, our Christian neighbor began saying how lucky the family Malpesh had been. We were lucky to have had a newborn in the house, she explained, an innocent baby to remind the marauders of their merciful Savior.

"To think what could have happened," the neighbor woman often said. "You see how I was right, that the world is not so wicked?"

With time it became clear that our neighbor's role in the madness was continually shifting in her memory. On the occasion of the third anniversary of my birth, she sat outside with us and shared the tea and cake of our small celebration.

"How lucky you were to have such neighbors who would speak out on your behalf," she said to my parents. "And how lucky the boy is, that true Christians were nearby to safeguard his birth!"

We all laughed along with her. "Yes, how lucky!"

The moment the neighbor woman had gone, Mama spit on the ground. When I looked at her in horror, she pinched my cheek until I howled.

Ever after, whenever the conversation turned to my entry into the world, my mother repeated a refrain first spoken on that April afternoon. In fact, the phrase became something of a birthday blessing. "Lucky as a butcher's goose," she liked to say.

In time, Father came to say this about the family as a whole, and whatever irony was first intended by the words began to fade. We had lived, after all, and others had not. What further proof of luck did we need?

Jews fled Kishinev by the hundreds in the years that followed. Whenever Mama expressed her wish that we join them, Father reminded her that it was only through Mr. Bemkin's connections that the men who attacked the Malpesh home had been among those arrested for crimes committed during the riots.

"How could we leave?" I once heard Father say. "In Kishinev I am an important man."

TRANSLATOR'S NOTE

Any attempt to render a written work in a new language is bound to create some distance between the text and the translation. Usually this distance is regarded as a change not only of means, but of value. Consider the way an untranslated text is referred to always as "the original," which by implication makes the translation, regardless of the level of creativity employed in its execution, "the unoriginal."

Yet how could a translation be anything but original in its own right? In the movement from one tongue to another, there is after all what the French philosopher Paul Ricoeur has called a "surplus of meaning." Text and translation are never exact equals; there is always something added, or lost.

Take for example the phrase spoken when Malpesh's father Abram marched through the goose down factory barking orders at his Russian and Moldovan workers. I have rendered his command simply as: "Pluck with pluck, my pluckers!" and I will be the first to admit this does not quite suffice. The words Malpesh actually put in his father's mouth were these:

> *"Lomir umdekn di dekn mit tetikn tenerkes,*
> *mayne kleyne, lustike teklekh!"*

Obviously, this is a longer statement than the five words I have used in its place. And more than length has been sacrificed in the move to English. The original, to begin with, is something of a tongue-twister. With the shifting "d" and "t" sounds, and the repeated use of the syllables *ik* and *ek*, it is in fact a line of near-nonsense verse displaying something of the limerick-like quality of Malpesh's early poems. Little of this comes across, however, in a literal translation:

> "Let us uncover the [geese's] bottoms with active hands,
> my tiny, cheerful dolls."

While awkward in English, in Yiddish the sentence practically dances from the lips. No doubt Malpesh wrote it this way to convey not only meaning but also something of his father's joy at being on the factory floor, and perhaps also the extent to which this joy made him oblivious to the suffering to which Malpesh himself was so sensitive, as we will see in later notebooks. It is also interesting to note that though Malpesh never mentions that his father was a direct influence on his poetry, here he seems to hint that this was indeed the case.

How does one convey all these intentions in a few words? Throughout this translation I have often chosen the path of least resistance. "Pluck with pluck, my pluckers" does not fully capture Malpesh's use of language, but I have made use of it as a simple play on words that would be impossible to render in Yiddish, just as Abram's more elaborate wordplay would be impossible to render in English.

In this and in all the other interpretive choices I have made, I have tried to be true to Malpesh's spirit, ever aware of the surplus of meaning lost, and reminded constantly of another contribution Ricoeur made to the art of translation. "If it is true that there is always more than one way of construing a text," he wrote, "it is not true that all interpretations are equal."

IT SHOULD BE ACKNOWLEDGED, lest there be any misunderstanding, that I am something of an amateur in the translation business. I was neither bred nor educated for this sort of work. Though I dabbled in languages in college, I am not one of those polyglot internationals—summering in Yupik, wintering in Tagalog—who overpopulate the field. It seems many such translators enjoy flitting between tongues the way a philanderer enjoys keeping a number of mistresses. While I am perhaps lesser in ability because of it, I come to the art more honestly than that. I am, in other words, an amateur in the original sense: I did it for love. I did it for a girl.

I have said I was mostly alone in the Yiddish book warehouse in the months before meeting Malpesh. Though that is true, I doubt I would have met him at all were it not for the one companion I had, an assistant who worked half days twice a week—a Mount Holyoke College student by the name of Clara Feld.

She was, she told me within five minutes of our acquaintance, a *baal t'shuva*—"a born-again Jew," she said, who had recently discovered the "emptiness" of her secular upbringing. She had opted to remain on campus through the summer to attend an intensive Judaic Studies seminar, which in turn had led to an internship with my employer. Raised in New Jersey, star of her high school tennis team, Clara Feld now wore a uniform of long-sleeved peasant tops and black skirts that swept the floor. Whenever she walked into work, she breathed in deeply the musty air, loving the place, she explained, for its "overwhelming Jewishness."

Yet for all the affectations of her newfound orthodoxy, her connection to the work we were doing was far more personal than mine.

"I have this box full of letters written by my great-grandmother," she told me. "They're in Yiddish, so I can't understand a word of them, but they're like my prized possession." She seemed to get choked up a bit at the thought, then added, "You're so lucky to be spending your days preserving the history of our people."

As she spoke, she lifted her hair from her shoulders and twisted it into an auburn knot, which she pinned to the back of her head with a pencil. With no other skin showing, the nape of her neck would drive me to distraction for the rest of the day. I saw no reason to deny what she believed me to be. I saw no reason to deny her anything at all.

"You ought to bring in those letters sometime," I suggested. "Maybe I could help you read them."

"Maybe I will," she said.

LEARNING TO PASS, it turns out, is less a matter of acting than *not* acting. You can become part of a given scene, situation, or people (*"our* people," as it were), simply by letting yourself serve as a mirror for those around you. When I was still in college, when I still thought I might make a good priest, I spent some time in a Trappist monastery. I found that by exerting as little of my own personality as possible, I was able to fit right in. The monks in no time came to call me brother, believing I was destined to make vows as one of their own. Passing begins with the assumptions of those around you. The best thing you can do to maintain the illusion is to come as close as possible to doing nothing at all.

Of course, it helps when there is assumed to be a sharp divide between the place a passer comes from and the one he enters through his deceit.

"The goyim are a curious people," Malpesh once said to me, before he had discovered who and what I was. "Not curious that they want to know things," he clarified, "curious that they don't."

For him the gulf between who he was and what "they" were was so vast that humanity seemed irreconcilably divided between the less than 1 percent of the global population who were Jews and the more than 99 percent who were not. Such was the divide

I crossed in my failure to disabuse Clara Feld of her assumptions about my religious and ethnic affiliations. It was a divide that was never so clear to me as it was in her immediate vicinity.

The warehouse we occasionally shared occupied the top two floors of a former textile mill that was more than a century old, a vast red brick block teetering on the edge of a stagnant canal. In its prime it had been the kind of place that could turn a third-rate river town into a city rich with jobs and manufacturing revenues. Now it was leased for two dollars per square foot to businesses that couldn't afford to rent a more respectable space in the suburbs.

On the mill's first floor there was a small tailoring operation, staffed by two dozen Vietnamese ladies who never seemed to come or go. Whenever I arrived at the warehouse in the morning, escaped for lunch at noon, or went home at night, I could hear the workers sewing and chattering through their main entrance, which they kept propped open with a folding chair in apparent hope of a breeze wicking off the canal.

The second level was occupied by a furniture shop. I have no evidence of dual use other than the affirming "One Day at a Time" and "Easy Does It" posters that decorated the walls on either side of the shop's minifridge, but it appeared to double as a drug and alcohol rehab program. The workers were damaged-looking hard cases with bruises on their necks; and from the shouts that drifted out to the stairwell, I guessed they were prone to slipups and displays of sudden anger.

As different as these two populations below the book warehouse were, they had one thing in common. To those on the first and second floors, we on the third and fourth were known simply as The Jews.

I was often puzzled by the plurality of it—most days there was only me, after all. Yet it was a welcome reminder as well that I was part of something. There had been others who had performed my job in years past; there would be more to come. No doubt they would nearly all be Jews, and so the name was more fitting than not.

At any rate, there was nothing derogatory about its use, as far as I could tell. In fact, one of the Vietnamese women was rather friendly about it. Of all the workers I'd seen through the shop windows, she was the only one who ever seemed to come out. As she dressed in stylish suits and garish jewelry, I supposed she must've owned the place. Whenever I ran into her in the parking lot beside her Lexus SUV, she would look me over, frown at my beat-up Celica, and ask, "You with the Jews?"

"Yes," I would answer, and she would cheer "Hi!" by which I can only assume she meant "Bye," because at that point she would invariably climb into the driver's seat and roar out of the parking lot.

It was the same with the furniture makers. My only contact with them came because they had a habit of leaving the door to the freight elevator open, making it inoperable on any other floor. Not a week went by when I didn't find myself poking my head into the shop and yelling over the whine of band saws that someone should please shut the safety gate. The five or six workers kept their heads down with cigarettes dangling from their lips as they cut piles of dresser knobs and shelving planks. They wore no ear protection except for knit caps pulled down to their goggled eyes. Eventually I'd walk through the sawdust cloud that hung below the rafters, past the minifridge and the AA posters, and close the elevator myself.

On my way out I would often hear one worker say aloud, "Who was that?"

"The Jews," another would say.

In such an environment, *not* passing would have required a concerted effort. And, worse, it might have been disruptive. Why bother insisting I was not a Jew when such insistence would only confound everyone around me? And what about my own attractive coworker? As Malpesh wrote, "A man is in his pants what he is not in his heart."

Summer days inside the warehouse felt as though the earth had tilted closer to the sun. Heat that was merely oppressive in the parking lot became unbearable in the entryway and just got worse on the march up the stairs. With windows sealed shut and the stairwell railings scalding to the touch, it was almost a relief to reach the top and arrive at work each day. Four flights up, our maze of metal bookshelves baked with the accumulated warmth of all the floors below, filling the place with a musty smell like incense mixed with newsprint. A few industrial fans blew the burning air around.

Twice a day, once for UPS, once for regular mail, I brought up the recent deliveries from the loading dock. When Clara was there, she helped. Together we would pile the boxes onto pallets and, using a pallet jack to wheel them into the freight elevator (a steel cage twelve feet wide by ten deep), we'd bring them to the fourth floor. There, we'd position the boxes in the gust of the fans and unpack the books as loose pages flew to the rafters.

I have mentioned that it was during this time that I began to develop a grasp of the language. It might be useful to explain how exactly this came to be. To the extent that there is ever truly a single moment of discovery—a shining light of comprehension where before there had only been the murk of limited understanding—it occurred one morning in July. While digging through a box of books sent from Montreal, I came upon a slim, bright yellow volume with an abstract drawing of a bearded man on the cover. Turning the book on its side, I studied the collection of characters I took to be the author's name. It did not look like the other Yiddish names I had read—something about the placement of vowels in relation to the consonants. So I organized the sounds of the letters in my mind, and then tried to speak them aloud. First the beginning three letters: *hey, ayin, mem*. "Hem." Then the second three: *yud, nun, gimel*. "Ing." The final four: *vav, vav, yud, yud*. "Vay."

"Did you say something?" Clara asked.

I ignored her, focusing now on the words I guessed were the title. The last was one I recognized from Hebrew; just two letters, *yud, mem. Yam*. Sea.

About 10 percent of Yiddish is taken directly from Hebrew. Within the language these borrowed words are called *loshn kodesh*, the holy tongue, because it is drawn directly from Scripture. The *yam* of this yellow book's title was the same *yam* into which the prophet Jonah was thrown, the same waters where Leviathan haunted the depths.

I sounded out the title and read it to myself, "*Der alter un der yam*." I knew enough German to guess those two instances of *der* might be "the," and *un* seemed close to "and." I looked again at the bearded man on the cover and now recognized him. I reread the author's name. "Hem-Ing-Vay." He wasn't some hatless rabbi but an American icon. Then it dawned on me: *Alt*. Old.

"The Old Man and the Sea!" I shouted, holding up the book triumphantly.

Clara looked skeptical. "Hemingway was Jewish?"

I couldn't tell if she was joking, but I didn't much care. Nothing could dampen my spirits. Standing in that awful heat, boxes and books scattered around me, I had completed my first translation; that it was only five words long and essentially an untranslation of a book title I had known since high school didn't matter in the least. Suddenly my warehouse clerk's life was filled with a million solvable mysteries, and I had stumbled upon a code key that could unlock them all. From that day on, whenever I unpacked a box of books, I'd pick up each volume, pronounce the name of its author, and hope to come across something familiar that might spur me to understanding. Within the first week I discovered Yiddish translations of Dickens, Shakespeare, Tolstoy . . .

As July turned to August, the heat inside the warehouse caused the books to sizzle on their shelves. Filled with nearly a century of moisture and the oils of readers' fingers, they hissed in the arid air, yielding up the scent of warm paper. Just looking at the maze of books, such a fire hazard, all that potential energy, I had soaked through my shirt by noon. So I sat and I read.

Three days each week, alone among the bookshelves, with boxes piling up at least as high as they'd been in June, instead of sorting through them, I'd position myself by the largest of the metal fans and work my way through page after page. I did so haltingly, with a Yiddish-English dictionary by my side, from the moment I arrived until it was time to go home.

On Clara's days in the warehouse, she'd join me in the relative cool, and we'd look over her great-grandmother's letters. There was a ritual to this: Clara sat in the same spot each time and selected a letter at random. Then I'd read aloud a line or two in Yiddish, doing my best to translate on the fly. Yiddish script was so much more difficult to decipher than the typefaces I'd read in the books that most of the sentences went only half translated, "Something-something-something . . . *on the train to Birobizhan, which* . . . something." This caused me no end of frustration, but Clara was enthralled by just the margins of the story that seemed to be emerging.

One stormy afternoon we tried for an hour to make sense of a short note, but the legible words amounted to not much more than "the baby is getting so big . . ."

"That must be my grandmother!" Clara exclaimed. She moved in close to my side and peered at the letter in my hand. The idea that these strange markings held clues about her family was thrilling to her. Outside, thunder boomed and lightning lit up the warehouse windows, and it was exactly the kind of commotion that seemed to be going on inside her. She looked up from the letter and held me in her gaze, her eyes shining. "It really says that?" she asked.

"Yes, it does," I answered, then looked down at my watch and guessed that the mail might be waiting on the loading dock, possibly getting wet.

"We'd better go down and get it," I said.

We rode the freight elevator to the dock, and sure enough, rain was falling hard on two dozen boxes. Darting in and out of a thunderstorm's downpour, we grabbed them by their sides and pulled them under cover. In three minutes only one box remained in danger, and this one was already so waterlogged that its cardboard corners came apart in my hands. When I lifted it to my chest, a small blue book fell out onto the concrete. Clara retrieved it as I wrestled the ruined box to the safety of the elevator.

Dripping and exhausted by the exertion, I pulled the elevator shut as we caught our breath. Clara was examining the book she had saved from the rain. It was no bigger than a pack of cigarettes, but, even wet, it was impressive. Gold letters gleamed on its hard blue covers, as did a seven-armed pitchfork design that appeared to represent a menorah. Clara ran her fingers along the spine.

"Isn't it beautiful?"

"Yes," I agreed, and took a quick look. "Some kind of prayer book."

"You can tell so fast?"

"Yeah. Look at the ornamentation. Doesn't it make you want to pray?"

"Are you teasing me?"

"No," I said. "Just think of the hands that have held it. It seems so well loved. And look here—" I opened the book to its inside cover, where a few lines of Yiddish mixed with Hebrew. "This word is *tehilah*. Prayer."

Clara stared down at the book with renewed wonder, then up at me.

"Can I tell you something?" she asked.

"Sure."

Smiling, twisting her finger in her hair, she said, "I never knew anyone so . . ."

I pressed the button marked "4," and we began to rise.

"So?" I asked.

"Jewish!" she cried and pushed me against the elevator wall. She kissed me so hard my back hit the buttons and we stopped with a crash, halfway between the first floor and the second. Through the safety gate we saw a gang of furniture shop carpenters taking a coffee break.

"Hey, look at the Jews!" one of them said.

Four-eyed with goggles raised to their foreheads, a cigarette loose in each set of lips like a snaggly fang, they could have been another species. Whoever or whatever I was at that moment, I knew I wasn't one of them.

Reaching behind me, I pressed the button marked "4" again, and up we went, the soggy book pressed between us like a bride's bouquet.

❧

"Translation is an intimate act," Malpesh once told me. "So much is made of the sharing of fluids, the pressing of bodies, as if chemistry or anatomy were the realm of the highest order of human exchange. But how is it not the sharing of language? Who but a writer in a lonely room could impregnate the thoughts of so many?"

"And where does translation fit into that scenario?" I asked.

"For a writer who has outlived his tongue, there is no other means of contact," Malpesh said. "Without a translator, who would unzip the words?"

gimel

THE EDUCATION OF A POET IS NEVER A straightforward affair. One does not attend a poetics academy or sit at the knee of a master, cleaning his toes. Rarely does a boy become apprentice to the village tinker of words. It is instead the kind of learning that falls upon you for no good reason, like bricks from the sky. Only later can the poet look back and remember that he himself threw these bricks into the air. Where? When? Why? Perhaps he writes to find answers to these questions, or perhaps he hopes the right words will be for him an impenetrable umbrella.

In Kishinev's religious school I learned my *alef-beys* in little more than a week and quickly advanced beyond the other small boys. By the time I was ten years old, I was moved to be with older fellows, studying in the yeshiva behind the synagogue.

"Yeshiva" is a rather grand word for the four dank walls that housed our studies. Since the death of Moishe Bimko, there had been no Jewish butcher in that part of town, and so, after a year of standing empty, the *shoykhet*'s slaughtering shed was swept of its feathers, scrubbed of its blood, and given a house blessing as the new community study hall. Before this, the older boys received their instruction in the synagogue attic, scraping their scalps on roofing nails when they stood to pray. Now, with Moishe Bimko's work table and chopping block replaced by backless benches and narrow desks, the sons of pious families became men who wrestled with books in a room where many a beast had been slain. For this privilege, each boy paid a tuition fee of one penny per day.

As was the custom, we sat by levels of achievement in this makeshift study house, which meant that, though I could scarcely see the lesson board over four rows of shoulders and heads in front of me, I was positioned in the back and told I must work my way forward. The seat closest to the front was kept empty by our teacher, an excitable man to whom we referred only by his title, Der Lerer, for fear that invoking his name might invoke also his wrath. The honored place nearest him was what he called "Rashi's Chair," and only when a boy understood the complexities of the Talmud's greatest mind could he claim it. Only a handful dared to try.

In the back of the room a boy five years my senior sat beside me. He was called Chaim, which did not mean much to me when I first met him, but thinking back now, I realize he did indeed give me new life. To this day when glasses clink and even the goyim say, "L'chaim," I think of the boy who taught me as much through his presence as his eventual absence, for the circumstances of his departure from Kishinev instructed me more in the ways of the world than all of my prior or subsequent schooling combined.

Chaim Glatt was a gaunt, gangly adolescent, with pimples glowing red beneath the fuzz of his beard. He said little but kept his nose always tucked in an enormous volume of Talmud. For a boy who seemed to study without ceasing, he had not advanced very far through the yeshiva's ranks. I was amazed he still sat in the room's cold back corner, and so I puzzled over him whenever the teacher looked away. He passed the days smoothing a finger over his wisp of a mustache, staring with empty eyes and slackened jaw at the book before him. Occasionally a line of spittle would drip from his gaping lips to the rough surface of the desk below, which often held not just his books but both of his elbows and much of the twigs that were his upper arms.

48

The boy was a mystery! Was he unable to learn? Was he destined to be an old man with a child's brain? If so, Der Lerer would have thrown him out, as he had several other boys that year.

"Kishinev needs cobblers as well as scholars," the teacher would say as he sent the expelled boys to his cousin the shoemaker. "Soon we will all leave here, and without proper soles beneath us where will the Torah be?"

Once or twice each week Der Lerer took note of Chaim's failure to pay attention to his lessons and, assuming the boy had been dozing behind his book, would try to catch him out. Yet that's when Chaim proved he indeed had his wits about him. Always he provided an answer that was not only correct but carefully chosen so as to require no further elaboration.

When Der Lerer called out to Chaim one day, "Glatt, are you listening? Would you be please be so kind as to lower that volume you are hiding behind and tell the class one of the five ways a *shoykhet* might make a kosher animal *treyf?*"

The rest of us had spent the better part of the previous week memorizing these arcane terms from the Shulchan Arukh. Through endless repetition of the Hebrew terms *sh'hiyah, chaldah, darsah, hagramah,* and *iqur,* we would struggle to remember that the forbidden knife techniques in kosher slaughter were also known as pressing, pausing, piercing, tearing, and covering. For an hour each day that week we had repeated a tuneless jingle:

> *Pressing, pausing, piercing, tearing,*
> *Is the way unclean to make*
> *Pausing, piercing, tearing, covering*
> *cut the cow and make her* treyf

Each time through, the song left out one of the five phrases, and so attention had to be paid to include the correct terms. It was meant to keep us from mindless repetition, but in fact it guaranteed it.

When called upon to answer Der Lerer's question, any other boy would have jumped to his feet and recalled the rhyme, though he likely would not have known the meaning of the words.

"Glatt, are you listening to me?" Der Lerer asked again. "Lower that volume and recite! Or are you embarrassed that you have not been paying attention? Are you unable to memorize a simple list? Can't you name even one way a *shoykhet* might defile a beast during slaughter?"

Without so much as a glance above his book, Chaim said, "Der Lerer, before you ask again, let me remind you that *pressing* me to explain the obvious might lead to me *pausing* my reading, which would cause me to look upon you with such *piercing* eyes that you would soon be *tearing* your beard out by its roots for fear of what I would do to you if you uttered another word. Considering this, don't you agree that it would be best for my *covering* to remain where it is?"

It was clear to the rest of the class that any additional interrogation of Chaim would have forced Der Lerer to betray his own ignorance. The sad eyes our teacher displayed at such moments gave the impression that his most indifferent student was training him like a dog.

One night I told Father about this, and he said there were from time to time remarkable prodigies in every Jewish community. He would not be surprised, he said, if Chaim had already moved far beyond Der Lerer's capacity to teach him.

"But why then does he sit in the back with me?" I wondered. "Why hasn't he marched forward and seized Rashi's Chair?"

"Perhaps he has learned enough to see your teacher's incentives for what they are: prizes for children," Father said. "If what you tell me about this boy is true, it would not be unheard of if behind his volume of Talmud he has hidden some advanced text of mystical knowledge. The Zohar, perhaps, or some other work of the Kabbalah. When the rabbi hears of it, this fellow Chaim will probably be shipped off to become some sort of holy man. A terrible waste, if you ask me. Such a boy would likely have a fine head for business."

At the start of the next week in the yeshiva, I greeted Chaim with a new sense that I would like him to be my friend. He did not look up from behind his volume, the covers of which he drew around him like a wall, but a voice rose from behind it.

"I am very busy, little Itsik," Chaim said. "If you have a question, ask Der Lerer. You paid him your penny, not me."

"What if I paid you a penny, too?" I asked. "Then would you tell me the secrets you have learned?"

He turned a page behind his wall. "Do you have another penny?"

Of course I did not—though the family Malpesh lived more comfortably than most, my parents knew better than to send a small boy out with money into the maw of Christian Kishinev—but I told him I could get one.

"Can you get one every day?" Chaim pressed. "If it's my secrets you want, you can't just buy one and be done with it. Secrets need company, and they need to eat. You must feed secrets with more secrets. They'll turn on you if you don't keep them coming, do you know this?"

I nodded my head as if I understood and then sat down at my desk. Ignoring most of what Der Lerer said in the hours that followed, I spent half the day wondering what in the world Chaim meant about feeding secrets with secrets and the other half scheming how I could acquire the treasure it would take to find out.

At home that evening, I lied to my father. I said that Der Lerer had raised the fees at the yeshiva. Doubled them, in fact.

"It has always been one penny," Father said. "Why now two?"

I had prepared myself for this question and could not contain my joy at having anticipated it. "Der Lerer is getting married," I declared, "and having babies!"

Father raised an eyebrow like a goose's arched neck. "How have I not heard such wonderful news? When will this take place?"

"Next week!"

"Next week married or next week babies?"

"Both! All! Married and babies!"

I must admit now that at the age of ten I was uncertain of the scheduling or mechanics necessary for such events. Yet my father said nothing. He only studied my face and then suggested, "If you have the need for an extra penny every day, perhaps it is time you begin working as well as studying."

From the kitchen my mother called out, "Itsik is too small for working!"

"I worked from my babyhood!" Father said.

"What work will he do? Who will hire a child?"

"I will hire him!"

"At the factory? You'd have him work with all those goose pluckers, tied like a goy to a killing machine?"

"That killing machine makes the bed you sleep in, buys the bread you eat, and pays your daughters' dowries. He will work as I once worked."

Mama entered the room, drying her hands but refusing to wipe the sour look from her face.

"He's only a boy."

"Now he will learn a man's sacrifice."

"If he learned a woman's sacrifice, he wouldn't be a shit-shoveler but a saint."

Father sidled up to Mama and tried to flatter her into agreement. "You're quite right, Minah. And don't we men struggle our whole lives to be worthy of a woman's sacrifice? How will Itsik ever earn the love of his *bashert* if he does not learn early how to support her?"

"*Bashert*?" I asked. I had never heard the word before.

"*Bashert*," Father explained, "is destiny, and so it can mean many things. In this case, *bashert* is the person with whom you are destined to spend your life. The one God has prepared for you, for

52

when it is time to start your own family. She has been there from the beginning, always closer than she seems, and is simply waiting to be found."

I was confused by this talk of beginnings. From the stories my parents had told, I knew that all those who were present at my beginning, my birth, were family—all but one.

"Is my *bashert* then Sasha Bimko?" I asked.

Father and Mama exchanged looks that were all at once puzzled, distressed, and surprised.

"What makes you mention Sasha Bimko?" my mother asked.

"She was there at the beginning," I said.

Father pushed a laugh from his beard. "Excellent reasoning, Itsik! Yes, Sasha Bimko may well be your *bashert*. She is an older woman, so you best start working to prove yourself worthy!"

"First working and now *bashert*!" Mama sighed. "Why must you fill his head with nonsense?"

✼

DESPITE MY MOTHER'S PROTESTS, Father won the day. Through the next months I worked at the down factory two hours each morning before heading to my lessons at the yeshiva. Before sunrise, it began: moving mountains of goose droppings to the dung furnace from the depluming room, just as my father had done before he became manager.

"I did it for years, so I can tell you from experience: there's a science to it," Father said as he showed me his technique my first day on the job. "No, in fact, it's an art. It's as if you're a painter and the landscape you're painting is not a mountain vista but a gray stone floor. Just as the mountains on a canvas must be discovered by the artist, so too must you uncover the surface of the stone."

"Stone?" I asked. If there was anything like stone in the room where we stood, I could not see it. The shop floor appeared to be made less of any hard substance than a buttery goo. And the color was anything but gray. In one corner of the plucking room the floor was green; in another it was daffodil yellow. A wide ring around the depluming machine included all the hues of the morning sky: feathery white and veiny purple and red like my mother's borscht.

"The stone is several inches down," Father said. "Can you believe beneath all this muck is clean, blank slate? Tabula rasa! You'll be a painter who removes color rather than adding it. And this is your brush!"

He handed me a shovel nearly as tall as I was.

"Don't you recognize it?" he asked with wet, nostalgic eyes. "Oh, but how could you? My shoveling days were long gone by the time of your birth."

It was, he explained, the very tool he had used through all his years of cleaning the same floor.

"You can even see where I held it," he said, pointing to two spots on the rough wooden handle that were worn smooth as soap. "Back then of course there was no depluming machine. It was all men and muscle. Do you know we now make twenty times the down we did ten years ago? Such progress!"

Father looked around the room with a devouring gaze, smiling at the sight of his invention. It truly was a beauty to behold: a wood and iron frame like the skeleton of some long-dead animal, dressed with leather belts and copper wheels holding spikes that glinted in the early morning light. Was I aware then of the bitterness my father must have felt to be only manager and not master of this monster he created? Did I ever wonder at the logic that Bemkin, the owner, should grow ever more fat on my father's skills?

"Such progress," he said again, then breathed a heavy sigh so long that I thought it would fill the factory from the muck-covered floor to the air vents in the ceiling above.

"And yet the shit remains. Use your hours with the shovel to dream of all the things you would rather do in life, and it will help you succeed. Forget what you're shoveling. You could as well be building a castle in the clouds as carving paths through goose slop."

I took to the task with vigor, eager first to follow in my father's footsteps, second to show him that his son could work as hard as any man, and third, of course, to get the pennies that would buy whatever secrets Chaim had to share. Father's suggestion that the work would lead to thoughts of what I would rather do with my life proved correct almost immediately, yet my dreams were soon drowned out by the honking laments of geese in their final moments. Close to half of the birds survived the plucking process and were restored to their pens to grow more feathers for another round; the rest expired either as their skin was picked raw, or as the fatal spike pierced their necks. These last especially drew my attention, with their poor white heads pinned to the moving belt of the machine, their black eyes staring out at me. What did they make of this final vision, I thought—a boy standing idle with his shovel covered in shit? They seemed to know that with my child's hands I'd just scraped their last act of living off the floor.

"The one drawback of the depluming machine's efficiency," Father said, "is that the noise level of the factory has increased twentyfold along with the amount of down we're producing. The pluckers would like to stop up their ears with cotton, but I forbid them from impeding any of their senses while they're working."

The result of my father's belief in unimpeded senses was that many of the pluckers had become rather deaf. Better for them, if you ask me. Their affliction meant they were spared what I was not: the endless bleating of mother geese calling out to stolen goslings, the cackling *ack-ack-ack* of powerless ganders unable to fight with their legs clamped to the copper wheel. Worst of all were the sounds that came every ten seconds as a new bird reached the end of the machine's cycle. The dead birds fell to the floor with a dull, wet *thwop*. And those lucky enough to have survived? How like an infant's cry was the complaint of each denuded bird as it joined its cousins in a flock that would fly no more. Who could dream in a sleep of this calamity? My daily hours on the factory floor resulted only in a single, inescapable fantasy, an early-morning nightmare: that I too would be lost among the condemned fowl.

One day this vision got the better of me, and Father found me sniffing back tears as I scraped a stubborn patch of muck beneath the interlocking gears that moved the depluming machine. All at once, my shovel felt so heavy that it dropped from my hands, and Father had to catch it as it fell to the floor. Before he could inquire what it was that had upset me, Mr. Bemkin happened upon us. He was a giant of a man, or at least seemed so to one as small as I was then. His face was as wide as my chest, and white as milk. To say it looked like a goose's rump would be too obvious, but it would not make it less true.

"Ah, *la famille Malpesh!*" the factory owner said with a flourish. "*Père et fils.* You are nearly the spitting image of your father, like the funhouse mirror they have at the carousel. Major Malpesh and Minor Malpesh—which is the real and which the reflection, eh?"

"Good morning, Mr. Bemkin," my father said. "You are back from your travels, I see."

"Yes, but not for long. Bemkin Down has become the rage of Paris, and I soon must return. I know all will be in good hands while I'm gone . . ." As he spoke, the factory owner took note of the shovel in Father's grasp. "Back to your roots, Monsieur Manager?" He gave me a sly wink, as if I would approve of him teasing my father, then he put a hand on my shoulder. "Perhaps if Major Malpesh has the shit-shoveling covered, Minor Malpesh would like to come to my office for a sweet, eh?"

At that moment a sweet would have been most welcome. Who would worry over doomed geese or a teased father with a bit of sugar on his tongue? Yet before I could voice my pleasure at the suggestion, I found the shovel pushed back into my hands.

"Very generous of you, Mr. Bemkin," Father said, "but Itsik has a floor to clear, and then he must rush off to his studies."

"Of course. Another time." The owner shrugged, and headed off to the stairs that led to his office.

I didn't dare express my disappointment, but it must have been visible on my face, for my father began to lecture me.

"With your pay you can buy your own sweets," he told me. "We work, he pays us. It's an even exchange. We do not need his charity." He paused a moment and then added quickly, "And you have no business in his office. He often sleeps there to escape his wife, and it's not appropriate for an employee to be involved in his private matters. Do you understand?"

In fact I did not understand, but I nodded gravely and went back to work.

As the days passed this way, I thought less and less of my dark fantasy of becoming one of the birds destined for the pillows and bedding of Bemkin Down. Perhaps my hearing was becoming poorer by the hour because, despite their crying, I thought less and less of the birds themselves. Soon there was only the certainty of the task, an increased focus on the movements of my arms and my hands and the shovel they held. I could feel myself becoming stronger, as if I were not a boy three years from bar mitzvah but a man who scraped and grunted for his daily bread.

In time, I came to feel that the sweat and the smell and the deafening squawks were worth it. With my pay, not only did I buy the occasional sweet, I was saving pennies in a jar I hid deep in my mother's cupboard. And of course, though sometimes I forgot this was the point of my labor, I slid a penny to Chaim each morning at the start of Der Lerer's lessons. For this he shared with me his secret books and instructed me in their meaning. And what books! They were not sacred texts, as my father had suspected. Chaim's interests were further still from what he or Der Lerer could have imagined.

I will never forget the wonder and fear inspired by my first peek behind the big volumes pinning Chaim to his desk. Once I had placed my first penny before him, he glanced this way and that to be sure no one else was nearby, then he tugged me by my collar to the other side of his wall of books. There, propped up against the open pages of his volume of Talmud, was a book the likes of which I had never seen. I stared for a moment and at first did not understand what I was seeing, for this hidden text was not Yiddish or Hebrew or Aramaic, nor any language we used in yeshiva, but—

"Russian!" I cried. "You're reading Russian!" Before I could say anything more Chaim reached out and smacked the words from my mouth.

"If you don't keep quiet, you'll have no secrets from me, penny or no penny."

"Russian!" I said again, now in a stunned whisper. "This is what you're reading while we study Talmud?"

"Of course. I finished the religious books Der Lerer offers long ago, and some he does not offer—"

"My father thought you must be reading the Zohar, or another text of the Kabbalah."

"Grandmother stories, the lot of them. Real learning is not to be found in the ramblings of the rabbis, not even the mystics. You'll see once you've read even a page of Pushkin or Turgenev. And you'll thank me for being so generous as to give you a new world for just a penny a day."

His power of persuasion was considerable. Standing close by Chaim's side, sharing air with this likely prodigy and his illicit reading, I stared at the open book, its Cyrillic type as exotic and enticing as a treasure map. I closed my eyes and leaned in close to the pages, inhaling their foreign scent, ready to be led anywhere by this perfume of wood pulp and ink. But then, suddenly, reason took hold again.

"A costly bargain!" I cried. "For my penny you would give me a book I can't understand?"

"Little Itsik, you know more Russian than you think. The family Malpesh doesn't live in the Jewish Quarter, after all. Don't you ever speak to your Christian neighbors?"

I blushed at his question. It was a widely held opinion that my family must live in the lap of luxury because of our address, and further that we received special treatment because of my father's position at the factory. Usually this was a source of pride for me, but now it felt hurtful to be set apart.

"That is only speaking," I said. "Reading is different. The letters are so strange!"

"What strange? You're surrounded by them every day. Can't you read the signs on the Christian shops? Can't you tell which window is the Russian butcher's and which is the banker's? Don't you know which church is named for the lady saint and which for the man saint?

"On your way through Chuflinskii Square today, try to read every Russian word you see. When you get home, write what you remember on a page and bring it to me. Tomorrow, if you impress me, and if you bring another penny, I will share my books with you. And note my phrasing: *share*. I will not give you a book for a penny. I am not a book dealer but a freethinker. You will pay me for my services, my brain, not my supplies. Do you understand?"

As usual I said I did when I did not, nodding in earnest that of course I understood entirely. For clarity's sake, though, I could not help but ask one last time, "How much, then?"

"A penny a page," Chaim said.

What happened next was to me a kind of magic, for Chaim was right. Walking my usual route home from the yeshiva through Chuflinskii Square, I now and again paused at certain shops that previously had failed to draw my curiosity. When I stood staring in the Russian butcher's window, I saw the word *noga*, and I knew it was chicken legs. At the Russian baker, I read *bliny*, and I knew it was the pastry that the Christian boys next door often asked my mother to prepare. At the office of the newspaper *Bessarabets* I was able to decipher a few words as well. Two men standing nearby were discussing one of the articles displayed in the window.

"It seems Jewish labor agitators are causing trouble across the district," one of them said.

No sooner had I heard this than I spotted evidence in the headline. The Russian equivalents of "labor" and "agitator" took some effort, but when I saw the word *zhid* I knew immediately that it meant "Jew."

How was it that I could read these words? I had never tried before, at least not consciously, but now it was as natural as seeing. It felt no different from looking upon a dog and thinking of the word *dog* or a horse and thinking of the word *horse*. Strange that the image of a thing can have this reflection in the mind. Or perhaps it is more of a shadow; this rendering that lacks flesh and weight is only a silhouette of letters, lines and dots that truly represent the thing itself.

I wondered about this into the evening, loitering in Chuflinskii Square with thoughts of the shadows cast by words until the sun had left the sky. When finally I reached home, I hurried past my parents without a word of greeting.

"What son treats his mama so?" my mother called after me, but I rushed on.

"He is of that age," I heard my father say.

Though usually I lingered out of sight and listened whenever my parents discussed their concerns over me, on this day I climbed the stairs and hid myself in the room where my sisters slept before they married. There I spread out on the floor and wrote as many Russian words as I could remember on a blank page Der Lerer had given for the evening's assignment. Beside each set of foreign letters, I wrote my best guess of its Yiddish equivalent, then the Hebrew. How could so many different words mean the same thing?

"VERY NICE, LITTLE ITSIK," Chaim said upon seeing my list of words the next day. "Do you see how much you knew without knowing you knew it? That is something Der Lerer will never teach you. You have already within you all the knowledge necessary for living. It's only a matter of unlocking it. The books I give you will be keys to the wisdom that is hiding in your head. . . . Now, where's your penny?"

I had barely been able to contain myself at the factory that morning. The excitement I felt was so great that it lingered even now, as if my anticipation of what Chaim would teach me exceeded the actuality of receiving the lesson. I had passed my hours clearing the depluming floor in patterns that followed the shapes of the new letters I had learned. If the Russian workers took note that I was covering the floor with the Cyrillic markings of their alphabet, they did not say so. In fact, they seemed barely to notice me at all. That day at least the feeling was mutual; as I carved letters in the piled shit around the goose pluckers it was as if they stood not on a factory floor but on an empty page. What were they but more words, stacks of letters in ankle boots, going about their tasks as obediently as would the parts of a sentence of my composing?

"Your penny, Itsik," Chaim said again. "I'll not say another word until I have your penny."

I placed it before him, and he smiled.

"That's more like it. And now, here is the first page of your book of secrets." Reaching into his coat pocket, he produced a

61

scrap of paper folded into a square that fit in the palm of my hand. "Go on, take it," he urged, and I plucked it as I would a moth from a flame.

When I flattened out the page before me, I saw line after line of cryptic Russian letters. Only after I had studied them for a moment did I notice that one side of the page was rough along the edge.

"Who has so many books that he would tear one apart?" I asked.

Chaim grinned. "Not me, I assure you. This page is not from one of mine. Don't worry, though. I took it from a place where it will not be missed."

It amazes me still how a boy told not to worry will simply shrug and not worry. I lifted the paper from the desk and held it close to my face.

"What is it?" I wondered as I gave it an exploratory sniff.

"It's a story," Chaim said.

"A story?"

"The story of a man who kills an old woman, then falls in love with a prostitute who teaches him about God."

"A Torah story?"

"No. A Christian story. A Russian story."

"A story full of secrets?"

"There's no other kind," Chaim said as he turned away. "When you have read both sides of this page, I will give you another. Note the words you don't understand, and I will explain them for a penny apiece."

"More pennies?" I lost control of my voice, nearly shouting for the whole class to hear. "There must be two hundred words I won't understand!"

"Shhh! Five for a penny, then. And don't ask before you've tried to figure out the meaning yourself. Without context we understand nothing."

So went what remained of the tenth year of my

62

life. In the mornings I broke my young back on the factory floor of Bemkin Down. Then for hours my time was filled with words on torn pages. I soon learned they were by a man called Dostoyevsky, but on first encounter they were pure revelation to me; words not written but rained from the heavens. I drank them through uncountable days, soon asking for five or ten pages at a time, finishing one book and then another. Chaim suggested my understanding of the books would increase if, after every significant turn of events, I wrote my own account of what I had read. I could not yet write fluently in Russian, so I did so in Yiddish, and what a thrill it was to watch as such a story poured from my pen!

All the while, I paid accordingly. I bought no more sweets with my earnings, saved no more pennies. Every last coin went to Chaim. As my savings jar emptied of money, my head filled with pages. I rolled my book of secrets into a scroll and kept it sealed and hidden in the darkest corner of my mother's cupboard.

My parents did not think ill of me when they heard I had not progressed beyond the lowest ranks in the yeshiva. My education had taken an unforeseen turn, but they didn't know it, so they just pitied me. For now my tutor and I both sat in the coldest row of the study house with volumes of Talmud opened before us, a great wall that Der Lerer did not dare breach, or perhaps he could not be bothered. Still, I always kept an ear open to his lectures, which ensured that even eighty years later there would be for me no Rashi without Raskolnikov, no Rabbi Akiba without Alyosha Karamazov. Raskolnikov I especially admired for the simple childish reason that the old woman who meets his ax reminded me of the Christian lady next door. Lucky as a butcher's goose, indeed!

And yet I also knew that my secret learning came at a cost. How could I forget the daily labor I endured to remain housed within this new castle of the mind? Surely there was a better way to keep myself in the pages Chaim provided.

When I asked my father how I might support myself through intellect rather than sweat as he had learned to do, he looked at me with a silence so heavy that I began to suspect he believed I would work with my back all my days. He and Mama were sitting at the table drinking tea; it was only her pleading eyes that caused him to offer any answer at all.

"When you have breathed in so much shit that your intellect is forced to the surface," he finally said, "then, perhaps, you'll find another way."

My mother moved her chin and raised her eyebrows, urging him on.

"Until then you must save your pennies," he continued. "Spend a little, of course, but keep track of your expenses. One day, should an idea come upon you, you will most likely need resources to make it a reality. Remember this, and you will avoid the mistakes your father made: if you do not own the resources, you will not own your idea. Repeat that to me so I will know you understand: If I do not . . ."

"If I do not own the resources," I said obediently, "I will not own my idea."

"Very good, Itsik," Mama said. "I have been so proud of you, the way you are always going into the cupboard to inspect your jar of coins. It seems you are making a new deposit most every day, yes? We know you will be a great success."

Father grinned at the mention of my jar of coins, and now joined the conversation more comfortably. "And what sort of resources have you amassed, my young entrepreneur? Might we see the treasure, or is it buried in your pirate's chest?"

He looked down on me then with a face filled with pride, a face that said, Maybe my son sits in the back of the class at the yeshiva, maybe his intellect will never come to the surface, but he works hard, he will make something of himself. Then I realized he expected me to show him my jar of pennies, and I felt my face burn. My eyes, as if creatures with their own instincts, started to blink uncontrollably.

"What is it, Itsik?" Mama asked. "You seem suddenly flushed . . ."

My mother's cheeks went pale with concern, but not Father's. Seeing my reaction to his simple inquiry into my savings, he must have suspected what I dared not confess, for he slapped his palm down on the table with such force that his tea jumped from its glass.

"Show me the jar!" he said.

THE NEXT DAY at the yeshiva I informed Chaim that I would no longer have pennies for him.

"My father insists on holding my earnings for me," I explained.

"Why is that?" Chaim teased. "Have you been irresponsible with your wealth?"

"He asked where all my money had gone," I admitted. "I told him you had it."

Chaim looked at me sharply.

"And did you show him all you have learned through our arrangement?" he asked.

"Show him? How does one show learning?"

"There is nothing that cannot be shown. Look here." He took a small notebook from the pocket of his waistcoat and flipped through pages showing rows of numbers and notations. "Do not think for a moment that because I am of literary leanings that I do not pay proper attention to my accounts," he said. "Every penny I make, every book I read, every page I give to you, it is all recorded here. You will find that if you begin to keep track of what you read and what you earn, what you take in from the world, you will naturally begin to take note of your actions, what you put out. Never mind what Der Lerer says about his holy books. All one needs to live a moral life is a proper system of accounting. Tell your father I told you that."

"I'm afraid I cannot," I said. "He has forbidden me to speak with you."

Chaim's face suddenly glowed red beneath his beard.

"Forbids you even to speak with me! What did you tell him of our arrangement! Did you tell him you gave your pennies to me freely and received something in return?" he demanded. "Or did you lead him to believe I picked them from your pocket?"

"I tried to explain, but he wouldn't listen. He said if I paid good money for scraps of paper I was a fool and you were no better than a thief for taking advantage."

"Scraps of paper?" Chaim scoffed. "I give you a new world, and you let him call it garbage. Is that what you think, that I have robbed you?"

I held my tongue because in truth I did not know what to think. It surely did not occur to me then that I was being asked to choose between two fathers—father of my flesh and father of this new fire inside me—but on some level I must have understood, for the complexity of the situation caused in me a total paralysis; I could not speak. Any word would either betray my blood or deny my will to continue learning.

Yet Chaim did not sense the respect my failure to answer signified; in fact, my silence seemed to give offense. As he raised one volume of Talmud and then another before him, it felt to me like a gate swinging shut.

"Go back to your children's lessons, little Itsik. I had begun to believe you might be an intellectual, but I see now I was wrong. Maybe if you try very hard you will finally advance through Der Lerer's ranks, eh? Rashi's Chair is waiting for you."

daled

Chaim withdrew from me not as the
sun sets, with brilliant colors and lingering warmth, but as a candle
is snuffed out. For many days, I walked in the smoke his light left.
I wandered by the shops whose signs he had first challenged me to
read: the Russian bakery, the Russian butcher, in particular the offices of *Bessarabets*, the newspaper that had caused so much trouble for
the Jews of Kishinev but now only shone for me, with its window
full of the week's clipped headlines, as a beacon of forbidden
knowledge. Through Chaim this language of Christians and
anti-Semites gave me a viewing glass on the wider world. I stood lamenting all it seemed I had lost along with Chaim's friendship: the
Russian tongue, the Russian stories. How to explain the passion I
now felt for these things?

I was entertaining just that thought when I felt a stinging sensation on the back of my neck. I saw smoke in the air above me
and knew that it was not of the metaphorical variety, for it made
the air smell acrid in a way that metaphors rarely do. Then, all at
once, it was as though I had been stabbed behind the ear with a
kitchen knife.

Swinging around on my heels, I found myself facing a gang of
Russian boys. How many? Three, four, five, ten . . . Their leader
was a little shorter than me. He held a stubbed-out cigarette between his thumb and forefinger. I put my palm to my neck and first

felt ash, then a hole in my skin, slick with the weeping of a new wound.

"You're on the wrong side of the street," the leader said. To his left and his right, his fellows alternately grimaced and cracked smiles of enjoyment. One instant they were squinting their eyes and flaring their nostrils to give the impression they were wild men, outlaws; the next they were giggling and jumping in place like the children they were. No amount of play-acting could hide their glee, for there was no better sport in Kishinev than a young Jew caught alone with his guard down.

"If you want a newspaper, you should be over there." He pointed across the street with his cigarette, then reached out and slapped my face with his other hand. Though the force of the blow blurred my vision, I could still see clearly what he was indicating—a narrow door in a brick building with a hand-lettered sign that read *Frei Yidishe Shtime.* "The Free Jewish Voice." I had been up and down this street ten thousand times and thought I knew every Jewish business in the city, but somehow I had never taken notice of this particular doorway before.

"The Jew paper is over there," the leader said. "My father runs the *Bessarabets,* and he doesn't want any Jew boys looking in his window. Got it? So you better run to your own side of the street before—"

The Russians tightened their circle around me, but I was already on the move. Others in their memories might have stayed for the fight, and doubtless if those memories were in written form, they would prevail. I, on the other hand, am a poet for whom truth is a constant companion, a steadfast lover and brother-in-arms, so I ran, ran from the clutches of those future pogromists, ran precisely to where they said I should run. What pride is there in a bloodied nose, a split lip, a blackened eye, after all? For the poet there is only pride in living to tell the tale.

In an instant I was across the street and had opened the door of the *Frei Yidishe Shtime* without breaking stride. Once inside, the assault on my senses was such that I nearly turned and ran back the way I had come.

Later in life, the scent of a newsroom would be an odor I knew as well as my own skin. There was always something deeply organic about it: the ink, the paper, the heat, the gaggle of gruff men too concerned with deadlines to wash their clothes or their hair: all of it combined to create an unmistakable air. It's a dirty smell, and my first encounter with it nearly sent me into a swoon. I began to back out the door, but was stopped by a commanding voice.

"Who are you? What do you want?"

A large man with a mustache hiding his upper lip and wire-rimmed glasses that looked much too small to be perched atop his considerable nose was resting inky hands on his aproned belly. He alone had stopped his work to pay attention to me. The other workers, six young men similarly ink-stained, rushed between tall tables arranged here and there throughout the shop.

If I spoke at all in response to the mustachioed man's questions, it was but a squeak, a squeak that must have sounded like "Malpesh."

He squinted at me. "Are you perhaps the son of Manager Malpesh, of the down factory?"

I nodded that I was, which only brought closer scrutiny.

"To what do we owe the pleasure of a visit from the prince of Jewish Kishinev, eh?"

All I could think to say was, "I didn't know there was a Yiddish newspaper in this part of town."

"We are a new operation. I am the editor. We opened our office outside of the Jewish Quarter so that we might better report on the Christian actions against us. It's risky work but it must be done. . . ." His voice trailed off as he studied me, as if he was weighing whether or not I was worth the breath required to speak his words. Apparently he decided I was not, for he said, "Ah, but what would the manager's son know of work, eh? Your world must be cushioned with feathers."

"I work," I protested, "two hours every morning. I clear the floor at the factory."

"Please forgive my impudence, Master Malpesh," the editor replied with a courtly wave of his hand. "And forgive my ignorance as well. I have never been inside the down factory, and so I must ask: Clear the floor of what?"

"Goose droppings," I said.

He smiled sadly, then laughed. "We poor Jews! Even the rich among us are defiled by goyish excess."

"It is difficult work," I said. "I am up before dawn and nearly break my back."

"I'm sure, I'm sure," the editor nodded. "Take no offense, my young friend. Our work is not so different. You shovel shit, I shovel words. Come, I will show you what I mean."

He put his meaty hand on my shoulder and led me to one of the half-dozen tables that filled the room. When he saw that I was too small to see what was on the tabletop, he hoisted me up and held me like a parcel under one arm.

"You see?" he said. "All day long I move letters, one at a time, from this jumbled pile to the inking tray, here."

The shop's tables, I now saw, were covered with wooden blocks of varying sizes, each one carved with a single letter; they were literally the building blocks of words. There were also blocks carved with every imaginable mark of punctuation. He lifted one displaying a cartoonish "!" and put it in my hand.

"Have you ever held a shout before?" he asked. "How about a question?" He found a "?" block in the pile of punctuation marks and placed it in my other hand. "Did you know that this is how a story is built? Inch by inch, line by line?"

"Oh, I know about stories," I told him. "I have written many and read many more."

"I was also raised on Torah stories—" he began to say, but I cut him short with a boast.

"Not just those," I said, "I know Russian stories, too, stories about Christians and crimes and punishments."

"Is that right?" He lowered me to my feet and looked down on me with new interest. "We are always looking for those sorts of stories. Perhaps when you are older you will write for us. We are in need of young men who live by their wits. Come and see me again when you have a story to tell."

Back at home that night I turned again to the pages Chaim had given me, still lamenting the fact that he would no longer be my guide to their meaning. To my surprise, however, I found that I no longer needed one. When I went back to Raskolnikov and *Crime and Punishment,* I discovered that I no longer read in the halting, grasping way I had under his tutelage. Now, reading those tattered pages was less like work and more like breathing. Like *being,* for while I read the story, I *was* the story. Raskolnikov's thoughts and fears were mine, and his crimes were also mine. How could another life be so fully experienced, I wondered. How could I be simultaneously a boy made of flesh and a man made of words?

I paused in these ponderings only long enough to wander into the kitchen to find a snack. I stopped in my tracks when I heard my parents talking—talking, or so it seemed at first, about me. Before they noticed my presence, I hid myself behind the curtain that divided the room.

"I believe I should have words with Mr. Bemkin about Itsik's bully, the boy Chaim," Father said. "I have seen him lately around the factory. In Bemkin's company, oddly enough."

"Has he given the boy a job?" my mother asked.

"If he has it is a poor choice. The factory could do without Chaim's help."

"Perhaps Mr. Bemkin feels he knows better what kind of help he needs," my mother said.

"Well, it seems I know better what Bemkin Down does not need. Scandal we do not need. Already there are rumors."

"Rumors? You know better than to believe such things. Wasn't it rumors that darkened Passover ten years back?"

"Rumors we can live with. It's what often follows them that worries me: Blood."

"Whose blood?"

"Whose always?" Father said. "Nothing good will come of allowing that boy to be involved in Mr. Bemkin's affairs."

"What good can come from meddling? If you make trouble, you will find trouble. Let Bemkin worry for Bemkin for once, and Malpesh worry for Malpesh."

"You worry enough for all of us. It's not as if he can fire me. My reputation among his clients is too strong. There has never been a word spoken against me. So long as that is so, my position is safe and I am free to speak my mind."

I could not see their faces as they argued, but my mother's silence at that moment was the sort that drained the blood from my cheeks. It was the silence of prophecy unspoken. I knew from the time it took my father to speak again that she was likely standing before him with her eyes closed, her neck bent with the weight of what she foresaw.

Finally my father struck an optimistic tone, as if he could sweep all her doubts aside. "Men of business see things differently than housewives do, Minah," he said. "I will simply inquire what interest he has in the boy and voice my reservations. He will recognize this is a matter of business, not a personal judgment. And that will be the end of it."

The next morning, I heard nothing specific of the disagreement that greeted my father's decision to ask Mr. Bemkin about Chaim. I only witnessed the aftermath, in which Father marched across the factory floor shouting commands—"Keep working! Pick up the pace!"—to any worker who looked up. Only when Father was out of sight, did Mr. Bemkin call to me.

"Minor Malpesh! Come here a moment, will you?"

He was standing at the bottom of the stairway that led to his office suite. With his hand raised to the height of his shoulder, he looked more as if he was waving farewell than beckoning me closer.

"Join me in my office," he said as I approached. "I've a favor to ask . . . and sweets to offer!"

I stood my shovel against the wall nearest the first stair, then followed him up. It was an open stairway, climbing at a steep grade to a balcony that overlooked the factory floor. I had heard my father mention how Bemkin liked his workers to see him watching them.

"He stands out on the balcony like a pope," my father had said once, "as if the goose pluckers would stop their work to cheer at the very sight of him. When they don't, he starts down the stairs in a huff and berates the first man he meets."

Going up seemed considerably more difficult for him, and as I climbed behind his massive legs, I wondered why Mr. Bemkin would want such a spectacle as a fat man losing his breath after ten stairs to be seen by those whose respect he hoped to command. As we reached the balcony, the backs of his trousers showed spots of perspiration. I paused for a look at the factory floor and was relieved not to see my father anywhere below.

By the time I entered the office, he was already sitting at his desk, an enormous boat of dark wood that made even a man his size seem tiny. I stood near enough to touch it, but I could barely see over the top. The rest of the suite was no less lavish. Porcelain lamps gave the room a soft glow from marble tabletops perched on carved legs of oak. An ornate samovar stood on a sideboard like a miniature silver elephant. Heavy velvet curtains partitioned the room from another space I couldn't see.

"Tell me, Minor Malpesh," Bemkin said, "do you read Russian?"

So surprised was I by his question that I offered nothing in response. He took my silence to mean no, and I did not correct him.

"Ah," he said, "perhaps someday you will. Here, have a sweet."

He reached into a bowl beside him and with his stout fingers scattered a rainbow of hard candies on the corner of the desk, then he dipped an ivory-handled pen in a jar of ink and began to write on a blank page in front of him.

"This will only take a moment," he said. "Please help yourself to the candies. Don't be shy."

As he wrote, I noticed the considerable library that filled the wall beside his desk. I scanned the spines of the volumes, which seemed to be organized not by author but by color. There were blocks of books bound in red leather, brown leather, blue leather, and black. Bemkin must have noticed my interest, for he said, "You know, we're not so different, Minor Malpesh. A boy like you can't read those books, and a man like me doesn't have the time. Maybe we could be friends, eh?"

I continued to scan the shelves. Every Russian author Chaim had ever mentioned to me was there. Glancing back toward Bemkin, I saw that he had returned to his writing. He moved the pen feverishly, occasionally pausing to mop his brow with a handkerchief. His focus on the task at hand was such that I ventured to move more closely to the bookshelves, stooping to the floor to have a look at a volume that had caught my eye.

"Yes, yes, just play on the floor, boy," Bemkin said. "This won't take a minute more."

Hidden out of sight, I slid his copy of *Crime and Punishment* off the shelf, eager to inspect it. What an unexpected delight! This was the book I had come to think of as my first love, yet I had never seen it between covers. For a year now it had been for me a nest of pages in a jar—an appropriate form, I thought, for the true messiness of life it revealed. That such an expansive story could be contained between two covers was to me a mesmerizing possibility. How does a world live in a block of leather and dead wood?

Upon opening the book, however, I discovered it was not *Crime and Punishment* at all. In place of the text were—blank pages. Hundreds of blank pages. Each had been cut to size and all stuffed between the elaborate endpapers to give the book shape. The missing pages, I realized, were in my jar at home. Was this why Father wished to warn the factory owner about Chaim? Did he know Chaim had been slaughtering Bemkin's books and selling their innards to me?

"All right then," Bemkin's voice called out. I managed to slide the book back silently and stood to face him. His face dripped as if he'd been caught in a rainstorm. Struggling to stand, he held out a folded piece of stationery.

"Please take this to the *Bessarabets*," he said. "Do you know where to find the office of the Russian newspaper?"

"Yes," I said, and took the note from his hand.

"I'm certain your father will be pleased that you have helped me in this matter," Bemkin told me as I made for the door. "Only don't mention it to him just yet. If you complete your assignment successfully, it will mean a great boon to the factory. Then we will tell him you were responsible, and he will be so proud. But for now, this must be done quickly and secretly. Do you understand?"

I nodded vigorously, then charged out the door and down the stairs. As soon as I was outside the factory walls, beyond Bemkin's reach and his sight, I unfolded the page. I could not read all the words—the factory owner's penmanship was abysmal, and he had sweated so much on the paper that it was smudged in several places—but I could read enough of them: "Jewish," the note said, "labor," "agitator." One word stood out especially because I had never before seen it rendered with Cyrillic script: "Malpesh."

I knew instantly that I must not bring this note to the Russian newspaper. Instead, I went to the yeshiva, where I hoped to find Chaim, with whom I would plead to read the note for me. With my imperfect grasp of the language, I could not be certain, but the more I studied it, the more I believed the note said something derogatory about my father. I believed Mr. Bemkin was informing the editors of the *Bessarabets* that Manager Malpesh was an organizer of Jewish labor elements in his factory, and as such was a threat to Christian Kishinev. If only I could find Chaim, I could confirm my suspicions.

Alas, Chaim was not at the yeshiva. The back row was empty, and the other boys claimed not to have seen him. Der Lerer asked me to please take my seat and pay my penny, but I ran from the room and back into the street, still clutching Bemkin's note in my hand.

Could any of it be true? No. I knew it wasn't. When I reached the open expanse of Chuflinskii Square, I tore the note into pieces and scattered it in the wind. Bits of white paper flew into the sky like the feathers my mother told me had greeted my birth. I was no stranger to fibs as a boy—what child is?—but to encounter this evidence of a lie concocted by an adult was to me an unnerving experience. I watched Bemkin's note fly into the air and felt relieved to be rid of it, as if all lies could be undone by exposing them to the light.

I walked home full of pride for my secret ability to decipher Bemkin's note, and the brave act this ability had inspired. Forgetting to return either to work or to the yeshiva, I thought instead of the hardships from which we would now be preserved. Thanks only to my intellect, Father's reputation would not be besmirched in the Russian newspaper. He would remain a respected figure; the name Malpesh would still be held in esteem by Jew and Christian alike.

My mother was delighted to see me when I appeared in the kitchen well before the hour I usually arrived. Though of course she did not know of the day's excitement, when she gave me a large slice of potato pie with cream, I thought of it as my just reward.

This prize was quickly eaten, though, and soon even the memory of its sweetness left me. For when Father came home that evening, he gave me a beating.

"Why did you leave the factory with your work unfinished this morning?" he demanded to know. "I returned to the depluming room and found your shovel propped against the wall with the floor still covered in muck. You should not expect special treatment just because you're the manager's son!"

He cuffed me about the head with such force that I could scarcely catch my breath, let alone provide an answer. My mother screamed that I was just a boy.

"You should have pity and not take out your misery on him!" she cried. "Your frustration will crack his skull!"

As if shamed by this, Father bent me over his knee to strike me as befits a child. When the spanking was over, he ordered me to my room, but not without one final word of punishment.

"And no reading!" he said.

To hell with him, I thought. I had saved his neck only hours before, and look how he repays the favor. Hidden in my room, I opened my jar of pages more to prove to myself that I could than because I truly wanted to read.

I spread my loose pages on the floor around me, arranging them as if they were the spokes of a wheel, with me at the hub. Let Father find me now, I thought, then he will see how I regard his commands. Half hoping, half dreading that he would burst through the door and find me defying him, I collected the pages of the seventh chapter of *Crime and Punishment* in my hand and began to reread them. It was among my favorite sections, for it had fewer of the philosophical ruminations that so dragged for a reader as young as I was then, and far more of the dramatic moments that to me made reading seem worthwhile. It was the chapter in which Raskolnikov resolves to do away with the pawnbroker, lured on by a force he cannot name.

Usually the sights and sounds of Dostoyevsky's St. Petersburg were enough for me to forget my cares. But that night, as I turned the pages, questions came to me that perhaps would have come to others more quickly. As I followed Raskolnikov's progress up the stairs of the pawnbroker's apartment building with hatchet in hand, I thought of my destruction of Bemkin's note and suddenly felt less a hero than a fool. As the pawnbroker opened her door and found Raskolnikov waiting there for her, I wondered what my scattering of the note had accomplished. Couldn't he simply write another one? How could a boy my size prevent a man his size from doing anything at all?

By the time Raskolnikov had gained entrance to the wretched woman's room, I knew what I must do.

THE DOWN FACTORY at night was a different place from the down factory in the morning. The windows, which at sunrise assumed a hue as pink as flowers, at midnight were black as machine grease. In the depluming room, the next day's geese were sleeping in their boxes. A communal snore rose from their corner of the shop floor. As I walked by them, I could not help but note how peaceful they seemed. Did they know they were dreaming their last dreams on earth?

I found my shovel where I had left it and hefted it in my hands. As quietly as I could manage, I crept up the stairway to Bemkin's office. Even with great effort, each step seemed to creak as loudly as a rusted wagon wheel. At the top of the stairs the door was shut tight, but with the echoing wheeze of the sleeping geese filling the building, not even I could distinguish the creak of the hinges as I slipped into the factory owner's suite.

Inside, the curtains were open, but the sky above the factory was filled with clouds; not even a faint glow of moonlight entered the room. Through the dark I moved forward a few inches at a time, tapping the floor before me with a cautious toe before committing to a full step. With every movement, I felt I should turn and go back the way I had come but was compelled forward just the same. What had I read of Raskolnikov? Ah, yes, this was it: *The moment he brought the hatchet down, all his strength returned to him.*

As I crept across the floor, a cloud must have moved as well, for the moon's beams now cast light on the top of Bemkin's desk. There, glinting, I could see his inkwell and pen—the very weapons he had used against my father.

I circled around to the back of the desk and climbed to stand on the cushioned chair where Bemkin had sat to compose his lies. My shovel had become heavier than ever it seemed while I was shoveling shit on the factory floor, but no matter. Taking a firm grip of the handle, one hand in each of the spots my father had worn smooth through years of labor, I lifted the blade high above my head and brought it down with all the force my young arms could gather.

A terrible crash followed, and a spray of drops shot up to wet my face. Blood? Had I chopped off my own foot? Some of it dribbled to my lip and I stuck out my tongue to taste. Ink. *Success!* I thought, then lifted my shovel and brought it down again and again, and again. With one strike I snapped the nib of Bemkin's pen, with another its ivory handle, with another I beat the shards of the glass inkwell into grains as fine as sand. Bemkin would find it difficult to write more lies about Father now.

From the darkness I heard a loud thud, and only then did I realize I was not alone in the room. In a flash of light, the velvet curtains parted and the factory owner stood before me, backlit by a bedside lamp next to a four-poster bed half hidden in shadow. He'd been an imposing figure in daylight, that enormous face of his stuffed into a collar and tie, but that was nothing compared to the great nude assemblage of milky white limbs that towered before me.

"Who?" he shouted.

An instant later, any fear I felt turned to sheer amazement. For as Bemkin stumbled to a chair where his pants lay in a ball, I saw behind him the spindly arms and sunken chest of—

"Chaim!"

Leaping from the bed, my former tutor gathered his clothing in seconds. Without breaking stride he scooped a stack of books from the table and made for the door. Before he left, he turned to look at me.

"Keep up your reading, little Itsik," he said. "There's no end to the secrets you will find."

And then he was gone.

Bemkin hopped and cursed as he tried to stuff himself into his trousers. They were of the new style, with a button at the top and a zipper from the crotch to the waist. He fit his calves and thighs into the trouser legs like meat into sausage casings, but his organ still stood with the blood of sleep and would not be contained. Pushing and bending this way and that, he could not conceal himself. He looked down at his belly, then at the unjoinable flaps of his pants, and, upon seeing that he was in an impossible situation, let out a sigh of defeat.

Only then did he look toward his desk and see who it was that had invaded his privacy.

"Malpesh!" he yelled, and yanked his trouser zipper upward with a force that would have knocked me to the ceiling had it been so directed. When the zipper's teeth tore across the flesh in their path, Bemkin let out a cry that in the silence of the factory echoed through the depluming room and woke the geese from their sleep. I will never forget the honking that followed.

I ran down the stairs and raced into the street. Instinct told me to head home to my mother's embrace, but instead I fled to the office of the *Frei Yidishe Shtime,* driven by a force that silenced all other impulses. Despite the hour, I found the editor stooped over his composition table.

"I have a story," I told him. I remember it as a shout, but it might have been a mumble. Whatever my volume, it prompted him to look up and squint while he wiped his hands on his apron.

"So soon?" he asked.

"Yes."

Perhaps my panting breath convinced him, or perhaps he was merely humoring me. I do not know. But what he did next changed my life, for he gave me a pencil and a page of blank newsprint and said to me, "A boy with a story must write." I remember this clearly, his simple words. Even today I repeat it to myself when I stare down at an empty page. *A boy with a story must write.* What truer sentence has been spoken? What thought could be as simply declarative and yet so forcefully imperative at the same time?

I wrote as though I had sprung a leak. One side of the page became crowded with letters, and then the other. When I was finished, I slid it across the table to the editor. He read it over—first barely glancing down, then staring with intensity, stroking his mustache. Finally he asked, "Is this true?"

"Yes," I said.

The editor laughed.

"Very good, my boy! That fat bastard had it coming. We'll run your story immediately. But first we must change a few things." He went through and amended every instance of the factory owner's name, altering it by two letters. Through each *ayen* he drew a *vav* and after every *mem* he added a *pey.*

"Bumpkin?" I asked. I had never heard the word before.

"It's French," the editor said. "Or maybe Dutch. It means a witless person, a fool. We use pseudonyms because the truth sometimes is too true. If we published this story about such a powerful figure, he would use his connections to close us down, or worse. However, if we publish a silly poem about a silly man who puts his putz in a vise, he will never dare to admit it is him, though everyone will know."

So it was that my first published words appeared the next morning. The editor broke my sentences into couplets and filled four columns of his poetry page with a work he entitled "The Bumpkin's Bris." All the Jews in Kishinev wondered if this Malpesh who wrote such biting verses was the same man who managed the down factory.

"No, it is his son," the know-it-alls explained.

"A prodigy!" others said.

My parents felt otherwise. They could not fathom why I would attack the factory owner, either in act or in print. When I tried to tell them about Bemkin's note, Mama begged me not to tell tales and Father put me over his knee. He hoped to smooth things out with his employer, but Bemkin avoided coming to the factory altogether. Each evening, Father smoked in silence at the dining room table.

In the yeshiva that week, the older boys looked on me with new respect and urged me to march forward and seize Rashi's Chair. Instead, I only moved my seat across the aisle and took the place that had belonged to Chaim, who had disappeared from town without a trace. I did not then fully understand what it meant to see Chaim jump from Bemkin's bed, but I did grasp, in some childlike way, that the books I'd been buying for a penny a page had been purchased for a much higher price.

Had I been told then that I would meet my tutor again years later and half a world away, I'm sure I would not have believed it. Even for a boy as full of surprises as Chaim was, I thought I would never again be as near to him as I was that morning when I filled the space in his empty chair.

As it happened, I held this seat only a short while. Just days after the publication of my poem, the *Bessarabets* ran a story that Bemkin had concocted, the same set of falsehoods he had asked me to deliver. That I had believed destroying one pen-and-ink set and chopping up his desk would prevent him from spreading lies about my father is now beyond my understanding, but I did, I truly did.

In the end, the only effect my act had on Bemkin's intentions was that he added a new character to his tale. The Russian newspaper reported that the Jewish labor agitator Abram Malpesh had not only tried to take control of Bemkin Down, he had sent his son—"a brute who had worked from childhood on the factory floor"—to kill the Christian owner.

The renown that followed did not bring with it acclaim or admiration, just an early-morning knock on our door. When the police officer in charge, Captain Kolykov, saw that the menace he and his deputies had come to question was just a small boy, they contented themselves with arresting my father alone.

My mother protested that there had been a terrible misunderstanding, that the vandalism in Bemkin's office was only a child's prank, not an attempted murder. Kolykov allowed that this might be the case, and told her that she should be thankful he too had a son. Then he advised her it would be best if I left town, perhaps went to live with relatives in the country.

"He will not be a child for long," he told her, "and there's no telling what will happen to a young man who acts without thinking."

"If only!" my mother moaned. "In fact, he thinks too much."

"It amounts to the same," the captain replied.

All the while I stood between them, hiding in my mother's apron. I only glanced out to say good-bye to my father, and wept when I discovered he was already gone.

Captain Kolykov reached down and patted my shoulder as kindly as the situation allowed.

"I hear you're quite the poet," he said, and the words burned so much that they dried my tears.

"Yes," I admitted. "I am."

TRANSLATOR'S NOTE

Historians will take issue with a number of details found in Malpesh's account of his early life, and rightly so. Viewing himself as a poet rather than a documentarian, he gave little or no thought to the importance his remembrances might have as an eyewitnessed chronicle of events. Those who would read him as a primary source of information concerning Jewish life in czarist Russia should keep in mind that, both as a writer and as a man, Itsik Malpesh seems to have been unbothered by inconsistency.

Particularly troublesome in this regard is his conflicted representation of Kishinev, which at many points in the narrative is depicted as a fairly modern urban center, but at others seems something of a little town out of time—closer to a *shtetl* than a *shtot*, as the Yiddish would phrase it. But even the most casual study of the late Imperial period of Russian history shows that Kishinev was indeed a large and growing metropolis. Today known as Chisinau, the capital of Moldova, it is a major transport hub, home to thirty-six universities, and among the more popular entertainment destinations of the former Soviet republics. During the poet's time in the city (1903—14), each of these industries (trade, education, tourism) existed in nascent form. A careful reading of Malpesh's work suggests that he was not attempting—at least not consciously—to obscure this fact. As he notes early on, Kishinev's population was over 100,000 at the time of his birth. Elsewhere he mentions that it was sizable enough to support several churches ("Do you know which church has the man saint and which the lady saint?"), industries engaged in international export ("Bemkin Down is the rage of Paris"), and a bustling business district that included both the daily Russian newspaper *Bessarabets* and at least one periodical, the *Free Jewish Voice*, focused on the substantial Jewish community.

Yet while Malpesh freely acknowledges all of this, the landscape of his memory nonetheless feels confined to a few streets, as if the city turned on an axis running from the Malpesh home on Aleksandrov Street to the goose down factory a short walk away. The center of this world is perhaps the carousel in Chuflinskii Square, the pole around which the saga of young Itsik swings—though never, curiously, does he mention taking a ride on it himself.

The differences between the Kishinev of history and the Kishinev of Malpesh's recollection might be explained by the simple truth that a man's memories of being a boy are, as often as not, a boy's memories. They are memories of a complex and dangerous time filtered first through the experiences of one too young to fully understand their meaning and filtered again through the will of the poet to make sense, and art, of what he has seen.

Only occasionally did I raise such concerns with Malpesh in conversation. Owing to my own relative ignorance when I first encountered his work, I did not mention any of the larger issues of accuracy outlined above, merely some incidents that, to my mind, strained a reader's confidence in his reliability.

To cite just one example: in his account of the hours leading to his birth, Malpesh reports that his mother bit through a small book while in the throes of labor. "Mama had bitten clean through Grand-mother's prayer book," he writes, "and now had nothing to stifle her screams." The original text does not indicate whether this prayer book was the popular collection of Yiddish verses and

Bible tales known as the *Tsena-Rena*, or a Hebrew *sidur* of the type that the Malpesh family might have used in the synagogue, but it was likely one or the other. In either case, to judge from contemporaneous examples of each, it would have had two leather covers and at least fifty or sixty pages in between. Even allowing for the inventions inevitable to a story told of events before a narrator was alive to see them, I had to admit that I found the suggestion that his mother bit through such a book hard to believe.

Malpesh waved off such concerns. I recorded his response to this specific question among my translation notes, as it was characteristic of the disdain with which he deflected doubt:

"I have never seen a woman in childbirth," he told me. "But I am told it is not unlike the process of bringing a book into the world. In both cases the life of the one bearing the burden is so altered that every given is changed. In the making of my book, I myself was driven to break every commandment given by God. *Every one.* If the Law itself could be torn apart by the turmoil of creation, do you believe the leather covers of a prayer book would be spared?"

As was often the case when working with Malpesh, this remained the last word on the matter.

Now that I have broached the subject of Yiddish and Hebrew devotional literature, it occurs to me that there is more to tell regarding that other prayer book, the one Clara Feld discovered in a wet box on the warehouse loading dock during the summer before Malpesh first entered my life. Strange as it may seem, it too played a role in the making of this translation. In fact, if not for that book, it's unlikely this one would have come into being.

From the day she found it, Clara carried what she called her "pretty little prayer book" wherever she went. When we sat outside the warehouse at one of the picnic tables that overlooked the canal, she'd cradle the book in her lap. If I happened to mention that we should find a place for it on the bookshelves, she only said, "Soon, soon," and slipped it back into her purse. The chances of her giving it up grew slimmer still when she began using it to hold photocopies of her great-grandmother's letters. It seemed that in her mind, the letters and the prayer book had become a matched set. Her great-grandmother's words were so timeworn and particular that Clara had accepted she might never know their meaning, but the orderly progression of text in the prayer book was full of promise that it might be understood. That she couldn't read more than a few words on any given page didn't matter at all as far as she was concerned. To her, it had the look and feel of a tradition her family had lost, and that was enough. She liked to run her fingers over the lines of Hebrew letters and say her own silent prayers; prayers she imagined to be very much like those others had said while touching the same holy pages.

By this point I hadn't yet read about Malpesh and the attachment he felt to a jar filled with stolen chapters of Dostoyevsky, but it strikes me now that Clara's bond with her prayer book was likely the product of a similar longing: access to a new world, a way of living and being that was totally foreign to her upbringing. How strange the history of "our people" is: Prayers in a Jewish language were now as exotic to a Jersey-bred tennis star turned *baal t'shuva* as stories in a Christian language once were to *yeshiva bocher*. One difference, of course, is that Malpesh came to read Russian fluently, while Clara still had trouble telling the third letter of the Hebrew alphabet from the fourth.

And yet, if I was Chaim to her Malpesh, I did not do a very good job of it. Given all that the prayer book seemed to mean to her, it took me much longer than is excusable to have a closer look at its contents. In part this was because the book rarely left her grasp, but also, I admit, I enjoyed knowing that I could explain it, but wasn't doing so. This would seem rather manipulative if not for the fact that she enjoyed it, too. It actually became a kind of game for us. Translation may well be an intimate act, as Malpesh said, but apparently the withholding of translation can be as well. Whenever Clara opened the book in my presence, she made a show of refusing to ask for help, waiting for me to say, "You want me to take a look at that for you?"

"Oh, don't you get all Jewisher-than-thou on me," she'd say.

"I'm not," I'd laugh. "I'm just saying, if you get stuck on a particular word—"

"I'll keep that in mind," she'd say, and we would sit in silence a few minutes more until she decided to throw me a line—"Fine, if you insist on being helpful . . ."—and then she would ask for a definition, or a pronunciation, or a reminder of a particular rule of grammar.

It was like some sort of linguistic mating dance, a dance we performed to music we'd discovered hidden among the books. Included in the boxes were a fair number of audio recordings, both cassette tapes and old-fashioned hard wax LPs, that allowed us to listen to an endless Yiddish sound track as we sat reading or talking. There were Borscht Belt dialogues by the comics Shimon Dzigan and Israel Schumacher; silly show tunes by the belle of the Lower East Side stage, Molly Picon; and of course that bilingual swing hit, the Andrews Sisters' ode to the romantic possibilities of loose translation:

> *Bei mir bist du sheyn*
> *Please let me explain*
> *Bei mir bist du sheyn*
> *Means you're grand*

That happened to be the tune playing when Clara said to me one day, "Okay, smart guy. How about this word. It's spelled: *Alef-mem-tof* . . ."

"What about it?" I asked.

"Well, for starters, is it Hebrew or Yiddish?"

"Depends on the context," I said. "It's *loshn kodesh*. Do you remember what that means?"

"Holy tongue?"

"Right, so it's a word from Scripture that can also be used colloquially. In Hebrew it's pronounced *'emet'*; in Yiddish it's *'emis,'* which is what you might say when you agree with someone, or if you want to insist that something is true."

"So what does it mean in Hebrew?"

"I'll tell you if I can take you to dinner."

"You drive a hard bargain."

"*Emis*," I said.

After work that night we decided to go to Kronbloom's, the only kosher restaurant within driving distance of the warehouse. With the shelving room locked up and the alarm set, Clara and I started down the stairs. It was still August, but the heat of the previous weeks had mostly left the building. Even four flights up, we could tell someone had propped open a door at the bottom of the stairs. A fresh-smelling breeze wrapped around us, blowing wisps of stray hair across Clara's face. When she lifted her left hand to tuck the loose hairs behind her ear, I reached toward her right. The backs of our fingers brushed together at the knuckles. She was not yet so religious, she had told me after our first kiss, that she avoided all physical contact with the opposite sex. Now, as I noticed her lips curl up at the corners, I reached to take her palm in mine. But she was already holding something. The pretty little prayer book.

"Oops! Sorry," she said. "I sometimes forget I'm holding it." She tucked the book into her back pocket, then grabbed my fingers. "It's funny how attached I am to it. Have you ever let a book become a part of you?"

"Not one I can't read," I said.

"That's mean!" she snapped, and tugged her hand away from mine. She still seemed to be smiling, yet her eyes pinched as though I had slapped her. I wasn't sure if she'd heard my answer as the joke I'd intended or a barb I had not, but before I could ask, or apologize, we heard a high-pitched voice below us, wafting up the stairwell.

"Who is mean?" the voice said. "Someone is mean?"

Clara and I exchanged surprised, embarrassed glances. When we reached the bottom of the stairs, we saw that the voice belonged to one of the Vietnamese ladies from the alterations shop, the woman I always took to be the owner. She was dressed in her uniform of tight-fitting black pants, bright pink top, and a tangle of plastic necklaces.

"Hello, Jews!" she said. "I thought it might be you."

Her voice rose in a playful singsong, using each word to hop a half-step up the scale. We nodded a greeting but continued past her, walking quickly out to the parking lot.

"I've been hoping to run into you," she said, following closely behind us. "I wanted to give you some, ah, comic book. Comic book from my church."

"Comic book?" I asked.

"Your church?" Clara said.

She pressed three scratch-card-sized pamphlets into my hand. I looked down and saw that they were bilingual evangelical tracts, English text in red, Vietnamese in blue. One of them was titled "God's Special People" and showed Jesus sitting in a circle with five bearded, yarmulke-topped rabbis. When she reached out with another handful, Clara hugged her prayer book to her chest and shook her head, no, no, no. The Vietnamese lady shrugged.

"Okay, you read his!" she sang, then hurried away toward her car. "You come church sometime! Address on back!" A minute later she waved good-bye from the open window of her Lexus. "You welcome!"

"I just don't understand Christians," Clara said. "Where do they get off telling people what to believe?"

"She's an evangelical," I said. "Telling people what to believe is pretty much the point."

"But they're just so . . . *predatory*," she whispered, as if we were in a bugged room. "It's like they're always sneaking around, waiting to get you. What are we supposed to do about it? Run? Hide? Fight?"

"Eat," I said.

KRONBLOOM'S KOSHER DAIRY had the half-lit feeling of a diner that, like its clientele, had seen better days. The part of town it occupied had been an immigrant stronghold when Jews were the newest and poorest arrivals in the city. The restaurant was still decorated with black-and-white photographs from that bustling era. It was the only place to go when keeping kosher was a concern for workers at the factories nearby. But as its customers' lives improved, its business faltered. According to Mrs. Kronbloom (who was still behind the counter after all these years), most of the regulars had either died or moved to Florida.

Clara loved that about the place. If its tables hadn't wobbled and its seat cushions hadn't been torn, she wouldn't have taken it seriously. The better I got to know her, the more I understood that her born-again religiosity was like something pulled up from the sea. She expected the trappings of her new life to have a whiff of rediscovery.

We chose a booth by the window and ordered kugel and coffee. After the coffee arrived, Clara said, "Shouldn't she be a Buddhist or something?"

"Who?" I asked. "The waitress?"

"No. That woman in the parking lot. You wouldn't think she was a Christian to look at her. I mean, it's surprising, right?"

"Because she's Vietnamese?"

"Yeah."

"I don't really like that kind of Christian either," I said, "but she does have some choice in the matter."

"Choice?" she said.

"Sure. She can be a Christian if she wants."

"I just think people should be what they are."

I couldn't tell her that I'd been so unnerved by the encounter—by the strangeness of someone trying to convert me to something close to the faith I was born into—that I had put it out of my mind as soon as it was over. But Clara insisted on going over it again and again. It almost seemed as if she enjoyed it. Brief and harmless as it was, perhaps this was the first time she'd felt that her religious sensibilities had been assaulted, and she was reveling in the experience.

We talked in circles about this for close to an hour. Our food arrived, we ate, the plates were cleared away, and we both continued to hold positions that precisely reflected our peculiar situations. Clara spoke in general terms about the importance of tradition, the need to recover lost ways of living simply, while I spoke in general terms about the importance of making up your own mind about such things and going your own way. I knew that every word she spoke was a justification of the type of person she was trying to become, and she assumed I was playing devil's advocate on behalf of leaving all the old ways behind. After all, wasn't I making a career out of preserving the history of our people?

When she pressed this point, I just stopped talking; the ground was too unstable to go another step in any direction. She ordered a milkshake to celebrate winning the argument. I asked for the check.

Finally, Clara decided it was time that she told me something that might explain her fervor. "I'm sorry it's taken so long to bring this up," she said. "I just didn't know what you'd think . . ."

What she told me then was this: She had a brother, an older brother whom she had always looked up to. He had gone off to college first—"To Utah, which we thought was kind of far but no big deal . . ."—and then, like a lot of kids, he'd come back home after his freshman year with a few new facets to his personality.

"A Mormon!" Clara said. "He tells us he met a girl, started going to church with her, and before you know it, my brother is wearing these short-sleeved button-down shirts and talking about going on a mission."

She took a long drag on her milkshake, sucking on the straw until she brought up only air.

"A mission!" she said again. "What Jew ever went on a mission! I actually heard him on the phone once, saying to one of his Utah friends, 'I used to be Jewish.' As soon as he hung up, I said to him, 'Michael, what the fuck! *Used to be* Jewish?' And he was like, 'Clara, please. Give me a break.' I haven't spoken to him since."

"What about your parents?"

"What about them?"

"Do they still speak to him?"

"I have no idea. I'm not speaking to them either."

Clara, I was beginning to understand, had a few more issues than I'd realized. I had somehow taken her for a natural citizen of the new world I'd discovered for myself. Now she was turning out to be just another exile.

"Why aren't you speaking to your parents?"

"Because it's their fault! Maybe if they'd given Michael something to believe in, he wouldn't need to go tagging along to some Mormon girl's church. But they don't know anything about where we come from. As far as their concerned, we're just from New Jersey."

We sat in silence for a few minutes, her burst of anger hanging in the air between us. Then she said, "That's what I like about you. You're the kind of Jew who really knows how to be a Jew." That's when she reached across the table and took my hand. "Let's go to your place, huh?"

* * *

93

OFTEN IN THESE TRANSLATOR'S NOTES, I have quoted the sayings of Malpesh himself, either as he spoke them to me, or as I have translated them from statements I found in his notebooks. No doubt he would have had an appropriate aphorism for a man who seduces a woman by pretending to share the faith to which she aspires. Malpesh had an eye for the greedy pursuit of endeavors that have only guilt as their ultimate end. But at this point, bringing Clara Feld back to my apartment for the first time, I had yet to read a word he had written. And so, the words that came to mind that night were those of another, better known memoirist: "Lord make me pure . . . but not yet." I spoke them aloud as we drove from Kronbloom's toward home.

"What was that?" Clara asked.

"You heard that?"

"I'm sitting two feet from you."

"It was nothing," I said. "Just something Saint Augustine used to say."

"And why are you saying it now?"

I made one halfhearted attempt to right the situation. "Well, you're trying to reconnect to your religious side, right? You're supposed to be a *baal t'shuva*. You know what that literally means?"

"A master of the return," she said.

"Right. I'm just wondering if this will slow down your return—"

"Let me worry about my return, okay?"

Inside my apartment, Clara walked directly to my bookshelves and scolded me for giving her a hard time about taking the pretty little prayer book from the warehouse. For months now, I'd been gathering a small Yiddish library of my own. In truth, it probably rivaled the Judaica sections at most of the colleges in the area: I had the complete works of Sholem Aleichem, issues of obscure literary journals published in Warsaw when Poland still had Jews, as well as a collection of works in English that were filling in the gaps in the education I'd been able to glean from a language I still struggled to understand. There was Irving Howe's *World of Our Fathers*; Ruth

Wisse's *A Little Love in Big Manhattan; The Complete Stories of Bernard Malamud*. She studied the books and said they were beautiful.

"So are you," I said.

Easy as that, we forgot everything that had caused us to argue an hour before. We forgot the parking lot evangelist and Clara's Mormon brother and the parents she wasn't speaking to. When she fell against me, pushing me toward the bed, then pinning me to it, I even forgot myself.

"In *Yiddish!*" she cooed.

"What?"

"Say it in Yiddish!"

"Say what?"

"That I'm beautiful . . . please."

Searching my limited vocabulary, I came up only with the Andrews Sisters, so I sang it for her, my face half buried in her hair.

"*Bei mir bist du sheyn . . . Please let me explain . . .*"

"And how do I say *Yes! Yes!*"

That much I knew. "Yo!" I shouted. "Yo!"

"Yo-yo?"

"'Yes' is 'yo.'"

"Oh."

She bit my chin, she bit my neck, and we rolled together with the thrill of it, this shtumping in Yiddish. I grabbed her *tuches*. I kissed her *pupik*. I gave her lessons in *loshn kodesh* until she screamed.

Loving a believer is not quite as world-changing as becoming one, but lying by Clara's side that night, I wondered if it might not be far off. Though I hadn't prayed in a year or more, once she drifted off to sleep, I thanked God for Clara's pretty little prayer book. It had brought us together, and I was happy.

hay

WHEN I WAS A BOY, I HEARD MY FATHER
mention many times the prevailing fear of his own youth: that of
being snatched away from his family by goblins who lurked in the
shadows. He'd been no more superstitious as a child than he was
as a man, he insisted, and in fact he had been right to be afraid.

In those days, there had been an unfortunate arrangement that
existed between the czar and the Jews. The czar's army needed
faces to plug the gaps between its collars and its caps, and Jews
were thought to be the one portion of the populace that had faces
to spare. In every town the Jewish community was required to
hand over a certain number of young men to fill quotas in the
ranks. After all the young men had been taken, boys who could
not yet sing their *alef-beys* were stolen away.

Of course to a boy a father's fears can only seem a jest. Like
every other detail of his life before I was born, I never took his
tales of child-snatching *khappers* seriously. To me they were bed-
time stories, no matter when he told them.

"Itsik, this is not a matter for mirth," he once said to me.
Without realizing it, I had been smiling with delight at the
sound of his voice, its rich tones like a kaddish echoing in
a barrel, as he recalled the playmates who had disappeared
from his school days. Father had always been an earnest man,
yet he seemed transported as he summoned up the names by

96

which he would forever know the friends of his youth: Baruch the Snitch, Fancy Shmuel, Dovid Holes-in-His-Pants . . .

When he saw the expression the marriage of his deep voice and these childish nicknames inspired in me, he reached out and squeezed my wrist.

"Don't grin at the mention of lost children," he scolded. "They lived and dreamed as you do, even if they breathed their last a lifetime before."

Such warnings seemed designed only to heighten the drama of the telling. After all, my father was a man of inspired imagination. Hadn't his goose machine come to him in a vision? His tales of Jewish boys taken from their parents seemed to me of similar origin. I was certain the *khappers* he described so vividly had been created especially for my amusement.

"My family had very little then, so I was at particular risk," he told me. "The richest members of the community would pay outlaws to steal away the children of the poorest. When the czar's men came looking for the required number of Jews, the urchins would be brought to the synagogue steps, and mothers of every class would wail at the sight: boys—boys your age, Itsik!—their heads shaved to the skin, their little bodies dressed for the front. Twenty-five years they were required to serve. We never saw any of them again.

"The lucky ones died," he added. "The less fortunate were lost in other ways."

More jokes, I thought. What fate was worse than death?

"They were converted," Father said. "Soon they had no idea who they were, where they had come from. But no matter. Gone is gone."

Father looked mournful at the thought, closing his eyes and drawing his lips into his beard. He loosened his grip on my arm.

"Before the *khapper* got him," he continued, "Dovid Holes-in-His-Pants said he would be happy to join the ranks. 'Abram,' he said to me, 'it will be such fun to have a sword and a horse!' We knew what he wanted most was a new suit of clothes, something to keep the wind off his skinny knees. He screamed for his mama when they got him."

My father never followed such memories with the suggestion that I should be good or the *khapper* would get me next, but that was the gloomy implication. As are all gloomy implications, it was easy to ignore. I was far more interested in other details.

"Father, did you have a nickname when you were small?" I asked.

Deep within his beard, his cheeks turned red as roses.

"You did! You did!" I cried. "What was it?"

"It was nothing. The mindless humor of childhood."

"Tell me!"

With a heavy sigh, he asked, "Have you never considered the words that can be formed from the parts of your name?"

"Itsik?"

"No," he said. "Your family name. *Malpesh.* None of your playmates have tried to convince you they know its true origin?"

I shook my head, and Father shrugged saying, "Children today are either less cunning or less cruel." He seemed content to end the conversation there, but then as if moved by my ignorance, he asked, "You do know what a *malpe* is, yes?"

"Of course! I remember them from my picture books!" I made a chimplike face, puffing my cheeks and pulling my ears.

"Yes, yes, that's a *malpe.* Now," he continued, dropping his voice to a whisper, "what fills the bucket when it is time to tinkle?"

I dared not answer. Mama had smacked me for saying such things in her presence. Having never before heard the word pass my father's lips, I feared I was being drawn into a trap.

Finally, I managed to force out a whisper, "*Pish?*"

He nodded solemnly. "Yes, it is better spoken softly, so God won't hear."

Silence passed between us for a long moment. Father studied

my face as if searching for signs of turning wheels of thought behind my eyes. My parents endlessly watched and hoped for indications of intelligence in their son. They did not yet know that in some sons, knowledge could mean ruin.

Nor did I. One does not set out to destroy one's family for the sake of discovering himself any more than he sets out to tinker with letters in order to find hidden import within. Yet sometimes it simply happens: suddenly he understands that words and people that seem permanently connected may come easily apart, and those that have nothing to do with each other may be joined to reshape the world.

Sounds and their meanings echoed through my brain. *Malpe . . . pish . . . malpe pish . . .* If indeed they were moved by turning wheels of thought, then those wheels were attached to a conveyor belt transporting words through a disassembly line, plucking them and stuffing their letters into burlap sacks: *malpe . . . pish . . .* Together they made something altogether new but somehow not unlike its constituent elements had been. *Malpe . . . pish . . .*

"Monkeypiss!" I shouted. "Monkeypiss! Malpesh can be heard as *malpe* plus *pish*! Was that your nickname?"

"It's true," my father admitted. "They called me Abram Monkeypiss."

Unable to contain my giggles, I fell over on my side. In a moment the embarrassed catch in Father's voice turned into laughter, full and deep.

"Did all the boys say this?" I asked.

"Most, yes."

"Did Fancy Shmuel?"

Father laughed until tears rolled from his eyes. "He did! He did!"

"And Baruch the Snitch?"

"They all did! There was no escape!"

"Even Dovid Holes-in-His-Pants? He called you Monkeypiss?"

At the mention of this last name Father choked on his laughter, but he could not stifle it completely.

"It was the last thing he said to me!" he said. "God help me, I can still hear his voice. We were walking together through the market when they grabbed him. A merchant's cart like any other came racing between the stalls, and just like that he was gone.

"The moment before, we were side by side. He kept daring me to steal an apple from the fruitseller's wagon. When I refused, he said he would get one himself. He stepped away from me into the street, and the next instant he was yanked into the air, screaming. *Monkeypiss, help me! Find my mama, Monkeypiss!* Monkeypiss. I hated the name and was embarrassed to hear it shouted so. I am sorry to say I was relieved when the cart turned a corner and his voice was heard no more."

Father wiped his fingers over his eyes, then smoothed them downward over his cheeks and chin, spreading glistening tears into the dark tangle of his beard.

"Many times I have wondered what would have become of him if I had gone to steal the apple instead. And what would have become of me."

Good *kheder* boy that I was, I sensed a moral to this story and wished to show that I understood.

"Like Adam he was punished, then?" I asked. "For taking the fruit?"

Father shook his head.

"Scripture should not be used to explain what befalls us," he sighed. "Dovid Holes-in-His-Pants was only hungry and poor. If the Creator punishes us for satisfying the hunger He created, we are doomed from the teat. This prospect I cannot bear. No, the *khappers* who got him had nothing to do with God's law. They were simply devils, and devils grab all they can."

SUCH WAS THE PREVAILING MYTHOLOGY of my youth. Thus instructed, it was with great confusion that I later discovered that members of the species against which my father had so often warned me were not actually devils, but men. This knowledge came to me—God's laughter echoes without end—not long after that dark day when I had seen my father taken away. It occurs to me only now that as the Kishinev police led him from the comfort of our parlor, Father perhaps supposed the goblins of his youth had seized him at last.

Once he had gone, with the scent of Kolykov's tobacco still hanging between us, my mother told me the police captain had been right: I had to leave that very morning. It was, she'd said, the only way Mr. Bemkin might be persuaded to have mercy on his loyal manager.

"When you are older, you will know where a man's pride resides, and you will understand what sort of injury you have inflicted," she said. "Until then, trust that your mother knows what is best. Mr. Bemkin is no fool. He understands that his factory will fail without your father, but just the sight of you will throw him into a rage that knows no reason."

Into my hands she pressed a cloth-wrapped package of cheese and bread. She then disappeared to her room and returned, holding a cream-colored envelope.

"Of all those who have left Kishinev these past years, I have only heard from a few. You never knew the family of Moshe Bimko, the butcher, but they knew of you. The day of her departure, the widow Bimko held you in her arms and wept bitter tears that she would not see you grow. Now perhaps she might."

She slid the envelope into the pocket of my coat.

"Ten years ago she took her daughter and left for Palestine; she never made it beyond Odessa."

Mama wiped her eyes with her hands, then her hands on her dress.

"Go and find her," she said. "I kept her daughter Sasha safe once. Now she will keep you safe."

I did not know then that this would be the last time I would see my mother, but I know this now, as I write. And so the years permit me what the moment did not, the possibility of letting my eyes linger upon her, of taking her hands in my own and holding on, refusing to let go. How healing memory can be: my mother when she lived had hands harder than a man's. The cracked tips of her fingers were often so dry they split and bled. Yet when I hold them now in my memory, they are soft and warm. And though I know she said to me that day, "Go, Itsik. Go and end the misery your life has meant to this family since the awful day of your birth," in my mind she found words that gave me the courage to turn and walk out the door.

IN ADDITION TO THE BUNDLE of food and the widow Bimko's letter, she had given me also enough money to take the train to Odessa. Because I was young and felt I had learned something about the value of a penny from my dealings with Chaim, I thought it would be better to keep my coins in my pocket. At the train station I asked the direction of Odessa, and began to walk.

Summer was in high bloom, the roadside lined with crocus flowers. Heavy with guilt for all that had befallen my family, I moved through a landscape empty but for the orphan making his way slowly southward. Orphan, I say, for though my father still breathed somewhere deep in Kolykov's jail and though my mother still sighed in her now-quiet parlor, already I thought of myself as entirely on my own. In my memory's eye I see myself now as if separate even from the man I would become; I see that lonely boy from above, dragging his feet on a rust-colored road, the black cap on his head like a pen point moving across an empty page.

For company I had only my nascent self-knowledge: I was not merely a boy bereft of his family but an exiled poet, as the newspaper clipping in my pocket confirmed. As such, even a world blurred by tears presented possibilities. Can any solace equal that which is found by finding the proper words for all we encounter? By sunset of the first day of my exile, I had discovered that to name the birds as they flew was more powerful even than to shoot them to the ground, as the poet owns not their fall but their flight, not one limp carcass but the wind that lifts all wings. With these and similar thoughts, I walked for miles composing poems, my footfalls marking meter, the air before me the only page.

> *By purple flowers*
> *I strolled for hours*
> *Until the moon climbed high*
> *In the flower-purple sky.*

They were awful verses, to be sure. Yet they so occupied me that a full day and night passed as though a moment.

Only upon waking the next morning did I realize this was not some grand adventure. I found myself in the shadow of a linden tree, thirsty as a stone, surprised to awaken for the first time not wrapped in the comfort of a Bemkin Down featherbed. Even when I attempted to transform my despair to poetry—*I rose from the dew / wet with God's tears / His hand he withdrew / and left only fears*—I knew I was utterly alone.

I considered briefly turning back and retracing my steps the way I had come, begging my mother to allow me to resume my unremarkable life. But which way was home? I turned and faced the morning sun; then turned again to the massive tree that had given me shelter in the night. Where had either been the day before? Did the linden branches point north or south? Should my shadow now be followed or should it follow me?

A merchant's cart clamored up behind me. Though I recall it all now quite clearly, at the time my eyes still were fogged with sleep and I saw the world as if through lenses smeared with cooking grease: clanking and scraping with two dozen pots dangling from either side, the cart wobbled with every turn of its wheels. A woman not yet my mother's age, her hair hidden under a green kerchief, urged on a single horse from a rough wooden bench. Beside her sat what looked to me to be an enormously fat child. It was unclear how old the child was, nor could I judge if this was the woman's son or her daughter. The corpulent figure was so fully wrapped in shawls and blankets, it could have been a golem made of its mother's weekly washing.

The woman called down to me, "You'd better run, boy, the *khapper* is on his way."

"*Khapper?*" I replied. Until then I had only heard the word from my father. Was it possible he had sent her? Was this a password he'd concocted, so that I would recognize his emissary?

As the cart approached, the horse wished to halt, turning its big head toward me. But the woman had no intention of stopping; she snapped the reins to hurry her steed along.

"Yes, the *khapper*. So run! Run, or he'll snatch you out of your boots!"

"I would rather be snatched than stranded," I said.

"You'll get no ride from me. My poor auntie is ill, and we haven't time to delay."

I searched the cart for other signs of life other than the woman and her rotund child, but saw none. Only then did I notice that the figure at her side was dressed not just in blankets but a coarse cloth peasant skirt that draped below its dangling feet. It had a black mourning scarf tied tight around its head. Within the dark cave the scarf made, I thought I saw too many eyes—three? four?—staring back at me.

"Your aunt?" I asked.

The woman turned from me to study the road behind her, where a rising cloud announced the approach of a second cart. She threw another blanket over her companion, who now was hidden fully from view. But the aunt or the child or whoever it was did not seem to appreciate this additional covering. It began to flap its arms and kick its legs until the blanket fell, and then the scarf. The heads of two boys appeared gasping for air, their mouths open toward the sky like hungry chicks in a nest.

"The devil take you if you tell," the woman said. "The *khapper* may get you, but he'll not have my boys." With a shout she set her horse to a quickened trot.

A moment later, I was alone on the road again, now a fixed point between two moving plumes of dust. As evidence of the woman and her disguised children shrank into the east, approaching from the west a larger cloud grew and grew until I could hear within it men's shouting voices and a thunder of horse hooves.

I stole behind a stand of trees a quick sprint from the roadside, then watched as a cart and its team of mares raced by. They were six of the most frightening creatures I'd ever seen, and if I wondered why so many were needed, it was only for an instant. As the cart raced by, I saw what sort of goods these merchants carried. The cart held on its back a wooden pen for livestock. A hand no bigger than my own reached out through a break in the slats.

ONE CANNOT WRITE of memory without wanting to explain with every inkstroke all that was once unknown. How else to explain our most extravagent missteps, our absurd movements tempting rebuke, other than to declare that we rode the crest of the history and did not lounge on the waiting shore? No, riding the crest is not quite right. The words I write now are merely notes from the undertow.

It so happened that not long before my departure from Kishinev, a man was shot in Sarajevo, and so Russia was again at war and many more men would be needed for shooting. The news had not yet reached us, but the general draft, which had been ended decades before, was now being revived. As in my father's youth, boys were pulled from their *kheder* seats and sealed in uniforms as though in green woolen graves.

This time the conscriptions would be so extensive that the quotas of previous generations meant nothing. Nonetheless there arose in certain disreputable circles rampant speculation in the coming market for draftable Jews.

As I watched what I now understood to be a *khapper*'s cart speed away, I did not know what an entrepreneurial lot they must have been; I knew only they were best to be avoided. Rather than return to the road in either direction, I decided it might be time to consider exactly where I was trying to go.

Though it had not left my pocket since I left home, the envelope my mother had given me was damp with the morning dew. Softened by moisture, its corners tore as I reached inside to retrieve the documents which with I had been entrusted.

The contents of the envelope were these: a letter dated the previous fall, October 1913, and a photograph of a woman and a girl posed on a tasseled divan. The full content of the letter I cannot recall—there were perhaps holiday wishes; I am certain there was a street address in Odessa. Otherwise, what can be said about words lost to time? They had been conceived, recorded, transported, received, perhaps enjoyed . . . thoughts frozen like a sound that never ceases to echo, and then they were gone. Such is the fate of all words, even a poet must admit.

Unlike that poor lost letter, however, the photograph I still have in my possession. It shows a woman and girl in the shining, front-buttoned dresses of bourgeoisie. Their faces could be reflections of each other, two pale ovals framed by hair so black it blends into the dark curtain that serves as the photograph's backdrop. Both mother and daughter have thin lips holding the smallest suggestion of a smile; both have chins held high enough to display long and graceful necks. The only differences between the two are those of age and affect. The mother's eyes, wrinkled at the edges, are cast downward; the daughter meanwhile stares directly toward the camera, as if peering beyond the bounds of the photograph, as if studying whomever would dare to look at her. On the reverse of the image is an inscription: "See how my Sasha grows! She is fifteen now and quite the young lady."

Never had I seen such a young lady. Kishinev surely had its share of beauties, but before that moment I had not been capable of seeing beauty in all its risk and possibility. Now, as a boy not yet twelve but older in mind and circumstance, I was free to entertain fantasy without fear of notice or punishment. Lacking the words to understand the feelings that stirred in me at the sight of her image, I simply stood and began to walk. I clutched the photograph before me in an outstretched hand and sang aloud the street addresss the letter contained—"*At twenty-four Yaponchik Street / I'll find the girl I am to meet!*"— following the sound of it as if knowing where I was going gave me instantaneous knowledge of how to get there.

Alas, it did not. To my ignorance of the historical and political significance of the times in which I was living, we must add also a rather poor sense of geography. It never occured to me that Odessa might be much farther from Kishinev than a boy could walk in a single day, or even four or five. As night fell for a second time on my exile, the air grew cold and sharp. My humble package of bread and cheese was reduced to crumbs. My feet burned with ten thousand footfalls. Unable to continue, unwilling to simply collapse at the foot of a linden tree as I had the evening before, I had no notion of what to do with myself. I attempted once again a feat of poetic distraction—*Words, will you be my bread / when my pack carries stone? / Songs, will you be my bed / when the bitter day is done?*—but it was little use.

The rumbling of my stomach drowned out even the provocations of my newfound muse. Though by moonlight I could still

107

discern the outline of the dark-eyed girl in the shining dress, the comfort I imagined she might bring only heightened my awareness of all that I lacked, all that I had lost.

At the moment at which despair nearly devoured me, I caught sight of a flicker of hope. Truly a flicker, for off the road, partially hidden in a stand of birch trees, I could see a small fire burning.

My senses sharpened as I approached: the smell of roasting meat. The clang of a cooking pot. A murmur of voices. The birch trees stood gray-white in the moon's glow. With the fire flashing deep within, they seemed like so many ribs protecting a pulsing heart.

At the edge of the woods, I was relieved to see a familiar cart. With its collection of pans and cookery, I knew it must be the wagon of the woman with the two boys who warned me of the *khapper* earlier that day. Her lone horse stood, unroped as far as I could see, beside a birch trunk. He scraped at the dirt and pushed his nose into what seemed to be the pile of the blankets and shawls the woman had used to disguise her sons, though neither they nor their mother were anywhere to be seen. When the horse looked at me, his face was stained red, as if he had found some nice berries to munch.

I raced toward the fire, certain the woman would not turn me away now that the *khappers* were nowhere in sight. All that greeted me was an immense cloud of smoke, so thick the blaze within was now barely visible.

As I neared the campsite, I began to shout, "I'll never tell about your auntie! I'll never tell about your auntie! If only you'll feed me some beans!"

Just then the wind picked up and the smoke cleared as if it had been inhaled by the trees. Seated on logs facing the fire were two men—vagrants, by the look of them. One was bearded and large, with a cap pulled low to his eyes. The other was smooth-faced and thin as a blade, his cheeks so gaunt his ears had the appearance of two coins stuck in either side of a carrot.

"Praise the Lord, another one," the smooth-faced one said.

The bearded one let out a booming laugh. He spoke to his companion in Russian, "I don't know why we kill ourselves chasing 'em if they're gonna start coming to us."

"Don't scare him off, now." He showed a big grin in his bare cheeks, pushing his hat up so I could see his watery eyes. Upon his chest rested a dark wooden cross on a hemp cord. He placed a hand over it, then he called out to me in Yiddish, "Hello, boy! I see you are a traveler like ourselves! Are you far from home?"

"Yes," I said.

"Where are you headed?"

"Odessa," I replied. "I must get to Odessa."

"That's a long way off, especially at night. Rest by our fire! You can continue in the morning."

Through the trees I heard the wind sing a lullabye. Back near the roadside, I heard the abandoned horse neigh. I heard pots and spoons knock together and ring like bells. Behind me was only darkness, before me only light.

"I am called Dov," the smooth-faced one said, "and my friend is called Wolf, but we are friendly animals. Sit down and warm yourself!"

No sooner had I settled in front of the fire than I was drifting off to sleep, muttering prayers of thanks that orphans are never forgotten by God.

ვოვ

EVEN BEFORE MY EYES HAD SHUT COM-
pletely, I began to dream. I dreamed that my body left the ground
and rose upward, quick as a cork through water, into the heavens. Before me burned a bright warm glow that could only be the
Shekinah, living spirit of the Almighty. As if blown by a strong
wind, the divine flame flickered and jumped, and I, blown by the
same wind, began to float from its heat. The air around me grew
cold and dim, and the sky I had glided through now offered the
resistance of a bumpy road. With every shake and jolt, a memory
of the holy light I'd beheld seemed to fracture in my skull and fall
out through my ears. Shards of memory dropped to earth like hail,
tapping the tops of my shoes before disappearing into the abyss
below.

Soon I was adrift in total darkness. I cried out to the void around
me, "What have I lost?" Then I shouted again and again, "What
have I lost? What have I lost?"

A hand clamped across my mouth.

Not a dream hand but flesh and bone, it smacked my lips and
cheeks with a force that shook my teeth. Flat on my back, I opened
my eyes to a gallery of twisted faces, all barking commands.

"Shut your hole!"

"Hold still!"

"Keep quiet!"

I struggled to sit upright, swinging my fists until the commands ceased and the faces pulled away to avoid my blows. Only then did I see that the voices belonged to boys my age.

There were perhaps a dozen of them, all seated bent beneath a canvas tarpaulin stretched across slatted walls barely taller than my seated height. Light shone in beams through rips and holes in the canvas, giving the wood-plank floor the appearance of having been spattered with gold paint. A few of the larger boys kept their heads tucked into their shoulders, turtlelike, or else sat curled into balls, their faces buried in their knees. The little fellows meanwhile seemed able to move quickly without bumping their heads, and settled comfortably into spots of their choosing.

The cramped quarters apparently had created an inverted pecking order, for after the initial volley of whispered threats and commands, it was the smallest boy among them who spoke to me first. Like a few of the others, he wore the sidelocks and black cap of a Hasid nearing bar mitzvah. Despite his size, he displayed wisps of a beard on his chin. He stood in a half-crouch, crowding in on me.

"Where did they grab you?" he asked.

"Who grabbed me?" As far as I knew, I'd simply awoken under rather strange circumstances. I could remember no grabbing.

"The two men who locked you in here. Where did they grab you? Where are we?"

"They didn't grab me," I insisted. "I saw their fire through the trees, so I asked for food."

"You mean you walked right up to them?"

His jaw hung open; his sidelocks dangled on either side of his open mouth like curtains drawn back to reveal an empty stage. Reading this expression as a sign of respect for my bravery, I said, "Yes. Yes, I did."

He turned and whispered to the others, "Another fool, that's all we need."

"I'm not a fool!" I shouted. "I am a poet!"

He reached out and slapped me.

"You'll be a dead poet you don't shut your mouth. Don't you know where you are?"

I surveyed our cramped quarters. There was a thin carpet of straw and dirt beneath us, and a pile of rusted tin cans gathered at one end of the enclosure. Otherwise it appeared in the darkness to be a wooden box stuffed with boys. With my heart no longer racing, I became aware of the sensation of movement. I had not been dreaming the bumpy road, I realized, but actually feeling it. The jump and sway of the walls and floor reverberated through my spine, rattling my bones.

"Some kind of cart?" I said.

"The worst kind," the little Hasid said. "The *khappers* have got you. Haven't you heard? There's a war starting up, and they want Jews for the front. They mean to sell us when we reach the next town."

"*Khappers?* But the men I saw at the campfire were Jews!"

"They're Jews like I'm the czarina."

"One spoke to me in Yiddish, I swear it."

"And the devil sings psalms. The one called Dov speaks Yiddish but wears a Christian cross. What kind of monster might that be, eh?"

I sat in contemplation of this riddle for some time. Until that moment the possibility that the tongue of our people could be separated from the covenant we had with God had never occurred to me. It was said that in heaven all souls know Yiddish, but on earth it was only we Jews who were sufficiently spiritual to speak the language. Even in the market, where a common vocabulary for haggling was required, one spoke to the Russian merchants in nods and gestures. Certainly they understood a few words of our language, and without doubt most Jews knew their language fluently, but all concerned acted as if it was in their best interest to keep a linguistic distance, believing mingled words could be as polluting as mingled blood.

As the cart bumped along, the light from above shifted, and for the first time I could see clearly the faces of the boys with whom I shared this rolling prison. I had never seen any of them before, but they could have been plucked off the streets of Kishinev. The little Hasid made introductions, of a sort. Pointing to a boy who was so thin his poor neck seemed to strain beneath the weight of his head, the Hasid said, "That one I call 'Pipke Pumpkin Pole.'" Of a boy who was as thick through the middle as I was tall, he said, "Fat-face Feivl."

Not all of his nicknames were such a mouthful. An otherwise handsome young man picking incessantly at his nose was simply "Nose," while a gangly fellow beside him who could not tear himself away from his ears was called "Ears." His own name, the Hasid said, was Meyer the Bully, and he smacked me again so that I would remember.

Through all this, indeed since the moment I had opened my eyes and found myself in the company of Meyer and Pipke and Nose and Ears, there sat across from me, leaning against the opposite wall, another boy with sidelocks, praying as if he were in shul. He had a bird's beak of a nose and the lazy eyes of a turtle, but neither of these features had played a role in his naming.

"That one doesn't stop with the prayers," Meyer said. "He hasn't moved from that spot in days. Just sits there davening like he's waiting for the messiah. Isn't that right, Hershl Shveig?"

The boy glanced up but didn't break from his devotions. His lips moved as might those of a younger child lost in the marketplace, endlessly repeating the address of his parents' home.

"Hershl the Silent?" I asked. "Is that really his name?"

"Nah, I gave it to him. Doesn't he look like a Hershl Shveig?"

As if to show he was not always silent, the boy called Hershl at that moment began to sing a wordless tune, a *nigun* like those sung by the great rabbis as they reached for the spiritual heights. He was perhaps a year or more younger than me, and yet there was something truly holy about him. The sound of his small voice, with its tone so haunting and sincere, silenced even Meyer. It was as if his voice alone reminded the other boys what had befallen us, that we were being taken against our will far from the places and lives we had known.

The light shifted again and sent a beam into the far corner of the cart. There, with arms latched around each other, were the two brothers I had seen looking like hungry chicks in a nest of women's clothing the day before.

"Didn't I see you yesterday?" I whispered to them. "Your mother had disguised you, yes? I'm the one she left on the roadside."

The hungry chicks said nothing.

"No hard feelings," I added. "We're all in the same lot now."

Still they only stared.

"Where is your mother? Is she sending for help?"

Finally one of the brothers spoke up. "They told us she would wait with the horse," he said.

All at once the image of the horse with the red-stained snout made sense to me. It had not been merely a pile of clothing and blankets I'd seen him inspecting, not merely berries that had been his lunch. I could not bear to share this image with them, and so I said only, "I'm sure she is waiting for you, then," and we rode along to the singing of a boy named for his silence.

Lulled by the rhythms of Hasidic melodies and the rocking of the khappers' cart, we moved in and out of sleep, made aware of the passing of days only by the beams of light that moved across the floor before they disappeared.

From time to time we would call out to our captors, "Where are we going? We are hungry and thirsty! When will you let us out of here?"

Most of our cries went unanswered. Only once did the flap at the front of the cart open in response. The smooth-faced vagrant I'd met at the campfire peered down upon us, grinning as if inspecting birds in a dovecote.

"Dov, have mercy!" Meyer the Bully called to him. "We know you don't wish for us to die back here."

"Have no fear, my little Jews," Dov said in flawless Yiddish. "We do the Lord's work."

"And we'll get a few rubles in the bargain," Wolf added in a laughing Russian voice.

When the flap closed as suddenly as it had opened, and the two men continued discussing our fate, we had nothing to do but sleep again and gather our strength. On waking we began our protests anew.

"We're hungry!"

"We're thirsty!"

"Have pity!"

"For shame!"

We had shouted ourselves hoarse when the flap opened and a tin of beans rained down onto our hats and at our feet. Instanly we all fell upon it, forgetting our common complaint long enough to kick and jab and throttle each other for a mouthful of dirty beans. With more shouting, other delicacies followed: stale bread, dried meat, mealy fruit. Four or five times the *khappers* dropped scraps of food through the flap. Whatever the items, Meyer the Bully, quickest with his fists and feet as well as with his tongue, began to claim his share before overseeing the distribution of the rest. The same system prevailed when a jug of water was dropped with a thud among us.

Thereafter, talk came in bursts of argument: one boy had a crumb compared to the crust another had; one took a large swallow from the jug when he'd been instructed only to wet his lips. Such disputes ended quickly, resolved by our shared fate and by the fact that before any disagreement over food or drink could escalate, its object had inevitably disappeared, snatched up by one of a dozen hungry mouths.

Did days, weeks, months, pass this way? I couldn't say. Time lost its meaning. My only solace came when I removed the envelope my mother had given me from my shirt. Using whatever light I could find, I examined again the photograph of Sasha Bimko.

Who was this girl? I wondered. Why did she look at me so? And was that a scar above her eye? My own plight seemed nothing when I considered harm coming to her, even if such harm had come so long before that now only a faint mark of it remained. My mother had told me Sasha had been present at my birth and that she had been injured that same day. But when we met, would she think me a child? After all, I was only as old as her scar.

These thoughts and others, all concerning Sasha Bimko, occupied me through the long stretches of darkness and sudden flashes of light. As I rode with no other distraction but Hershl Shveig's hasidic melodies, the two became linked in my mind. Songs of longing and desire, of long-endured exile and long-promised return.

Perhaps he sang them to God. As I learned his tunes and began to hum along to the bump and sway of the cart rolling toward our fate, my songs were only for her.

"Up! Up, my little Jews!"

We awoke to shouts from the open gate. We were nearing our destination, Dov said. Now they wished us to clean ourselves.

"But try anything funny," Wolf added, "and we'll pound you into the ground."

It seemed to be early in the morning, though we had been locked away in the dark so long that any amount of light would have been just as blinding. Pulled from the cart one by one, we found ourselves standing in a clearing by a slow-moving river. The air smelled of crocus flowers, and I breathed it in giant gulps, only now realizing how stifling the cart had been.

"Get moving," Wolf said. "To the river." He picked a long, thin branch off the ground and swung it at us like a riding crop.

"If you have bugs on you, we won't get a kopeck for your scrawny hides."

We ran from him, toward the water, and would have run through it and beyond had not the first of our ranks to reach the river's edge let out a howl.

"It's cold! It's too cold!" Pipke Pumpkin Pole shouted.

"We'll freeze to death!" Ears agreed.

"Aw. Too hungry, too thirsty, too cold," Wolf shouted in a mocking tone. "Get in there or you'll get a beating!"

Obediently, we dropped to our knees and began to splash the icy water on our faces and our arms. It was so bracing I hoped it might wake me from this awful dream, that I would look up from my cupped hands and find myself in my mother's kitchen, washing for dinner in her gray metal basin. Would my father be there too? I wondered.

Wolf shoved my head into the water.

"All the way in!" he snorted. "Shirts off! Pants off! Scrub!"

When Wolf had satisfied himself with our cleanliness, he allowed us out of the water. What a pathetic sight we must have been! Twelve wet boys naked as trees, we stood shivering on the muddy bank, our bare feet now dirtier than they had been. Hershl Shveig's sidelocks lay pasted against his face. Nose unplugged his finger and water dribbled from his nostril to his chin. Fat-face Feivl put embarrassed hands across his womanly chest.

"That's right, that's right," Wolf said. "Just dry off in the wind."

Dov meanwhile had made a fire and boiled water in a metal pot. He allowed us to crowd around the flame and sip tea, sharing from a single cup.

Wolf squinted at this small act of generosity.

"Why waste our tea?" he asked. "Are you getting soft?"

"No, I simply know how much they can stand," Dov responded. "I know a little tea will keep them from running for the woods or back into the river. I know the smallest kindness now will outweigh all the suffering they have endured."

"You think you're the brains of this outfit, eh? How do you know so much about what our little Jews are thinking?"

"I know because I know their fears," Dov said. "When I was their age I was grabbed myself."

"You, grabbed?"

"I used to be a Jew."

"You, Dov? No!"

"Being grabbed was the best thing that ever happened to me. One minute I was stealing apples in Kishinev, the next I was in the induction center, baptized and given a gun."

All at once—the way that letters fall together and form a word, a sentence, a poem—I was certain I knew the identity of my captor. His name alone had not given me any indication—Dov was a common enough name—nor had his mention of his city of origin. If my father had been correct, countless boys had been stolen away from our town. No, it was the fact that in his trousers he now had a healthy rip in the thigh, showing through to pale white skin beneath. Perhaps it was my youth, my hunger, my delirium, it did not occur to me that as a distinguishing feature a rip in the trousers was hardly unique and was certainly not one likely to be carried through the decades. But no matter, I was convinced.

"Dovid Holes-in-His-Pants!" I shouted. "I know who you are! You are Dovid Holes-in-His-Pants!"

Wolf turned to Dov. "What did he say?"

"Something in his pants," Dov answered.

"Holes!" I shouted. "Holes!"

Dov just stared, squinting when I locked my eyes on his own.

"My father is Abram Malpesh! He saw you lifted by the *khappers*, right out of your shoes!"

He said nothing, studying my face.

"You know him!" I insisted. "You know him!"

"What is this little Jew jabbering about?" Wolf asked.

"I have no idea," Dov said.

"Monkeypiss!" I shouted. "Monkeypiss!"

The other boys stood by watching, with their bony chests bare to the morning light.

"Monkeypiss!" I called the name out with all my power, believing I could force understanding with volume. "Monkeypiss!"

"This boy speaks nonsense," Dov said as he advanced on me. "He'd better keep quiet when it comes time to sell him. The induction officers don't care for lunatics in the ranks."

"Mutes they don't mind," Wolf said. "If he doesn't hold his tongue, I'll cut it out and feed it to the dog."

"Now, now. It won't come to that. We aim to save them, remember?"

"You aim to save them. I aim to put a few coins in my pockets."

An instant later I was lifted off the ground, tucked under Dov's arm. I saw the world then as if I was flying, but there was no mistaking this for my dream of heavenly flight. He threw me back into the cart with such force my eyes went dark.

When I awoke, I was surrounded by the other boys. My fellow inmates barely looked at me.

"They told us there'd be no more food, thanks to you," Meyer the Bully said. "If we get out of here alive, I'm going to kill you."

True to their words, the *khappers* did not lift the flap, not even for a jug of water, through the long day that followed. With nothing to fight over, there was little to say. The only sound came from the rolling wheels and the occasional humming and singing of Hershl Shveig. He sang songs without words as endless as our journey seemed.

For my part, I passed the hours that followed studying my photograph of Sasha Bimko. Could it be I would never meet this girl who had suddenly and irrevocably come to dominate my thoughts? Was it then that, somewhere deep in my heart, I began to compose my first poem to her? Rocked by the sway and jolt of the *khappers'* cart, I found in that rolling prison a rhythm by which to join memory and longing, for her face began to seem to me at once all that I had lost and all that I hoped for. Her face was the unlocking of the poet's eye, for in it I saw that what is lost and what is found always resemble each other, in the fleeting nature of the moment if nowhere else.

"Hey Apeshit!" the little bully called out to me. "Apeshit!" He picked up a pebble and flicked it in my direction, pinging it off my forehead. "Apeshit, I'm talking to you."

"My name's not Apeshit," I said.

"Your name is what I say it is. What's that you got there?" he motioned toward my hands, where I cradled the image of Sasha and her mother.

"A photograph," I said.

"I see it's a photograph, Apeshit. Who is it?"

"My muse," I said sadly.

"Your shmooze?" He snatched the photo from my hand.

"Muse," I said.

"Your cooze?"

"Muse!"

"Oh . . . *muse*," he said. "I beg your pardon. Tell me, Mr. Monkeypiss . . ." He stuffed the photograph down the front of his trousers. "Would you mind if your *muse* lit my *fuse*?"

"Don't speak of her that way!"

"Oh calm down. I'm only passing the time—" He removed the photo from his pants and looked at it, his eyes growing wide. "Well, well, Monkeypiss. She's not half bad—"

"And don't call me Monkeypiss!" I howled.

"Hush up. You can't fight what the world wants to call you. And it suits you perfectly. I wish I had thought of it! The way it rolls off the tongue . . . Mon-key-piss . . . Mon-key-piss . . . Mon-key-piss . . ."

Meyer began chanting it rhythmically, bouncing a fist on his knee with each beat.

"Shah!" I cried, to no avail. There is of course nothing a group of boys likes more than a chant that sends one of their number into a rage, and so they all were chanting it now.

"Mon! Key! Piss! Mon! Key! Piss! Mon! Key! Piss!"

Or nearly all. The only one who was not was Hershl Shveig. He sat smiling mutely at me. No longer singing, perhaps for fear of associating his gentle tune with this harsh chorus, he wore a look of such dumb innocence I wondered if he might be some sort of angel, bereft of its wings.

Unaccountably, it was toward him that I directed my fury. Who was this boy to pity me? I wondered. We all were trapped, kidnapped by *khappers*, in the midst of being transported to war, probably death. And yet he looked on me with wide eyes of compassion, as if my lot as the momentary target of a crowd of frightened boys was deserving of a lament.

Without warning, I reached out and slugged him, popping him in the nose with such barbaric force that the chanting around me stopped immediately.

Nose dislodged his pinkie, Ears withdrew his thumb. Pipke Pumpkin Pole strained to look up in disgust. The hungry chicks yelped in one voice, "Hey! What did he ever do to you?"

Even Meyer the Bully let his jaw go loose in shock. He had struck me at least a dozen times by then but still spat out, "Monkeypiss, what the hell?"

"You call me Monkeypiss again, and I will tear out your sidecurls and tie them around your neck."

I frightened even myself. Where was this rage coming from? Hershl Shveig surely did not deserve it, but when I looked toward Meyer's hand and saw how he gripped my photograph of Sasha Bimko, the sweat on my brow boiled to steam. One hand cocked in the air in a threatening fist, I snatched the photograph from his grasp with the other, then fell back breathless. Directly across from me, not more than three feet away, Hershl Shveig sat, covering his face and weeping.

From behind his cupped hands he formed the first full word we had heard from him in days of captivity—"Why?"—uttered with such fervent desire to comprehend what had happened to him that it might have been the yearning of all our hearts, though it was his chin alone that dribbled green and red with snot and blood.

Just then the cart came to an abrupt halt.

"Now you did it," Meyer said. "They're going to kill us."

Outside, I could hear voices, but no distinct words, just the murmur of street and commerce. Before any of us thought to yell out to whomever might hear us, the cart flooded with blinding light. The canvas had been lifted at the back of the cart, and the gate swung open. None of us moved. Then Dov's gaunt face appeared, a dark outline in the white light.

"Nobody make a sound," he said in a harsh whisper. "You'll all get out of here soon if you just keep your mouths shut." Again he spoke in Yiddish. How could our mothers' tongue continue to betray us?

When he had gone, we again sat in silence, listening to the world beyond the walls of our wood and canvas prison. None of us recognized any sounds of home. Meyer the Bully pushed me down and climbed up to the top of my shoulders to steal a glance through a gap in the tarpaulin. We strained our ears to listen as he narrated what he saw.

"There's a man in uniform, coming down the steps."

"Good morning, Mr. Induction Officer," I heard one of our captors say.

"Wolf is speaking to him," Meyer said, "and now Dov."

"We are merchants and we are interested in selling our wares—at a deep discount—to the czar's army."

"Patriots, eh? What have you got to sell?"

"Before we talk business, I wonder if you might settle a dispute my friend and I were having. Hypothetically speaking, Mr. Induction Officer, what sort of reward would be offered for a dozen or so conscripts?"

Meyer said, "God help us. We're doomed." His leg slipped off my shoulder and he came tumbling to the floor. I used the opportunity to reverse our roles, kneeling on his back, raising myself up, and peeping through the hole.

What I saw was this: the officer—sporting a pince-nez, white mustache, and field cap—seemed to be studying the faces of our captors. They might have chosen better than to pass themselves off as merchants, or else cleaned themselves up a bit to look the part. Traveling merchants are far from elegant, of course, but these men had grass in their hair.

"Offering rewards for conscripts is tricky business," the officer said. "Suppose they have already been drafted? In such a case you would essentially be selling stolen property. Such property, if it existed, would be confiscated immediately, and whoever had sought to profit from it would likely be jailed. Hypothetically speaking."

"Of course, of course," Dov said. "That is just what I was telling my friend here. But wouldn't you agree the important thing is that these boys find their way to service, no matter the means? I myself was inducted at an early age and am forever grateful. Were it not for my induction, I would have lived and died a Jew and not the Christian man you see before you today. So you understand, it is my hope only to help the neglected find the comfort offered by the czar and Our Lord."

"Yes, a noble cause, I'm sure," the officer said. "But take my word for it, gentlemen: we have no desire to promote kidnapping of the sort that existed a generation ago. The czar's army is quite proficient in adding new recruits to its ranks, without resorting to the use of mercenaries. Now, do you have wares to show me in your cart?"

The two *khappers* looked at each other. "No, sir, no," Wolf said quickly. "Nothing you would be interested in, I'm sure."

"I'll be the judge of that, eh?"

"Allow us to arrange our wares."

"Come, come," the officer said. "We've a war to win, no time for niceties."

Again the cart filled with light. The officer stared in at us for an instant, then snapped around on his heels and began blowing a metal whistle.

Twee! Twee! Twee!

The flap dropped shut, and again we were in darkness. Beyond the canvas walls, we heard clacking footfalls and shouting, and then the floor of the cart seemed to yank away beneath us. I tumbled from atop Meyer, and we both tumbled into the others. The empty bean tins scattered and clanked against each other such that they sounded like a rattling of prisoners' chains.

Suddenly Russian voices surrounded us: "Halt! Halt!"

We heard the crack of gunfire, and then similar bursts from combustion engines.

"Do you hear that?" the hungry chicks cried out. "They're coming for us! We're saved!"

Meyer said, "The czar's army is after us, and you think we're saved?"

From the front of the cart, I heard Wolf's voice.

"We'll never outrun them if we don't lose weight! Climb back and throw them out!"

"But I had hoped to save them!" Dov said.

"Get them out, or we'll all be lost!"

With a quick tug, Dov pulled the tarpaulin from the slatted walls, leaving us exposed to the air. As Wolf drove the team on faster, faster, faster, Dov jumped down among us.

"I am sorry, my little Jews! I had hoped to get you to the army, where you might be saved as I was saved. I'm afraid you will have to find another path!"

He grabbed the two boys nearest to him each by one arm, and with a strength that was surprising for his slim build, he launched one after the other into the air, over the side of the cart as if we were a ship struggling to stay afloat.

"Off you go! Go with God!" he called after them. "Who is next?"

Out went the hungry chicks. Out went Pipke and Feivl and Nose and Ears, all crying for their mamas as the *khapper* tossed them from the cart.

Behind us a great green beast of a military vehicle jugged along in pursuit. It swerved to avoid the boys in the road, now being thrown directly in its path.

I knew my turn was coming, but I couldn't stop watching the flight of my fellow captives. Pipke bounced his heavy head off the steps of a bank; Feivl plopped into the dirt of a courtyard, where a tire bumped over his legs.

Finally out went Meyer the Bully, so obviously a mere runt now, not a threat to me or anyone at all. Dov lifted him like a loaf of bread, then tossed him as if he was feeding ducks.

"Out you go!" Dov cried. "Out!"

It seemed I was the only one left, and Dov looked on me with such hungry eyes, I was sure he thought I was as well. Then, behind him, I noticed a lump of a boy lying still and silent as his name. Hershl Shveig, slumped over after I hit him, was now apparently unconscious. Or pretending to be. Either way, he did not stir. I could not imagine my fist had done such damage, but there was proof behind Dov's legs.

"I am sorry, Hershl Shveig," I said.

Then, with a running leap, I learned to fly.

Before landing, I heard one last shout from the *khapper* as the cart clamored away.

"Good-bye, Monkeypiss!" Dov shouted. "Be sure to thank your father for the salvation of my soul!"

TRANSLATOR'S NOTE

One day early in September, Clara and I were unpacking boxes when the phone rang at the far end of the building. I ran to get it, but I was too late. No one was there when I picked up the receiver.

Back in the book pile, Clara sat on an unopened box with the prayer book in her lap, caressing it with the tips of her fingers. Now that the semester had started, she had added a number of Judaic Studies classes to her self-study in the warehouse. She'd also begun meeting with the wife of a Lubavitch rabbi at the local Chabad House, to learn firsthand about the role of women in Orthodox practice. With so many Jewish texts in her dorm room these days, she had decided to leave her prayer book at the warehouse, figuring that each time she saw it, she would understand a little more.

Running a thumb over the letters on its spine, she read slowly aloud. "*Der Bris Hadash.*" She looked up, proud of her accomplishment, for she had pronounced the words more or less without a mistake. "That's like a 'bris,' right? A circumcision?"

"Yes," I said, "but *bris* actually means 'covenant.' The idea is that when a baby is circumcised, he's entering into a covenant with God."

She nodded seriously and said, "Yeah . . . and the other word, that's like *kodesh*, like holy?"

"Close," I said. "It's not *kodesh* but *hadash*. New. So the title is 'The New Covenant.'"

"*The New Covenant*," she said dreamily, almost singing the words. "Sounds like me! Except I don't need a circumcision, I just wear long skirts!"

Strange, I thought, but I had never noticed the title of Clara's prayer book, or if I had, I hadn't given it much thought. Now, though, something about the sound of it made me want to breach our translation-as-flirtation protocol.

She sat down to silently flip through a few more pages, probably expecting me to wait and wonder vaguely if she needed any help. But instead I walked over and took the book from her hand.

"I think it's time I had a look at this," I said.

It was indeed a lovely volume. But then I noticed something unexpected. As near as I could tell, the first four sections were called, in Yiddish, *Matti, Markus, Lukas, Jonan.* I flipped to the first page of the fourth of these sections and read aloud, "*In onheib iz geven dos vort.*" In the beginning was the word.

I tipped my head back and laughed as I handed the book to her.

Clara smiled, eager to be in on the joke. "What? Is it a funny prayer book?"

"I hate to break it to you, but it's not a prayer book at all," I said. "At least, not the kind we thought it was."

She glanced down, then up, then down again, looking a bit confused. "So what is it?" she asked.

"I think it's a Yiddish translation of the New Testament."

The color drained from Clara's face. She stared down at the book in her hands as if it were a murder weapon, a bloody dagger, a smoking gun. She didn't know a lot of Yiddish, but she used it then.

"*Shlekhte bukh! Shlekhte bukh!*" she barked. *Bad book! Bad book!*

Without another thought, she wound up the serving arm that had made her the terror of New Jersey high school tennis, and *Der Bris Hadash* went flying high into the air, soaring above the bookshelves, its pages flapping. It must have caught a gust of wind from the industrial fans, because it flew half the length of the warehouse before it crashed and skidded across the floor.

"A Christian book, *here*? Is no place safe?"

"It's okay, it's okay," I said. "It's just a book."

"It's not! Don't you get it? They are everywhere! We can't get away!"

They? I thought. *We?*

I located *Der Bris Hadash* and dusted it off as I walked back to the unpacking area. Checking the title page to see where it might be shelved, I saw that the translation had been completed by one "Rev. Hershl Shveig."

"It may be a Christian book," I said, "but it's a safe bet the guy who translated it was a Jew."

Clara looked at me as if I had said something that defied all logic.

"How could he be?" she asked.

THAT NIGHT WE WENT BACK to Kronbloom's. Instead of the nonstop chatter we'd had last time, we sat in silence over knishes and black coffee. After about ten minutes, Clara excused herself and went to the ladies' room. When she returned, it was as if she'd found something written about me on the bathroom wall.

"How do you know so well what the New Testament says?" she asked.

Could she see my face flush? Did I stutter when I answered?

"I don't know it that well," I said. And it was true. I didn't. Sure, I'd read bits of it in Greek, but never more than a few lines at a time. I'd never come close to reading the whole thing. Even when I thought I was a believer, I never had much patience for the druggie swirl of Revelation. I tried to explain all this, with the exception of the "when I was a believer" part, but she wasn't buying it.

"You looked at one page and knew what it was. I wouldn't know that." She stared at me hard, then looked away.

"I studied religion," I said. "Like you're doing now."

"I'm not studying *religion*," she said, "I'm learning about *God*."

After we ate, we drove back to my apartment, where Clara wondered aloud if maybe I was too secular for her. That was her word, "secular," as if her budding religiosity was being dragged from its heavenly flight by my knowledge of such things as profane as the works of Bernard Malamud and the Gospel of John. Before going to sleep, I admitted that maybe I was. Some time later, I rolled out of bed in the darkness. In the bathroom, I studied myself in the mirror and thought, If by "secular" she means liar, she's got you nailed. When I returned to the bedroom, she was sitting in a chair by the bookcase.

"You're awake?" I asked.

She was staring down into her lap, where her hands were cupped and trembling. In the bowl of her palms she held a small picture of Jesus, his finger pointing to his sacred heart. It must have been tucked into one of my books. On the back, I knew, was printed the Lord's Prayer and the name of my father's mother.

"What's this?" Clara asked.

Surely there was a story that could explain it. Surely a religion major who was now a collector of used Jewish books had gathered other odd artifacts through the years. Surely the fact that pictures of Jesus had become kitschy consumer items could get me out of this awkward situation. Yet in the middle of the night, standing naked in a doorway as dark as the womb, who could deny his past? Who has the strength to pretend?

"From my grandmother's funeral," I said.

She looked again at Jesus, shaking now between her fingers. "Your *grandmother's*?"

Before I could explain myself, she was dressed and out the door.

THE NEXT DAY at the warehouse I couldn't help but pick up *Der Bris Hadash* where I had left it, and, much to my surprise, I found it to be a fairly sophisticated literary translation. From the structure and word choice of certain sentences, I came to believe that the translator had worked from the original Greek, which made it an interesting artifact, if nothing else.

Wondering when such a book would have been published, I began scanning the pages for a date. There was no year listed anywhere in the front matter, and I likewise found no indication of how old the book might be when I turned to the back. One thing I did find, how-ever—tucked snugly between two pages of the Acts of the Apostles—was a copy of one of Clara's family letters, apparently forgotten when she sent the book flying through the air. "Something-something-something," I read, "the baby is getting so big . . ."

Just then the phone rang. It was Elaine from human resources. Elaine had been the woman who hired me. We'd hit it off, I thought, but in the months since, we'd had very little contact. The tone of her voice made it immediately clear she wasn't calling to just say hello. Clara had called, she told me.

"Called in sick?" I asked.

She quit, Elaine reported, and wondered if I knew why.

"No," I said, "but I'll be sorry to see her go."

"She was saying some strange things. Maybe you can come over to the business office, and we can talk about it?"

"There's an awful lot to do here," I said, "but I'll see what I can do."

Elaine took a long breath, and I held my own, waiting for the other shoe to drop, for Elaine to announce that Clara had told her everything, had told her that I was a liar and—oh shit, was I her su-pervisor? was she technically my *employee?*—a sexual harasser, and probably a Christian missionary to boot. Just then the phone's sec-ond line rang. I had another call.

"Could you hold on, Elaine?"

I pressed a blinking button marked "2" on the receiver. Before I could get a word out, I heard a storm of wheezing coughs.

"Hello?"

Then I heard a man's voice, faint and hoarse.

"I have them," it said.

"Hello?"

"I kept them for you. But you must come soon."

"Sorry?"

I heard what sounded like a long intake of air, then a sucking sound as the voice regathered itself.

"Forgive me. I am looking for the people who come for the books."

"Oh! Yes, you've called the right place. Can you hold one moment?"

"But—"

I pressed the button marked "1" and asked, "Elaine?"

"Still here," she said.

"I have a call about a book pickup, can I call you back?"

"I'll wait."

When I clicked back to the other line, it seemed the fellow had not understood that I'd put him on hold. He was in mid-sentence and speaking excitedly, as if he hadn't stopped talking long enough to realize I'd left the line.

"—which is why I cannot move them," he said. "There are too many thousands, and I am old."

"Thousands? Thousands of what?"

"Thousands of books, I said it already!"

"Is it some sort of library?"

"No! A moment ago I told you. No library. An office. Knobloch."

The office, he explained, perhaps for the second time, was in Baltimore, and I had to come for the books right away.

"There is construction," he said, "tomorrow, next day, the books will be gone." He gave me the address and said again how urgent it was.

"Baltimore is quite far from here, sir."

"For these books it will be worth it. If not to you, they will go to the trash."

The light on the phone kept blinking; Elaine was still holding. That's when it occurred to me: I could either drive all day, or face a human resources inquisition in the business office.

"Okay," I said. "I'll leave right away."

"Yes. You must."

"Could you hold again, Mr. Knobloch?" I asked. "I have another call to end, but I need to get some further information from you." I pressed the blinking button and heard Elaine breathing. "I can't come today, Elaine."

"We need to talk. In person. Clara is making some claims that if true will cause us to reconsider your—"

Before she could say another word, I uttered the phrase with which no one dared argue in our organization: "Emergency book rescue," I said. "I need to leave right away. How about if we talk the moment I get back?"

"When will that be?"

"Soon as I can," I said.

I clicked back to the waiting, coughing, wheezing voice, which, it seemed, had given me a temporary reprieve.

"Mr. Knobloch?"

"Not Knobloch!"

"You're not Mr. Knobloch?"

"The books are in the office of Knobloch, but Knobloch is dead."

"To whom am I speaking, then?"

"I am Malpesh," the voice said. "I am . . . the poet . . . Itsik Malpesh . . ."

A silence followed as I waited for him to say more. The silence was such that I thought he might be catching his breath, and in that moment of waiting I glanced down again at Clara's abandoned prayer book and forgotten Yiddish letter, both still in my hands.

"Itsik Malpesh," he said again. Then he cleared his throat and added a hopeful lilt to his voice as he asked the question I would come to realize meant everything to him: "Perhaps you know my name?"

The Memoirs of Itsik Malpesh

zayn

I HIT THE UNFORGIVING EARTH OF THE church courtyard with such a wallop it rang the bells in the steeple above. They were noon bells, clanging from a huge white sentinel that looked out over a gray expanse of cobblestones as if it were a lighthouse on the edge of an endless sea. Only instead of light this tower sent out a gut-mashing alarm I have never fathomed as remotely related to prayer. It was the same sound I'd heard every day of my youth in Kishinev, the sound that reminded us hourly whose God owned the air.

I composed an ode to those bells at the instant my head felt the ringing and my rump met the road:

> *Christian bells and Christian stones*
> *sting Jewish ears, break Jewish bones.*
> *What is the sound that will linger on*
> *When all good from the earth has gone,*
> *when even children's hopes are trod upon?*
> *Bim-bom bim-bom bim-bom bim-bom.*

That was the last sound I heard as I looked up into a sky as blue as my mother's dairy crockery. Then the world went black.

* * *

I AWOKE TO A SENSATION I would soon discover was common in the city in which I'd landed: hands moving in and out of my pockets, shaking my feet to see if coins might fall from my shoes, then unbuckling my belt to discover if I'd stashed any rubles with the treasures between my thighs.

Let me remind you I was not yet old enough to plead for closer contact at the slightest grazing of my inseam. No, I was still a boy, and I sat up with a start, yanking the flaps of my pants back into place.

Only then did I see two women crouched over my knees, their hair wrapped in dark scarves, their skin etched with lines of age. They began to laugh and poke each other at the sight of me, as if startled and amused to discover that I was alive.

"Sorry, sonny," one of these witches cackled. "We thought you were dead!"

"I told you he was breathing!" the other said.

"Even a corpse is entitled to a few last breaths."

I scooted away on my backside, fumbling to refasten my pants. The witches moved after me, still crouching, grinning all the while.

"Don't worry, little one! We won't hurt you. We never hurt a soul! We're not wolves, after all."

"No, no, not wolves. You can understand our mistake: The dead get dropped before the church sometimes—"

"To get a decent burial."

"—and we lighten the load for the priests."

"Not wolves at all! We only like to pick the bones."

"Didn't pinch you a bit, did we?"

"We were careful not to jostle you too much."

"That's the sort we are, we take extra care."

They each put a hand on my back, as if to soothe me, or perhaps to help me to my feet. It took a moment to realize they were in fact continuing their search, patting me down for any bulges of wealth they might have missed.

"Extra care," they said again as their bony hands rubbed my

shoulders. "Extra care. We didn't need to be so gentle. Don't you have a few coins for our trouble?"

"I have nothing!" I cried. "I don't even know where I am!"

All at once the truth of that statement washed over me. I had been snatched by the *khappers* a day's walk from Kishinev. I had traveled in their rolling prison, what, four days? Five? Had we traveled north or south? East or west? These were just the beginning of my questions. The great stone church looming over me now was twice as large as any I had seen before; it was made of white marble that to me looked carved from the clouds. I could have been in Paris or Rome, for all I knew of the world.

The two witches looked at me with pinched eyes; one crinkled her lips like a wilted rose.

"Poor thing, doesn't know where he is!"

"What's to know? Odessa is Odessa."

"Odessa?" I asked.

"Of course, Odessa. Where else would we be?"

Odessa! You protest that this cannot be so, that the odds of this are too low. Yet if it seems unlikely that the *khappers* had delivered me to the very place where my mother had sent me, I must remind you that I would not be telling the story were this not the case. Is there a greater contrivance than life itself, after all? Who can look back on the course one's days have taken and not see one impossible coincidence after another? Even from before the beginning: what are the odds that your mother would meet your father? A silly question, as that is simply what happened, if it happened, and so here you are, if you are. There are no odds about it.

So too my arrival in Odessa. How and why would I be anywhere else? Where else did a Yiddish writer born of the Old World, destined for the New, belong? Odessa, with its endless stairway sloping down to the harbor like the curve of a woman's back. Odessa, full of wide boulevards pulsing with a dozen languages, as if words were the blood that pumped through its veins. Odessa, at once the navel of Europe and the nipple of Asia: there was no greater titillation than to know it, and yet one knew that from it one could either drink deeply or fall into the bowels of the earth. No other city ever felt so right for Jews, if only because no country, no continent, no grand plan, could fully claim Odessa as its own.

But still I was amazed to find myself there. I looked left and looked right, believing I might see the widow Bimko and her lovely Sasha walking toward me across the church courtyard's wide expanse. They would be dressed just as they were in my photograph, both in black, but not mournful. No, there would be joy in their eyes, and they would carry comfort with them as if such a thing could be lifted and brought to anyone in need. The fates had been good enough to deposit me just where I'd hoped to be, so why shouldn't my hosts be here waiting, perhaps with a hot pot of *cholent* at the ready?

Searching the courtyard, however, of course I did not see them. The only figures I could see were a number of bearded priests carrying bundles from a cart into their church.

Beyond them, on the far end of the courtyard, I saw what seemed to be a boy about my size, similarly lying in a lump on the stones. Another of the *khappers'* captives tossed off as dead weight? I tried to remember who had been ejected just before I flew from the cart, and the face that came to me was that of Meyer the Bully. He seemed to have been less lucky in his landing than I had been. He didn't stir at all, only lay there like rags in a burn pile.

The witches spotted him just as I did.

"Another one!" they sang, then ran off to pick him clean.

Gathering myself, finally struggling to my feet, I was dismayed to discover I no longer had the letter from the widow Bimko. I checked my pockets, I checked my shoes, I checked my hat. No letter. Mercifully, my photograph of Sasha Bimko was just where I'd hidden it, tucked into my shirt, where the witches had not had a chance to look. Only because the address had been fixed in my memory as a bit of verse did I know where I should be going, though still I had no notion of how to get there.

To be a ghetto people has its uses, however. In those days, in that world, to find one Jew was to find them all. To be a Jew outside the fold was to be pulled back as if by gravity. Even today, while I have not darkened a synagogue door in more than fifty years, to walk by this shul or that—always on the other side of street—is to feel the ancient hooks sink in.

Such was the feeling I stood and waited for in Odessa. When it did not come quickly, I undertook a tactic of last resort. If all else failed, we could always ask the goyim, who never ceased to tell us where we should go.

I caught sight of a priest lingering by the freshly unloaded cart before the massive wooden doors of his church. Dressed entirely in black and with a long dark beard to match, he looked not unlike the Hasidim of Kishinev, though of course I knew he was as different as could be in all the ways that mattered. Normally I would not dare approach such a figure, but he seemed to be the only one nearby.

"Excuse me," I called to him in Russian. "Please forgive the intrusion, but could you tell me where the Jews live?"

"Not here, thank God," he said.

"Nearby?"

"Far from the truth."

"In which direction should I walk?"

"Away from salvation, if that's where you want to go."

This continued for some time and need not be repeated here. It will suffice to say that in response to my simple request for directions this zealous fellow treated me to a lesson in the Christian creed such as I had never heard. In Kishinev, Christians kept to themselves except when it came time to conscript Jews into the army or kill them in the street. In Odessa, it seemed another matter.

The priest kept up his sermon as I wandered away. But the fates still were with me. It wasn't long before I spotted a Jew making his way along the street. With his black capote and earlocks, I surmised that if he wasn't headed toward the Jewish Quarter, he was heading away, and it was only a matter of time before he would return, and so I took off after him.

When finally I worked up the nerve to stop him and ask how I might reach the widow Bimko's address, he fixed me with sad eyes and said solemnly, "The Holy One, blessed be He, weeps for the world that a boy should want to find such a place on the eve of the Sabbath."

But still he pointed me in the right direction.

"How could I avoid it without knowing where it is?" he said.

IF THE INN AT 24 YAPONCHIK STREET had ever been the fine establish-ment the widow Bimko had described in her letters to my mother, its better days were by then a distant memory. Vagrants congregated at the top of the stone stairs that led down to its basement entryway, where a door flecked with peeling paint hung loose on its hinges. Perhaps in an earlier era this had been the last threshold passed by thieves on their way to a dungeon or torture chamber, for it was positioned as if purposefully hidden from the comings and goings of life on the street. Even in the bright, seaside light of a summer after-noon, it seemed to me to be an access point to some dank Gehenna where demons did their worst. I descended to a depth nearly twice my full height; the only evidence of the world above were the shards of orange and brown roof tiles that littered the steps; even these looked like the devil's broken teeth.

Inside was no more inviting. Cracked basement windows let in rays of shabby sunlight, which were immediately absorbed by clouds of smoke emanating from men occupied with cigarettes and schnapps.

In fact, 24 Yaponchik Street appeared not to be an inn at all but a drinking establishment. With Friday evening fast approaching, when usually even the impious made a point of busying themselves as if they intended to rush home for the Sabbath, the tavern was nonethe-less filled. Half of the patrons leaned against a bar of dark wood, the other half sat in chairs arranged along the far wall. Between these two groups, a narrow strip of floor opened before me.

I gathered up my courage and prepared to step forward to inquire if this was where I might find what was left of the family Bimko. No sooner had I lifted my foot, however, than a voice rang down from beside the bar.

"Pick a side, boy," it said.

My leg stopped in midair, my shoe hovered inches above the floor. Only then did I notice that like the bar and the tabletops and indeed even some of the patrons' shoulders, the corridor of wide planks ahead of me was thick with grimy dust. If not for its blue-black hue, it might have resembled newfallen snow. I glanced left, and I glanced right: faces looked from me to the floor and back again, waiting to see if I would dare move forward onto a path that seemed to have gone untrodden for some time.

The voice from the bar continued in a harsh, Russian-inflected Yiddish: "How can you dance at two weddings with only one ass to shake?"

"I don't understand," I said.

"In the Underground," he said, "you can be on one side or the other, not in between."

Further explanation came from the opposite side of the room, in the form of a string of puzzling yet familiar sounds rising from the beard of a stout fellow in a black watch cap. He held out a hand full of thick, potato-colored fingers, offering me his palm as if I would have eternal friendship if only I walked toward him. I hesitated, not least because it took me a moment to realize he was speaking in Hebrew, as if beseeching a congregation from the bimah, "*Bakharu lakhem ha yom etmi ta avdunim.*"

Who had ever heard the *loshn kodesh* outside of yeshiva, shul, or the Sabbath table? The very thought of it—Hebrew in a tavern, and a dirty tavern at that—seemed outlandish, even scandalous, to me. And it seemed all the more so when I played his words back in my mind and was able to discern that he had indeed spoken a line of scripture: "Choose for yourself this day whom you will serve."

The man at the bar laughed like a braying goat. He bore no small resemblance to one, in fact, with his pointed chin and a young man's eager attempt at a beard.

"Shove the Torah up your ass, Zinnenoff!" he snorted. "No one is fooled by your phony reverence. We see where you stand on Friday night."

On my left the man who had spoken Hebrew switched to Yiddish and spat back, "Watch it, Shmolnik, or by *shabbos* evening I'll stand on your grave."

"And on *shabbos* morning I'll wake with your wife!" Shmolnik replied.

The older man opened and closed his mouth as if hoping a response would come to him, or else that no one would notice his silence if he just kept moving his lips.

"I'll leave her speechless, too!" Shmolnik laughed. "I bet she's never had a real Yiddish pen dipped in her inkwell."

Zinnenoff stamped the floor and turned to the men surrounding him. "You see? Epithets and fornication! That's all his 'mother tongue' is good for."

"Better fornication than constipation!" Shmolnik shouted. "Zinnenoff's Hebrew will plug up your intestines and leave you as bloated as he is! Never trust a language with no verb meaning 'to defecate.'"

"We have such a word!" Zinnenoff protested. "We have such a word!"

"Where is it in the scriptures or the commentaries?" Shmolnik asked.

"*Peresh! Charney-yownim!*"

"Nouns, only nouns. And zoological nouns at that! Ox dung and dove droppings. But what is the verb for what humans do? If you don't find it in the tomb from which you draw your lexicon, how can you stuff it with straw and put it on display?"

"Taxidermist!" a little fellow next to Shmolnik shouted. "Embalmer!" He seemed prepared to go on, but Shmolnik put a hand in the air to silence him, "That's enough. Let the mummy-maker speak."

"You know as well as I that we have expert linguists creating new words every day! Even words for the coarse purposes you describe. Since the last meeting of the Hebrew Language Committee, we have several!"

"What a relief!" Shmolnik said. "I've been waiting all day." He put a cupped hand to the back of his trousers. "Tell us quickly, what are they?"

Zinnenoff opened his mouth to reply but then went red as kiddush wine behind his beard.

"I don't recall them just now," he admitted. "But I assure you they are graceful neologisms, and very useful!"

"Behold the Hebraist's dilemma!" Shmolnik declared. "Even he lacks the words to describe how full of shit he really is."

Zinnenoff slammed a fist down on his table. His schnapps glass jumped, wetting his hand with clear liquor that seemed to strain his ability to keep his fingers from his mouth. He tasted them finally, and as if by the jolt of liquor he found his words.

"And the Yiddishist," he said, "rolls like a pig in the filth of the shtetl!"

On both sides of the tavern men leapt to their feet; those already standing lifted outraged arms into the air. From my right, ringing down from the men at the bar, I heard Yiddish insults that would have made a gangster blush ("An ear to my ass hears more eloquent speech than yours!"); from my left, from the gallery against the far wall, I heard Hebrew invectives that might have been pulled from the mouths of the prophets. ("*Lech le azazel, ben zona!*" *Burn in hell, you son of a whore!*)

Two Jews, three opinions, as the saying goes. Multiply that by two dozen men crowded into this cave of an underground tavern, and you will have some idea of the volatility of the scene. Why such rancor between Jews? I should explain: At some point in its thousand-year history as the language and heart of our people, Yiddish began to be seen by some as vulgar slang, and by others as a political statement. The world was gripped then in a mania of nationalisms—every tribe declared itself a nation and called for its own national language to set itself apart from all the rest. For Romanians and Moldovans it was easy: Romanians spoke Romanian; Moldovans spoke Moldovan. But for Jews? Who was to say if Yiddish or Hebrew or Aramaic or Ladino should be the unifying voice of the Jewish people? How do Jews settle anything? With shouting such as has not been heard since Babel.

In fact, on the day I first learned of this lingusitic divide, the two factions became so taken with their quarreling that they soon forgot the presence of the boy caught between them, the boy somehow ducking though still balanced on one leg, not wishing to choose sides. My left foot remained awkwardly perched above the open patch of floor that kept one language from the other. For two, three, four minutes I strained to maintain this foolish posture, until my muscles began to ache and drops of sweat stung my eyes.

Finally, with a great sense of relief, I lowered my foot. The sole of my shoe touched down soft as a feather in the dead center of their no-man's-land. I would have called less attention to myself had I smashed a gong.

Once again all voices were directed at me:

"Pick a side!"

"One or the other! Where do you stand?"

"*Ivri, daber ivrit!*" Zinnenoff bellowed. *Hebrews, speak Hebrew!*

"Living Jews should speak a living language!" Shmolnik cried.

"You must choose!"

"Leave him be," a voice rang out above the din. Instantly, the room went silent.

The man bellowing behind the bar was large enough that it was no surprise he was able to command the attention of every man before him, but in truth it seemed not to be his size that was the source of his authority. Unlike many of the others who wore uniforms announcing their allegiance to this cause and that—Shmolnik an obvious revolutionary in his red and black shirt, Zinnenoff a Zionist with his pioneer's neckerchief poking from his pocket—the man behind the bar dressed in such a way that he could have been either a religious Jew or an atheist freethinker. Was his white beard kept thick and long as an homage to Moses, or was it to Marx? Did his heavy black homburg conceal a yarmulke, or merely a bald spot? It was impossible to tell. He had a presence and bearing one wanted to observe closely, if only to come to a conclusion about the man himself.

He continued my defense with a lecture to the chastened crowd: "Where will any of you be if all this Jewish shouting sends a Jewish boy out the door? I will tell you. You will be where you've always been: pushing your children once again into exile. Do not make a boy pay for men's petty differences!"

Zinnenoff shouted, "Minkovsky, you know better than anyone: it is for our children we fight—for the future!"

"What kind of father would allow his children to speak an ancient language in modern times?" Shmolnik fumed. "You'll make a generation of golems, animated by words the world doesn't understand!"

"Another word from either of you, and your business with me is done," the white-bearded one, whose name I gathered was Minkovsky, said. He then turned and declared to both sides, "Back to your drinking or I'll lock up early! If you want to argue over nonsense, take yourselves to the synagogue."

Chairs scraped, glasses clinked. In a moment, when the usual murmurings of a tavern had returned, Minkovsky looked down his nose at me.

"We don't need any beggars here, boy," he said.

As a child of relative privilege among the Jews of Kishinev, I had never been called such a thing, and did not like the sound of it.

"I am not a beggar," I said petulantly.

He looked me up and down with such rigor that I had no choice but to do the same, and I was embarrassed by what I saw. How far the son of the factory manager had fallen! My shoes were caked with mud, the knees of my trousers shredded by my tumble onto the churchyard stones, my jacket torn by the witches at the pockets and the collar. I reached to straighten my hat and discovered there was straw from the *khappers'* cart still clinging to my hair.

"Well, you look like a beggar," Minkovsky said.

"But I'm not!" I insisted. "I am a poet!"

"Poets we need even less than beggars." He called out again to the drinking men, "Who here is a poet?"

Hands and shouts rose from both sides of the breach.

Zinnenoff snorted. "You, a poet, Shmolnik? You write ladies' literature, grandmother stories. Nothing for serious men!"

"And you write hieroglyphs," Shmolnik replied. "A dead language of dead words for dead readers buried in the sand."

Zinnenoff flung his glass with such speed it whistled as it flew by my nose, then smashed against the bar. A flurry of crystalline shards blew back and whited my shoulder, burning my cheek. Shmolnik saw me wince.

"For our children, Zinnenoff?" he asked, shaking a fist in the air.

The little fellow beside him called out, "Fraud! Liar! Pogromist!"

He was the first across the breach, and others immediately followed. Shmolnik lifted a chair and carried it from one side of the tavern to the other, holding it high above his head, as if it held a bride. Then he brought it down with a crash across Zinnenoff's back.

Minkovsky emerged from behind the bar and took me by the back of the neck, pushing me forward.

"You see what you started, Mr. Poet?"

He steered me to safety through a door and directed me to crouch in the entryway of a windowless side room, dark as shadow beyond the few feet of light that leaked in from the tavern. Only then did he see my stricken look—had I truly caused all this turmoil?

"Don't worry. In truth this has nothing to do with you," he assured me. "The disagreement between Zinnenoff and Shmolnik flares up once a week. Sabbath evening brings it to a head: when the worldly days meet the holy day, the advocates of each feel judged."

"I never imagined men might come to blows for one day over another," I said.

"I speak in a metaphor, boy," Minkovsky said. "It is not about days of the week, though it might as well be." He craned his neck to look once again into the quarreling mob, still roiling like water in a pot.

"They're newspapermen," he explained. "Half write in Yiddish, the other half in Hebrew. Half are Zionists. Half are Socialists. Half are religious. Half consider themselves freethinkers. Half are native-born, and half have come, as the saying goes, to live like God in Odessa. Of those, half believe in God and the other half don't, which makes me wonder if they intend to live like one who does not exist. Of course, half the men in here don't know what they're talking about. Half do. Half might, depending on how much they've had to drink. And half never will."

"That's a lot of halves," I said.

"You can see why it's crowded. So many factions make strange bedfellows even in a single man. I call this bar the Underground simply because it is underground, yet many men come here thinking they will meet comrades with whom they can blow up their enemies above. Every day a new species of true believer appears at my door: Socialist Zionists. Socialist Yiddishists. Socialist Hebraists. Yiddishist Zionists. Socialist Zionist atheist Hebraists. The only combination I have not yet seen is a man who claims simultaneously to be both religious and not."

Minkovsky struggled to his feet, his breathing as heavy as his arms and legs looked to be.

"But what do I know of these questions? I am just a tavernkeeper," he said, "it serves me to be all things to all men. To see some logic in every argument. My customers are another matter, however."

Back in the main room the scuffle had settled down, but the debate raged on.

"Language must be the first revolution!" Zinnenoff said. "Every conversation we Jews hold in Yiddish or Russian delays the day when we will speak the holy tongue in the Promised Land!"

"Holy tongue! Bah! The idea is a plague," Shmolnik scoffed. "And your Promised Land will grant promises only to the elite. The language of revolution is the language of the people!"

Minkovsky turned back to me. "But what is it you want here? You're too young for schnapps. Or for revolution."

"I'm looking for the widow Bimko, and for her daughter Sasha."

He studied me with sharp eyes.

"What do you want with them?"

What did I want with them? I wasn't entirely sure. There are moments in the writing of this history when I am forced to acknowledge that the events I am describing were experienced by a boy pushed along by the whims and intentions of others, sometimes benign, often less so. What did I want with the family Bimko? I told Minkovsky everything I knew about the subject, and I hoped that somewhere in this recitation I would discover an answer for myself.

"My mother sent me," I began. "I had to leave Kishinev, and my mother says those with shared misfortune are landsmen of a country without borders. She says once she kept Sasha safe, and so now Mrs. Bimko should keep me safe. She says Sasha was present at my birth, and so now I must find her!"

"Kishinev, eh? Has the draft come to Kishinev? They are taking boys away?"

He assumed I was on the run from the army, which was partially true but not entirely. I decided to let this misapprehension stand. The saga of Chaim and Bemkin and my father's imprisonment was a burden even as a recent memory; it would only become heavier if I spoke of it by way of explanation.

"You are wise to come to Odessa," Minkovsky said. "A boy could hide here from God, so avoiding the czar's army will not be a problem. Come with me."

I followed his heavy steps up a narrow stairway, each fall of his foot squeaking like a goose as the wood groaned in duress. His breathing grew heavy, and the stairwell echoed with such a symphony of squeaks and wheezes and groans that we might have been passing through a livestock barn.

"This is your tavern, then?" I asked.

"It is."

"And the inn is on the upper floors?"

"Inn? It has not been one for a very long time. No one would live here now if the widow did not need a place to sleep."

"And Sasha?" I asked. I felt the poems I had begun to compose to her burning a hole in my heart.

"Better to ask Mrs. Bimko questions about the family Bimko."

At the top of the stairs, Minkovsky rapped lightly on a brown door, then pushed it open, though I heard no response.

"Be brief, she is not well," he said.

Inside, a woman sat alone by a curtained window that let the only light into the room. She held back one side of the curtain as if peering out into the street.

"Mrs. Bimko?" I asked.

"Who's that?" she asked.

"Itsik Malpesh," I said. "Son of Abram and Minah Malpesh."

Hearing my name, she looked away from her window and stared across the tiny room. Only then did I see the widow Bimko clearly. She was a grave woman, her skin tight on her bones. The light within her eyes was set so deep in her hungry skull, it might have been a match burning at the bottom of a well. From what my mother had told me, she had been plump and joyful in Kishinev—a butcher's wife, after all. In Odessa, she looked as though she ate only when food fell into her mouth. She had not given any indication of hardship or illness in her letters to Kishinev. An emigrant's shoes turn gold, as the saying goes. Who would write back misfortune when good news is sent as cheaply as truth?

With no word of greeting, she said finally, "Kishinev's misery follows even here." Then she returned her gaze to the opening between the curtains.

The image of her lonely vigil so burned into my soul that decades later I composed a verse about it, though by then it was as much about my loss as her own. I wrote as though she sat still before me:

> By the attic window
> a widowed soul waits,
> Searching the horizon
> for love's return
> Yet even the shadows
> From corners are chased
> When, lit by this burden,
> her black eyes now burn.

A boy is just a boy, however. At the time I was unable to see beyond my own floorspace in any room I entered; I assumed she had been watching out her window for none other than myself.

"My mother sent me," I said. "She hopes I might stay here for a time."

Only as I spoke the words and studied the surroundings did I realize the widow was in no position to take on a boarder.

"What I mean to say is," I added, "she thought perhaps I could be a help to you."

Yet the widow Bimko did not seem to care in the least how I phrased the explanation for my unexpected arrival. In fact, she seemed not to be listening to me at all.

"The sun sets at last," she said, rising from her seat to stand before a low table, where she lit the Sabbath candles and said the blessing.

In the dim light, I saw between the candlesticks a photograph of Sasha, the only decoration in this lonely room. She lit a cigarette off the Sabbath candle.

"Good *shabbos*," I said. "Can you tell me, will she return for dinner?"

Mrs. Bimko looked up from her cigarette with a puzzled expression.

"Who?" she said.

"Your daughter," I said. "Sasha."

"Ah. Sasha. My daughter," Mrs. Bimko replied. "My daughter is not here."

"Yes, I see." I spoke loudly now, in case the old woman was hard of hearing. "I wonder when she might return?"

Mrs. Bimko squeezed her cheeks together and sucked at her cigarette, causing the lit end to brighten in the darkness of the room. When she exhaled, I could no longer see her face. It was as though a storm cloud spoke when I heard the words, "She is in the desert."

"The desert?"

"My Sasha went off to Palestine," Mrs. Bimko said. "A parade of fools walked into town, and she joined them. She is gone."

"Palestine? Why?"

"A dreamer! She wants to farm the land, grow vegetables. I tell her, We have dirt here. She says, This dirt is not our dirt. I tell her, Your father was a butcher, you were weaned from my breast to cow's blood; what do you know of potatoes? She tells me, We do not grow potatoes. We grow oranges.

"Oranges! Did you ever hear such nonsense? I told her, in Eretz Yisroel you grow oranges. In Odessa we grow old."

"You speak to her?" I asked.

"What?"

"You say you speak to her, only how do you speak to her, if she is in Palestine?"

Widow Bimko squinted.

"Perhaps she wrote me a letter?" she said. "Yes, it must be that. She wrote to tell me of the oranges. Each one is as big as a peasant's head, she tells me. I said to her, Ah, but a peasant's head is juicier. Oh, how we laughed over that."

149

She drew on her cigarette.

"So you have spoken to her?"

"Who?"

"Sasha."

"My Sasha is in the desert," she said, then went back to her waiting.

LATER THAT NIGHT, over a *shabbos* meal of black bread and pickles, I heard the full story from Minkovsky.

Years before, he told me, 24 Yaponchik Street had indeed been an inn, and a reputable one. Reputable enough that when the widow Bimko arrived in town and told the rabbi of the Butchers' Shul that her husband had been the ritual slaughterer of Kishinev and she wondered where a pious woman and her daughter might stay, they sent her to Minkovsky's door.

"I had a wife then," Minkovsky said, "and I teased her that she kept the place as if she expected Queen Esther for tea. 'I am the only Esther in this house,' she would tell me, 'but still it should be worthy of a queen!' My Esther welcomed the widow Bimko as if she were a long-lost sister. Of course we had heard everything about the violence in Kishinev, so it began as charity. But over the next two years they became the best of friends. They were friends until the end."

"The end?" I asked.

"Two years after the widow arrived, Esther went out to the market one day and didn't return."

"Where did she go?"

"First to the hospital, then to the world to come."

He perhaps could see the questions in my eyes.

"Do you think Kishinev is the only place so full of the chosen as to be visited by a pogrom?"

I shook my head, no, but the truth is, I had lived a life untouched by such things except as someone else's memory. What boy knows his parents' ghosts, much less knows enough to fear them?

"What I didn't realize at the time—and this is why I tell you all this now—was that I had lost Nachum as well."

"Nachum?"

"My son. He was just a boy then, younger even than yourself. Yet he never recovered, or forgave."

"Forgave who?"

"Me, to begin with," Minkovsky said with a steely gaze. "But not just me. He never forgave Odessa. The streets, the people. He felt as though his home had turned into a gallows. He was too young to realize it had been one all along. That he had played in the shadow of a noose he thought was a swing. And so his disillusionment was total, whereas mine was—well, can one become disillusioned when one had no illusions to start with? My Esther and I, we knew that Jews here lived on borrowed time. We had planned to emigrate. I have a brother in America, and we were perhaps two years from joining him there. With Esther gone, I could not imagine making the trip. And then there was the widow to consider. To be honest, I perhaps considered her too much, with not enough attention given to Nachum. He was left to his own devices, I'm sorry to say. Left to follow whichever wild ideas caught his eye.

"Last year a contigent of *fusgeyers* came through Odessa singing songs about the glories that awaited in Zion. Do you know of the *fusgeyers*? Young Jews making a show of their strength by marching all the way to Eretz Yisroel.

"They seemed to Nachum a Jewish army, and that was exactly what he thought was needed. They boarded a boat, beating drums and raising their voices with 'Hatikvah' all the while. It was only in the morning that we realized Nachum had made good on his threats.

"When the widow reported that Sasha was also missing, we realized they both had gone.

"I was not surprised. If to the Bimkos you are practically family, as you say, you must know this already: Sasha Bimko is a dreamer, a fighter, and stubborn as a plague. When she learned that the life in Eretz Yisroel is a hard one, she would not allow the thought of going there to be driven from her head. Never mind that her departure returned her mother to the state she was in when they arrived here. She said, 'Here it is hard with no hope; there it may be harder still, but the hope will outshine the gloom.'

"She challenged me to find a reason for Jews to remain in Odessa, or in all of Russia, and I could not. I tried, of course.

"'Your mother,' I told her. 'You should stay for her.'

"She said to me, 'This is not what I asked. My mother is only my own; what of the people, where will they find comfort?'

"To this I had no reply," Minkovsky said.

Before I had been drawn to the face of Sasha Bimko, but now I knew I was drawn to her soul as well. How does a boy of eleven know in his heart what his destiny will be, with whom it will be locked? He doesn't. He simply speaks, and in speaking he makes his destiny.

"I will follow her, then," I said.

"Your devotion is admirable, but your timing is poor," Minkovsky said. "Even a boy must know a war has begun. The port has been closed. Our pioneers are stranded in one world, and we in another."

"No matter," I said. Isn't the power of words greatest when they are being used to convince oneself that what we perceive is the only reality? When a boy swears an oath, he does so without consideration of a single implication; truly, he does so without thinking at all. And yet in the saying, in the formation of the words, they become truth.

"One day I will find her," I said, and I believed this no less than God must have believed when he said, "Let there be light."

The Memoirs of Itsik Malpesh

khes

IN THE MORNING, THE FIRST OF WHAT would prove to be perhaps five hundred Sabbath mornings in Odessa, the first Sabbath morning that I did not greet with prayer, Minkovsky asked if I had any talents to speak of. I replied with a flourish of my published poem, waving the scrap of newsprint from the *Free Jewish Voice* as if it were the flag of a conquering army.

"As I told you yesterday, in Kishinev I was a poet of some renown," I declared, unfolding my clipping as evidence.

"*Work*," Minkovsky clarified. "Do you know how to *work?*"

I chose not to tell him of my years shoveling goose shit in my father's down factory, for fear he might have similar labors in store for me. Instead, I told him I had spent time in a typesetter's shop. How much time, or rather how little, I kept to myself. Only then did he seem interested in my page of newsprint.

"Did you do this?" he asked.

"Yes, it is my first publication!"

"The *type*," he said. "Did you set the type?"

"Yes," I said. "I mean, I know how to do it. That is, I have seen it done."

He produced a small magnifying glass from his vest pocket, and peered through it at my page. Reflected in his spectacles, I could see the letters grow larger, then smaller, as he moved the glass from right to left.

"Poets I can find by the bushel," he said. "Can't walk five feet in Odessa without some fallen kabbalist pushing his tortured Pushkin verses on me. But to set type is a real art. And this is not badly done. Of course, the lines are too tight and the ink smudges like a runny nose, but otherwise it seems the work of a skilled hand."

I looked with renewed admiration at the letters on the page, realizing for the first time that my composition was not the only act of creation they displayed.

"With the war I'll be busier than ever," he said. "An apprentice would be useful."

"Apprentice for what?"

"Do you remember the argument that greeted your arrival yesterday?" he asked.

Did I remember? Could he not see the flecks of red that remained on my cheek, the lasting gift of Zinnenoff's flying schnapps glass? I touched my chin and imagined I felt a stubble of embedded shards.

"I remember," I said.

"Why is it, do you suppose, that two such warring factions would choose to keep company? In part, it is because deep down I believe they know they need each other. What is Hebrew without Yiddish? What is Yiddish without Hebrew? As they say, a man without woman is like a mouth without a tongue; he can eat, but can he taste? Such is the way with my patrons, they each need the salt and spit of the other. But there is another reason, as well. Do you know why they come here every day?"

"To drink?" I ventured.

Minkovsky shook his head, his white beard moving like a brush across his chest. "They can get schnapps anywhere. In fact, they could get it cheaper elsewhere. They come to me because I fulfill another need."

"Need?"

"What might journalists need in equal measure to liquor? If

clear schnapps makes up half of their blood, what do you suppose also runs through their hearts and turns their veins blue?"

He led me down the narrow stairs, into the tavern, and then across the floor. When he reached the dark strip of grime and dust that after he opened his doors would once again divide his fractious clientele, he hopped over it, despite his bulk, with a grace that spoke of endlessly repeated motion.

"Some would scrub this line away," he said. "To tell the truth, I don't mind it. As petty as their squabble is, it does provide some needed organization. It is like the crease that divides one page from another."

I followed him into the darkened room he had hidden me in the day before. He lit one lamp, then another and another, until the bare brick walls jumped with light and shadow. The room was much bigger than the closet I had imagined it to be, and it was not filled, as I had supposed, with brooms and mops or other unused cleaning supplies. No, spread before us was a scene much like the one I had stumbled into in Kishinev, in the office of the *Free Jewish Voice*—printing blocks and composition and boards, rollers and presses dark with grease, shelf after shelf of yellowed newspapers. As in the tavern, everything in this back room was covered with blue-black grime.

"Yes," Minkovsky said. "Ink. I have tried to contain it in this room, but when we go to press it seems to float where it will."

It had been little more than a month since I saw printing equipment for the first time, and yet the world and my place in it now seemed so changed I accepted without hesitation that these formerly foreign objects and machines were about to become part of my life.

"You're a printer?" I asked.

Minkovsky shook his head, wagging a finger in front of me.

"No, no," he insisted. "Printers get themselves into trouble. I am only a tavernkeeper. But a tavernkeeper is first of all one who understands the inner workings of both men and the words they use. To pour drinks all day is to watch speech slowed down and speeded up. It is to become aware of the composition of every thought, the way it is built incrementally, as if by bricks. Many a time I have a conversation with a patron that stalls as if the bricklayer has lost his trowel, or the ladder has collapsed beneath him. A half-spoken sentence hangs there like a half-built wall, not quite serving its purpose, but marking the spot where it will stand. I suppose that's why I have this equipment; I sell schnapps and print papers, each informs me in the construction of language.

"The Yiddishists and the Hebraists, they all come to me thinking I sympathize with their side and merely tolerate the other. They don't realize that I see them as the same, because I am less concerned with the words than with their component parts, letters, puncuation, even the spaces that keep one word from another. A question mark or a period is as important as an *alef* or a *mem* or a *tof*. Together they add up to one truth, yes. But each has a truth of its own."

There were at the time no fewer than eight hundred regular newspapers, journals, and magazines in Odessa: the two produced in the back room of Minkovsky's tavern were far from the best, even among the Jewish publications. The majority of these were in Russian, and were produced on schedules ranging from the weekly to the "once now and again when the messiah comes" variety. Minkovsky distinguished himself by printing and distributing the only daily publications in both Hebrew and Yiddish. He did so by reproducing—on narrow, two-sided sheets of stock the weight and color of cigarette paper—largely unedited transcriptions of the world's news as filtered through the inebriated ramblings of his clientele. He named each of his periodicals after his rolling-paper-thin printing stock: *Papirosen*, for the Yiddish, and a newly coined word, *Cigariot*, for the Hebrew.

The unorthodox editorial approach he took with both of these publications occasionally led to commentary that could be found nowhere else in Odessa. Such was the case when the great writer Abramovich wandered by chance into the bar and discussed at length the similarities between his wife's kugel recipe and the changing po-litical situation in the Balkans; "We may be separate noodles now, but in time we will all cook into a clump and much violence will come of our separation," said the famous writer, who was greatly surprised to find that his schnapps-fueled predictions were headlines the next day.

Minkovsky's technique for gathering this exclusive information was to sit at the bar, keep the liquor flowing, and write down all that he heard, plucking words from the smoky air as if with a butterfly net.

"After all have left, I compose the page with blocks in the back room," he told me. "I have discovered that the material becomes more interesting the longer I allow them to drink, but the longer they stay, the more is said, and the less time I have to compose and print the pages.

"You'll begin with de-composition. I rarely have time to take the blocks off the composition board. So after I print, you will clean and take them apart."

"And then?"

He showed me to a shelf in the back of the room, where perhaps a hundred composing boards stood stacked, one upon the other.

"You'll have plenty to keep you busy," he said.

The next day I began work as I would every morning during my decade in Odessa, by climbing a ladder to the top of the tower of composition boards, bringing down four or five, and then going line by line, picking letters off two at a time, and depositing them in the correct section of a partitioned wooden box designed for that purpose.

In the beginning it was as though I had forgotten two

languages at once, both the language of my home and that of my religious education. To have them broken into their elements made them unrecognizable. The work was long and monotonous: imagine a typewriter that removed words from a page at a pace equivalent to that of a single bloated inchworm eating a rosebush from roots to thorns. Each composition board required of me an hour or more as I lifted the blocks, studied them, and went searching for the proper box for every letter.

Yet by month's end, I'd memorized the locations of all the different boxes and knew each block by touch. The *alef*'s curves and angles; *beys*, like a cresting wave. *Gimel*, called "camel" for a reason, with its head looking here and there like a beast in the desert. *Shin* like a candelabra. *Reysh* like an eagle's claw. *Tof* like a horse walking into the wind. It was in Minkovsky's backroom print shop that I came to understand the kabbalists' lessons about the significance of letters as the building blocks of creation. Each told a story if one took the time to read it.

It was in this way also that I followed the news of the day, particularly of the war. During my first fall in the city, when Odessa was bombarded from the sea, 24 Yaponchik Street shook to its foundations more times than I can recall. The air filled with dust; stacks of composition boards toppled in explosive bursts of wooden blocks. Words that had been so carefully composed broke apart and scattered on the ground; the same letters with which God made the world clacked like dice on the stone floor, the unchanging elements of the game of chance called life.

The years that followed were perhaps best experienced by a boy far from home, for what did they bring other than an endless homelessness to all? Every month more men went missing from the Underground. At first it was the czar's army that got them. Later, it was the civil war. In either case, Minkovsky initiated a ritual of feting the lucky inductee on the night before he was to report to duty. The man of honor was seated in a chair and plied with a drink Minkovsky made especially for the occasion. The draftee never had more than a couple of gulps before he fell over backward with a stained blue grin on his face.

"Three parts schnapps, two parts alcohol ink," Minkovsky explained the first time I saw this. "If you get the mixture just right, he'll sleep through his induction and miss the train to the front."

"And if you get it wrong?"

"He goes blind and crazy. Better that than the trenches."

Noble as Minkovsky's plan was, it was at best a short-term solution. One army or another always found the recruits, and off to war they went with lips as blue as the sea.

"The stain is temporary," Minkovsky explained. "But it may last long enough to get him a medical exemption."

There was no record of my existence as resident of Odessa, and so I avoided conscription even as I came of age. One day to the next, one war to the next, daily existence for me changed little. There was never enough to eat no matter who claimed to be in charge.

Foreign soldiers came and went, first the Germans, next the French. Then, with the shifting sands of revolution, came the White Army, then the Red. I knew little of the differences then, and can remember little of them now. What I knew of Red and White during those years was limited to this: they were the colors I saw when I rubbed myself raw each night, thinking of my beloved.

My ignorance was a symptom of a larger epidemic. Soon enough I was writing stories as well as setting type and printing pages, yet what I knew of the world was limited to what I learned in the Underground, and what my ill-informed sources knew they had only picked up like litter in the street—sometimes literally so. More than once we heard old events repeated as breaking news by this fellow or that who had just walked into the tavern with last week's *Papirosen* stuck to the bottom of his shoe.

I have often wished I saved some of those editions, more as time capsules than as examples of a poet's juvenile works. They were, as any newspaper is, rough drafts of history. The difference, of course, was that those tissue-thin, spit-white sheets were rough drafts written in a language that history itself would soon destroy.

Today I remember only scraps of the content we produced, such as the headline with which we led our report on the treaty ending Russia's official involvement in the Great War:

PEACE DECLARED
Germans, Russians agree to kill only Jews
Which was followed soon enough by our coverage of the Bolshevik rise to power:

WELL, NOT PEACE EXACTLY
October revolution ousts February revolution,
further revolutions to follow

Then came stories of life under the new regime:

FAMINE, DISEASE RAGE IN CIVIL WAR'S WAKE
At least we have our health, sources said

In time our concerns of war and the hardships that followed became replaced with fears of more insidious enemies. After a lull in which it seemed all the men who might be taken to this front or that had gone, there once again seemed to be men missing from the Underground each week.

Those who remained spoke in hushed tones of the Cheka, the secret police. They pronounced the name as if they were speaking of a particularly unsavory fellow they knew, the sort of man who might borrow money, seduce your sister, insinuate himself into your confidence only to broadcast your secrets about town, and then, adding insult to injury, shoot you in the back of the head.

"We used to take comfort that it could get no worse," Minkovsky said. "But I would choose Cossacks over the Cheka any day."

When men went missing now, their departure was neither announced with weeping nor saluted with toasts. It happened silently: a man would pass an evening pleasantly enough in his usual seat, then he would stand to say his good-byes and find himself joined by strangers on his way out the door. We never saw any of them again.

"If the Cheka would at least announce themselves, I could serve them a few of my ink cocktails and we could put them out to sea."

"You think alcohol affects them?" Shmolnik asked. "To get drunk you need blood. To have blood you must have a heart."

"An ink cocktail could knock out a stone."

"If they had the soul of a stone, it would be an improvement."

Wild stories were told of the tactics of the Cheka. Shmolnik insisted he knew a man who'd had his arm strapped to a table and was made to watch as his hand was set on fire.

"And this was a writer for the party's own paper!" Shmolnik said. "He made the mistake of taking the wrong perspective toward 'the end of history.' Since the October Revolution was a revolt against the February Revolution, he wondered if the latter should properly be called a counterrevolution, and if so, whether the Bolsheviks were in fact not revolutionaries but *counter*revolutionaries. When his comrades took this as a treasonous remark, he insisted he was simply making a linguistic point. 'Bourgeois!' they shouted. Then the Cheka gouged out his eyes."

"That is not what I heard," Zinnenoff said. "I heard that the Cheka doused him with water and froze him in the street."

"You've got it all wrong as usual, Zinnenoff. I'm certain the Cheka gouged out his eyes. Then they put sugar on his nipples and dropped five rats in his shirt."

"You must have him confused with another. After the freezing, they stuffed him in a barrel with ten thousand nails, then rolled him down the Potemkin Steps."

"Don't make your case through exaggeration. You couldn't find ten thousand nails in all of Odessa at the moment. If there were so many nails, we would find a way to eat them."

"A hundred would do it. The Cheka poke them through the boards at angles so they tear as well as stab. As the barrel picks up speed, the points slice as cleanly as a single blade."

"And how do you know so much about the Cheka's tactics?"

"It's simple physics," Zinnenoff said.

"So now you're a physicist? And where did you learn that, the Song of Songs?"

"Enough!" Minkovsky said. "Gone is gone. He was a nice fellow. A fine poet as well."

"A poet?" I said. Through much of the conversation, I had assumed they'd been talking politics and so paid it little mind. Mention of a poet brought it home. "Why should they care what poets say?"

"Cheka finds words dangerous."

On that point Shmolnik and Zinnenoff agreed.

"They'll come for all of us," they said. "It's only a matter of time."

THROUGH ALL THIS, Odessa's Jews kept drinking, kept talking, kept reading, and so Minkovsky, with my help, continued to record the news as it was overheard in the bar. Often the news was such that publishing it decreased our readership significantly. Such was the case when we printed reports that soon the port would close to emigration. Overnight our circulation was cut in half. Some of our former readers made it out of the country, just as many went to jail.

Other news we didn't need to publish, as it was evident all around us. Faced with endless external hardships and dwindling numbers, the Underground's warring Jewish factions had the good sense to reach a truce. Of the Yiddishists and Hebraists, only

Shmolnik and Zinnenoff continued to feud, and even they recognized that their disagreement was based more on personal animosity than loyalty to the cause.

When there were too few partisans of either side left for the breach between them to serve any practical purpose, Minkovsky put me to work scrubbing the line away. I worked at it for two solid days, first scraping, then sweeping, then mopping the floor's wide boards until it reflected perfectly the dingy light that filtered through the windows at noon. So pleased was Minkovsky with my efforts—inky dust is nothing compared to goose shit, after all—he then added to my chores regular cleaning of the house from basement storeroom to the attic apartment three floors above.

Ink still floated in great clouds from the printing room each night when we went to press, but nonetheless the daily scrubbing seemed to have a positive effect on both the walls and those who lived within them—most notably the widow Bimko. While for a year or more my presence seemed to go unnoticed by the mother of the girl I loved, she gradually came to greet me when I entered her suite of rooms. She even smiled from time to time when she caught me lingering by her mantel, where her shrine to Sasha's image stood, ethereally haloed by candlelight in the evenings, thick with dust in the morning light.

Not a day went by that I did not compare myself to this photograph. The picture of course did not age, but I did. I felt older each day, while her face remained untouched by age or anxiety or famine. It felt as though we were in a footrace; she had been faster at the start, but by sheer will and endurance I was gaining on her now. Her mother seemed invigorated just by the watching, though in truth I never felt she was cheering me on.

"My Sasha is too old for you, Itsik," the widow Bimko would tell me. "You are a boy of sixteen, she is a woman of twenty. For all you know she is married to an Arab, the fourth of six wives. Don't be heartsick over a fantasy. Find yourself a nice Odessa girl."

Her position on the matter never changed. A year later, she had ceased watching out her window each day, had begun once again to busy herself about the house. She was sweeping the stairs one day when she found me sitting alone, sketching Sasha's face on a scrap of cigarette print.

"Itsik, truly, you must forget her," she said. "You are a boy of seventeen. Almost a man, yes, a young man with life to look forward to. But who is Sasha now? A grandmother, no doubt; days pass quickly in the heat. Her Arab children are certainly grown and breeding, and her husband has moved on to younger wives. What would you want with a used-up old woman who sleeps with the camels? Be reasonable. Find yourself a nice Odessa girl."

Later still, after another year had passed, she had fully descended the steps, occasionally even attempting to pour drinks in the Underground. It was from behind the bar one night that she read over my shoulder yet another of my endless verses to her daughter's memory.

"Itsik, why do you torture yourself?" she asked me. "I am certain, I feel it in my motherly bones: Sasha, may she live in blessed memory, has been wrapped like a mummy and lodged beneath a pyramid. Have pity on me and do not keep her memory alive. Your love for her is too painful to watch. Let her rest, she should find peace. Find yourself a nice Odessa girl."

Shmolnik heard this advice and added some of his own. "Don't listen to her about that nice-Odessa-girl crap. What you've got to do is find yourself a not-so-nice Odessa girl. You're young! You should live. Do you know that next door there are plenty of not-so-nice Odessa girls? Russians, sure, but they like the taste of the kosher."

What did I know of such things? While bent over Minkovsky's letter blocks I had grown to my full height, but still I was young, and I remained haunted the way only the young can be by the twin, self-devouring beliefs in fate and love. What had begun as a childish inability to recognize fantasy as only that had become an adolescent preoccupation and was now turning into an adult obsession. With few certainties in life, I knew without doubt that Sasha Bimko had something to do with my origins. It was not merely that meeting her had become a matter of religious importance. It was far worse: she—my thoughts of her, my dreams of her—was the closest thing to religion I then knew.

Imagine my torment when Minkovsky told me I had slept long enough among paper stock and bottles of schnapps. "I have spoken to the widow," he said. "We agree you ought to sleep in the attic, in the extra room."

"Sasha's room?"

"It has not been so for nearly five years, Itsik."

"Ah but it was, it was!"

The "extra room" in the widow Bimko's attic was to me the Holy of Holies. Many an idle moment had been spent with my hands to its threshold, my fingers on the doorknob. She had touched these surfaces! Touching them, I imagined I was touching her, which frequently brought about an embarrassing arousal.

"The widow is too old for you!" Shmolnik would shout upon seeing me.

"Oh, to be young!" Minkovsky laughed. "I haven't stood with such attention in forty years. Only a teenage boy could make a tea delivery into a burlesque."

"Just keep zipped up, Itsik. I'm told widows are ravenous creatures," Shmolnik said, jabbing his elbow into the older man's side.

Minkovsky pretended to blow his nose so that we would not see his cheeks turn red as beets beneath his beard.

We were, I suppose, a cobbled-together family. All bereft, all orphans in a sense, we each filled a role in the others' lives. If Minkovsky occasionally called me Nachum, or the widow Bimko from time to time called out "Sasha?" when I entered the door, I pretended not to notice, and they pretended their tongues had not slipped. No one admitted we were joined together by loss.

I wish I could say it was my parents whose loss was my greatest wound. In truth I thought very rarely of them. Far more difficult was grappling with the absence of Sasha Bimko each day. I looked for signs of her constantly, and of course found them wherever I turned. The feelings of loss were endless, everywhere; to be in the room where she once slept, but never to know her . . . I have since known bereavement, so I will not say the feelings were quite the same. But my vision was similarly clouded.

Once in her room I found a silky brown strand I took to be a cutting of her hair; from childhood perhaps, or from her decision at age sixteen (as I imagined it) to be free of childhood's braids.

I tied it around my wrist and wore it as a remembrance of my devotion.

"It's a talisman," I said one day. "A love spell. The gyspies say if you wear a scrap of clothing or hair that once belonged to your beloved, she will one day come to you to reclaim it."

"A rat's tail," Minkovsky said. He reached out and pinched my bracelet with two fingers. "Even our pests are starving. I have never seen one so thin."

I was growing too old for his teasing.

"Rat's tails don't have hair!" I said.

He leaned in more closely and gave my talisman a sniff.

"I have been wondering what happened to the widow Bimko's cat."

Do not believe for a moment that I failed to realize this preoccupation was madness. What else did a boy have during wartime, when the great city of Odessa stood like a mourner with his head hung low? I had never known it in its glory, of course, but even I could tell something was missing from the streets of my adopted home. I know now that it was nothing other than hope, which like divinity we came to know by many names. Zinnenoff called it Zion. Shmolnik called it Revolution. In my innocence, I called it Sasha Bimko. Which of us was the bigger fool?

The Memoirs of Itsik Malpesh

tes

As for Minkovsky, he called it America. The word was always on his lips, even if it was for him a promised land of last resort. Europe, he knew, had been ravaged by war. Russia was becoming increasingly inhospitable to Jews. Every report he heard from Palestine caused him to fear he had lost his son.

"Why could he not have run off to America?" he wondered. "New York is practically a province of the Pale of Settlement, but my only heir runs off to starve and fight Arabs in the sand."

"America is so much better?" Zinnenoff asked.

"Without a doubt," Minkovsky said.

"For the young maybe."

"Yes, yes. It is a young country. Perfect for a boy Itsik's age."

"A man Itsik's age," Shmolnik corrected.

"Yes, quite right."

"I agree. A man like Itsik could go far in America."

They spoke of me as if I were not there, and yet they carried on theatrically, casting occasional glances, as if acting out a scene for my benefit.

"I have an associate there, a man who once was in the printing trade in Odessa. Knobloch—did you know him?"

"Tsvi Knobloch?" Shmolnik asked.

"That's the one. But he calls himself 'Harry' now. In America he has done quite well for himself. I've lived in Odessa sixty years and I own a hole in the ground. Five years in New York, Knobloch owns a building with his name on it. Do you know how he built this empire?''

Shmolnik and Zinnenoff shrugged.

"Yiddish newspapers! Every Jew off the boat reads the Yiddish paper to find out how to become American. Can you imagine? In fact, Knobloch sends word he is expanding his operation to fill the need. He says the future of Yiddish is in America, and I believe him.''

"The future of Yiddish! A contradiction in terms!'' Zinnenoff said.

Shmolnik poked him in the ribs.

"If you can say that in Hebrew, I'll buy the next round.''

"One day, Shmolnik,'' Zinnenoff said dejectedly in Yiddish. "One day.''

"Until then, schnapps is on you.''

"We'll toast to Zion,'' Zinnenoff said.

"And to America!''

"To anywhere but here.''

They raised their glasses to show their readiness for another round.

Minkovsky found a bottle behind the bar and held it up to the light. Empty.

"I'm afraid I will have to beg your patience,'' he said. "Come Itsik, I have a case of this in the printing room. I'll show you where.''

"Just return before the messiah comes,'' Shmolnik called after us, "which is sure to be before Zinnenoff learns to ask me for a smoke in his desert tongue.''

In the printing room, Minkovsky showed me the location of the case of schnapps, and then said, "Stay a moment. Those two can wait.

"This talk of America reminds me that I have not yet told you: I have plans with my associate in New York. He doesn't know it yet, but we are going into business together.''

He opened a large trunk in the dark corner of the room. It was full of printing blocks.

"He is expanding his operation, so surely he must need printing materials. I'm going to send every spare piece I have; and some that aren't spares. Better we should do without, and the language will live on."

"Live on?"

"Do you know why Shmolnik and Zinnenoff fight so bitterly? They both know that the Jewish future, like the Jewish past, can only be found through words. Not nations. Certainly not land.

"Do you know that in some parts of the world the earth breaks open from time to time and swallows whole cities? Millions devoured as if by a beast. It is true. That is how little land can be trusted, whether Palestine or Europe or Russia, it is the same: at any moment the streets of a city might become a gaping maw.

"Make words your homeland, Itsik. Make them your lover as well. I swear to you, if you do, you will never be homeless and you will never be heartbroken. You will rise each morning and know that the world is yours, no matter in which corner of it you wake."

"You sound as though you are giving me a farewell speech," I said. "Are you going somewhere?"

"Have you seen the big steamship in the harbor?"

"Yes," I said. It was hard to miss. So few ships had come into Odessa since the war.

"The *King Alexander*," Minkovsky said. "It travels mainly between Constantinople and New York, but once a year it makes its way up the Bosphorus to the Black Sea and takes on freight in Odessa before returning to Constantinople for passengers. I have made arrangements for this trunk to be on board when it departs tomorrow."

"Seems like quite a lot of preparation for a trunk full of carved blocks."

"Not just blocks."

"So you are going? How?"

"Not me."

"Who then?"

"What would you say to accompanying this trunk to the New World? You would be my emissary. One day I would join you."

"Me? How? Even if I wanted to, the port is closed to emigration."

"There are other ways."

"Mr. Minkovsky, it is a kind offer. But you know that my heart longs to be with Sasha."

He looked at me for a moment with intense sadness, but then clapped his hands together as if his mind had moved on to other things.

"A pity!" he said. "Well, let's join our friends for a drink. Shall we?"

Back in the tavern, Minkovsky set the bottles down, then took a clear jar filled with blue liquid from beneath the bar.

"Friends, I must tell you how loyal our young Itsik is," he announced. "Just this moment I offered him passage to America. No, he said, he would prefer to stay with us."

"Well! Let's drink to his loyalty!"

"Yes!"

Minkovsky poured the two waiting glasses. Then he set a third before himself, and another in front of me.

"We're celebrating!" he said as he poured.

I was about to lift my glass when Minkovsky said, "Itsik, don't be rude. Almost ten years in Odessa, and you don't know that it is the custom to close one's eyes when drinking to loyalty?"

"It is?"

"Of course!"

"It goes without saying!"

I closed my eyes and raised my glass again.

"Not so fast! Now you must wait as I fill the glass completely."

I heard the trickle of liquid added to liquid.

"Now may I drink?"

"Yes, yes! In a single gulp!"

I threw it back and nearly gagged.

"Ach!" I spat. "This tastes like ink!"

"Ink? No!"

"Not mine," Shmolnik said.

Zinnenoff added, "Let's have another and see."

"Everyone's eyes closed?" Minkovsky asked.

With my second gulp, my tongue felt as though it had been injected with molten lead. The one that followed turned my teeth to smoldering ash.

I opened my eyes and saw the three of them staring back at me. Their glasses still stood full before them.

"Itsik, have I ever told you the story of how there came to be a Jewish press in Odessa?" Minkovsky asked.

My head moved right to left and back again as if out of my control. My hands likewise acted on their own, tightening around my glass as if holding on to a branch above a cliff.

"Not so long ago, there was a fellow who kept asking permission of the local authorities to print a newspaper for Odessa's Jews. No, came the response again and again, always from local officials who knew that if the Jews had a press, then the Jews would have a voice, and who would want to listen to what they had to say?

"Well, it came to be the czar's birthday, and our intrepid Jewish printer had an idea. He composed an ode—in Russian—in honor of the czar and the motherland. You never saw such praise! He sent it to the man himself. Then he asked permission for it to be translated and published in Odessa's Jewish newspaper. Yes, of course, the czar wrote back. Such a poem as this should appear in all newspapers of every language, especially the Jewish paper in Odessa. When the printer showed this proclamation to the local authorities, what were they to do? They knew better than anyone that there was no Jewish newspaper in Odessa, because they had been preventing the establishment of one for years! But the czar had just mentioned it. Now there had to be one.

"So what's the moral of this story?" Minkovsky asked.

"That a clever Jew can find a way out of any unpleasant situation," Zinnenoff said.

Shmolnik let out a wicked laugh. "I'll remember that when Cheka comes to put a rat up my ass."

"No, no. The moral is only this," Minkovsky said. "We are nowhere at home except in our *alef-beys*. Every place we find ourselves is temporary. But our *words*—can you still hear me, Itsik?—our *letters*, these are borders that cannot be breached."

As he spoke, his edges seemed to soften, until his beard blended into his vest and his head became his hat and the words I heard seemed to emanate not from a man but from what remains of a man once he has left a room, a scent, a shadow, or something between these two.

"Mr. Minkovsky, I think I may be drunk," I said.

He reached across the table, wrapped a thumb and a finger around my wrist, and lifted it into the air. When he released his grip, my hand fell with a thump, as if my fingers were five tiny sacks filled with sand.

"Yes, I think you're right," he said.

He climbed to his feet, walked around to my side of the table, and then wrapped his arms around my waist the same way he'd held my wrist: effortlessly, all-encompassingly.

"You are a good boy, Itsik. You've been a great help to me these past years," he said. He held me beneath the arms; Shmolnik and Zinnenoff each took a foot.

And then the widow Bimko was at their side.

"Be gentle with him now."

"Please forgive us for deceiving you," Minkovsky continued. "In years to come you will understand that it was out of love."

They carried me into the printing room, past the composition boards and inking trays, and then set me down in what felt like a cradle, or a shallow grave, flat on my back. A wall on each side rose two feet above me. Widow Bimko spread a blanket across my chest.

"Rest here," Minkovsky said. "You will sleep through the night

172

and maybe through the day as well. And in truth perhaps through another night . . . Or two . . . Three at the most.''

He took the glass from my hand and studied the liquor that remained, thick and blue, opaque as quicksilver.

"In any event, you will wake eventually," he said.

Shmolnik reached down and tussled my hair.

"Give my best to the girls in New York."

Zinnenoff stooped to take my limp hand.

"*Lehitra-ot*, Itsik. Until we meet again."

Widow Bimko kissed her fingers, then pressed them to my forehead.

"Forget about Sasha," she said. "Live life where you are!"

Minkovsky said a few more words, but though I heard them, I did not immediately comprehend.

I nodded to them each in turn, and then they closed the lid.

For what seemed the next several hours, I slept comfortably. Only when a swaying sensation caused me to shift in my bed did I feel something dig into my scalp. Groping in the darkness—it was, it seemed, as dark a night as I had ever known—I located the sharp-edged object, rolled it between my fingers, and knew instantly what it was. A wooden block. I held it in my hands, traced the shape with my thumbs. No doubt about it: *alef*.

I grabbed another, it too had an outline: *beys*.

Then another: *gimel*.

In this way I drifted back to sleep, naming the letters with which God had made the world. As if from inside my skull, I heard Minkovsky speak, replaying the last words I'd heard in Odessa, finally understanding them:

"You are our message in a bottle," he'd said. "Remember that as you float across the sea. Remember the castaways who have sent you off so that they would not be forgotten. Bring these letters as a message to a world that looks away as another island sinks below the waves."

THE EDUCATION OF A POET, as I have said, is never a straightforward affair. It is in fact an endless education. However, there are moments that in retrospect seem to offer singular instances of learning.

For me such a moment came that night—or perhaps it was the next day, or the next, the next, the next—when finally I stirred from my drunken stupor. Eyes open in the darkness, awoken by a faint scent of sea breeze mixed with ink and urine, I found myself locked in a trunk filled with wooden printing blocks. Their corners cut into my clothes, their edges came together to pinch my skin. With every frantic move I made, the blocks rolled beneath me and scraped gashes in my back. Terrified as I was, I knew then that this would always be a poet's lot: to be isolated, alone, grasping for answers, with letters as his only company and his constant torment.

I shouted, yes, of course I shouted. I screamed myself hoarse and was picking splinters from under my fingernails for days to come. But there were quiet stretches as well, hours at a time when I lay limp and exhausted, struggling to steady my racing heart.

During those lulls between frenzied efforts to free myself, I took solace in the work I had mastered through the previous years. With my fingertips as guides, I sought letters one by one. And the name they made preserved me.

Eventually my cries were heard, and I was released by a crewman deep in the hold of the *King Alexander*. Far from the nearest port where I might be ejected, he allowed me to join the rest of the rabble in steerage.

Yet in my mind I remained locked among the printing blocks. As I wandered the decks and breathed the salted air, my fellow passengers—speaking languages I had never heard, wearing costumes I had never imagined—seemed to me so many jumbled letters, all waiting to be assembled into stories, poems, songs; moving together across the wordless ocean, empty as a waiting page.

TRANSLATOR'S NOTE

THERE IS LIKELY TO BE SOME DISCUSSION, in certain circles, as to which more established Yiddish literary figure, if any, Itsik Malpesh most resembles.

Indeed, much of the life story recounted in his notebooks is nearly indistinguishable from that of other poets of his generation. The broad strokes of this collective biography are as follows: Raised with a traditional Jewish education in Eastern Europe or the Russian Pale of Settlement, at a certain point in middle adolescence the budding Yiddish literateurs of the early twentieth century discovered secular literature, and with it the outside world. Upon reaching adulthood, as many of these young writers emigrated as did not. Those who left settled mostly in the United States; smaller numbers went to Canada, Argentina, or Palestine. Those who remained clustered in urban enclaves such as Warsaw or Vilna (then known as the Jerusalem of Lithuania), vibrant cultural centers where Yiddish flourished even as intimations of the coming cataclysm could be seen in every European nation Jews called home. Regardless of where they came of age, all of these young writers, in one way or another, left the religious environment of their youth behind. Few found commercial success through their writing. Instead, they sought work in whatever occupation fate or family put before them.

In this sense, Malpesh can and should be considered as both

part and representative of a larger community, the only significant difference between himself and his peers being that, as he often repeated, he has outlived them all.

Having spent a lifetime as not just a writer but a reader of Yiddish literature, Malpesh seems to have written about himself as if he lived in the world of Yiddish fiction rather than Yiddish fact. This is not to say he intentionally invented details of his life, rather it is simply to suggest that he lived in a world more shaped by books than by his physical environment. How else to explain the striking similarities between the portrait presented of young Malpesh the would-be poet and, for example, the rhyming imp Hershel Summerwind created by the fabulist Itzik Manger (1901 – 1969)? Likewise, Malpesh's narrative of the Kishinev pogrom bears marks of the influence of the short story master Lamed Shapiro (1878 – 1948). The account of his life in the shadow and then the wake of World War I seems to echo the childhood anecdotes of his Nobel Prize—winning contemporary Isaac Bashevis Singer (1904 – 1991). As we will see in subsequent chapters, Malpesh's recollection of his life in New York would seem very familiar to Morris Rosenfeld (1862 – 1923), Moishe Leib Halpern (1886 – 1932), or any of about two dozen others who struggled with poverty even while becoming well-known poets on the Lower East Side.

Through all these life stages, meanwhile, Malpesh's memoirs display a blend of straightforward narrative and apparent allegory which seems to borrow from the three progenitors of Yiddish literature: I. L. Peretz, Sholem Aleichem, and Sholem Abramovich, also known as Mendele Mocher Sforim.

These and other questions of influence and intent must remain constantly on a translator's mind. How much is the telling of one life story determined by the lives of others? To what extent does writing about one teller of "forgotten tales in a forgotten tongue" amount to writing about them all?

When I asked Malpesh about some of the similarities between

his work and that of other Yiddish writers, his rambling answer ranged from philosophical to defensive to purposefully obscure.

"To be the last is to stand for the rest," he told me, "even if the rest wouldn't have stood for it."

That he, and indeed many of the characters presented in his memoirs, bear a resemblance to well-known figures from the literature, he did not dispute. Yet he did not regard himself as owing a debt to anyone.

"There was a certain uniformity to what we produced all those years ago," he said. "No one knew anything of genuine novelty. When Yiddish poets began composing their poems, simply to be writing something other than Talmud commentaries was revolutionary enough. Back then we could not help it if we all sounded the same. We all had our 'black trees bent like rabbis,' our 'tefillin heavy as chains.' We wrote to become something other than what we had been. We wrote striving for what we could be.

"Yet the longer one lived and continued to write, continued to write even as the language died, the more likely new styles would emerge.

"In the early days, everyone was obsessed with the *knaytch*," he told me. "Do you know this word? It is the sudden turn of the story or poem, when all at once the writer's meaning is revealed. In English, *knaytch* is the 'twist.' It is the same word a baker might use if he is making a pastry. But a writer is not a baker. A writer should be more like a butcher. And not just a butcher but a *shoykhet*, like Moshe Bimko bent over his sharpening stone.

"Do you know what kind of knife a *shoykhet* uses? When a *shoykhet* kills an animal, he must select the right blade—a *halaf*—for the size of the beast. It may not be the sharpest knife, or the most deadly, but it is the most graceful.

"A writer's work is not very different. Faced with poems and stories of all sizes, one uses whatever style is most graceful at the time. If in reaching the end of a story I need to borrow Bashevis's *halaf*, or Manger's, or Halpern's, so be it. I will use it, wipe it clean on my sleeve, and say, 'Thank you, Moishe Leib. Your *halaf* got me out of a jam.'

"This is a reason for many of the similarities between my work and others. We all learned to dispatch our stories with the same set of knives.

"And perhaps they all borrowed from me, did you ever think of that? Who is to say that in those other stories, it isn't my *halaf* that you see?"

The Memoirs of Itsik Malpesh

yud

IT WAS MID-MARCH WHEN I STEPPED OFF the *King Alexander*, making my first glimpse of the American sky more gray than it might appear in the typical immigrant dream. Cold as it was, I wore only the lightweight jacket that on the other side of the world had barely protected me from the Underground's subterranean chill. With no luggage to speak of, the distance I'd traveled in three weeks was shown now not by any outward change to myself or my choice of clothing, but by two smudges of white chalk, one on my sleeve, the other on my lapel. The first came when a ruddy-cheeked health inspector took my pulse and slashed a line across my arm declaring me satisfactory in both hygiene and disposition. I then moved along a line of men and boys until I stood in front of another inspector, who, though I could not quite understand him, seemed to inquire where I had come from and why.

For such questions, I was prepared. Deep in the third-class hold, I had followed the example of my peers. I learned from the sweating mob of Russians and Gypsies and Jews that the mindless and repeated recitation of words I could not comprehend was the surest way of gaining access to the place that in every language was called the Golden Land. I learned to recognize variations on questions regarding my skills and education by listening for three syllables that to my Yiddish ears would sound as though they began with a *vav*, a *kaf*, and a *shin*. To this collection of sounds I trained myself to answer, in English, "I am a printer," with such authority and assurance that any official would not merely believe me but would attest to the importance of my work.

I pinched myself whenever I said, "I am a poet," by mistake. That I could arrange words into the elements of a salable product would help my chances, I was told. That I could do the opposite—turn the tangible world into something so flimsy as a structure of words— would likely see me labeled an atheist, an anarchist, or worse.

"Vo. Kay. Shun?" the inspector said.

"I . . . am . . . a . . . pee . . . rin . . . ter," I managed to reply.

The inspector eyed me suspiciously, and then quizzed me in Russian.

"Place of birth?

"Kishinev."

"Port of departure?"

"Odessa."

"Race and creed?"

"Creed?" I asked.

"God," he said.

"What about Him?"

"Don't hold up the line, friend. What do you call Him? What's His name?"

"He has many names," I answered, "but I haven't spoken any of them in years."

With a stab and a flourish he inscribed my second chalk mark, this one meant to identify what sort of person I was. Scanning the lapels of my fellow inspectees, I saw there were two kinds: X's and O's, Christians and Jews. When the inspector had finished labeling me, I stood before him with a large egg of a circle above my heart, uncertain what to do next.

"Welcome to America," he said. "Please move along."

"Thank you," I replied, and I meant it.

True, I was an accidental immigrant. I'd been tricked into visiting these shores. To use the words I had learned when I attempted to describe my plight to members of the British crew of the *King Alexander*, I had been "shanghaied," "bamboozled," "crimped."

Yet I was not one to hold a grudge, and I was no fool besides. I had not been deaf to the talk in the Underground that New York was now the home of the great Yiddish writers. Some had insisted Warsaw was the place for a budding poet, but wasn't the father of all Yiddish literature buried here? Even in Odessa we had read news of Sholem Aleichem's funeral, of his burial in Queens, of the hundreds of thousands who took to the streets to pay homage. Such an army would have turned the Whites yellow and the Reds brown. There was no doubt that here Yiddish would thrive. And so too might its poetry, which by then had become my passion, my reason for living.

As for my other passion, my Sasha, though the distance between us now was greater than ever, I began to realize that I had her right where she had always been: on my pages, in my written dreams. Daily I gave her wet kisses through the nib of my fountain pen. In this way she had kept me company through the long ugly trip across the ocean. Somewhere en route, over the depths that separated me from her last living relative and the only place I'd hoped she might eventually return, I had made peace with the likelihood that I would never lay eyes on her. That likelihood, in turn, had set my hand moving such as it had never before. My poems now would not be written merely for her or about her, for me they would *be* her. If my longing for her was all I would know, I would nurture it as though it was the future she and I would never have.

Climbing aboard the ferry to Manhattan, I carried in one arm my valise of poems; in the other, a page Minkovksy had slipped inside. There he had written the address for his associate's printing shop, to which I was to deliver the trunk that had nearly been my grave.

I located Minkovsky's trunk on the main deck, arranged among the other pieces of luggage too large to bring through the tightly packed inspection queue. It was easier to ride in than to move, however. I must have been quite a sight: a man of scarcely 140 pounds slung across the top of a four-by-three-by-two steamer trunk, unable to budge it an inch.

A dark-skinned deckhand laughed and said something in a foreign tongue—English, I assumed, though it was the first I had heard of it beyond my memorized résumé. In response I could only raise my hands in acknowledgment of my failings and hope his laughter was not malicious. He spoke again, and my confusion must have shown, because another man passing by explained, "He says, Whatever you've got in there ain't worth breaking your back."

The deckhand kicked a small board with wheels toward me. It knocked into the trunk with a hollow thud. He grinned, sliding one hand under the other in repeated motion. It did not occur to me that he was miming the action he wanted me to take: to slide the wheeled board under the trunk. I thought instead it was some sort of American greeting, so I did the same in return. He repeated his gesture, now more earnestly, punctuating each slide of his hands with emphatic pointing first to the wheels, then to the trunk. I added reciprocal gesticulations, and together we stood there moving our hands as if we were swimming toward each other, though neither of us moved in any direction.

Finally, he marched toward me, lifted the trunk, and slid the wheels underneath. He then reached down, tied a length of rope around the wheels and the trunk, and spoke again. It was barely a word, just a consonant and a vowel, and to me it meant nothing. Did I owe him money for his service? Did he think I had given him my trunk? He made the sound again and waved his hands at me as though he was swatting a fly.

I looked here and there for the man who had served as my translator, feeling totally helpless. When I spotted him, he was standing beside a woman and a small boy, each dressed in Old World clothes that made the cut of his American-made suit seem a costume from the future. I supposed he had come over in advance of his family, which was not at all unusual. From the grimace he wore, I wondered if he now resented their arrival. Wrestling with their oversize luggage, he pretended not to notice my attempts to regain his attention. I coughed, then waved, then in desperation called to him in Yiddish, "Would you be so kind?"

He shot me such a glare, it was as though I had accused him of a crime.

"A single word you don't understand?" he shouted at me. "The *shvartze* says, 'Go!' 'Go!' One word he speaks, and you stand there like a cow with your mouth in your collar. How do you expect to make it in this new land if you can't comprehend the simplest instruction?"

At that moment I had trouble understanding even my own language. Had he called the deckhand a *shvartze*? In Russia we used this word to refer to the most pious among the religious Jews. The more layers of dark overcoats and *shtreimels* they wore, the more *shvartze* they were said to be. Here it seemed this same word refered to a particular variety of non-Jew. Was it not only English but all language that I was now unable to understand?

My reluctant interpreter spit on the deck and glared at me with wild eyes. His wife looked on apologetically from behind; his little boy put a hand to his face and seemed ready to cry.

"In my day we took some time to learn our English before we got off the boat," the man continued. "They should've locked the gates in 1920!"

His little boy spoke up. "But Papa, if they locked the gates, how would we get in!"

"Shah! Now, go! Go and get out of the way so all the nations can drop into the bucket and join the stink."

Behind me a throng had gathered, swelling like a river behind a dam, all waiting to exit and descend the ferry's ramp. Others called out, in Yiddish, Russian, Greek, Italian, as well as languages I could not name. From the context their collective meaning was unmistakable: they wanted me to move, to make way for the final steps of their arrival, which now pulled them with the force of gravity.

I wrapped the deckhand's rope around my shoulder and set off down a wide walkway, from the swaying river to what appeared to be solid ground.

No sooner had my foot met the wood planks of the dock than two boys, American-born by the looks of them, called out to me in flawless Yiddish.

"Excuse me, sir, but I believe we are countrymen!" the first boy said.

The second added, "Perhaps you know our father, Mr. Shloime Shnarklish? He was supposed to arrive on this ship, and I am unable to find him!"

One of them had hollow cheeks and ashy hair hanging down in front of the half-closed eyes of a turtle. The other was round-faced and redheaded, with freckles as bright as a flame. They were the most unlikely brothers I had ever seen, which only made me feel worse for them.

"I'm sorry, my boys, but I'm afraid I don't know your father," I said.

"We have been waiting for months!" the ashy boy said. "Our baby sister is hungry and now our mother has gone off to work in the shops and we don't know what we will do . . ."

"A pity that Jews have it so hard in this land of dreams!"

"Perhaps you have a coin or two or a scrap to eat?"

"I have no money, but I do have a poem that I think will brighten your spirits—"

"How about in the trunk? It's bigger than the room my mother and sister and brother and I share. Not a scrap or a coin anywhere inside?"

"I'm afraid what's in the trunk is not mine. In fact, I am only in this country to make sure it reaches its destination."

They eyed it hungrily. Then the freckled one took his cap off his head and waved it as though batting flies, though I didn't see any flying around him.

"Must be worth quite a lot to go through all that trouble," he said.

"To some," I said. "But here, here is the verse I had in mind . . ." I fumbled with my satchel, unable to retrieve the page while holding the handle in one hand and the rope attached to the trunk in the other.

"Shall we hold the rope for you?" one of the boys asked.

"And your bag?" the other said.

"Very kind, very kind," I said.

I found the sheet I was looking for, then handed the smaller boy my valise of poems, speaking all the while. "I'm impressed to see boys your age so well mannered. When I was ten I often found myself in a bit of trouble. . . . I only wish I had more than a verse or two to give you . . ."

With their hopeful faces staring up at me, I began to recite:

> We ride life's waves
> as if made of driftwood,
> From our roots cut, fallen,
> and cast on the deep
> How then will we rise
> and learn to walk as we should
> When we come to the shallows
> to search for relief?

I was preparing to move into the inspiring second stanza when I looked up to see what effect my poem was having. To my surprise, there were now not two boys but many—eight? ten?—crowded around me, each in an identical cap. When I looked down, I saw only a miniature mob with dirty faces.

You are water-logged, drowning,
but fear not, floating youth!
Branches hardened by the ocean
have strength deep within.
The beach beckons with sunshine,
glowing like truth,
The shore will rise to meet you
as the tide rolls in.

Only when I had finished did I look again into the crowd, now searching for the boy who had originally called out to help. I looked into one face, then another. They stared back blankly. Others cried, "Read more! Read more!"

"I would be happy to," I said, "but where are the boys who had been in such need?"

"What boys?" some said, and others: "We are all in need! Why deprive us because they wandered away?"

Finally the smallest boy among them said, "Turtle and Fishl are long gone, chump! You'll never catch them now!"

A bigger boy cuffed him on the ear and then smiled.

"This one's soft in the head, doesn't know what he's saying. We never heard of any Turtle or Fishl."

Turtle? Hearing the name I knew it could only refer to the ashy boy with the half-closed eyes. By then—too late!—I had become suspicious. Pushing aside one boy and then another, I carved a path through the crowd. I prepared to take up Minkovsky's trunk and be on my way, but it was nowhere to be seen.

I scanned the dock from the ferry's creaky bridges to the distant stairway that led to the city above. There, about one hundred steps away, I saw Turtle and Fishl racing away, one before the trunk, one behind.

I tore off after them.

"Stop, you American thieves! I'll break your lying heads!"

Turtle shouted back at me, "You'll have to catch us, Driftwood!"

"How will you run with so many leaden words in your head?" his brother taunted.

They sped away, at first aided by the slope of the dock, then hindered by it as it climbed uphill.

I was nearly upon them when a red-nosed policeman appeared at my side. Apparently he'd witnessed the theft. We both huffed up the hill, and by the time we reached the top, the boys had run out of both energy and places to hide.

Turtle first smiled wickedly at me. Then he saw the officer at my side. He kicked the trunk in frustration, flipping the lid back. Inside, Minkovsky's wooden printing blocks, my bed for the better part of the passage from the Old World, appeared shabby in the New York light. They looked like only what they were: small hunks of wood, carved with ancient runes, chipped from use, stained with ink.

"For this we get caught?"

"Charlie Smooth will drain us dry!"

"How much do you owe him?"

"Too much already."

Turtle gave the trunk another good kick, this time with less anger but greater intent. He kicked it again and sent the trunk rolling, back down the hill we'd just climbed, back toward the pier and the boat tie-offs and the immigrants milling about in their new home, hands in their pockets, nowhere to go. Minkovsky's trunk rolled toward them with gathering speed. A wooden box full of Yiddish printing blocks on a set of rusty wheels, it screeched and clamored and jugged like a locomotive leaving the station, bumping along weather-worn planks that had brought uncountable languages to the city above, planks that now were sending the carved representatives of one of those languages down, down, down.

Yiddish is often thought a trifle of a tongue, harmless, homey, schmaltz and borscht served on your *bubbe*'s challah. How much damage could it do? This much: Minkovsky's trunk knocked over a ladder with a paint can balanced on top, it caught the corner of an egg merchant's cart and sent her wares flying, it kicked a blind man's cane out his hand, it crushed toes and tore dresses and made immigrant mamas cry for their children to clear out of the way. And it kept rolling.

The officer blew his whistle, took off down the ramp. I followed. Behind us, the boys we had raced to catch melted into the crowd that had formed to watch this spectacle, a crowd that let out a sound that was somewhere between a gasp and a cheer when Minkovsky's trunk reached the bottom of the ramp. It splintered the planks that kept the dock from open air, and flew out, over the river.

I reached the edge just in time to see it fall, slapping against the surface of the water with a smack and a crash. Leaning over after it, I watched the trunk fill with black water and sink into the abyss.

Gone! All of it gone. I sent my own tears down into the water at the sight of what was lost. It felt as if all my years in Odessa had been contained in that case.

As my tears dropped down and joined that hungry river, bits of wood bobbed up from the depths. I strained to see them, and they were of course—what else would they be?—an *alef*, a *beys*, a *gimel*, a *daled*. . . . As the trunk sank, its contents shot to the surface. A hundred or more printing blocks floated in a cluster below me, out of reach.

The waves rolled in and dragged back out, and I watched the blocks move farther and farther away. They floated eastward in loose formation, like a defiant Yiddish armada on its way out to sea. Tiny. Absurd. Unsinkable.

I gathered myself and wandered back up the ramp. The police officer said a few incomprehensible things to me, but I only shook my head over and over, unable to tell him that I did not understand.

He left me to my misery, and I sank into the crowd entering the city. With eyes downcast on the stones of the road, I could have been anywhere. The same feet had run through Kishinev's streets, the same had made their way to Odessa. I closed my ears to the foreign sounds all around me and composed a verse as I plodded along. Alone, with nowhere to go and no way to get there, I wondered if this was the end of me.

> The poet's shoes walk
> the same road in any country
> On stones which do not care
> Where he came from or why
> With each footfall, he learns
> What the stones know already:
> That silence is the only poem
> We hear when we die

I floated with the crowd, a river of people such as I had never seen. I wished for something, anything familiar. I dreamed of, who else, my Sasha appearing before me. Perhaps she was here, waiting for me, perhaps . . .

"Hey, Mister," a Yiddish voice called out.

I looked up. It was Turtle. Had I the strength I would have fixed on him a gaze of burning rage, but in my state I could only stare blankly. Then I saw that he held in his hand my valise of pages. I could have wept with gratitude.

"You say you're from Kishinev?" the boy asked.

I nodded.

"Come with me. There's someone you should meet."

"Why should I trust you after you robbed me?"

He looked me up and down, then shrugged.

"You have nothing left to steal."

The Memoirs of Itsik Malpesh

khaf

WATCHING MINKOVSKY'S PRINTING BLOCKS float out to sea, I feared for a moment that I might have seen the last of the most stable element of my young life, the beleagured runes of the *alef-beys*. Where would I be without those odd shapes that had sustained me from murderous Kishinev to starving Odessa to my captive journey across the ocean? What would become of a boy who knew his name only as a collection of symbols lost to time?

I soon discovered that I had nothing to fear. As Turtle announced our entry into the Lower East Side ("Of what?" I asked. "Of the world," he said), it became clear that I had arrived in a place more crowded with Yiddish letters than the city of my birth and the city of my adolescence combined.

Even had the streets been empty, it would have been obvious this was a city of Jews. Everywhere I looked, there were carved wooden shingles and letter-press posters, paste-posted bills and throwaway pamphlets, stacks of daily papers waiting for the newsboys to shoulder, hard candy boxes and bubblegum wrappers and cigar bands, a hundred varieties of printed litter, all of it Yiddish, all of it stamped with the same ancient curves and angles that in Russia had begun to seem marked for the grave. Naturally, there were scores of butcher signs, tailor signs, and bookseller signs, expected Yiddish placards hung before expected Yiddish storefronts with expected bearded Jews in the windows. But there also seemed to be no end to the New

World purposes to which our Old World language could be put: there were signs for Yiddish beauty salons, signs for Yiddish telegram shops, signs for Yiddish sellers of lipstick, compacts, and synthetic wigs. There were signs for Yiddish detective agencies specializing in husband-finding services, guaranteeing prompt payment of alimony or photographs of the grave. There were signs for Yiddish baseball betting parlors, signs for Yiddish American citizenship classes, signs for thousand-seat Yiddish theaters, signs for Yiddish teahouses blocked from view by the lines that stretched out their doors.

And the signs were only the beginning. I followed Turtle down sidewalks thick with fur-*shtreimeled* Hasidim, shtetl-bred anarchists, yeshiva-boy Socialists with stripes of party affiliation stitched to their shirts. Litvaks and Galicianers argued over the ownership of the corners where they hocked their wares, while the Yekkes, German Jews who'd crossed the ocean a generation before, passed by more recent immigrants with sniffs of disdain and insults tossed off in their newly mastered tongue.

In the lives they'd left behind they never would have met, but here, five thousand miles from the land of their births and their feuds, they walked with common concerns: making it in America; no longer running from Cossacks, pogromists, and secret police; becoming members of a people who belonged. Not even in Odessa, sitting at the bottom of Europe and Russia like a greasetrap on a drain, had I seen such a variety of Jews. Here was Babel before the tower, I was sure, for here, despite having been scattered across the earth, men and women from a dozen nations spoke with one voice. Yiddish floated above the streets of New York and turned the air a guttural gray. All that could climb from such a haze were the great cloud-parting buildings, rising in the distance like fingers of the hand of God.

Not that I gave God a thought at the time. Not at all. It would be difficult to pinpoint the exact moment at which I lost my faith, but I'm certain that by then, my twenty-first year, the beginning of my life in the "Golden Land," the point at which I knew and owned less than I had previously thought possible, my belief too was gone. As I walked the streets of Manhattan for the first time, any childlike religious reverence I had yet within me was jostled and bumped to the side of my soul by godless awe at my manmade surroundings and the thickness of the crowd.

"Come on, this way's faster," Turtle said.

He made a quick step from the crowded streets into a fetid alley-way, an endless network of clotheslines above us, all empty but for a few shirts that had frozen solid in the March wind. They clacked against each other like shutters, while feral children made games of stalking the headless shadows the laundry cast on the tenement walls.

"Who is this friend of yours?" I asked my guide. "And why should I want to meet him?"

"He's a very important man, and you will be grateful for the in-troduction," the boy answered. "Before I joined his gang, I was get-ting grabbed by the cops every week. Now that they know I'm with Charlie Smooth, they leave me be."

"His gang?" I said. "You're taking me to see a gangster?"

"Hush up, greenhorn. It's not like that. Charlie Smooth takes care of us. He gives us everything we need."

We walked on, block after block through a city that seemed to have no edge, no thinning of the crowd. I began to get winded but followed dutifully, aware that if Turtle abandoned me, there might be no end to my wanderings through this wretched urban maze.

Finally my impatience got the better of me, and I blurted out, "And where will we find this important man of yours?"

By way of answer, Turtle threw a stubby finger into the air, point-ing ahead to a double-arched structure looming over the four- and five-story buildings that made a canyon of the streets. In steerage I had heard the names of the great skyscrapers of New York repeated endlessly. Surely this must be the biggest of them all.

"The Woolworth Building?" I asked.

Turtle laughed.

"What a dummy! That's the Brooklyn Bridge!" he said. "You're not so bright, eh? Are you sure you come from Charlie Smooth's hometown?"

"I don't know anything about your Charlie Smooth!"

"If you did, at least you'd know something."

We continued on. With every step, the bridge seemed to grow before us. Soon I could see that it was in fact made up of not one tower but two, joined by a roadway that cut across the sky like a second horizon. In a few minutes we reached a ramp thick with men and women strolling without a care over the dark water below.

"Are we going across?" I asked.

"Only halfway," Turtle said.

We walked out over the river, to a height that seemed to me as great as a mountain. The wind intensified as we left solid ground far behind, blowing such that men held on to their hats and ladies gripped their dresses for fear they would flutter and expose their knees. Turtle seemed too young to care for this possibility, but worn out as I was from my travels, I watched for it as if the smallest glimpse of American flesh would bode well for my American future. Every gust of a breeze brought a flash of hope.

When we reached the stone tower that held aloft this vast stage of human comings and goings, Turtle ran to the edge of the promenade, lifted one foot over the railing, and said, "Quick! Before anyone sees!"

With a hop he was gone, disappearing as if having jumped to the river below.

I peered over the railing and saw that he stood on a gray metal platform, midway between the pedestrian level and the automobile roadway below. I climbed the railing and then lowered myself carefully to join him. As soon as my feet touched down, Turtle was again on the move.

"This way," he said, ducking through a gap beneath the promenade. I followed tentatively at first, but then had to rush to keep up with him. With every step I stumbled while he darted in and out between iron beams and cable reinforcements. He made sudden turns with the grace of a gazelle while I ducked and staggered for fear of hitting my head. Inches above us, the footfalls of hundreds of shoes clopped toward the city and away.

Turtle didn't stop running until he reached the gray brick of the support tower, where he quickly located a window-sized opening that looked like a cavity dug into the wall.

"Charlie Smooth says they left this space for storage when they built the bridge," Turtle said. "The city forgot it was here. So it's ours now."

"Ours?" I said. "How many are you?"

He climbed into the hole without a word, creeping forward like a caterpillar until even the soles of his shoes disappeared into the darkness.

"Turtle?" I called. When I heard no answer, I climbed in after him. The hole—something of a tunnel, actually—was a tighter fit for me than it had seemed for him, but with a minute or so of wriggling and sliding, I managed to make my way through.

I fell into a room crowded with cots and pallets, sleeping space for perhaps fifteen—more if they were all the size of my guide. A warm gust of air greeted me as I stood, providing a feeling of warmth for the first time in weeks. From the corner of the brick-walled room a pot-bellied stove glowed orange in the darkness, and its heat combined with the sight of the blankets and bedding made me want to close my eyes and drift off to sleep. I placed my hand on one of the bunks as I passed and was surprised by the softness of the covering. Not at all what one would expect in the lair of pickpocket urchins. There was also something unmistakably familiar about it. I gathered up the blanket in two hands and smoothed it across my cheek.

"This is Bemkin Down!" I said. "From Kishinev! Where did it come from?"

"I told you, Charlie Smooth gets us whatever we need."

Turtle led me to a door frame without a door and held his hand up when we reached the threshold.

"Wait here," he said, and took two steps forward into another room, slightly smaller than the first. It was dominated by a wooden desk facing out from the far wall. A Yiddish newspaper hung above it like a barricade, with two small boys, one on either side, holding the page by its corners. Though I could see no one older than ten or twelve years, a man's voice rustled the paper from behind.

"Heard you had a little trouble at the dock," the voice said.

Turtle stood upright as if stricken.

"I can explain, Charlie. It was—"

"You know the price of explanations, don't you?"

Turtle stepped toward the desk, put a penny on the corner, and began to gush.

"I thought we had a mark, but when I found out he was a landsman of yours, I knew I should bring him in."

A page turned behind the wall of newsprint.

"That's not how I heard it. I heard you botched the job, let a perfectly good steamer trunk get away. And you got caught by the cops in the process. I don't have enough trouble with the cops?"

"But I brought him."

"Who?"

"Your landsman. Says he's from Kishinev."

"You think I left Kishinev because I wanted to meet men from Kishinev?"

"But—"

"I don't care where he's from. Just shake him down and throw him in the river. You hear me?"

When he lowered the paper, I couldn't believe what I saw—or

rather who, for I knew the face hidden behind the page of Yiddish words.

THOUGH NOW A FULL-GROWN MAN with a bulging Adam's apple, he had the same adolescent mien I remembered, a sadly smirking mug full of pimples that glowed like summer berries in the sun. And while he wore no beard now, nor a skullcap, there remained something pious about him—perhaps it was the way he kept one finger high up on his cheek, twirling a sidecurl that had long since met the barber's shears.

"Chaim?" I said.

He stared at me a moment. "Little Itsik?"

"Chaim!" I shouted.

"Chaim?" Turtle asked.

"Don't look so surprised," my old tutor said to the boy. "Why not *Chaim?* Hasn't Charlie Smooth made a *life* for you?" He turned to me and smiled. "I'm no longer called Chaim, Little Itsik. My new pupils know me as Charlie Smooth."

As he spoke this last word, he offered a smirk and ran a rueful hand across his cheek. Though he was now as clean-shaven as any young American, he still was plagued by a beard of acne that followed perfectly the lines of his facial hair when he had allowed it to grow. It was late in the afternoon, a time at which a conspiracy of stubble and weeping sores left his cheeks the black and red of molten lava cooling to rock. He would later tell me that those who believed his "smooth" to be simply a nickname—and not, as I knew it to be, a rough translation of his family name, Glatt—supposed he had been so tagged by cruel youths with a talent for irony. In fact, the irony was his own; he liked the distraction created by the unlikely joining of his skin and his name. He used it almost daily, he told me, introducing himself to strangers on the street who would invariably stammer and stare at the sad spectacle—a man with a graveled complexion declaring himself "smooth"—while his boys picked their pockets clean.

Taken aback as I was to find myself standing before this figure from my youth, I should not have been surprised to discover him here—in America, in New York. Of course, in my memory it had been I alone who had left Kishinev . . . I who had left and, in leaving, I who had frozen the world behind me. And yet even in the grip of this fantasy, I should have recalled that Chaim had left before me.

As I soon learned, he had come across by way of London, immediately following his early-morning exit from Bemkin's bed. And unlike myself, a boy passed from place to place by the whims of fate, Chaim had pointed himself toward a single goal and attained it. He'd left town with a sufficient supply of earned cash and pilfered valuables that he had traveled first class all the way, running out of money only when he hit the East Side, and not lacking it for long. In no time he had learned to apply his talents to the streets of his new home, he told me. Which talents I didn't ask.

"Itsik, you look as hungry as all Russia. Don't they feed you over there? That's a joke. I read the papers. I know about the famine and the rest, so when I say, 'Don't they feed you in Russia,' it's *funny.* Get it? No? Oh, but don't worry. American humor took some time for me, too."

I studied my old friend. Was it the years or the crossing of the ocean that had changed him? Or had he stayed the same, and it was I who saw him differently?

"Humor, Chaim?" I said. "I'm surprised. I remember you as a serious young man. It was you who filled my head with Dostoyevsky, remember?"

"I've moved on, Little Itsik. A real intellectual looks for ways to apply his learning to the world, not merely to library shelves. And anyway, I found a new favorite writer not long after I left Kishinev. In London."

Chaim threw a big brick of a book down in front of me. Its text was in Yiddish, but the author didn't sound like a Jew.

"Dickens?" I read aloud. "A Yiddish writer?"

"English," Chaim said. "This volume is a translation, but I can read him in the original now."

I hefted the book in my hands.

"Are English writers paid by the pound? What kind of story could need so many pages to tell?"

"It's the tale of a wise and generous Jew who takes in orphans and trains them to make their way in the world."

It would be years before I would read this book—in English myself, I am now proud to say. Only then, remembering our conversation about it, would I realize Chaim had found a new model of living in its pages just as I had in *Crime and Punishment*. I did not know then as I looked around this bunker filled with orphan boys and budding criminals that Chaim perhaps thought he was another Fagin. Given what became of his example, I have often wondered if he read through to the end.

"Take it, read it. Like old times we'll learn from the same book," Chaim said. "I'll even ignore inflation and charge you the same rate as years ago to explain the words you do not know."

I put the book back on his desk.

"No, thank you," I said. "The last book you gave me got me into too much trouble."

"Perhaps later," he said. "Remember that it was your old friend Chaim Glatt who told you this: Trouble is the true American vernacular. When you can speak it fluently, you'll know you've found a home.

"But forget books for a moment. You're new in this country, and you have a lot to learn. Lucky for you, you'll have me to teach it."

OUR LESSONS BEGAN RIGHT AWAY. That night, Chaim took me to eat at the Automat on Thirteenth and Broadway. From outside, it was the brightest place I had ever seen. White light radiated from the windows such that our shadows were cast behind us on the sidewalk as we approached. We might as well have been walking into the sun, and my steps were as cautious as if we were. The Statue of Liberty, Ellis Island, these beacons had meant little to me when I'd seen them the day before. In truth I had barely noticed them. Only now, standing with Chaim before the Automat, did I see clearly the America I had imagined in all its blinding possibility. I thanked my old friend as he held the door for me, and in response he said, "It's nothing. The least I can do. And dinner's on you, right?"

I had not been off the boat more than twelve hours, so of course I had no money. I began to answer, intending to claim that in fact I was not hungry enough to eat, though in truth I was famished. Before I could speak, Chaim let out a hooting laugh.

"You greenhorns!" he said. "You never know a joke when you hear one. Look at you, you're white as a baker's pecker! You think your old friend would stick you with the bill?"

I stammered a reply, confused by the whole situation.

"I know you have no money right now," he continued. "When I arrived, what did I have? Less than you, I'll tell you that much. You have a landsman who's going to show you the ropes. Just stick close, and you'll see how to make something of yourself in this country."

At the change counter, Chaim slid a bill to a woman behind glass and then made her count the coins—twenty of them—twice before he accepted them from her hand.

Speaking to her in broken English, he slid ten of the coins back. She glared at him, them counted off five smaller coins and pushed them through the opening. Chaim slapped his head theatrically, spoke to her in more English, and slid back to her the five small coins along with a few of the larger coins. He placed his hand on the rest of the larger coins and slid them into his coat pocket without looking at them. When the change girl pushed three even larger coins in his direction, he asked her a question that prompted her to point to the hand that he'd used to cover the coins on the counter. When he moved it, there was nothing there. The change girl glowered. With a few more words in pleasant tones, Chaim pushed all the coins from their various transactions across the counter and pointed at the bill he'd given her originally. She looked repeatedly between the bill and his face.

"Never let them shortchange you," he whispered to me as she deliberated. "Believe me, I'm in business so I know. Shortchanging is the only way these places stay afloat. You've got to make them count and count and recount. Give the girl a wink so she thinks you're only hanging around to take a longer look, but watch she doesn't drop one of your nickels in her lap. They think if it's between their legs, you'll be too shy speak up."

When finally she relented and gave his bill back to him, he reached into his pocket and produced one of the coins he'd slid from the counter. He pushed it under the glass and said in practiced English, "Faryoo, shveethart."

The woman took the coin without a glance, waving us on as though she was swatting flies. She called out to the man behind me, who was tapping his foot impatiently.

Chaim grinned as he took me by the arm.

"You hear that? 'Next,' she said. You see how that sounds like *nacht?* Well, that's what American girls say when they want to get to know you better but suspect society wouldn't approve. They say 'next' so you'll know to come back later, at *night,* when no one will see you, right? Come on, let's eat."

Beyond the change counter, Chaim passed by a table that had not yet been cleared. He lifted a spoon from a coffee cup, shaking it dry before sliding it into his pocket. Then he directed me toward a wall of glass and shining metal. He put four coins in my hand.

"Just drop the money in the slot next to the sandwich you want," he told me as he pointed to a row of tiny windows that opened like doors. Behind each was a slice of pie or a bruised pear; whitefish on toast with a pickle; two hard-boiled eggs. Chaim saw me hesitate, reaching to this door then that, coins shaking between my fingers.

"Just pick one, Itsik!" he said. "You're in America now. If you taste it and it's no good to you, you just pick another."

Chaim took a coin from my hand and dropped it in the slot next to a toasted cheese sandwich. When he opened the window, the clamor of the kitchen behind the wall of food poured out as if a leak had been sprung. With his hand resting on the plate as if pausing in a moment of indecision, he looked left and right, then back toward the change counter. An instant later the spoon he'd lifted from the table was in his other hand. Pushing the handle into a small opening that caught the glass door's latch when closed, he turned the spoon as if it were a screwdriver.

"Catch that, will you?" he said.

"Catch what?" I began to ask, but before the question was fully formed I saw what he meant. The coin I'd just dropped into the slot was coming back up, ejecting itself from the wall like a tongue sliding out between puckered lips. Chaim turned the spoon again, and another coin followed, then again and again.

Green as I was, I knew this was a theft. I looked around in horror.

"It's my first day here!" I whispered harshly. "I'd rather not spend it in jail."

"Shah!" he snapped. He pulled his spoon out of the catch and pointed through the open Automat window. "If we can hear the kitchen, they can hear us."

When he closed the window, we again heard only the low murmur of a dozen diners and their clinking silverware. I stood there holding a plate in one hand and a fistful of coins in the other, unsure what to do next.

"Look at that," Chaim said. "You've been here twelve hours, and you've already turned a profit."

I looked into my palm and counted sixteen nickels.

"Chaim, I don't feel good about this," I said.

"That's because you can't read the signs all around you." He pointed at the wall. "Look there, see what that says: It says, 'Tuesday Special: All you can eat.' That one? 'Wednesday Special: Two for one.' In America, prices are flexible. They change. You've got to learn that money moves here. It's not like Russia, where we hide it away. Got me?"

"Money moves?" I said.

"Oy, Itsik, I forgot you were such a dummy. I remember you told me your mama worried you were too smart for your own good. You should let her know she has nothing to worry about.

"It's like this, see: When you breathe in, you need to breathe out, right, or else you'll turn blue and fall over dead. In America, the same is true with money! You must give to get and get to give. You think I only collect from those kids who shook you down? No, no. They cost me a bundle. I feed them, give them a place to sleep, put clothes on their backs. *Investment.*"

This last word he said in English, and I tried to sound it out, as if wearing the word on my lips would help me understand it.

"In-vesh-men?" I asked

"Listen, I'm going to give you your first English lesson. Say this slowly: You . . . wanna . . . breathe . . ."

I stared at him, unable to speak. He reached out and tugged my ear.

"Say it!" he said. "You want to breathe."

"Yo vanna breet," I said.

Chaim stuck his tongue between his teeth and made a sound like a leaking balloon. "*Th tht thhhh,*" he said. "Like that, with your tongue on your teeth."

"Teh-heh, teh-heh, teh-heh," I said.

"Close enough," he said. "Try again: 'You wanna breathe . . .'"

"Yo vanna breet-heh," I said.

"Good, now this: 'You got to spend.'"

"Yo gotta shprend."

"*Mazel tov*, Itsik. Now you talk like an American. So eat something already before you fall over dead."

I ate gladly, endlessly, growing more comfortable with this means of gathering food with every coin I plunked into the glass-windowed wall. I was midway through a second slice of apple pie when I remembered the task I'd been charged with and stood up with a start.

"Minkovsky's associate! I must find him and explain what has happened to his printing blocks!"

"What? Find who?"

I dug through my valise for the note and read the name aloud. "Knobloch."

"Knobloch?" Chaim's eyebrows arched like two black birds taking flight. "*The* Knobloch?"

I showed him the address.

"That's *the* Knobloch all right. The guy's a crook! What business do you have with a sweatshop slave driver like him?"

"He's not!" I said. "Look here. He's a respected publisher. And I can't believe you of all people would call anyone a crook."

"Knobloch may dabble in publishing, but he creams his coffee with the blood of working stiffs. Not me, mister. I'm a regular Reuven Hood compared to that guy."

"All I know is, he needs the printing materials I brought from Odessa! The materials your boy Turtle launched into the sea!"

"You think American newspapers use junk like that? Even the Jewish ones? Nah. That crap was strictly for the Old Home. You're better off rid of it."

"But I promised."

"What's a promise on the other side of the ocean? Believe me, it makes no difference to him now."

"If a poet doesn't keep his word, what's a word worth?"

Chaim laughed. "Oh, I heard all about your poetry. You think I don't have a mama in Kishinev? She tells me your poetry sent your poor papa to prison."

I fell back in my chair.

"Don't worry, Itsik. Come stay with us under the bridge tonight. In the morning you'll go to Knobloch and explain everything. Trust me, it won't be the end of the world."

I ate the rest of my meal with my appetite stilled by suspicion, knowing I needed as much nourishment as I could get, yet wary of both my old friend and my new home. With my reason for being in New York first sunk into the sea, and now doubted by Chaim, I wanted nothing more than to return to Odessa, where despite war and famine and the Cheka, I had somehow felt safe. At least there I had known the dangers by sight and by name, and I knew how to avoid them. Here there seemed to be new threats lurking beyond every door—some new, some old but dressed in different clothing.

On our way out of the Automat, Chaim had just begun another English lesson when a young man with blond hair and no hat approached as if he had been waiting for us to exit.

"Hello, friends!" he called to us, speaking the strangest Yiddish I had ever heard. "I can see you are new in this country! I would like to welcome you and invite you to a meeting of recent immigrants." He held a pamphlet before him as though it were a ticket to the circus, his arm fully outstretched, overeager to stuff it into my hands. "Here you will find the address, and a few inspiring stories of our mission."

I reached out to accept the pamphlet, but Chaim smacked my hand.

"Stick it, friend," he said.

The blond man smiled.

"Please speak more slowly, if you don't mind. I have only learned recently your language."

"No kidding," Chaim spat, then rolled words out of his mouth like stones. "In. Your. Ass. Friend," he said. "Stick. It. In. Your. Ass."

The man laughed.

"And it is such a colorful language, isn't it! I can see you are reluctant to hear my message today, but no matter. We're all brothers, we all come to the truth in time."

Chaim knocked the pamphlets out of his hand.

"God loves you just the same!" the man said.

"Your God can pull my *petzl* and shoot himself in the eye."

Grabbing my wrist, Chaim pulled me away as I began to stoop to pick up the pamphlets, which now were blowing down the street in the evening breeze.

"Strange," Chaim said. "They're not usually so stubborn. I wonder what made him think we were greenhorns?" Then he caught sight of my sleeve. It had seemed like weeks since I had landed in New York, but in fact it had been less than a day. My sleeve was still white with the chalk from the Ellis Island inspection. Chaim reached over and brushed away the chalk from my arm, shaking his head.

"You gotta blend in, Itsik. Anyone spots you as a greenie, you're a marked man. Then they all will be on you."

"They who?"

"Christians and thieves, Itsik," Chaim said. "You know they're teaching missionaries Yiddish to try to snag immigrants fresh off the boat? They even have a few converts working for them. They watch for poor suckers like you who look like they stepped out of a Sholem Aleichem story, then they're on you like dogs.

"How do you think my boys made you for a mark? You're just lucky we got to you first. The ones that don't pick your pocket will rob your Jewish soul."

lamed

MINKOVSKY HAD TOLD ME OF HARRY KNOB-
loch's success in the Golden Land, but he'd made no mention of
the fact, and perhaps he did not know this himself, that his associate had become quite well known since leaving Odessa. As I soon
learned, in certain New York Yiddish-speaking circles Knobloch
was a household name.

Though he had never met the man, Chaim knew just where to find
him. He even drew a map. I studied it for half an hour, trying to make
sense of the grid of avenues and streets.

"You sure you don't want Turtle to take you?" Chaim asked.

"Take him where?" Turtle said.

"Remember the warehouse on Delancey where you found those
bundles of ladies' underwear last year?"

"The place with the loading dock as big as Washington Square?"

"That's the one."

"That was quite a haul."

"One of the biggest."

"You robbed him?" I asked.

"Who said *robbed?*" Chaim huffed indignantly. "Turtle only *found.*
Is it the boy's fault somebody lost a gross of ladies' underwear just as he
happened to walk by?"

I didn't think it would be in my best interest to visit Knobloch in
the company of a boy who had "found" some of his merchandise, so I
insisted I could locate the address myself.

Following Chaim's map, I soon stood before a massive gray building that dwarfed anything in my experience. It was bigger than Bemkin's down factory or any of the churches in Odessa, perhaps even larger than the *King Alexander*. That such a place could be the kingdom of one man was unbelievable to me—one Jew even more so. And yet there was the evidence in black and white as well as Yiddish and English, a sign on the door that read:

KNOBLOCH INDUSTRIES
INTEGRATED BUSINESS INTERESTS

I climbed three flights of stairs to an office where I was pleased to find a secretary who spoke Yiddish. She was a plain girl, eyes of a rabbit, with a twitching nose to match.

"I need to see Mr. Knobloch," I told her. "It is a matter of great importance to his publishing business."

The secretary lowered her glasses to the tip of her nose and studied me without the aid of the lenses. I tried not to think of what sort of impression I would make, on her or on Knobloch himself. As the clothes on my back when I stepped off the boat the day before had been in dire need of washing, I had borrowed a suit from Chaim. A fine suit, and I was grateful for it, though because he was now at least six inches shorter than me, the sleeves ended midway between my hands and my elbows, and the striped trouser legs showed so much stocking that I might as well have been wearing knickers. Topping off this costume, I wore a ribbon-banded straw boater that seemed unseasonable for March but was the only hat Chaim had to spare. I looked like a gondolier.

"A matter of great importance, is it?" the secretary said with barely disguised amusement. "Is he expecting you?"

"Expecting me?" I glanced again at the note Minkovsky had sent along; he didn't mention whether or not I was expected, only that the printing blocks were expected. Perhaps such an expectation would have extended to me if in fact the printing blocks were by my side, but as they were not, I was unsure what to say.

"To be honest, I don't know."

"Well, you are not in his appointment book, so I must admit that I don't know either. Let's find out, shall we?"

From the lobby the secretary led me down a long corridor, its wooden floorboards squeaking with every step I took. She walked briskly yet gracefully, somehow with no squeak of her own. I struggled to keep up, which only increased the frequency of the embarrassing sounds beneath my feet. I searched for something to say to cover the noise. On either side of us the walls were filled with photographs of the great Yiddish writers: Sholem Asch, with his bulbous nose and horse-brush of a mustache; Sholem Abramovich, with his grandfatherly gaze and his gnomish whiskers; Sholem Aleichem, with his delicate pince-nez balanced over an impish grin.

"Funny, but I never noticed how many Sholems were writing in Yiddish these days," I said.

"And why is that funny?" the secretary asked.

She shot me such a look I couldn't speak. Did she want me to say more, or had she wished I hadn't spoken at all?

"Not funny, I mean, only peculiar," I stammered. "That is, a coincidence, or no, not a coincidence, but . . ."

"Perhaps you mean to say, 'Odd there are so many men of *peace* in such a volatile business,' eh? Or do you mean, 'If only more old writers would rest in *peace*, the younger ones could find a publisher . . .'"

She rattled off half a dozen plays on the name Sholem and its meaning, peace, as if knowing full well that each was the sort of quip I had hoped to make but had failed to summon to my lips. She seemed to take joy in making me smaller with each pun, making my steps closer together, and their attendant squeaks quicker, sharper, as though I was walking a pirate's plank made of an enormous duck's bill.

I must have turned some color indicating my embarrassment—red or white, I don't know which—because when we reached the end of the hallway she touched my arm gently.

"Please forgive me," she said. "I have walked many young men with an interest in Yiddish letters down this hall. I have heard so many lines about Sholem-this and Sholem-that from so many disreputable writers. I could not bear to hear the same from a nice young man such as yourself." She smiled. "I can see you have just arrived from the Old Home, and that is torment enough."

She opened a thick oak door and announced my arrival to whoever was waiting inside, "Mr. . . . ."

"Malpesh," I whispered, saying it slowly.

"Truly?" she whispered back. "Malpe-pish?"

"Yes."

"Mr. Monkeypiss," she announced.

"Malpesh!" I corrected. "Malpesh!"

"Mr. Malpesh," she said.

Inside, I heard a voice say, "Who?"

"He'll see you now," the secretary told me, then turned on her heels and walked back down the hall.

I stepped forward into a room that seemed to have no walls, so full were the shelves on all sides with books. It seemed also to have no windows, but I believed I saw cracks of sunlight breaking through several rows of oversize volumes behind the desk. This meager light provided the only sustenance for two potted trees that flanked the room.

A bald man with square glasses sat scribbling on a large page of newsprint with a red wax pencil. He did not look up to greet me.

"Didn't catch the name," he said.

"Mr. Knobloch?" I asked.

"You? A Knobloch?"

"Sorry?"

"Well, well! Always glad to meet another Knobloch."

"Mr. Knobloch, I'm afraid I am not a Knobloch. My name is Itsik Malpesh. I've been sent by Minkovsky, from Odessa."

He looked up with such a snap his glasses first jumped toward his forehead, then fell from his face, remaining hooked on one ear and dangling beside his cheek. He smiled warmly.

"Minkovsky? Ah! Good, good. Better you should be sent by Minkovsky than be another godforsaken Knobloch. They show up every week looking for handouts. But how is Minkovsky? Is he still chasing that widow?"

His words jumped out in a Russian Yiddish quickened by years in New York. Afraid I would miss something important, I stood mute before him, too worried to speak.

"Sit! Sit!" he said, so I did, lowering myself carefully to the edge of a large leather wing chair which faced his desk.

"You look hungry. You hungry? Thirsty? You want I should call my secretary and have her bring something in?"

The prospect of again seeing that woman was at that moment too much to bear.

"No, no. I'm fine," I said. "Truly."

"My sister," he said.

"Excuse me?"

"The secretary. She is my sister, Rachel. Big as Knobloch Industries is, we're a family outfit. And to tell the truth, my wife, she didn't want I should look at my secretary, so there you are."

And now I worried that not just his secretary but his sister thought I was a fool. I replayed our conversation in my mind while trying to listen to Knobloch's endless patter. In my nervousness I began to fold my hat in my lap, joining one side of its brim to another until it was the size of a matchbox. I didn't remember until it was too late that the hat was made of straw. With every fold I was in fact breaking it into smaller and smaller pieces. Soon I sat with a pile of yellow and brown bits in my lap, surrounded by a green ribbon that did nothing at all to hold the splinters of straw together.

Knobloch stood up behind his desk and seemed ready to move in my direction. I spoke quickly to keep him on the opposite side of his desk, from where it seemed his view of my lap was sufficiently obscured.

"I have never seen so many books in one place," I said.

"Yes, yes! I'm told I have the largest library on the East Side."

"These are all yours?"

"They are now."

"And all in Yiddish?"

"Some in Hebrew, some in German. Mostly Yiddish. You are a lover of literature, I take it? You may find this volume interesting." He picked a small blue book from his desk and again began to make his way to the other side.

"May I see that one instead?" I asked.

"Hmm? Which one?"

"Which one?" I said. In truth I hadn't settled on one before I spoke. I pointed to a spot high up on his shelves, tucked in a corner I supposed he'd be unable to reach. "That one."

He stood on his tiptoes and pulled a book from a spot just over his head. "This one?"

"No, no, that one." I pointed with my nose, then with my right hand, careful to keep the broken bits of hat contained with my left.

"That one there?"

"Yes. That's the one. I'm certain it's a book I've been looking for."

With great effort Knobloch dragged his desk chair to the corner of the shelves and proceeded to climb. As I'd hoped, he turned his back on me long enough that I was able to rise carefully from my chair and approach one of the potted trees flanking his desk. I dumped what was left of my hat into the soil, then like a cat I began to discreetly bury my embarrassment.

So relieved was I to be rid of this unexplainable pile of straw, I failed to notice that the door behind me had opened, and Knobloch's secretary, his sister no less, had entered the room. Holding a watering can, her eyebrows raised, she stood watching me now.

"May I help you find something?" she said to me.

"No, no. I've almost got it," Knobloch answered. "Our friend from Odessa was interested in seeing a particular volume. Says he has been looking high and low for it. To be honest I'm not sure what it might be. I have quite a few unread books in my library, I'm afraid to say."

Slowly, carefully, Knobloch climbed back down from his desk chair. As her brother descended, the secretary took another look at me, my hands now filthy with potting soil. Pulling a handkerchief from her sleeve, she poured a bit of water in it and handed it to me. I wiped my hands and fell back into my chair just as Knobloch returned to the floor.

He walked from one side of the desk to the other, fishing his glasses from his breast pocket, settling them on his nose. He held the book in front of his face.

"Here you are," he said, then read the title aloud: "Di Geshlekhts-fragn fun meydlekh: A madrekh mit ilustratzia." *The Sexual Questions of Young Ladies: An Illustrated Guide.*

"Well, I can see I have interrupted a very highminded literary discussion," his secretary said, then turned on her heels and went out the way she had come.

Knobloch seemed unfazed by the book in his hands. "To be honest, I have no idea what is in my library. In my youth I read everything that landed before me, but now who has the time? The shame of it is that now that I am established in business, I have no time to read, and yet my success has led me to relationships with various publishers. I receive all the new titles from every Yiddish publishing house in New York, Argentina, Moscow . . . And Odessa, of course. Is this why you've come? You've brought books from Minkovsky?"

"I brought printing blocks. A steamer trunk full of printing blocks."

"Wonderful! Are they in the street? Shall I send someone down?"

"They are not in the street."

"Well, where are they?"

"The East River," I said. "At least, that is where they began."

"Began?"

"If they have not sunk, they may now be farther south." I summoned up an image of my new land, and imagined the course Minkovsky's blocks might have taken since I saw them last. "Perhaps Florida?" I said. "Depending on the currents."

Knobloch scratched his head. "You speak in riddles, boy."

"Will you still be able to print your paper?"

He let out a shouting laugh, then checked his watch.

"Come with me," he said. "They should be just starting up on the typesetting floor. My old friend Minkovsky is thoughtful to send me printing materials. But this is a different world."

Knobloch led me back into the corridor at a brisk march. We had covered half the distance between his office and the secretary's desk—beyond two Sholems, but not yet to the third—when he suddenly turned a corner I hadn't noticed before. I quickened my pace to keep up with him. Though several inches shorter than me, he made up for his small gait by taking three strides for every one of mine. At the far end of this second corridor, he opened a door to a room wild with smoke and noise.

"This is the home of the newest Yiddish daily in New York," he said. "And it is soon to be the biggest: the *Naye Yidishe Tsukunft!*"

The *New Yiddish Future*. It was without a doubt the most optimistic name for a Jewish newspaper I had ever heard, and its publisher's expression now matched it note for note. Knobloch beamed at the display before us as a father might at an infant son, not a factory floor crowded with men and black metal. Yet the source of his pride was exactly that. The room we now entered was crowded with a forest of great metal machines, each one seven feet tall, four feet across, made of arms, wheels, and oil pans that seemed salvaged from a scrap yard and welded together with no apparent concern for function or form.

Knobloch shouted in my ear, pressing his lips close and hollering with all his breath, sacrificing inflection simply to be heard.

"You ever see! A linotype machine!"

"No!" I answered.

Seated before each machine was a man hunched over a horizontal tray that extended from the moving parts like a small desk, the one nod to human interface to be found on the indifferent bulk of the machine. The men moved their fingers like virtuosos playing two dozen pianos. A foreman stalked between them. Knobloch rolled his hand in the air, and the foreman walked to the wall, where he pulled a lever.

"Blood in the veins!" he called out. "Blood in the veins!"

The typesetters took up his call, each shouting it to his left, then to his right, to be sure everyone heard the announcement above the din of the machines. "Blood in the veins! Blood in the veins!"

"That means!" Knobloch explained. "The lead! Is in! The system!"

"Lead!" I asked.

"Between the weeklies! And the dailies!" Knobloch said. "There are ten million pages! Of Yiddish printed every day! In New York! The Yiddish press! Has gotten so big! We need the latest technology! To keep up! With demand!"

He paused by one of the machines and scooped up a handful of tiny gray slugs from a bucket at its side. The slugs were slick with grease, stained with ink. Each displayed a letter of the *alef-beys* on its end.

"Wooden blocks! Are useless! We print now! Only with metal!"

He poured a few slugs into my hand. I had never handled bullets, but I imagined they must feel something like this: heavier than they look, weighed down by both the density of their mass and the consequences of their use.

I followed him through the alley of machines. The noise was deafening, cataclysmic, like locomotives colliding. If the men at the typesetting trays noticed us, they didn't show it. They kept their gazes fixed on texts clipped to boards at chin height in front of them. Their eyes didn't move, their hands didn't stop.

"You want! To see! How it works!" Knobloch paused at the one vacant machine, its wheels and gears whirring in anticipation. "Look! Pull this arm! Isolate a line of liquid metal! Then you push this button! Releases the lock! On the keyboard! Then you type! Right! Into! The! Metal!

"Next! You pull! The cooling lever! Then slide! This knob! To the left! All the way! To the left! You go halfway! You'll split your line! And the whole page is fucked! Then you bang! Your fist! On the reset bar! And begin again! Got it!"

All around the room, the typesetters looked more like symphony conductors than men working with words. The thought that movement, bodies, could be so intimately, necessarily involved in the formation of sentences, stories, was a revelation to me. They repeated the gestures over and over, the full gamut Knobloch had just described in about three seconds. At the end of each cycle of movement a lead slug clinked into the printing tray.

"It takes! Forty slugs! To fill a column! Five columns! To every page!"

"That's! A lot! Of lead!" I said. "Where! Does it! Come from!"

Knobloch grinned. "I hoped! You would! Ask!"

Stepping into a corridor off the printing floor, he led me through one threshold, then another, each with an iron door several inches thick. In a moment we stood in an empty chamber with copper-colored metallic floor and walls. It was surprisingly quiet, considering the noise we had just left behind.

"Most of the dailies scrap the lead—they figure it's the cost of doing business. And sure, it's cheap. But I thought, why not just remelt it? Everyone told me, you do that, you get molten lead sloshing around the shop floor. Six hundred degrees. Everyone said I'd end up with stump-handed typesetters and the unions on my ass. So I decided to make one big bucket. Melt all the slugs at once, and then the lead drains back out, into the pipes.

"That's what this room is. The melting chamber. Once a day we fire up the furnace and drop the lead slugs in from the chute above your head." He pointed to a red light and a hammer-and-bell alarm by the door. "You don't want be anywhere near here when that buzzer sounds. Means there's just one minute until the fires kick in and the lead starts dropping to the floor. Molten lead will fill this whole room before we open the drain and let it into the pipes that feed the machines. This room is the heart of the operation. You hear them shouting 'blood in the veins' out there? Means the liquid metal is in the pipes, pumped from right here.

"My lead repurposing system will revolutionize the industry!" he cheered. "And mark my words, the Yiddish publishing industry is about to explode. You yourself are proof. Every day more Jews get off the boat. More readers, right? And they're young, like you! If I get them reading the *Naye Yidishe Tsukufnt* now, they'll be reading it their whole damn lives! And then their children!

"My competitors at the *Forverts* are trying to keep readers by helping them learn English. You ever hear anything so insane? What, they want to put themselves out of business? Not me. My thinking is, the best thing for Jews—and for Jewish newspaper publishers—will be to keep reading Yiddish. If we can help that happen, in ten years New York will be printing more pages in Yiddish than English, and it will all start right here!"

Knobloch raised his arms in the empty room, where words were turned to liquid and sent down a drain.

"Look around!" he cheered. "This is the future of Yiddish in America!"

WHEN THE TOUR of his printing operation was complete, Knobloch led me back to his office.

"Tell me, Malpesh, did you work for Minkovsky in the Old Home?" he asked. "You know a little about printing?"

"I did," I said, "and I do. But to tell the truth I have another vocation: I am a poet."

"A poet! Well, well. Knobloch Industries has a long history of making use of poets," he said. "Didn't you see my sign out front? 'Integrated business interests.' You know what that means? It means I have need for workers of all abilities and temperaments. In fact, I have a dozen or more poets working for me right now."

"A dozen poets working for you?" What an amazing country this

America was, I thought; where else would a rich man keep poets on his payroll?

"Of course! There are so many poets in this city, it would be impossible not to hire at least a few. Come back next week, and we'll see about putting you to work."

On the way out of the building, I made the mistake of reaching to my brow to tip my hat to the secretary. Then I remembered what had happened to my hat.

"Will we see you again, Mr. Monkeypiss?" the secretary asked.

"Not *Malpe-pish*. It is *Malpesh*," I said. "And I believe you will."

"Tell me, what did you think of my brother's library?"

"Very impressive," I said.

"Did he mention to you how he acquired it?"

"Yes, he told me of his relationships with various publishers. They send him all of their new titles."

"He is being humble to make his role seem so passive. In truth, the library has required quite a lot of effort on his part. For years he haunted the entry point to the city from Ellis Island. Many a man comes to these shores so certain he will make his fortune that he brings all his books along with him from the Old Home. Every Jew off the boat dreams he will have a house with an extra room in which to keep his books. They realize soon enough that they will be lucky to find a home with room enough for their families. And so the books must go. My brother tells them, I will hold your books for you until you are on your feet, but he knows they will never be back for them. I call it his Library of Broken Dreams. There isn't a week that goes by that a few more disappointed men don't wander in here and make a deposit."

She eyed me as if assessing my worth.

"Perhaps one day you will add to his collection," she said. "Did you bring many books with you across the ocean?"

"I brought no books but the one I am writing."

"I'm sure we could find a place for it," she said.

217

The Memoirs of Itsik Malpesh

mem

BACK UNDER THE BRIDGE, CHAIM WAS skeptical about Knobloch offering me work as a poet. His gang sat around their dinner table like Hasidim awaiting words from their rebbe, but for the moment I had his full attention.

"Don't trust him, Itsik. The man may dabble in printing, but he runs a sweatshop. That's how he got so rich. You think he built that building with pretty words?"

"He employs a dozen poets! Whatever else he does, he's clearly a patron of the arts. You should see his library."

"I've had dealings with businessmen and their libraries," Chaim said. "None of them for the good."

"Knobloch is different. He says Yiddish has a future in America!"

"Ha! The last thing you need to be doing is writing in Yiddish. English! English is the key to success in America. Look at me, I'm not even fluent yet, and I'm sitting on top of the world."

"English to me sounds like a language of coughs and lisps. I cannot imagine learning it."

"Nonsense!" Chaim shouted. "I don't know why so many of you green Jews make it more difficult than it needs to be. Yiddish, English, English, Yiddish. The languages couldn't be closer to each other."

He looked around the table. "Am I right, boys?"

"You're right, Charlie Smooth!"

"Itsik, look here," he said, gesturing to the center of the table. "What's this?"

"That, with the flaming wick? That's a *likht*," I said.

"Right. Well, in English a *likht* is a candle. A 'ken-dul,' all right? Just listen, and I will teach you how to remember this. First break the word down into pieces. Split *ken-dul* in two, and what do you have?"

I put my hands in the air, not sure what he was getting at.

"It's not a trick, dummy. Split it in two and you get *ken* and *dul*. Okay?" This last word he said in perfect New York English. He had an arsenal of such Americanisms: *alrite, yoobetcha, awgowaan*.

"Okay."

"*Ken* is 'to be able.' *Dul* is 'confused.' Are you with me? So a *likht* is called a *ken-dul* because when it is night, it should be dark, but if you put a flame to a *ken-dul*, the room gets light no matter the time. So it's opposite of the way it should be, you follow?"

When I said nothing, one of the boys chimed in, "I follow, Charlie Smooth!"

"Smart boy," Chaim said, and threw him a penny. Turning back to me, he finished his lesson.

"So a *ken-dul* is *able* to *confuse* night into thinking it's day."

Chaim nodded sagely. His boys sat in awe of their leader-teacher father-figure's powers of erudition.

"Every English word works this way, I promise you. It's a simple language so long as you apply your intelligence."

He lit a cigarette, inhaled deeply, and blew more wisdom into the air.

"Itsik, I know you are a grown man now and not a boy needing my advice, but listen to what I tell you. Get out of Yiddish as fast as you can."

"Get out of Yiddish?" I said. "How does one get out of a language? It's not as if it is a place."

"It's a ghetto as much as the Jewish Quarter in Kishinev was a ghetto. It may not have walls you can see, but believe me: everyone else can."

"I am a poet, Chaim. And for better or worse, Yiddish is my language. It's not as if I could pick up a pen and compose in another tongue. I am a child in Russian or Hebrew. In Yiddish I can write whatever I please."

"Forget Russian, and Hebrew as well. Learn English. Start now, here with us."

"It takes years to learn a language. Should my life be put on hold?"

"Better to say the alphabet in English than write sonnets in Sumerian. I don't care what Knobloch or anyone else tells you: Yiddish is not long for this world. These boys, here? None of them are too bright. America does not produce prodigies the way the Old Home did. But they will accomplish more than you or I ever will. You know why? They won't be burdened by Yiddish dreams."

"For a Yiddish poet, Yiddish dreams are not a burden."

"Tell me this again when you have been in America more than a day or two, when you want to shake the language but can't pry loose its jaws. Better to let it go now."

"It is not simply a matter of making a choice," I said.

"Isn't it?" Chaim grinned wickedly, then hammered his fist on the table, calling the room to attention. "Boys, listen! I have an announcement. From now on, we speak only English here, all right?"

The boys shrugged, switched languages, and continued their conversations as if Chaim had asked them to take their elbows off the table. They laughed, they joked, they seemed to toss barbs and insults as casually as boys do. And I could not understand a word of it.

"Don't go back to Knobloch. He loves the language of the Old

Home only because he has found success with it. If everyone for-got about Yiddish, he wouldn't have a constant reminder of how far he has risen above the circumstances of his youth. Stay here with us. You will learn the language by the end of next month," he said. "You'll thank me later, when you never have to write Yiddish again."

It was the coldness of his eyes now that made me understand the extent to which leaving the Old Home behind in every way possible was for him an existential necessity.

"Do you hate so much where you come from, Chaim?"

"On that subject," he said, "you wouldn't know what you were talking about in any language."

I LEFT CHAIM'S LAIR that night and wandered the streets for eight cold hours, convinced that it would be better to freeze to death in my own language than remain in a place where I didn't even know the word for warmth.

In the morning I found an opening for a boarder in an apart-ment five flights above a dirty alley in a walk-up tenement on Broome Street. The first floor was occupied by a pawnshop, and the apartment was that of the *balebusta* who ran it. She called her-self Mrs. Goldstein, but never during the years I knew her did I see or hear of her husband.

"You have work? You can pay rent?" she asked when I inquired about the room.

"I have a job waiting for me," I told her. "At Knobloch In-dustries."

"You will work for Knobloch? Fancy. Maybe you pay me now, you so fancy."

"That would be difficult. I haven't begun work yet."

She looked me up and down, and seemed to sniff, as if she could tell a good boarder from a bad one by smell alone.

"Do you love your mama?" she asked.

"I did. I do. I haven't seen her in many years."

"Ach, you sound just like my son! He has gone to California. To Hellyvood. He says he will bring his mama there one day, but he never comes back. Are you like this, you promise to bring your mother to the sunshine and then leave her in the mud?"

"No, ma'am. I never promised to bring my mother anywhere."

"Okay, then. You can stay. If every runaway son finds an abandoned mother, at least there is some justice in the world."

WHEN I RETURNED to Knobloch Industries the following Monday, I charged up the stairs to the secretary's office like a conquering hero. She had assumed my previous visit with her brother would come to nothing, and now here I was about to become his employee, not just some would-be scribbler but a professional poet working for a New York Yiddish daily. It did strike me as odd that my prospective publisher had not asked to read any of my poems before offering me a job, and so I carried my valise along with me.

"You!" she said at the sight of me.

"Itsik Malpesh, in case you have forgotten the name."

"I had not forgotten. You made quite an impression. Are you here to plant another hat?"

"I am here to begin my employment with Knobloch Industries! Mr. Knobloch has offered me a job. He tells me I'm to work with the poets. Perhaps you could direct me to the poetry department?"

Rachel grinned. "Of course! The poets work downstairs," she said. "A whole floor full of poets. Some prose writers, as well, and a few playwrights. I'm told there is a painter or two. All downstairs. Shall I show you the way? I would love to see your face when you first rest your eyes on the poetry department of Knobloch Industries."

"I'm sure I can find it, but if you wish to escort me, by all means ..."

I was feeling more confident around her now. Employed by her brother, as she was, I felt on equal footing. What's more: as I was employed for my literary abilities and she was merely a secretary, I thought she might now offer me my due respect.

She rose crisply from her desk and said, "This way, please, sir. To the poetry department!"

We walked the hall I had squeaked and creaked my way through on my previous visit. If any such sounds rang out now, I didn't hear them. I was light on my feet, bursting with words.

We entered a stairwell and made our way down one flight, then another. From behind a door I heard the most awful whirring and hissing.

"What in the world is that?" I asked.

"Ah, you can hear them scratching away! Listen to those pens at work!"

She opened the door with a flourish and said, "Poets first!"

But I could not step forward. What I saw beyond the threshold stopped my heart. The room was full of sewing machines. Big and small, all black metal and whirring with needles and wheels. Little men with grim faces sat stooped at every station. They looked up and glowered as one, as if I'd stumbled into the devil's workshop and Satan's helpers all at once smelled a human soul.

"Where are the poets?" I asked.

"You're looking at them!" Rachel said.

"But they aren't writing . . . they're sewing!"

"Some are sewing. Others are cutting. Some are pressing. They write on their own time. You know how many poets step off the boat from the Old Home every day? They're lucky to have work of any kind!"

It was then that I learned the nature of Knobloch's "integrated business interests." He had made his fortune in the garment trade, and was only now beginning to dabble in the publishing business.

"Paper is my brother's passion, but rags are his pay," Rachel explained. "He truly is a lover of literature, which is why he has given so many otherwise unskilled poets steady work all these years."

We walked the length of the floor, passing by the bent backs of perhaps forty cutters and stitchers and pressers, all curled like lizards over sewing machines or various hand tools, each facing the spinning wheels of a great assembly of belts and gears that moved sections of fabric from one station to another.

"Ah, here comes the foreman. He'll get you started," Rachel said. "He is a gruff fellow, but don't be too afraid. The workers call him Big Yekke, and to be honest I don't know his given name."

The large fellow wore an enormous grin as we approached, and began nervously smoothing his hair and tugging at his shirt collar.

"Good morning, Miss Knobloch," he said. "That is a lovely blouse."

If she heard him, she didn't show it, offering no thank you and not blushing a bit. She said only, "Mr. Foreman, my brother has hired another poet for your floor."

Big Yekke shot a wounded look in my direction, frowning as if he had just noticed me.

"You ever work in a garment shop?" he asked.

"I have worked since I was ten years old, but never in a garment shop," I admitted.

"That's what I thought."

"Be good to him, Mr. Foreman," Rachel said. "My brother seems to like this one."

"Of course, Miss Knobloch. I'll watch out for him myself."

We both watched her go. As soon as she had turned the corner, Big Yekke glowered at me.

"Okay, greenhorn. Come with me. You'll start on cleanup detail." He was an enormous and gruff man, with legs nearly as long as I was tall. Without hurrying, he was instantly several paces ahead of me. I raced to keep up as he ticked off instructions.

"Watch for big pieces when you sweep up the cuttings; put them in the fabric pile to be used again. Watch for broken needles; they can usually be repaired. Put them in the broken needle drawer. Sop up grease puddles with a grease puddle rag from the grease puddle rag bucket. Remember, you get paid for cleaning, not for walking, so if you're walking, make sure you're cleaning. And don't even think about skipping the latrine."

He led me into a windowless corridor and marched me down its full length. At the end he pushed open a narrow door that revealed a fly-filled closet containing nothing but a wooden bench equipped with a worn and dirty hole.

"This is used by the floors above and below, so you gotta scrub it twice a day."

"It looks like it hasn't been cleaned in years!" I said.

Big Yekke grinned.

"We've been waiting for the right man for the job." He pointed a fat finger into the hole. "You gotta get down in there. Can't just wipe the seat and call it done."

Into my hands he shoved a long-handled brush with a smooth wooden handle. It was not quite as tall as my shit shovel from Kishinev (or perhaps it simply did not seem so, as I was no longer as small as I had been), but holding it was an achingly familiar sensation.

"No! I cannot go back," I said. "I did not come to the Golden Land to go back to shoveling shit in a factory!"

I stormed past Big Yekke, bounding for the stairs. I crossed Rachel Knobloch's desk without a glance toward her, then creaked down the hall of Sholems and through the door to Knobloch's office without breaking stride.

My new employer sat behind his desk with his feet up and a book open before him. I reminded him I had worked ten years in Minkovsky's print shop and did not feel I should now be demoted to the position of sweatshop cleanup man.

"Get a hold of yourself, Malpesh. I asked if you could operate a linotype machine. You said no; would you like to change your answer?"

As badly as I wanted to work in the printing shop, I had to admit that the work I had done for Minkovsky was nowhere near as advanced—nor, as I would later learn, was it as dangerous. The *Naye Yidishe Tsukunft*'s typesetters were a hardened lot, a dozen men with one hundred fingers between them. The top men, Roth and Nomberg, had just six fingers each.

"But don't cry for them," Knobloch said. "They've never been better at their jobs. To hear them tell it, pinkies and ring fingers just get in the way."

Knobloch told me to feel free to spend a few hours in the type-setters' company, watching the linotypes in action, to see if working among them was really for me.

"In the meantime, give the garment shop a chance. It may not look it, but the place is full of poets! Scratch any man down there, and he'll bleed words. Was I wrong to think you might find a place among them?"

"But I had hoped I would be writing for the paper!"

"Don't get ahead of yourself. Show me whatever you write, and we'll look for possibilities. You know how many writers there are in New York who would kill to have a publisher say that to them?"

When I returned to the garment shop, I was greeted with know-ing glances and sympathetic smiles. The biggest smile belonged to Big Yekke, but it was not sympathetic at all. He pushed the toilet brush back into my hands and pointed me toward the windowless hallway and the stinking closet to which it led.

"This way to the Golden Land," he said.

TRANSLATOR'S NOTE

To use Malpesh's own idiosyncratic terminology, I suppose it could be said that if I used a *halaf*—the butcher's tool that he preferred to think of as a sort of narrative knife—to cut my way through impending troubles with both Clara Feld and my employer, it was Malpesh himself.

The day of our first conversation, his voice on the phone sounded to me like nothing so much as reprieve. Even as he gave me directions and I agreed to make the trip the next morning, I knew there was really no need to drop everything and head down to Baltimore. The Jewish Cultural Organization had a network of volunteers who bore the brunt of gathering donations from around the country. There was surely a local volunteer who would have been happy to pack Malpesh's books in a box and ship it via UPS, or simply to hold them until a more convenient time.

But with Clara apparently calling for my head, and human resources apparently willing to oblige, leaving town for a day or two seemed the best possible course of action. And though I didn't know anything about Malpesh at the time, his voice alone suggested to me that none of my coworkers would question an impromptu mission to rescue his books. Irate elderly Jews were the JCO's bread and butter. As a publicly supported organization, we bent over backward to please any and all potential donors, and we knew some were worth more than others. If anyone from the business office wanted to object, I had a two-word rebuttal that I knew would end the conversation: *Planned giving.*

I swept the top of my desk into my backpack and headed home, both to rest for the long drive ahead and to ensure I would not bump into anyone who might ask questions I didn't want to answer. That a photocopy of one of Clara's great-grandmother's letters was among the odds and ends that landed in my bag is just another stroke of luck or fate that determined this translation would come to be.

IF YOU EVER HAVE THE PLEASURE of driving from Massachusetts to Maryland, I would recommend leaving well before sunrise. When you time it just right and the traffic goes your way, you can cruise past New York City in darkness and watch the sky above I-95 turn orange, pink, and purple behind the smokestacks that bring Newark to life. By the time I checked my watch—8:30 AM—I was already on the far side of the Delaware Memorial Bridge.

I rolled into Baltimore by ten o'clock, ready to pick up the books, eat a quick lunch, and make it back home by midnight. It was JCO policy to carry an overnight bag in case something went wrong with the truck—a not uncommon occurrence—but all I'd packed was a dry shirt. After a couple of hours spent moving books, my back would inevitably be soaked with sweat and a change would be a relief—especially in what a native New Englander like me regarded as a semitropical climate.

It bears mentioning, before I describe my first visit to the city, that I actually like Baltimore. I truly do. In the early days of my work on this translation, I returned on several occasions and found more to appreciate each time. By now, a decade later, I have not been back in years, and I've heard it has turned itself around, but the events I am describing occurred in the mid-1990s. This was the Baltimore that had averaged a murder a day since the Reagan administration; the Baltimore of 10 percent drug addiction; a city with a slogan so far removed from reality—the City That Reads—it seemed designed for satire. With thousands of residents fleeing its crime, poverty, and hopelessness every year, Baltimore when I arrived was a city of mass exodus that rivaled the flight of Jews from Russia in Malpesh's youth.

Long stretches of the city were empty that late fall morning, and none more so than its former Jewish enclave, Corned Beef Row. Once home to a bustling retail and restaurant district, the area had died a sudden financial and cultural death when all but the most stubborn members of the Jewish population moved on.

That's where Malpesh had told me to go, as if I was heading to Washington and he'd directed me to the National Mall. When I told him I didn't know where—or what—Corned Beef Row was, he'd barked further, equally inscrutable directions. "Halfway down Lombard Street! Between the black ghetto and the German shul!"

It had been difficult to picture the place he described, where such unlikely neighbors were close enough to serve as opposing landmarks to find a single address, but as I made my way through downtown to East Baltimore, I felt I was getting close.

Along the south side, the 1000 block of East Lombard Street looked much as it probably had for a century: brick storefronts with delicatessen and barbershop signs in the windows, a mom-and-pop market or two, a lone bakery holding out against all odds.

On the north side loomed a ghost town of another sort. Three ten-story apartment buildings stood jammed close together, all surrounded by chain-link fences topped with razor wire. Keep Out and Construction Zone signs in English and Spanish mirrored the storefront signs, as if danger was a product on sale. Backhoes and bulldozers scraped around the ground below each tower like squirrels at the roots of a dead tree. The apartments themselves appeared deserted. I couldn't tell if they were still being built, or had been recently condemned.

When I saw, on the opposite corner, a battered three-level building butted up against a stone edifice adorned with Greek columns and a stained-glass Star of David, I was sure it was the place.

I pulled the truck into an alley around back, looking for a service entrance, which I hoped would have access to an elevator. Without one, I suspected I would spend the afternoon lugging boxes one at a time down three flights of stairs. Unfortunately there was no sign of either dock or elevator, just a spray-painted Dumpster behind another chain-link fence. I parked beside it, then walked around to the front of the building. Beside the glass and wood door, two columns of shabby white buttons suggested that as many as ten apartments could be found inside. Only three or four of the buttons were labeled. I pressed the one marked MALPESH. A moment later, a voice crackled through the speaker.

"Yes?"

"Mr. Malpesh?"

"Who is this?"

"I am here for your books."

"Books?"

"Yes, books. I am here from the Jewish Cultural Organization. You called us about picking up your books?"

"No, no."

"No?"

"Yes, I called. But no, they are not my books. They are Knobloch's books!"

"Of course. Should I speak to Mr. Knobloch, then?"

"Knobloch is dead! Please to wait just a moment. I will come down."

Through the speaker I heard the sound of a chair scraping backward, then footseps on the floor, then a door creaking open. When the footsteps disappeared, I leaned in and could make out the faint sounds of a television or a radio. I listened for several minutes and was able to discern that it was a talk show of some kind, though I heard only murmurs of questions and answers followed by an assortment of whoops and boos and applause. Then his voice returned.

"You come up instead. It is not yet time."

I tried the door.

"Locked," I said.

"I will buzz you."

He hadn't said which floor, or which apartment number, so I climbed slowly, pausing to listen at every entrance. There was an odd silence to the place; no sign or sound of life anywhere. The only illumination came from the first-floor entryway and dimmed significantly as I reached the second floor. When I reached the top, I was in total darkness but for a line of light that crept under one of the three doors. I put my ear to it and again heard the game-show noises, then the stomp-scrape-stomp-scrape of someone moving slowly across a room. I knocked and waited.

When the door finally opened, it did so only a few inches. A safety chain pulled tight at eye level. Beyond it, a gray face with huge plastic glasses stared out at me.

"For the books?" he asked.

"Yes," I said. "We spoke just a moment ago."

The door closed again, then opened, this time without the chain. The man on the other side moved away to let me enter, creeping backward a few inches at a time, sliding one foot then the other. He wobbled a bit as he did so, and steadied himself by tightening his grip on a wooden cane with a stainless steel handle. Only after he stopped backing up did I think of stepping forward myself. He was so slight, I was afraid a sudden movement on my part might knock him down. Several feet back from the threshold, he stood framed by the doorway in the apartment's dim light, which seemed to come only from a single lamp in the far corner.

"I am Malpesh. Come in. Come in."

As I entered, he looked behind me, into the stairwell. He seemed confused.

"Only you?" he asked.

"Only me."

"But there are many books."

"I'll do my best," I told him. "Are they here? In the apartment?"

"I will take you to them. But please to wait. We cannot go just yet."

Malpesh wandered away, into a kitchen of green tile, green appliances, and green metal cabinets. So monochrome was the room that my eyes were immediately drawn to the kitchen table, where a notebook lay open as if recently in use. Its yellowed pages glowed in the light of a window that looked over the street.

He sat down at the table and peered out the window, into the construction zone on the opposite corner. There was only one chair in the room, so I remained standing behind him. For the first two minutes, I thought he was catching his breath. For the next two, I assumed he had forgotten why I was there. After observing perhaps six or eight minutes of motionless staring, I feared he had fallen asleep, or worse. What does one do in such a situation? I had enough to explain to my employer without a dead book donor on my hands.

"Mr. Malpesh?" I asked.

"They have just finished their coffee break," he said. "Now we will have to wait until lunch, when they will not be so near the entrance."

Only then did I look out the window to see who he was watching. A dozen or so construction workers, all in hard hats, were going about their business jackhammering concrete, loading wheelbarrows with debris.

Leaning over the table, and seeing nothing of particular interest despite Malpesh's apparently mesmerized state, I let my attention fall instead to the notebook, which I realized was full of

Yiddish script. I squinted to read it and may have leaned in too close, because, with a quickness that surprised me for a man his age, Malpesh swatted shut the notebook's cover.

"You read Yiddish, Mr. Book Collector?" he asked.

"I am learning," I said, blushing at having been caught. "Forgive me for snooping. I'm trying to improve my skill with Yiddish script. I've been helping a friend read letters written by her great-grandmother."

"Ah. Of course. What is Yiddish today but a language of great-grandmothers? For a moment I thought you read literature. When you are finished reading ladies' shopping lists, I will give you something of value to read."

"Do you have a particular book in mind?" I asked.

It was then that he informed me of his status as the last great Yiddish poet in America, and of the story contained in his notebooks. He stacked them before me as a bricklayer might, piling ledger after ledger on the table as if sealing shut the window and its view of the demolition below.

"It is the story of a life, and so it is naturally a work in progress. For the last year I have been writing it."

He stood and left the kitchen, leaving me alone with the notebooks. For a long minute I stared down at the pile of pages with which I would soon spend so much time.

When he returned, he had a cap tugged low on his forehead, pulled down until its brim met his glasses. He zipped a maroon windbreaker to his chin. He leaned slightly on his cane.

"But later. Later. This book is safe," he said. "Other books are not."

I followed him out of the apartment, down the stairs, back to the street. Outside, the hard-hatted workmen now sat on buckets and overturned wheelbarrows. They drank from thermoses, smoking and flicking the butts high into the air. They were shooting the remains of their cigarettes toward a tilted basketball backboard. Beneath them all, I realized, was a decrepit court. It was covered with trash and broken concrete, but the free-throw lines could still be seen. In the center there was a painted circle; in the center of the circle I made out the words "Knobloch Towers" painted in red block letters.

"Knobloch?" I asked. "The same as the owner of the books?"

Malpesh shuffled on without a word; whether he was ignoring me or simply hadn't heard the question I couldn't say.

We turned a corner and finally stopped before a single-story brick building at the foot of the last tower. On the glass was an identical Knobloch Towers logo. Below it in smaller type were the words "Business Office."

"The books are in the back room," he said.

We stood staring through the door for a moment. Inside, the office was empty but for a black metal desk and matching filing cabinets, all covered with a skin of dust. Through a door behind the desk, I could see bookshelves filled with green, blue, red, and black volumes. There also seemed to be stacks of books on the floor. Malpesh said, "A shame. It is an excellent collection."

I tugged the door a bit, then waited for him to unlock it, but he only stood staring, leaving me no choice but to do the same.

Finally I asked, "Could you open it up, and I'll get to work?"

"Open?" He looked at me with startled eyes. "I don't have the keys."

"Then how do you expect me to get the books?"

"Around back, we'll go around back."

"There's a back door? Do you have a key for that?"

He said nothing, only shuffled away in silence. When we reached the rear of the building and found another door, this one gray metal, I asked again, "Do you have a key?"

Malpesh tugged the handle, then whacked it with his cane.

"We will have to find another way in," he said.

"You have no keys at all?"

"No keys."

"Could we call someone?" I asked. "Mr. Knobloch, maybe?"

"Knobloch is dead! How many times must I tell you?"

"There must be someone we can ask about this."

"No time to ask!"

"Mr. Malpesh, what exactly is the rush? The books look like they've been there for quite a long time."

"Tomorrow," he said. He whacked the door a second time with his cane, losing balance in the process, grabbing my arm to stay on his feet.

"What about tomorrow?"

"They are going to tear all of this down."

Once he had steadied himself, Malpesh again lifted his cane. It seemed he was going to again whack the metal door.

"Please don't," I said. "You'll only hurt yourself."

But then he swung high instead of low, sending the cane's handle toward a window above the door. It smashed with a sound like falling water, then he drew his cane back for a second attack. Three swings later, all glass within reach was gone from the frame.

He looked from me to the window and back again.

"Go!" he said. "The books are waiting!"

nun

So went my first months in America, then years. By day I worked in Knobloch's garment shop, earning nickels and dimes for ten hours' labor. When my shift ended, I climbed two flights of stairs to the printing operation, which ran through the night to put the daily edition of the *Naye Yidishe Tsukunft* on the streets by dawn.

In the beginning I received no pay for my time among the typesetters. Content to watch them transform text into freshly minted lead slugs with a weight and heat I had never before associated with words, I was ever hopeful that I would learn their trade well enough to leave the garment shop behind.

Perhaps to keep me from constantly looming over the shoulders of the linotype operators, I was given the task of running proof sheets between the copy desk and the typesetters. This was, I told myself, a vital role: as mediator between men of words and men of machines, I was the one who determined which pages were printed, and when.

Eventually Knobloch agreed to pay me an extra half dollar for every evening I spent in this work, and so I haunted the alleys between the linotypes into the early-morning hours before finally heading home to my rented corner of the rented room high up in the tenement on Broome Street.

It hardly mattered to me where I slept. Every spare moment in any location, I spent scribbling the verses that came to me as the machines' clamor filled my brain and pushed poems out through my fingers to whatever scraps of paper I could find.

And not only paper: in those days I wrote on empty flour sacks pilfered from bakery trash cans, on bits of wood from the fruit crates that littered Hester Street, on tin cans that clogged the overflowing gutters of the East Side like river stones. Sometimes I composed on the street itself, or, when I was sure no one would see me and mistake me for a common vandal, on the walls of the buildings that surrounded my every activity, like massive hardcovers enclosing the story of my days.

There was no place that was not fit for poetry. Always it was only a matter of finding the proper writing implement for the job. Pencil worked best on most surfaces, but charcoal snatched from the trash fires that weekly darkened the sky would do in a pinch. From time to time I even worked in needle and thread, carefully stitching verses into otherwise worthless strips of cotton left over from Knobloch Industries frocks. I suppose a sculptor who worked for a fishmonger would learn to carve his statues with a carp; the life and work of a sweatshop poet was no different.

In the garment shop I soon learned that I had company in my artistic pursuits. Knobloch had not been exaggerating: it seemed every other man bent before a sewing machine had a pen tucked behind his ear. Within a year I had graduated from roving cleanup boy to a piecework tailor, and the coworkers nearest my station turned out to be writers of some renown.

To my right there was Adler, the Romanticist, who, if his poems were an accurate reflection of his worldview, had apparently never met a machine that didn't weep, never met a machine operator who didn't sweat machine oil from his pores. By far the most accomplished poet of the lot, he'd had a regular engagement with the *Forverts* for ten years, and counted its editor as a friend.

"One day he will pay me enough so I can leave the shop!" Adler announced, but even he seemed to know this was a fantasy.

Occupying the two stations to my left were Glazman and Gutman, who had written for the Yiddish stage in Warsaw and were now looking for a break on Second Avenue. They were less supportive of my endeavors than Adler. In fact, as often as not I found myself either the butt of their jokes or an unwilling participant in comedic routines they seemed to be testing for the vaudeville circuit in the Catskills.

"Hey, Itsik," one of them would call to me. It hardly mattered which of them began these interactions; they traded off the straight man's role to keep me guessing. "Could you settle a dispute between me and my landsman?"

"What dispute!" the other would say. "I only ask a question, and to him it's a dispute."

"Listen," the first would continue. "My landsman here, he was—"

"Are you hungry, Itsik?" the other would interrupt. "Here, eat a little while we talk." He tore off a piece of his cheese sandwich and put it in my hand. "Eat! Eat!"

"So my landsman was shopping down on Delancey Street the other day, and he stopped to look in the window of the dairy store."

"The kosher dairy store," the other said.

"Of course! My landsman is a very pious fellow. So he looks in the window, and he sees a big hunk of cheese. Only when he goes inside to buy it, he notices that one side is entirely covered with flies!"

"Big hairy flies like you never seen!"

"So he says to the dairy man, 'That's not right! I thought this was a good Jewish dairy, but look at all those flies! They've got so much meat on them I bet they make the whole thing *treyf*!'"

"'What do you want me to do about it?' the dairyman says.

"'I demand you cut them off!'

"'All of them?'

"'All of them.'

"'Okay, okay, the customer is always right,' the dairyman says. He

238

gets out his knife, sharpens it up, and says, 'I run a good Jewish dairy, so don't worry about a thing. Come back later. I'll take care of it.'

"So my landsman walks off, buys a paper, sits on a bench by the park. He wonders if he was too hard on the dairyman. After all, wasn't the dairyman sharpening his knife, willing to make it right? So he takes his time getting back, thinking about this. When he reaches the store, he has a look at the cheese through the window, everything seems fine. But then he gets inside, he sees it's still covered with flies!

"'I thought you said you'd take care of it!' he says. 'Is this a Jewish dairy store or what?'

"'Don't worry! Don't worry!' the dairy man tells him. 'It took all morning, but they've all been circumcised.'"

Gutman and Glazman would then study my face for a reaction.

"Ach, he don't like it. I told you the timing was all wrong."

"The timing is fine. What does he know."

"Audience knows best."

"Audience knows best how to drive a writer to drink."

They seemed to forget that I was standing there with them, or that they had begun their story by asking me to settle a dispute. I waited for them to look again in my direction as I finished my sandwich.

"So what's the disagreement?" I asked.

Glazman pointed at the sandwich I'd nearly finished. "Gutman says the fly-penis cheese tastes kosher. What do you think?"

GUTMAN AND GLAZMAN rarely paid attention to me when they did not have new material to try out, so it was Adler who allowed me to tag along to my first visits to the literary hot spots of the Lower East Side.

It was from him that I learned that among the Yiddish literati of New York, the holy day wasn't Friday but Wednesday. On that evening alone I left the Knobloch Building in the company of the other garment workers with writerly ambitions. We all retreated to our separate garrets to dress in what finery we had, and scrub like mad-men to remove traces of oil or grime from our fingers, and then we gathered at a place called Goodman's, on Twelfth Street, crowding in together as if every week was Yom Kippur. On any given afternoon or evening there was something to see at Goodman's, a conversation to overhear, a debate to join, but Wednesdays were the main event. The readings held that night ensured that every Yiddish poet in the city was sure to be there, at least those who could get off work.

I sat on the edge of the crowd of established poets, hoping to be noticed but dreading the possibility and secretly relieved when the night came to an end and I remained as anonymous as when it began. I showed my poems to no one, supposing that when they were good enough, the world would somehow seek them out, like a tree's roots searching the dark earth for a source of nutrients. In the meantime, I carried them with me everywhere, in the same battered valise Min-kovsky had sent with me across the ocean.

Such valises were more common in Knobloch's shop than lunch pails. Some days it seemed everyone had pages he carried with him.

Everyone, that is, except for Big Yekke. Well aware of the aspira-tions of the tailors under his supervision, the shop foreman made it his mission to keep the poets from writing even on our meager lunch breaks.

"If you're writing on your break, I know you'll be planning before the whistle and revising until you punch the clock. We don't pay you for your pretty thoughts!"

"You barely pay us at all!" Gutman said.

"You pay us in grief!" Glazman huffed.

"Not in dollars but dolor!" Adler quipped.

Around the shop floor the other poets nodded in approval of his wordplay, then took it up as challenge.

"Not in groschn but grouching!"

"Not in rubles but rudeness!"

"Not in shekels but—"

"Shah, you damn poets!" Big Yekke fumed. "If you sons of bitches are so clever, I'd better shut the window so none of your best lines will blow out in the wind."

He marched along the wall of windows, slamming shut one after the other. The rest of the day we baked in the heat, without even the faint breeze of the garment district as relief.

That's the way it was in the shops then: we worked from sunrise, and by midday the walls would drip with sweat. When the equipment was cold, we were cold; when it grew hot to the touch from a few hours' labor, so did we. If we workers didn't compose poems while we worked, there would have been no telling us from the machines. Big Yekke would have preferred it that way. The poets hated him for it, and let him know in as many ways as they could imagine. Nearly as many ways, I should say. Because of the large number of poets and other independent spirits on the floor, Knobloch's shop had never attempted to unionize. We would-be writers preferred mistreatment to the perceived defeat of admitting we were tailors by carrying a union card that said as much.

I held my tongue in such disputes. Because I had seemed to have the favor of the boss since stepping off the boat, Big Yekke had not liked me from my first day on the job. I could understand his bitterness. He was perhaps forty years old, had come to New York as a boy, and had toiled in shops all his life. That a man like myself—a dirty and useless poet, no less—could stumble to these shores as a relative adult and land in the good graces of a man like Knobloch was for him too much to bear. I kept a small head around the shop, attempting to avoid Big Yekke whenever I could. I did not make it easy on myself. Carrying a valise of poems everywhere I went made me a marked man.

Through those early years my poems were in fact my only company. Yet I showed them to no one, with the exception of Mr. Knobloch. Perhaps he had merely been humoring me when he insisted I show him my poems, but he seemed to have genuine interest in me and my work—my true work, not the labor I performed for him on the sweatshop floor.

Once or twice each week I snuck away from the shop toward the end of the lunch break to climb the stairs to his office. With trembling fingers I held my most recent work while I tiptoed past Rachel Knobloch, who had begun to eye me less with suspicion than curiosity.

"More poems?" she would ask.

"Yes."

"Do you write every day?"

"Every moment," I said. "If not on paper, then in my mind."

"Does it help having a blank page for a brain?"

I had no response to her witticisms. I simply bowed my head and moved by as quickly as possible. And yet I could not ignore her. She fixed her gaze upon me the moment I crossed the threshold to the lobby. There was no other way to reach Knobloch's office, and so whenever I attempted to see him, I had first to brave contact with his sister.

"More poems?" she asked another time.

I nodded. Perhaps if I said nothing, I reasoned, she could find no way to tease me.

"More poems every day," she said in mock wonder. "Where do you find the words?"

In response I simply pointed to my head.

"Are they whispered by the bugs in your hair?"

Surviving the barbs of Rachel Knobloch became for me a regular running of the gauntlet. I hoped if I could weather her words, I would be a stronger poet. And becoming a stronger poet, as I saw it then, was my only hope of attaining a better life.

With each new verse I composed, I hoped I might persuade Knobloch that it deserved a place in the pages of the *Naye Yidishe Tsukunft*, but his response was nearly always the same. With a stroke of his chin, a nibble at the tip of his pencil, a few quick notations on the margins of my pages, he would finally nod and say, "A poet like you was made for my garment shop."

Some days I heard this as an affirmation, some days as an insult, but always he insisted it was simply a statement of fact.

"What better work for a poet than to cut and fold and join cloth from sunrise to sunset and then to apply the same skills to words when evening comes?"

"Does that mean that you think my work is improving? That one day I will be published in the *Naye Yidishe Tsukunft?*"

"Itsik, don't worry so much about publication! Isn't writing its own reward?"

MORE AND MORE it began to feel like the opposite, as if the impulse to put pen to paper was a curse visited upon those whom God had selected for endless torment. It was not merely the hardship of feeling one's work would never reach an audience; the humiliations were far more immediate than that.

One day as I hurried to complete a poem on my lunch break, I ran out of paper. I begged a scrap from Gutman and Glazman but quickly found myself caught in one of their spontaneous vaudeville routines:

"Hey, Itsik. I think I see some paper over by the window."

"Run and get it before someone else snatches it!"

"You know, maybe I'll use it myself!"

"Glazman, your words are best written in the dust on the floor. If the boy needs it, let him have it."

"So let him get up and get it!"

"Better grab it fast before Big Yekke returns and starts breaking pencils."

I ran for the paper and snatched it up before anyone had seen me. Only on the way back to my seat did I realized it wasn't just paper. Lumpy and fragrant, it weighed as much as a chicken. I unfolded one corner, then another, but before I could peek inside, its contents—bread and brisket and mustard-smeared pickles—tumbled to the floor between my feet. With a quick look up and down the composing aisle

I determined no one else had seen it fall, so I gave it a good kick toward a pile of sawdust and hurried back to my chair.

Regardless of its prior use, it was grand piece of paper for composing: square and smooth once it was wiped of all it had contained; free of markings but for a grease stain or two. A single shining pickle slice clung to the corner like a leech. I flicked it to the floor, then licked the tip of my pencil and pressed it to the page.

From across the shop I heard a shout: "Where is my sandwich, you thieving greenies?" Big Yekke had returned and was bellowing like a bull. "I put it down for one minute, and one of you bums sneaks up and grabs it?"

"Toss it, Itsik. Toss it!" Gutman whispered. "He'll skin you alive!"

"Keep it, Itsik! Keep it!" Glazman said. "Take a stand for your art!"

I raced to fold the sandwich wrapper and dispose of it in my shirt. I had risked enough grabbing it; I wasn't now going to lose such a prized canvas.

Big Yekke must have heard the paper rustling—we were all deaf from machines, but a fat man will always have ears for food—because he came charging in my direction.

"Malpesh!" he raged. "You stole my lunch!"

I was so startled I jumped to my feet, planting the sole of one shoe squarely atop the pickle slice. My legs shot out from beneath me and I fell to the oily floor.

Big Yekke spotted the pickle clinging stubbornly to my shoe, then he saw the sandwich half buried by the sawdust pile. He stooped to retrieve it, but by then it was too late. Machine grease dripped from the soft white bread; the meat lay limp as a tired man's tongue.

The sight brought the foreman to tears.

"*Meyn bruit*," he said in the German that emerged only at moments of great duress. "*Meyn bruit*." His sorrow lasted only a moment before it turned to blind rage.

Picking me up by the collar, he stood three heads above me. Then he brought his fist down like a hammer, as if to crack my skull. I was able to hide the sandwich wrapper in my shirt even as he bloodied my nose and knocked my hat to the floor.

When he had tired himself, he picked up his slop and went away weeping, eating what crumbs he could.

Adler ran to my side. "Itsik? Are you all right?"

"Yeth," I said. My tongue was swollen in my mouth; I could barely speak.

"You're sure?"

"Yeth. I am thure," I said.

The whistle blew, ending our lunch break.

"Thit! I am late for Mithter Knobloch!"

"You can miss a day, Itsik! You're in no condition to present your work!"

"I mutht! I mutht!"

Up the stairs I went, limping on the ankle on which Big Yekke had planted his foot while his fists explored my face. As I reached the last flight of stairs, I could see a shadow extending out of the lobby. It could only be Rachel Knobloch, waiting to torment me yet again.

"Running late today, Mr. Malpesh?" she called out to me. "Was there an important meeting in the poetry department?"

I tucked my face in my collar, pulled my cap down over my eyes.

"You are bundled up as if for a storm!" she said. "Or are you moonlighting as a merchant marine? Perhaps you have written a few nautical verses for today?"

She fully blocked the doorway. I stepped to my left, I stepped to my right, she would not let me pass.

"Is my brother expecting you, Captain? Or shall I pipe you aboard?"

I tried to maneuver around her, but wherever I stepped, she stepped as well.

"Mith Knobloch, will you never thtop teathing me?"

"I doubt it. Teasing you is a kind of rest for me; I feel much revived after. I'm told a trip to the sanatoriums of the Catskills might have similar effect." She cast an eye toward my valise of poems. "You might find that showing me a poem or two dulls the blade of my tongue . . ."

Perhaps it was the fact that my own tongue was cut and bleeding that made me feel I'd had enough torments for one day. When I lifted my hat to face her, she gasped at my black eye, my scratched cheek, at the red clot of snot and blood that plugged my nostrils and made breathing an ordeal.

"My poemth are not written for your amuthement!" I shouted, each syllable a strain. "I'd thooner thwaddle a dead fith with a Torah thcroll than thow you a thingle verthe!"

Rachel's face went slack. Her eyes welled with tears.

"There is no need to insult!" she said in a wail. She sat down, sniffling. "I only poke at you because it gives us a chance to speak." She let out a pitiful sob. "A dead fish? Am I truly so hideous to you?"

"You are not hideouth at all. I was only anthwering athid with athid."

"Forgive me. I thought I was being playful. I am not experienced talking to men I find interesting."

"Interethting?"

"Every week for five years you walk through here with that absurd valise like a door-to-door salesman. Finally I ask my brother what it is you keep coming back to show him. Poems, he says. Poems every week for five years? I asked him. Yes, he says. Poems every week for five years is either interesting or insane."

"Your brother thpeaks of my poemth? Does he thay if he thinkth they are good?"

"Good is beside the point. He says you are persistent, which is sometimes good enough."

"Mith Knobloch, I am thorry. I don't underthtand what you are thaying—"

"Enough Miss Knobloch!" she said. "From now on you will call

246

me Rachel. And after you have shown my brother your poems for the ten-thousandth time, you will come back here and ask me to have a glass of tea with you at the café. Tonight. Do you understand?"

"Yeth, Mith Knobloch."

"Rachel!"

"Yeth, Rachel."

"Good."

FOLLOWING FURTHER ORDERS later that night at the café, I allowed Rachel Knobloch to look through my valise of poems. She studied each one for a long time, while I sat nervously drinking my tea. After an hour of silence, she looked up, nodding seriously.

"I am pleased to know that you are not a terrible poet. Harry tells me he would not stand for me to marry a terrible poet. But tell me—"

"Marry?" I said, nearly choking on a blintz.

"Who is this woman you so often mention?" she asked. "She walks through your verses like a ghost. Never fully there, yet never far off."

I blushed at the question.

"A girl from my hometown. The daughter of a ritual slaughterer who died on the day of my birth. She is . . ." I considered several descriptors before I spoke. My beloved? My hope? My dream? My *bashert*?

"My muse," I said.

"Your muse?" Rachel laughed. "I have never known a man with a muse before. She must have made quite an impression on you."

"I have never met her," I said.

Rachel studied me in silence. Then she gathered in her hands all the pages I had written in my life, hundreds of them. She lifted the pile thoughtfully, as if she were a grocer weighing a hen.

"So many words for someone you have never met?"

"How many words have the rabbis written about God?" I asked.

"How long have Jews pined after Jerusalem with no hope of returning to Zion?"

"And so like the rabbis, you will spend your life lamenting the loss of a love you never knew? A home you never truly had?"

She placed my pile of papers on the table between us, pushing them across so they bent on my chest.

"Tell me: What is to be gained from writing all these songs for your butcher's daughter? What good will come of singing to apparitions, to dreams?"

"She is all my imagination has ever known."

"Itsik," Rachel said, "imagination is a lovely thing. But you must live life where you are, with real people, not with shadows."

She took my hand, squeezed it.

"I think you will find real people are far more interesting to write about." She leaned across the table and pressed her lips against mine, then lingered there, letting her breath warm my cheeks, fill my mouth. The pressure on my swollen lips shot jolts of pain through my entire body.

When she sat back, she was smiling.

"And they are better kissers as well," she said.

samekh

FROM THAT DAY ON RACHEL WAS OFTEN at my side. At first I chafed at the company—every moment I was with her was a moment I did not spend writing—but in time she came to be a comfort. No longer were my Sabbath evenings spent eating in bachelors' cafés or wandering alone along the river, looking with longing toward the ocean and what lay beyond. Now I was Rachel's regular guest at the table of her brother and his wife. The lovely meals prepared by Mrs. Knobloch were the closest to my mother's cooking I had tasted in twenty years.

Rachel, too, proved herself to be good company, especially during our exploratory walks of the city. We crossed over the Brooklyn Bridge at least once a week, and she never ceased to marvel when I pointed out the entrance to the storage room that Chaim had made the seat of his fiefdom.

"Truly you slept in the bridge, Itsik? You are not just telling grandmother stories?"

"A poet always speaks the truth," I insisted. "A true man of letters would never abuse words by twisting them into lies."

She gripped my arm as we walked, the wind from the river wrapping us even as we wrapped each other. Her arm slipped around my waist. Mine held tight across her shoulders. She was tangible and soft to the touch in a way my fantasies of female contact never were.

And, of course, there was one factor that endeared me to her above all else:

She liked my poems.

Never had anyone paid so much attention to my work, my ambitions. She even developed a sense of humor about my literary preoccupations that other women might have found threatening.

"I am grateful to your ghost," she would say, for so had she taken to referring to any mention of Sasha Bimko in my work. "If not for her, perhaps when I met you, you would've been married already. And then where would I be?"

As she hinted during our first lengthy conversation, marriage was foremost on Rachel's mind. She was several years my senior, and had by then been through two failed engagements. She had waited long enough, she declared, and had decided she would wait no more.

"She is only waiting for you to ask," Knobloch said to me when next I brought him my poems.

I closed my eyes at such suggestions. In a way it made perfect sense: hadn't I been snatched by *khappers* and later shanghaied aboard the *King Alexander*? It would only stand to reason that I would now be locked in the trunk of a marriage I did not want.

My excuses for delaying such a question were endless, but they all touched on the same theme.

"I appreciate your eagerness to see me join your family, Mr. Knobloch. But a man of business such as yourself must understand that I hope to first find success as a poet before I begin married life."

"Married life makes every man a failure, Malpesh. Better to start without success; you'll have less of a fall." Knobloch paused to look around his office, waving a hand in the direction of his library shelves. "There is a reason I line my walls with books instead of family pictures. Books don't look back.

"But let's focus on the issue at hand. What will it take for you to feel you are reaching your goals as a poet? Is it merely publication? You marry my sister, I'll publish whatever you want!"

"I am grateful to you for that," I told him. "But I must succeed without the help of nepotism, or what will my reputation be worth?"

"Very well. Let's determine how to measure the success you seek, and we will set about finding a way to meet it."

"When I read at the café and am recognized by the established poets of the East Side, then I will be affirmed in my art."

"Do they still read there on Wednesdays?" he asked.

"Yes, but I understand they are booked months in advance. Goodman himself determines who will read."

"Listen, you think I sell ladies' underwear for my health? I sell it because it makes me rich, and being rich makes people take my calls."

He picked up the phone.

"Rachel, get me Goodman."

A moment later he barked into the receiver: "Goodman? This is Knobloch. I got a poet here you really need to have read in your café. Yeah. Soon as possible. Okay? Okay."

Knobloch hung up the phone.

"Done," he said. "We'll get some kids to post the flyers."

"What flyers?"

"We'll have them in an hour."

Fifty-five minutes later, I held in my hand a hot stack of newsprint, each sheet filled with 40-point letters that read:

WEDNESDAY NIGHT AT GOODMAN'S:
ITSIK MALPESH,
SWEATSHOP POET,
SURVIVOR OF KISHINEV,
BARD OF ODESSA
NEW YORK DEBUT!

"We'll paper the town with them," Knobloch said. "Overnight you will be as well known as any Yiddish poet in America."

"But I'm not ready!"

"Not ready? You have five days to prepare. Then you'll get your affirmation, or whatever it is you need, and we'll formalize the engagement. All right?"

Goodman's never looked so crowded as it did that night. The tailors from Knobloch's shop filled the front row; the typesetters lined the windows facing the street. The established poets of the East Side sat in a clique toward the back, smoking cigarettes and talking among themselves, apparently oblivious to the event whose printed announcements had packed the room. Several of them even sat with their backs to the reader's podium, as if the featured poet of the evening was of no concern to them.

Looking out over the luminaries in the audience, I said to Rachel, "They are here, but they could not be less interested!"

"If they were not interested, why would they be here?"

"I've been to enough of these events to know that poets attend readings for only two reasons: firstly, so that others will attend their own; moreover, because they hope above all else that they might be witness to a disaster. Look at the smirks on their faces! I can hear them sharpening the knives!"

"Itsik, you wanted to do this to prove something to yourself. Forget about the other poets and just read your work. You can do no more than that."

Adler rose from the ranks of the established poets and made his way to the reader's podium.

"Ladies and Gentlemen! Tonight, a very special treat! We interrupt our series of well-known writers of the East Side to present the American debut of a poet who first published at the age of eleven in Kishinev. In years to come, those who were not will claim they were here!"

I took the podium in utter silence. Every gaze was on me, even those of the established poets. I felt one hundred pairs of eyes press into me, like letters being pressed into softened lead. My valise creaked loudly as I opened it.

"Get this man some grease for his poems!"

"Not too much!" another added. "I have a feeling there's plenty of schmaltz in them already."

"A little schmaltz wouldn't be so bad. I missed lunch!"

"Shut up, you Philistines!" Adler shouted. "It may be appropriate for the theater to shout before a performance, but poetry demands attention and respect. This is high art!"

Glazman hooted. "High art, he says! Malpesh can barely see over the podium. How high can it be?"

"I'm getting a nosebleed already," Gutman said.

I ignored them, and in fact was grateful for the interruption. It gave me a few moments to compose myself and spread my pages on the podium before me.

"This is from a collection of verse that I have entitled *Songs for the Butcher's Daughter*."

As I fumbled with my pages, Gutman and Glazman continued to bubble up with their acid murmurings:

"Why does it need a title if it has no cover?"

"Where have his poems been collected, in his hat?"

"Ah, but his hat has exclusive rights!"

"I hear there was quite the bidding war between his hat and his shoes."

"Yes, the shoes walked out, but the hat hung in there."

"Let the man read!" came a silencing shout. It came not from Adler this time but—when had he come in?—Chaim. It had been years since I seen him. And he was not alone. The boys at his side I recognized as Turtle and Fishl, now strapping young men, six-footers and then some. Chaim nodded in the direction of my hecklers, and his two protégés slid through the crowd, taking seats on either side of Gutman and Glazman. Fishl cracked his knuckles. Turtle rested fists the size of cannonballs on the café table that the two playwrights shared.

"Funny thing, Gutman."

"Yeah, Glazman?"

"Suddenly, I've forgotten all my material."

From then on there was no more heckling from the crowd, not a single interruption for the next twenty minutes as I recited poems I knew as well as my name.

No, recited is not quite right: I wept, I shouted, I sang.

> *Welcome, my countrymen,*
> *to the great Golden Land,*
> *Where coins fall like rain*
> *to a working man's hand,*
> *Where joy is as common*
> *as Coney Island's sand,*
> *Where if you believe all I say,*
> *you do not understand*
>
> *If this land is Golden,*
> *why am I made of lead?*
> *If our letters are eternal*
> *Why do some call them dead?*
> *Why do our children cross oceans*
> *Just to beg for their bread?*
> *Must our poets bleed on their pages*
> *just so they'll be read?*
>
> *Call me Isaac, call me Itsik,*
> *I haven't a care.*
> *For I am Malpesh, the poet,*
> *bard of Yiddishland fair,*
> *Who danced off the boat*
> *with no shortage of flair:*

Who will sing for your supper
if you'll eat his despair.

After this introduction, the verses I recited that night, in a shaky but determined voice, summed up my life and experiences, wrapping them around my long-standing fascination with Sasha Bimko, as if she were the Maypole of my days. By then was she more of a literary figure in my mind than a flesh-and-bone person living and breathing somewhere on the planet? Perhaps. Nonetheless, as I spoke of her, I felt her presence as I had never before.

Through verses scribbled and saved across two decades and three countries, through war, revolution, and emigration, I related the tale of a baby born in the madness of a pogrom and of the neighbor girl, the butcher's daughter, who at four years old had raised her fist and in doing so shamed the marauders into remorse. Whoever she now was, she would always be that girl to me.

Conceived on the Sabbath,
midwifed by a pogrom
The poet of Kishinev
waits for the one
Who witnessed his birth
while others did run
Who fought off attackers
though she was too young

To know what she risked,
or what might be gained.
Though her fists should be famous,
she will go forever unnamed
As God does by night
When sleep is sustained
When psalms come as breathing
And belief is unstrained.

In the verses that followed, she stood for all that was hoped for yet unattainable—was she God? was she Zion?—and yet as I recited there was also the new knowledge, or perhaps merely the new maturity to understand knowledge I'd had all along, that she was alive, and as such had a reality separate from all of my dreams. And yet she was also something to me that she was to no one else.

How is it that we are to others what we are not to ourselves? Does a word know its own meaning? Does a letter know the sound that it signifies? How then can we pretend to know what our lives are for?

These were the questions my poems raised that night. I cannot recall every line I spoke, but I know I closed with the following stanza.

> Come to me now,
> my lost butcher's daughter
> Meet me back there,
> in that city of slaughter
> I'll be the one who
> greets you with laughter,
> We'll find love in the rubble,
> our only hereafter.

When my recitation was finished, I exited the stage, ducking behind a curtain that hid the kitchen from the audience. I fell across a wooden bench, exhausted, exhilarated. In a moment, Rachel was at my side.

"Itsik, you were wonderful!" she said. "I'm certain that now my brother will give you a job writing for his paper. No more toiling in the garment shop for you."

From in front of the stage we heard a sound rarely offered by the audience at Goodman's.

"Is that rain?" I asked.

"No! It is applause, Itsik. For you! You are affirmed! I must go find my brother. There is so much to discuss!" She wrapped her arms around me and squeezed as though she feared I might come apart at the seams. "I will go find him. Then we'll all go out and celebrate!"

She had not been gone a minute when Knobloch himself appeared, apparently unaware Rachel had just run off to find him.

"Well done, Malpesh," he said. "Let's go out and celebrate. Then we can formalize that arrangement we spoke of. Here—" He handed me a wad of bills such as I had never seen. "Dinner should be on you, then you'll ask me permission to marry Rachel."

"Ask you?"

"Our father, may he rest in peace, would have wanted it so. And anyway, in this as in all things, my word is law. I'll find Rachel and we'll be waiting by the door."

A moment later, Chaim appeared.

"Good to see you, Charlie Smooth," I said.

He grinned at my use of his new name, which was now no longer so new. Then he ran a hand over his cheek, which was now as smooth as the name implied.

"Glad you noticed."

"But how did you know I was reading tonight?"

"I may keep company with fish and turtles, but I don't live under a rock." He pulled a flyer from his pocket. "I see my first pupil's name all over town, and you think I won't show up to hear him read? You ought to return the favor and come to see us sometime."

"Are you still under the bridge?"

"Nah, we left that place last year. I'm a legitimate businessman now. I opened up an entertainment room on Norfolk Street." He fished a calling card out of his pocket and handed it to me.

I read it aloud. "'Smooth Toys & Gifts, Inc.' A toy store, Chaim?"

"Tell the doorman you know me," he said. "Don't worry: he speaks Yiddish, so you won't have any problems dropping my name."

"Why would you need a doorman at a toy store?"

"We sell dolls of all kinds. But our biggest business is in baby bottles. For baby bottles you need a doorman."

A moment later he had already disappeared. I was a bit hurt that years now after I had seen him last, my old friend assumed that I still did not know English. That he was correct in his assumption was worst of all.

But on this night it didn't matter. I stood basking in my newfound recognition—my *Yiddish* recognition. Poets I knew by reputation alone approached, shook my hand. A few suggested I contribute to their journals. Others asked for introductions to Knobloch, as if I were the well-connected poet and they the amateurs looking for a foot in the door. "I'll see what I can do," I said.

Others complimented me for my honest accounting of the obsessions of memory. We were all immigrants, after all. We all had our forgotten families, our loves lost before they came to flower. "To write of this is to write of the condition we all find ourselves in," one poet said, "and to show us a way we might overcome."

To this I could only humbly say, Thank you. If I had overcome my obsession, it was news to me. Yet could it be that in speaking the story, I was free of it? I looked down at my pages, bundled in my hand like old papers gathered to start a fire. The story of Sasha Bimko was only a poem, I realized; it was not a prefiguring of my fate.

I bent to the floor and began to place the pages back into my valise. With a click of the latch, they were sealed away as if they were nothing more than a merchant's wares. I would take them out when next it came time to sell them, but until then they would not be a burden. There were other poems to write, other loves to explore. My eyes scanned the crowd and finally settled upon Rachel, who looked at me with a smile of invitation and hope—hope not of fantasies made real, but of life.

Just then a voice fell down on me like feathers floating to earth.

"It is good you are a poet and not a historian," it said.

I turned and found myself face-to-face with a striking figure. She had the same dark hair as any of the women in the room, but her skin was not the pale of a sweatshop slave or high-rise office worker. She looked as if she had spent her life in the sun.

"Do I know you?" I asked.

"You seem to think you do," she said. "But then, you seem to have a loose relationship with reality."

"And apparently you think you know me as well?"

"Oh, I won't pretend to know you. I also won't pretend to believe the sight of a little girl with her fist clenched could stop rampaging pogromists in their tracks."

"I'm afraid you must take my word for it," I snapped, my defenses rising. "After all, one of us was there, and one of us was not."

"That's where you're wrong," she said. "You were there, blind with blood and your mother's juices. I was there with eyes wide open, and I remember what I saw."

Rachel tugged on my arm. I ignored her. How could I look upon plain Rachel when there was this exotic creature before me?

I studied the woman from head to toe and up again. She wore her dark hair pulled back in a knot, fastened by what appeared to be a leather bootlace. The collar of her shirt was open, revealing a triangle of bronzed skin that drew the eye of every man who walked by. I remembered the paper-white features of the girl in a photograph I still kept among my poems. The only trace of who she had been was on her forehead, where a faint scar spoke of an ancient injury.

"You're not—," I said.

"I am."

TRANSLATOR'S NOTE

"A TRANSLATION MUST BE EITHER A CRIB or a thing of beauty," the early-twentieth-century Dante scholar C. H. Grandgent once wrote, "else it is worth nothing save to its maker."

In this somewhat cryptic summation of the translators' art, I read a prescription that to present a literary work in a language other than that of its composition, one must decide from the outset if one's intention is merely to convey, word by word, an approximation of the meaning of the text, or if it is to create a work with merit all its own. Grandgent's "crib" translation would merely safeguard the original, while the alternate approach would dress it up and take it out on the town.

Such an either/or attitude toward translation puts a particular burden on those attempting to work with a text that moves as freely between prose and poetry, pedestrian language and ornate, as does Malpesh's memoir.

In some ways, I have adopted the "crib" approach to presenting Malpesh's notebooks in English. His story, after all, is largely anecdotal in nature, told without much reliance on narrative tricks or lofty tone. Yet in taking this tack, I fear I have done a continual disservice to Malpesh's poetic gifts, which he considered of far greater importance than his abilities as a simple storyteller. And so let it be known that it is my fervent hope that through this mere crib of a translation, Malpesh's name will become better known among those with the requisite training who might revisit his poems for their own sake, preferably in their original Yiddish.

Of course, determining what sort of training is necessary for a proper poetic translation is difficult. As the old Italian saying has it, *Traduttore, traditore*. A translator is a traitor. With poetry it is even more complicated than that. Even in my meager efforts here, I have discovered how quickly the lines between one writer and another can become blurred. The translator transforms the orginal work, yes, but where did the original come from? It is often and rightly said that translation is interpretation. But is a poem, too, any more than an interpretation of experience? If both original and translation are works of interpretation, how does one know where the translation begins and the poem ends?

As Grandgent, among others, has also said, "It takes a poet to translate a poet," and I, sadly, am not one. It occurs to me only now that if Grandgent himself were to read this particular work of translation, he might come up with a third category. Neither crib nor thing of beauty, my work here is closer to a sledgehammer pounding square pegs into round holes. When engaged in such work, of course, it is usually best to ignore the damage done to each.

OF THAT OTHER HOLE through which this translation eventually came to be, the hole created by Malpesh's cane in the back of a condemned brick building in East Baltimore, I will say only this: the opening looked bigger than it was. It looked big enough, in fact, that I, the square peg in this metaphor, didn't bother to remove my backpack as I climbed onto a trash can, grabbed hold of the metal window frame, and climbed in. It was not until I heard the rip of jagged glass snagging canvas that I realized I was doing something not very smart and probably illegal.

Halfway in, halfway out, I imagine I would have looked like a hunter's trophy to anyone glancing up at the wall from the inside. It seemed no one had been inside in quite a while, however. The wall was crumbling beneath me. Just below my chin, six spikes of exposed rebar stabbed out of the concrete.

Below me, behind me, safe on the ground, Malpesh apparently noticed that my feet had stopped moving.

"Are you going all the way in, or do you like the view from there?" he asked. "You can reach the books already?"

"No, I can't reach the books. I'm stuck. My backpack is caught on something."

"Better you should take it off," he said. "I thought this before you climbed, but I don't presume to advise a professional."

"Thanks," I said.

"You want I should push?"

"No!" I shouted. "If you push I think I'll lose an eye. Let me try to get the backpack off."

I wriggled this way and that, careful not to move forward and impale myself. After a minute I had the straps off my shoulders and was able to slide forward, leaving the backpack hanging in the window frame, snagged on the glass. I did not land lightly.

Once inside, I was able for the first time to see the size of the collection. From outside, the building appeared to have two floors, but inside it was clear some substantial remodeling had occurred. Most of what had been the first level's ceiling and the second level's floor had been removed, creating a cavernous warehouse of a space filled floor to ceiling with books. I stood in a library with twenty-foot walls, every inch of which was covered with shelving, every shelf of which was filled to bursting with books.

"You are in?" I heard Malpesh say. "Open the door."

The Jewish Cultural Organization had perhaps 100,000 volumes in its warehouse. This place seemed to have even more.

"I'm going to need a bigger truck," I said.

"Quickly! Open!"

I moved toward his voice, toward the gray metal door.

"It needs a key on either side," I said.

"It can't be!" Malpesh coughed. "Such a fire hazard for a library! Get what you can. The workers' lunch break will soon be over."

"Okay, I'm coming out."

I climbed back through the hole, then pulled my backpack down after me. It had a six-inch-long tear in the side pocket.

"No books?" Malpesh asked.

"Mr. Malpesh, there's just no way," I said, holding out my wrecked bag for his inspection. "Look at this rip! That could have been my skin!"

The rip in fact was worse than I thought. A dagger of glass had caught not only the canvas of the pocket but the papers inside, pulling them up through the hole like Kleenex. Clara's grandmother's letter flapped in the breeze.

"Maybe I could go back in and get a few important books, but I'm afraid that's all. I can't crawl in and out through that hole a hundred times."

Malpesh wasn't listening. He was looking at the rip in my backpack. In fact, he was staring with such intensity through his magnifying lenses, I wouldn't have been surprised if the backpack had burst into flames.

"Don't worry, I'm not hurt," I said.

But he wasn't worried.

Something about the ripped pack had caught his eye. He pointed a shaky finger at the exposed piece of copy paper, its Yiddish script shaking in the wind like an earthquake reading on a seismograph.

"What is that?" he asked. "Where did it come from?"

"This? It's the letter I mentioned. Written by my girlfriend's great-grandmother."

Malpesh stooped to the ground with the help of his cane. Then, as carefully as he could with trembling hands, he pulled the page from the bag, through the hole. He shuffled to the stairs and sat to smooth the letter on his lap. He ran his fingers over the words, then cleaned his glasses with his handkerchief and held the bottom of the letter close to his face.

"Great-grandmother?" he said.

The Memoirs of Itsik Malpesh

ayin

SASHA BIMKO. TO SAY THE NAME WAS
hardly new for me. How many times had I been embarrassed to
find it absentmindedly on my lips, spoken aloud to a grocer who
had asked how many pounds of apples I'd like, or to a stranger
who had inquired only if I knew the time? How often had I spoken
it to myself, like a Hindu's mantra, a spell of protection and hope?
It was a name that rose up unbidden through the layers of my consciousness, a long-buried splinter forcing its way to the surface of
the skin.

Yet to see her face, her warm and breathing face, to see it and
know that it was not a vision or a fantasy . . . this was a revelation.
Many years later, when there came to exist a tanned, lean, intimi-
dating variety of Jews who called themselves Israelis, they would
seem familiar to me, for standing before me then—twenty years before their state came to be—was their prototype, perhaps their Eve.
Dressed in mannish clothing but nonetheless arresting in the sexual
charge that radiated from her like heat, the woman claiming to be
my muse and lifelong romantic obsession looked me straight in the
eye with such complete confidence I supposed—correctly, it turned
out—that she was a product of days spent in the fields of a kibbutz
and nights spent on duty guarding the perimeter.

"Sasha Bimko," she said as she held out her hand in greeting. I
took it in my own, and despite having worked with my own hands

for the better part of two decades, I was struck by the roughness of it. Her calluses suggested that she had held weapons, but it was her eyes that convinced me she had used them.

"Sasha?" I said. "Could it be?"

I had difficulty releasing her hand, fearing that the moment I did, she would see my fingers quiver like ferns in the wind. Yes, so unsettling was this slight contact that it caused me to tremble. Could it be that all my dreams had become real in an instant? The applause, the praise, the public acknowledgment of my passion, my words. And now this? No, no, I thought. What man would dream it? What fool would dare?

"Itsik, you look faint," I heard Rachel say behind me. Was she still standing there? Her voice was filled with concern, lilting upward toward an uneasy tone containing notes of both warning and plea. Concerned or no, she sounded to me at the moment only like a distraction.

"Please go," I said.

"Go?" Rachel and Sasha asked in unison.

"No!" I said to Sasha. "Yes, please," I said to Rachel. "I must speak with my . . . my . . . old friend."

"Don't you mean"—Sasha grinned—"your 'butcher's daughter'?"

Rachel's eyes darted between Sasha's face and my own.

"She? The butcher's daughter?" Rachel gasped. "From your poems?"

I could say nothing more, as I scarcely believed it myself.

Rachel put a hand to her mouth.

"Itsik?" she said imploringly.

When I made no effort to reply, she backed away several quick steps, as if she had just seen a man hit by a streetcar.

"I hope I am not interrupting," Sasha said.

"No, no! She is only my . . . my employer's sister."

Behind me I heard a small cry, and I turned in time to see Rachel rushing away with her face buried in her hands. It didn't occur to me to call after her, but I remember being somewhat relieved to see Knobloch waiting by the exit, holding her coat. She sped past him, out toward the street, with arms bare against the winter chill.

Knobloch saw me watching from across the room.

"Malpesh?" he called to me. "Aren't you coming?"

For him, too, I had no more words. In fact, I felt as though I would never have words again, except, perhaps, only one.

"Sasha!" I said, and then again, "Sasha!"

She twisted her lips. She wrinkled her brow. The scar on her forehead pinched like a flower folding for the night. Then she smiled—barely, but enough to quicken my breath.

"You are beginning to scare me, Mr. Malpesh."

"Mister! How does one I have known since birth call me Mister?"

"Hearing you read tonight, I realized I don't know you at all."

"You will," I said. "But how is it you are here?"

As Chaim had a few minutes before, she unfolded a flyer and held my own name before my face.

"I witnessed your first debut," she said. "How could I miss the second?"

ALL THAT FOLLOWED this improbable meeting could not seem more sudden. Yet to me every event of my life was leading to this moment, and so if in the telling Sasha's arrival seems something like a god dropping from the clouds as in the ancient pagan plays, I can only beg your understanding. Her arrival to me felt nothing like a convenient deity gently floating down from above. It was more like an avalanche. Far from solving the problems of the unwieldy narrative of my days, she simply covered over them, burying every possibility and intention I'd had previous to that evening, leaving me feeling as if history could be forgotten, as if both my present and future were now tabula rasa.

We left together, into the street. I said very little those first few moments, content to breathe the air next to her. This was my intention, at least. In my zeal to drink in her scent, I inhaled so deeply that my nose filled with the stench of our surroundings: pickles and rotting fish. Only then did I remember the café's unfortunate location. I coughed until tears poured from my eyes.

"Isaac?"

"Isaac? First 'Mr. Malpesh,' now you call me by my Hebrew name?"

"Forgive me," she said. "Hebrew names roll more easily off the tongue. Yiddish for me is a language of long ago."

I searched my memory for a scrap of Hebrew from my school days, something to show her that we shared more than a language and a past that was dead to her. When I found none, I was forced to ask myself what we truly had in common. A lost home, fathers unknown since childhood, mothers abandoned to their fates. We also each had a lifetime of fantasies devoted to the question of who she was, who she would be.

In truth, looking at her that night, I realized that I had spent more time wondering what would become of Sasha Bimko than I had worrying the same of Itsik Malpesh. My fate had always revealed itself to me each day with no greater meaning or effort on my part. Hers, meanwhile, had come to stand for the fate of the world to me. How to tell her this? How to explain that the poem she heard me recite, the poem in which her name is invoked as prayerfully as the psalmist's *selah*, how to explain that this poem was only the beginning of the devotional literature I had penned in her memory? How to explain that, yes, she had been my muse for as long as I had cared to put pen to paper? I dared not speak a word of it.

As slowly as we walked, words began to rise between us. We passed hours this way, first ignoring the cold as we warmed ourselves with conversation, then pushing close against each other as we strolled, each using the other as bulwark against the wind. From nowhere flurries fell and squalled about us. The cold nipped our cheeks as snow blew through the cross streets, intensified by the endless canyons the tenements made.

"I am a long way from the desert!" Sasha laughed.

"Just pretend it is sand!" I said.

We stumbled laughing through the door of the Automat on Thirteenth Street, where Chaim had taken me my first night in New York. How different my life was now, five years later! And yet no change had felt as transformative as the one I had felt wash over me in the hours since Sasha finally arrived in my life.

Suddenly I was the experienced New Yorker, she my greenhorn in need of lessons.

"Have you ever seen a place so bright as this?" I asked as we entered, the gleaming white-and-red tabletops polished to mirror shine.

"The Negev comes close," she said. "But this looks much more hospitable."

I handed one of Knobloch's dollars to the girl at the change counter. She counted off twenty nickels, pushing each one in my direction. I didn't try any of Chaim's sleight-of-hand schemes, but I did borrow one of his lines.

"For you, shveethart," I said as I slid a single nickel across the counter.

"Isaac, do you know English?" Sasha asked. "I am impressed! Surely you didn't learn that in Kishinev or Odessa?"

"I've been here five years," I said. "One picks up a few things."

"Spoken Hebrew was not so easily picked up. It is difficult to pick up a language when it is buried in the ground."

"I trust it was worth the effort?"

"The effort perhaps, but not the cost," she said cryptically, then rushed to change the subject. She pointed at the wall of glass doors displaying the menu items of the day. "What in the world is that?"

"Ah! This is a place where a desert girl like you will feel right at

268

home. Did you know that New York is primarily a hunter-gatherer society?" I took her hand and led her to the wall of glass doors. "First we hunt . . ." I studied the windows theatrically, creeping along and peering into each as though I was a pygmy peeking through jungle vines. "Then we gather! Pick one, and I will show you how it works."

"Hmmm," she said as she scanned the windows. Her eyes settled on a triangular potato pastry. "That one." I loved her for the choice alone.

At the beverage counter I ordered glasses of water and two cups of coffee, milk and sugar for me, black for her. We found a table and sat down, and soon the story of her arrival in New York began to come out, but only in flashes. There was reluctance in her voice each time we stumbled onto the subject. I never asked about it directly, as any mention of her recent departure from the land of Israel caused the broad smile she wore so comfortably to shrink to an expression of forced amiability. Through an hour of picked-over pastry and slowly sipped coffee, I came to understand what had happened: after more than a decade among the Zionist pioneers, she had had enough of the struggle.

"It was a great adventure for a time," she said. "But the land of Israel is not a place to grow old. And not a place to be alone."

"Alone?" I asked.

I remembered quite well that she had gone to Palestine with Minkovsky's son, but I did not ask about him, and she did not elaborate. Instead, she told me that she had returned briefly to Odessa to be with her mother.

"I found myself choosing between a place in which I did not wish to die, and a place in which I did not wish to live. And so I decided I would see for myself the Golden Land. Tell me, Isaac, is it everything they say?"

"It is nothing like what they say," I told her.

"Well, I certainly never heard of the way you Americans hunt for your food! Food from a wall! Who ever heard of such a thing? Do you know that in Jerusalem we push prayers into a big wall to get God's attention? In New York, you open a wall and pull out a sandwich. I think from this difference we can determine which city God favors, don't you?"

As soon as we left the subject of Israel, she spoke without ceasing, full of life and wit. I could not stop watching her, even as she did the least remarkable things: she gulped her water as though her throat had been permanently parched by her time in the desert. She arranged her fork and knife on the table so that they were perfectly aligned. She leaned back in her chair to loosen and then retie her hair. Several strands fell across her forehead, and I finally saw the face of the girl from the photograph. It truly was my Sasha, here at last.

I'd hoped my study of her was subtle, but she caught me watching her as she bit into the pastry that had been sitting neglected on her plate.

"Would you like a taste of my knish?" she asked.

My face turned as red as the table at her question. She'd asked it innocently, I knew, but it stirred in me such desire that my ability to speak vanished. I dried my forehead with my napkin and found myself unable to disguise the grin that seized my face.

"Why do you blush? Are you laughing at me?" she asked, wiping her cheeks. "Do I have potato on my face?"

"Has it been so long since you've spoken Yiddish?"

She laughed, somewhat sadly, I thought.

"I told you, I haven't spoken Yiddish since I left Odessa! You can't image the disdain for it in Israel. In Jerusalem they fight over it in the street."

"They fought over it in Odessa as well."

"Not like this. I remember the men who hung around Minkovsky's as well. Full of talk, of rhetoric about the proper national language of the Jews. Easy to talk about national language when there is no hope of nation. In the land of Israel, they fight as if choosing the right language will determine whether or not there will ever be a nation. The Hebraists in Palestine will not stand for anything that smells of the Jews they used to be."

"And what do they think Yiddish-speaking Jews smell like?" I asked.

"Do you remember that cloud of foul air we walked through when we left Goodman's? That reek of death and brine?"

Again I blushed, though now not happily. Now it was more in shame. She noticed my reaction right away. It would have been impossible to ignore.

"Forgive me. You must understand that in Israel there is genuine fear of Yiddish. It is as though they believe the language itself had something to do with our endless misfortune in the Old Home. For the last fifteen years I have been surrounded by those who believe there is nothing to be gained from speaking Yiddish and much to lose."

"You'll find that many feel the same way here."

A darkness settled over me. A reminder. It had been good of Chaim to come to my reading, but his insistence that my language was a dying animal still stung. That its death throes could be heard even in Israel was news to me.

"Oh, never mind all that!" Sasha declared suddenly, emphatically, in a way I would soon realize was characteristic of her. Hers was a willed and willful optimism, and she would not stand for less from those around her. "You were full of mirth a moment ago!" she chided, then held up her plate in offering. "Here, please. Taste my knish. It is here waiting for you."

Again a blush and grin came unbidden to my face.

"What? Did I misspeak again? Did I say something embarrassing? You must tell me!"

With the slightest smiles, the hint of intention, she brought me out of my gloom.

"It was only your word choice. On a first date it is a scandal!"

"Which word?"

I glanced down to her plate. She followed my gaze to her half-eaten potato pastry.

"Knish?" she said. She seemed to think for a moment, and then she too was blushing. Her cheeks turned such a deep shade of violet, it was as though she had stood on her head.

"Oh! I had forgotten its other meaning! What you must think of me!"

"No, no," I assured her. With one hand I caressed her arm; with the other I reached across the table and snatched a morsel from her plate. "I would die for a taste of whatever you offer."

"Have you always been so bold, Isaac, or is it the influence of America?"

"It is the influence of you," I said.

She drained her coffee in a single gulp, then asked, "Can we get liquor here?"

"No," I said. "But I know where we can go."

PROHIBITION WAS OF COURSE the official rule of life in New York, but not once in my five years in the city had I met anyone who lived by it. Of the dozens of drinking establishments within walking distance of the Automat, I decided to take Sasha to the one speakeasy I knew of where the doorman spoke Yiddish. If I took her anywhere else, she was sure to realize I'd exaggerated my facility with the local tongue.

We walked down Broadway to Houston and from Houston to Norfolk, where a set of stone stairs led down into a black abyss untouched by streetlamps. A half dozen men milled about at the top of the stairs, smoking cigarettes or just leaning against the wall.

"Just like Minkovsky's, isn't it?" I said. "Don't worry. It's safe."

Sasha surveyed the men around the stairwell, then the darkness into which we now descended.

"It hadn't occurred to me to be worried," she said. "Do not take it as a boast when I tell you I have seen much worse. I doubt even one of these men is armed."

I banged on the door and waited for the eye-level view slot to slide open. When it did a moment later, red light and smoke plumed from the hole.

"Toy store's closed, friend," a voice said through the hole. "Come back in the morning."

"I am a landsman of Charlie Smooth," I said.

"How do I know you're not a cop?"

"How many cops you know speak Yiddish with a Kishinev accent? Open up. We're only here to drink."

The door opened as if I had uttered a magic spell. I was impressed with myself until I realized who had been behind the door. He stared at me with half-closed eyes, grinning like an amphibian.

"Turtle? Why didn't you just let me in?"

"Sorry, Itsik. House rules. Charlie says we always have to ask, 'How do I know you're not a cop?' He says it's part of the ambience."

Sasha touched my arm as we entered. "To think when I saw you last, you were an innocent baby!" Sasha laughed. "Now look at you, a friend to doormen! A regular at speakeasies! My mother would be shocked!"

"Your mother was part of the crowd that gave me my first drink."

Inside, there were about twenty people sitting close around cocktail tables. We found a booth in the back, far from the hubbub of the rest of the crowd, where we talked late into the night.

Spurred on first by the intoxication of shared history and then by other spirits, we spoke of interrupted childhood and fatherless adolescence, pausing in the tellings of our life stories only when the waiter appeared to offer more booze.

We started with beer, then switched to schnapps to toast our common heritage—"To Kishinev! To Odessa! To New York!"— and soon found ourselves bleary-eyed and clumsy, letting our knees bump beneath the table, letting our fingers brush together above. When the waiter returned a sixth time to the table, we asked him to leave the bottle. It was around that time that we discovered, without much surprise, that the first drinks of our lives had been taken from the same set of glasses. Mine had been the ink cocktail Minkovsky had served me before my departure from Odessa; hers had been vodka pilfered from the Underground's supply.

"It's a pity we did not meet there," she said.

"We missed each other only by months."

"I know. I heard from my mother of your arrival."

"I am surprised to hear she wrote you at the time. She was not well then."

Sasha flashed me a look of anger, narrowing her eyes as if I had accused her of causing her mother's condition. "It's not polite to assume one knows more about another's family," she said.

"She was like a mother to me as well."

Again, in an instant, Sasha flashed a new mood. Full of barely disguised rage one moment, playing coy the next.

"Does that make us brother and sister then? A pity . . ."

A moment later she was smiling, but as the schnapps flowed, more and larger cracks emerged in her optimistic facade.

"There is a purity to longing, to searching and striving for something," she said. "Once you have it in hand, there is only the ugly business of holding on to it."

I assumed she was speaking of Palestine. As I held her, my fingers beginning to take firmer purchase, and I felt the glow of what was hoped for attained, I wondered if the same might be true for the love of another.

"That may be true of land, but not of people."

"Land?" she said. After considering it for a moment, she gave a sad laugh. "Palestine, you mean? I hadn't thought of it that way. But yes, I suppose it's true."

"What were you speaking of, then?"

She drained her glass.

"It is not the time to discuss this, Isaac."

Now I was the one with the quickly shifting mood.

"Oh, don't sulk! I will tell you. I am speaking of Nachum Minkovsky."

My assumptions of the life she'd had before she arrived in New York became facts over the course of that first few hours. She had gone to Israel with Minkovsky's son. Had she loved him? Yes, she had loved him.

"And now he is gone?" I asked.

"I chased him, he chased the land. Then the land killed him, and what did I have left?"

"Killed? Forgive me, but are we speaking in metaphor?"

"You are indeed a poet, aren't you? He was shot dead last summer in Jerusalem," she said. "There was nothing metaphorical about it."

I poured two more glasses, full to their brims.

"To his memory," I said.

We both drank; I poured again.

"And to no longer being alone," I said.

She drained her glass. "Yes, it's nice to have company in a new city," she said. "Thank you for your kindness, especially as I believe I interrupted your plans for the evening."

"Plans?" I shook my head at the word. "You know the old saying, Man plans, God laughs?" Emboldened by schnapps, I wrapped her hands in my own. "Finding you has been my life's plan for twenty years, and God has laughed at me every step of the way, moving you farther with each step closer I tried to take." I raised my voice above the speakeasy's din. "But now I laugh at God, and let Him plan what he will!"

"Isaac, you're drunk!"

"Yes. But that hasn't made me forget what it is I most want to say to you." I put my hands on the table to steady myself as I looked

Sasha in the eye. "*All through life you were cast away from me. / Like a wave moving toward a distant shore. / Yet even a tide must return across the sea. / To crash upon a familiar beach, / on sands the water knew before.*"

She smiled, barely stifling a laugh of her own.

"Oh, Isaac. You speak to me as if every line has been rehearsed! Do you think just because thoughts are well spoken, they are true? That is the trouble with your poems. You have convinced yourself they are life. You prefer to ignore facts for the sake of making a rhyme."

"Facts? What facts do I ignore?"

She pulled me in by my collar. When her lips found my lips, it was for me a moment out of time.

"Never mind facts," she said. "Let's leave here. Where can we go?"

I stood up so quickly I nearly overturned the table. I was three paces away before Sasha grabbed my arm.

"Wait!" she said. "Bring the bottle."

DESPITE MY RUSH to find someplace private with Sasha, I wasn't immediately sure where that might be. I couldn't take her back to my rented corner of the rented room, where Mrs. Goldstein would be waiting with her bean soup and hot-water bottle. The Knobloch Building jumped to mind as a possibility, but the risk of running into either Rachel or her brother was too great. I had spent most of Knobloch's cash, so a hotel room was impossible.

Then I had it; I knew where we could go.

"I will take you somewhere, if you're up for your first American adventure," I said.

"Big talk! Who would have guessed the son of a goose plucker would be so suave."

"He wasn't a goose plucker!" I said. "He was a goose plucker manager! And I was a goose-shit shoveler, so why shouldn't I be suave?"

We stumbled out into the street, where the flurries of earlier in the evening had painted the city white. Slipping in the slush that had already formed in the gutter, laughing and warm with the schnapps in our veins, we hailed a Checker cab. I shouted in my best approximation of New York English, "Broo! Klin! Breege!" and we rolled southward through a canyon of buildings that could have served as a stage set of heaven. Sasha fell onto my arm and rested there a moment, both of us saying nothing as we listened to the taxi's tires glide through the snow-covered streets. I felt the weight of her head on my shoulder, and I made a great effort not to wake up, just in case the entire evening turned out to be a dream.

The driver let us out at the base of the bridge's pedestrian walkway, and I dropped a single silver coin in his hand. It was the last of the dollars Knobloch had given me earlier in the evening. Was it too much? Not enough? I had no idea, and I didn't linger to find out.

Taking Sasha's hand, we charged up the wood plank ramp that led to the crossing. In a moment we could see air on all sides and nothing else. The only people on the bridge as the snow whipped around us, we turned back every few steps to marvel at how easily all traces of the city had been scrubbed from the sky.

Below us too, there was nothing, and above, nothing. Only white, as if God had erased the universe to start from scratch, as if he was through with history and searching and loves that did not measure up to ideas of what love should be, as if he'd finally had enough—as had we.

I slipped on the wet planks of the walkway, and Sasha caught my arm.

"Where are we going?" She had to shout over the wind.

"Over the side!" I shouted back.

"And what is on the other side?"

"No, no. Not the *other* side. *Over* the side!"

I pointed south, past the guardrail, toward the oblivion beyond.

"Over? Are you mad?"

"Don't tell me the pioneer is frightened! I suspect you've seen far worse!"

It was not until I had swung both feet over the safety wires that I realized this was likely to be my last bad idea.

"It's safe! Don't worry!" I said, adding hopefully, "But I probably don't have to tell you that."

"Isaac, we've had quite a lot to drink, we are a quarter mile above a very cold river, and every surface is covered with new-fallen snow. This time, yes, it did occur to me to worry. Where are you going?"

With a small push of my arms I slid off the guardrail and landed with a loud thud a few feet below on the platform that kept jumpers from disrupting the roadway. Sasha peered down at me from above.

"I am not sure why you expect me to follow you!" she said. "Because we are from the same town in Russia, you feel obliged to lead me to my grave?"

"You will follow me because it will be a great story to tell our grandchildren!"

In response, Sasha scooped up a handful of snow, packed it into a ball, and threw it with frightening accuracy toward my head. It missed by inches, which seemed to be her intention.

"Did you learn that in the desert? I'd think with all your training, you'd have better aim."

"In the desert it would have been a grenade. Grenades only need to come close."

She climbed over the railing and hopped down to join me.

"This way," I said, taking her hand to lead her through the maze of supports and beams through which Turtle had been my guide five years before. A moment later, a moment in which Sasha's grip tightened on my fingers with every step, we reached the bridge tower and the tunnel entryway.

"Almost there," I said. "It's just inside."

Sasha poked her head into the hole, giving the tunnel a puzzled, exploratory look. Then she turned and studied me with equal fascination.

"Inside," I said again.

"You are joking with me. It's not nice to play tricks on the new girl in town."

"No joke. Inside."

"You first."

We climbed into the tunnel like two eager bees into their hive. I had done this twice before, but still I progressed awkwardly, using my hands to grip the walls and inch myself along while bracing my feet at right angles to my legs to keep my belly, and my clothes, from scraping on the tunnel floor. When I glaced back, I saw that Sasha moved gracefully in comparision. Crawling on her elbows and her knees, she slid forward as if she could crawl this way for miles.

"You learned a great many things in the desert, didn't you?"

"This I learned in Odessa. Did you never explore the tunnels that led from the Underground to the port?"

"Only once," I said.

We were through the tunnel in less than a minute, and then stood in the dark in the storage room. I struck a match and was pleased to see Chaim and his boys had not emptied the place completely. I lit an oil lamp with a cracked globe that stood on the table, and it cast just enough light for us to discern that a scrap of newspaper beside it was two years old. Sasha took the lamp and walked a slow circle around the room. Despite a few reminders that Chaim and his boys had lived here, it felt like a cave, cold and dank, with the sounds of dripping water echoing in the darkness.

"An odd sort of place to bring a girl," Sasha said.

"I've dreamed of you trapped in the back of a *khappers* cart and locked in a steamer trunk full of letters. I don't know if I'd recognize you if I had any more room."

"Ah, but you only recognize your fantasies. You've been waiting so long for your dream to walk through the door, how will you know the real Sasha Bimko when she arrives?"

"She is here now, that is all that matters," I said. "Wait one moment."

In the adjacent room, I lit another match and threw it into the woodstove with as many scraps of newsprint I could find. Then I kicked apart a broken chair and fed its legs into the fire, leaving the gate open so that the flames threw jumping light on the floor and walls.

"Okay, come in!"

Sasha surveyed the room in the firelight.

"You are full of surprises, aren't you?"

"You betcha," I said.

We fell to a bed Chaim and his boys had left behind. Damp and cold, smelling as if it had been floating in the river below, the mattress sagged where we landed, and together we sank as if in quicksand.

"This may be the end of us!" I said.

She reached a hand between my legs and grabbed me. "I hope it's not the end of you."

As she soon discovered, it was not even the beginning.

"Don't you find me attractive, Isaac?"

"Very," I said.

"Are you nervous, then?"

"Very," I said again.

"Don't worry. It's safe."

She held me, kissed me, guiding my fingers, then my skinny hips. Did I think for a moment I was the only man she had known in her thirty years? No, though she undoubtedly could tell my inexperience with every clumsy movement of my hands.

Despite my repeated fears that this night had been a dream, the most dreamlike hours of it only served as evidence that no vision could be so real. I realized this with every breath, with every inhaled

280

reminder that not only could I see Sasha's face and hear her voice, I could smell her. In twenty years of fantasizing about her, I had never imagined such a thing. If anything, in my dreams she smelled like a decades-old photograph. In person, beside me, I breathed deep and struggled to define the scent: it was like peppermint mixed with rosemary; no, it was like sage mixed with cinnamon; no, it was simply clean air and pure water . . . Hers was a scent never known near the shop floor or the printing house or the tenements. Simply put, she smelled nothing of the life I had lived since arriving on these shores. Nothing of the life I wrote poems to escape. Indeed she smelled of escape itself, escape to the place to which one belonged all along.

All through the night I held her hair to my face and breathed deeply.

"Is this what Jerusalem smells like?" I asked.

She made a sour face as she pulled away. With a quickness that spoke of combat training or military maneuvers, she rolled from me to the pile of clothes she had dropped beside the bed.

Finding a cigarette, she lit it and blew a cloud of white over us, making the room appear for a moment as scrubbed clean as the sky above and the river below had seemed.

"Sorry to disappoint you, Isaac," she said, "but Jerusalem smells like smoke."

pey

OVER THE NEXT FEW WEEKS, SASHA BEGAN
to tell me of her life in Palestine—and, eventually, of Nachum
Minkovsky's death.

"It was lovely before the war," she said. "We didn't go there to
fight, after all. We thought just being there would be struggle enough,
though in the beginning it felt more like a holiday. We lived in a settlement south of Haifa, overlooking the sea. We grew oranges. We grew
grapes. We made wine. For months it was exactly what we wanted
from a Promised Land.

"Then a few young people in our settlement—just a year or two
older than me—got it in their heads that we should help the British
get the Turks out of Palestine. We trained like soldiers, shooting guns
and crawling around in the desert sand. It was a great adventure, until
members of our group starting dying. One was shot in the Sinai, another was taken captive and killed herself. I told Nachum I wanted no
more of it, but he carried on.

"After the war, we moved to Jerusalem—"

"Moved together?" I asked, unable to resist the urge to ask nor
bear the response that I already anticipated.

"Yes, Isaac. Together," she said. "There are different rules in the
desert. And you'll find I live by different rules because of my time
there. I had hoped we would return to a normal life once we were
within the city walls, or that at least it would mean an end to the

fighting. It didn't. The fighting in Jerusalem is endless. As perhaps you have heard."

I had read in the Yiddish papers of the recent violence, the fighting between British soldiers, Jewish settlers, and Arabs in Jerusalem. But reading of it was nothing compared to hearing it firsthand. As often as new faces were arriving from the Old Home, I had never met anyone who had once stepped foot in Eretz Yisroel, no one who could even imagine what the sites of these skirmishes looked like. Sasha meanwhile spoke of Jerusalem with both the immediacy and bitterness that Adler spoke of Minsk.

"It was all on account of that damn wall," she said. "The one with the prayers stuffed in the cracks. Jews have access to it, but we're not supposed to build anything nearby.

"Some of the rabbis insisted on separating men and women, so they arranged a few chairs as a makeshift divider. One day an Arab happened to notice and wondered, 'What are those chairs there?' 'A mechitza,' someone said. 'A fence.'

"Of course word got around the Jews had built a fence at the Western Wall. That's how it started. It was a matter of days before stones were thrown; then came the British and their guns and the Arabs with theirs. Nachum thought it was a scandal to rely on the British for protection. He went to the Jaffa Gate with a gun of his own. I asked him, Nachum, will you shoot people so that a few zealots can continue to divide men from women? Is this why we've come here? To this he said to me, 'I'll shoot people so that Jews can do what they please in the land God intended for them.'

"He spoke of the land as if it was a soul mate, a lover. 'Our place here is bashert,' he said. That's when I realized he was as much of a zealot as the rabbis at the wall. He hadn't been before. He was a believer in the cause, yes, but before he had been a romantic soul, motivated by love. The love had gone out of him by the end.

"I came to see that the zealotry and the land feed each other. Before we had Zion, we longed for it; when we had it, we fought to keep it. I never thought I would say so, but having fought for it and left it behind, I don't know if I will ever long for it again. It seems that to be separated from it is to be cured of that particular madness.

"I am ready for all of that to be behind me," she said. "Enough death, enough fighting. I am ready to begin my life again."

I took her hand in mine. "Let us begin together."

"You are a kind man, Isaac. But I do not know if you are what I am looking for."

"What is it you went there looking for?"

"If it will not make you think I am terribly old, I would like to tell you a story from a time before you were born."

"You are only four years older than me, Sasha. How many stories from before my birth could you have?"

"Only one. Well, two—if you count the story of your birth itself."

"That story I know," I said.

"Some of it you know," she corrected; "the rest is a story for another time.

"But let me tell you of my other memory. In general I do not have many recollections of Kishinev, or of my father, but I do recall watching him go off to work each morning and being very curious what he did all day. We lived in a house near the synagogue, beside the butchering shed, so Papa did not have far to go, and all day long I could hear the mewing of sheep or the lowing of cows, the honking of geese—"

"I know the sound of honking geese well," I said. "It rings in my head like a funeral dirge."

"To me it sounded like a constant celebration. I was a child, so naturally I loved animals, and the first day I followed my father to the shed I supposed he went in there each day to play with them. Then I watched through a crack in the door, and I quickly learned the truth.

"For weeks I stole away at every opportunity to watch my father work. He was very good at his job. I am sorry to say I have witnessed my share of death since then, and never have I seen it arrive so peacefully. Papa soothed the animals before he brought out his blade, he even sang to them—the same lullabies he sang to me each night. He put them in such a state of calm that when he cut their throats they seemed to die almost happily, giving up their spirits as casually as an exhaled breath.

"It is a peculiarity of my raising that before I could speak, I understood the words associated with the slaughter of animals. I don't suppose you know this, it is not the type of knowledge passed along to most children, but there are a number of ways that a ritual slaughter can go wrong—several mistakes the *shoykhet* might make that will render the meat unkosher despite having no other imperfections."

"Oh, I know a few of these," I said. "We memorized a great deal of unnecessary information in *kheder*: pressing, pausing, tearing, covering, piercing."

"Very good, Isaac. You must have been a star pupil. Perhaps poets and butchers are not so different. You each must know how to make appropriate cuts, yes? And often you each are oblivious to the pain your work can cause."

"And did you find my poems kosher when you heard them?"

"Tasteless and overcooked, you mean?"

"Pleasing to God," I said.

"I suspect the only poetry God likes is his own. Who but God could write our reunion?"

"I might try."

"Don't. You would set it to rhyme and make us sound absurd. What was I saying before?"

"Your father."

"Ah, yes. My father was an expert and took meticulous care of his *halaf*. The five errors a *shoykhet* might make were never a problem for him. My mother claimed he made just one mistake in all his years at the knife.

"I don't know what possessed me the day I pushed open the door to the slaughtering shed. I entered as quietly as I could, and saw my father poised over the neck of a huge brown cow. Just as he began to draw his blade across its neck, I called to him, 'Papa!'

"The thing I remember best about my father is that he was always so thrilled to see me. At the sound of my voice he never failed to look up and smile no matter the circumstances, even in the middle of a task that required his full attention.

"Only an instant later did he realize that by looking up to greet me, he had paused in his cut. It was for less than a second, but a pause is a pause. He continued with his slice, but already he knew it was a waste. The animal would not be kosher and so would not be eaten.

"'Out, Sasha! Out!' he shouted at me.

"I wanted to do as I was told, but I stood there transfixed. Blood shot out of the cow's neck and covered my father's hands as if he was wearing bright red gloves. After that it was unlike any other slaughter I had seen him perform. When I had watched him without his knowing, he had always held the animal by the nose and spoke softly to it as it died. He believed a slaughter done in keeping with God's law gave the animal a less painful death; this belief made him calm, which in turn seemed to keep the animal at ease as well.

"But the day he saw me and paused, it was as though a spell had been broken. He panicked, and so the animal panicked as well. It rolled over onto its legs and bucked around the shed, knocking the butchering table on its side and scattering buckets of goose feathers everywhere. My father's other tools—knives and mallets and cleavers—fell from the wall and cut the cow's legs as it jumped. The poor beast kicked and swung its gashed neck so violently it seemed its head might fly off. My father couldn't get hold of it to finish the job until it had bled so much it collapsed on the floor.

"A moment later my mother grabbed me and pulled me out of the shed, but not before I saw Papa weeping over the animal as it died.

"Years later, when I learned my father had been killed by Christians in that same place, in the middle of that awful shed, the two deaths became inseparable in my mind. And now for some reason Nachum's is as well. When nightmares come to me, as they often do, I see a death that is somehow three in one. In my dreams I can't tell if it is Jerusalem

286

that is one large slaughtering shed, or if my father's slaughtering shed is a Jerusalem in miniature. When I wake, I remember it doesn't matter. In either place there is too much blood spilled over belief."

She closed her eyes, shaking her head.

"Belief," she said again. "The word nearly makes me sick. . . . And yet at heart I remain a pious man's daughter. You asked what I am looking for? I suppose I am looking for something to believe in that will not kill me or the ones I love.

"In Russia we believed in God, and where did it get us? In Palestine we believe in the land, and that will serve us no better. I came to New York because many people believe in America. I thought I would come here and see if this is a belief that will finally keep us safe."

"Do you know that after you left Kishinev, your father's slaughtering shed became a yeshiva?" I asked.

She looked up at me with surprise. "No, I did not."

"It was where I discovered what I believe."

"I suppose you were a good little boy, learning your Bible stories?"

"No, it is where I discovered that Bible stories were not the only stories, nor even the most powerful. It was there I discovered that I believe in the magic of words."

"Words? Words are as common as air. What magic could they have?"

"I believed if I wrote about you until my poems piled so high they could be seen from Jerusalem, then my *bashert* would come to me. And here you are."

She nodded seriously, as if considering the value of my belief, weighing it with unseen measures and scales. She seemed to wonder if one man's impossible faith, not in God or land but in poetry and fate, could be enough to sustain her.

"Words?" she asked again.

"Words," I said solemnly.

She took my hand and squeezed it.

"That will have to do."

The Memoirs of Itsik Malpesh

tsadek

FROM THAT DAY ON, IT SEEMED I HAD RE-
turned to the double life of my youth. I was once again a man with
two names, only now it was not a Hebrew name for the synagogue
and a Yiddish name for home. I was Isaac whenever I was with
Sasha; Itsik everywhere else.

Within a month, she moved into my room in Mrs. Goldstein's
apartment. It was rushed, to be sure, but she had nowhere else to go.

"My wife has finally arrived from the Old Home," I told my
landlady.

"What wife?" Mrs. Goldstein said. "I never heard of no wife."

In fact, I dearly wished Sasha was my wife, but she wouldn't
hear of it.

"Look what happened to the last man I was engaged to," she
told me. "And look what happened to my father. God is out to get
whomever I love. Maybe if we keep it unofficial, He won't notice."

"Did you say love?" I asked.

"Yes, Isaac. Love."

Again and again, I professed that I hoped to live properly as
husband and wife. Again and again, she resisted. Yet even as she
did, she offered me hope—albeit hope measured out in the smallest imaginable increments. We spoke occasionally of having an
apartment of our own, but each time Sasha convinced me to stop
short of ending our arrangement with Mrs. Goldstein.

"Why move?" Sasha said. "Soon she will be dead, and the apartment will be ours!"

We lived, I realize now, something of a half-life: together yet not bound; with shared history but no shared memories. She was the future I had long hoped for; I was a connection to the past she had thought gone forever. Where that left the present was never entirely clear. When I was with her, I lived as though the fantasies of a lifetime had become real, which only highlighted the larger reality of my life: when I was not by her side, it seemed little had changed.

Perhaps if I had followed the course that had been set for me—if I had married Rachel following my debut as a poet and public literary figure—things would have been different. Perhaps my writing career would have developed in the ways Knobloch had suggested were possible. I would have begun writing for his paper, and that would have led to others. I would have left the shop floor forever.

Unfortunately, my change of heart regarding Rachel had altered my professional prospects as well. Knobloch did not go so far as to remove me from my positions within his company, but he no longer showed me favor. He no longer even feigned interest in my poetry. He made no secret of the fact that the sole reason for this was that I had jilted his sister. Whenever we crossed paths on the shop floor, he shook his head, perplexed and annoyed by the sight of me.

"This is a bad business, Malpesh," he said to me once, not long after my reading at Goodman's. "Rachel has had other suitors. Big Yekke, for example. She turned them all away—for you. And she is no longer young enough to be marketable!" Hearing their employer raise his voice inevitably started the other tailors looking up from their piecework. He lowered his voice. "Forgive my bluntness. I am a businessman and I speak like one, but that does not mean I do not love my sister. And I do not like to see her hurt. She hears all the rumors, of course. Are we to understand you've taken up with that Arab woman we saw at your reading?"

"She is not an Arab, she is a Jewish pioneer!" I said. "And, yes, I have taken up with her. If you must know, I have been acquainted with her family since my birth. I am sorry for Rachel, but I had a prior commitment to Sasha."

"Nonsense. Rachel tells me you had never set eyes on her before that night. All you had was fantasy, a delusion!"

"How was it a fantasy if she is here now? Mr. Knobloch, I care for Rachel, but there is nothing I can do. Sasha, you see, is my destined one, my *bashert*."

"*Bashert!*" Knobloch scoffed. "An ugly word. You have free will, Malpesh. Or at least you did! You are a changed man since this woman entered your life."

"I am!" I said. "Thank God, I am."

I TRULY WAS, and it was only the beginning. Not just for me, but for the world. Just as my arrival long before in the battered city of Kishinev happened to coincide with forces of history that had nothing to do with my birth but everything to do with the life that came of it, Sasha's arrival in New York occurred simultaneously with the Depression in America and rising tensions overseas. Every day we printed such stories in the *Naye Yidishe Tsukunft*. It was the start of the 1930s, and every headline suggested this would be a decade, like all those before it, that was not good for the Jews.

When news arrived from Odessa that Minkovsky's printing operation had finally been shut down and that he and others associated with it had all been taken away, Sasha became obsessed with the welfare of her mother.

"Isaac, I left her once because I knew with Minkovsky there she would not be alone. But now who does she have? What does she have? We must find a way to bring her here, to be with us."

Before then, as an unmarried man unconcerned with luxury, moving toward engagement with the sister of a wealthy businessman, I had been able to get by on the most meager of means. So long as I had paper to write on, I had been content.

Now, however, money became my primary concern. I worked every shift available at Knobloch Industries, then picked up some piecework on the side. Whatever money came in beyond our daily expenses, we put in a jar and hid it beneath the bed. No one trusted banks, of course, and this way Sasha was able to watch our savings grow, ever hopeful that when the jar was stuffed to the top with dollars she would be able to see her mother.

"When it is full, I'll take it to the Western Union," Sasha declared, "and send her enough for passage to New York, plus a little extra for bribes. Then I will have a family again."

To hear such statements from her stung my heart. "Sasha, you know I would gladly be your family," I told her many times. "If only you would let me."

"When we have more saved, perhaps we can talk about that as well," she said.

With that hope I worked tirelessly. Yet for all my efforts, the jar filled so slowly, it seemed we were waiting for the dollars to reproduce on their own.

Filling far more quickly was my valise of poems. Each night after Sasha had gone to sleep, I took the case down from a high shelf in the corner of our room. With the rest of the apartment dark and silent, I crept to the table in Mrs. Goldstein's kitchen and wrote until morning.

I wrote new poems every day, but spent more time reworking the verses that remained most meaningful to me, those that told of the violence surrounding my birth and of the girl who raised her fists against the attackers. Now that the girl with the fist was the woman with whom I shared my bed, these stories from my youth seemed entirely new to me. The longer I spent revising, the more I understood the rippling effects of that reckless, childish, defiant act. Had little Sasha saved my life? My parents' lives? Her own? To think that a raised fist could do so much.

One night, from the other side of the apartment, I heard the door to our room open, and then footsteps. Sasha appeared, bleary-eyed and lovely in her blue nightdress.

"Praying to your God of words?" she said. "Don't stay up too late."

She continued on toward the door that led to the corridor and the humiliating shared water closet at the end. In the silence following the close of the door an image came to mind: I thought of that harmless fist raised now thirty years ago and imagined it aging before my eyes. I thought of that same little hand packing her bags for the desert, and then training to fight in an ancient city, and now being used to put money in a jar. An equally defiant act? The thought that a few saved dollars could be gathered to make a bridge across the ocean, to carry her mother to us, to save life. I sharpened the tip of my pencil and began to write:

> In the morning she was a tiny fist
> a girl no bigger than a whisper
> an angel sent to shame pogromists,
> and save a boy who was born to miss her.
>
> At noon she was a trigger finger,
> a girl grown bold as a battle shout.
> In daydreams, he would rise to kiss her.
> When his visions ended, his heart cried out.
>
> Now it is dusk and she's a fist again,
> a woman with the wisdom of a sigh.
> Lifting coins from the boy's own hands,
> she tells him, Saving dollars will save lives.
>
> In the night, when she's an open palm,
> Will the boy sit up and shudder,
> Where is the girl? Who is this woman?
> Have dreams aged since I was younger?

It was not the poem I'd intended. Before I could make sense of where these words had come from or why, I heard the door open and close again. When I looked up from my page, Sasha was standing over me. The sun was coming in through the window now, and she looked pale and frightened in the morning light.

"Sasha?" I said. "Is everything all right?"

"No," she replied. "I'm pregnant."

How MANY TIMES had I been teased, mocked, pilloried, for my belief in the magic of words? Sasha herself thought the notion helplessly romantic, so far removed from the workings of the world as to demand either laughter or scorn. And yet here were words from her own mouth that proved it. "I am pregnant," she said, and our lives changed forever.

To begin with, our financial concerns quickly came to constrict me like the stitches I pulled tight and knotted all day. Before sunrise I was on the shop floor; eighteen hours later I dragged myself home. A third of my pay went into the jar to bring Sasha's mother from Russia. A third went into an envelope "for the baby," which Sasha hid even from me. The rest disappeared as quickly as ever. Mrs. Goldstein inquired about the rent whenever I passed her room.

"Why don't you sell some poems, Mr. Bigshot Writer!"

She was mocking even the idea of it, of course, but desperately I tried to do just that. Every day when the lunch whistle blew I left the Knobloch Building and made a mad dash to every Yiddish publication in the city, offering up whatever new verses I had. The rejection letters I received now all hit the same note: circulation was down and dropping fast at all the Yiddish journals. The nicer notes praised my verses and expressed regrets. When I delivered "In the morning she was a tiny fist" to the offices of the *Freiheit*, for example, a secretary glanced at the name on top and handed me a pretyped letter that read simply: "Kindly refrain from further submissions."

"But you haven't even read it!" I complained.

"Let me explain something to you," the secretary said. "Fewer Yiddish readers means fewer Yiddish sales, which means fewer Yiddish pages and fewer Yiddish poems. You get it?"

"But soon that will mean fewer Yiddish poets!"

"The world will keep turning," she said.

That the world would turn without me was not a surprise, but now I felt in danger of being thrown from it as it spun.

THE DAY THAT CHANGED EVERYTHING began like any other. I left the house as the sun rose through Mrs. Goldstein's kitchen window. Sasha lay asleep in our bed, her belly growing like a boulder rolling down a mountainside toward a village below.

On the shop floor, only one thing was different: Adler wasn't there.

I noticed his absence immediately. Adler was always there. Not only was his station empty, the rank charge of competitive tension he brought to the air seemed missing. Possible he was home sick, of course, but it seemed unlikely. He had many mouths to feed, and it was unimaginable he would risk losing his job over a mere cough or rattle in the lungs.

I finally sought out Gutman and Glazman and asked them, "Where is Adler?"

They looked at each other with eyebrows raised to the ceiling.

"What, you haven't heard?" Gutman asked.

"He's gone." Glazman shrugged.

"Gone?"

"Just like that."

"I heard he was walking down the street, and the guy just grabbed him."

"Could've been anyone!"

"Why him?"

"A pity!" I said.

Gutman and Glazman looked at each other, then at me.

"Yeah, right. A real pity!"

"A pity it wasn't you, you mean!"

"Me, I'm glad it happened to him."

"I'm glad too."

"He deserved it! More than anyone."

"He surely did. On that we agree. He had it coming."

"What?" I shouted. "I thought you were his friends!"

"Every friend should meet such an end!"

I couldn't believe what I was hearing. "To be grabbed on the street, and then gone?" I was shouting above the din of the machines now. "That's an end to wish on a friend?"

Gutman held up his hands as if he was directing traffic.

"Wait a minute, wait a minute!" he said. "Who do you think grabbed him?"

"A mugger! A bandit! A killer!" I cried.

"Get a load of Mr. Melodrama!" Gutman laughed. "A killer, he says!"

"And those crocodile tears!" Glazman roared. "What, are you looking for a spot in our next production?"

"It was no killer who grabbed him!" Gutman hooted. "It was a translator!"

"Translator?"

"Yeah, get this: Adler was walking down the street eating peanuts from a bag. And this young Jew—American born!—this young Jew says to him: 'Aren't you Adler, the poet? My father sung your verses to me in the cradle.' Turns out he's a college boy, a professor no less! An *anthropologist*. Says he wants to translate Adler's poems into English, take him on a tour of colleges to give students a taste of the Jewish experience."

"The Jewish experience." Glazman sniffed. "Tie them to a couple of Cossack horses, they want the Jewish experience."

"The *American* Jewish experience," Gutman clarified.

"Adler's feet may be in America, but his experience is in Minsk."

"That's why they want him, the college boy says. He's *authentic*. A real live immigrant Jew!"

"*Mazel tov* to Adler! He's a Hottentot! He's a pygmy at the zoo!"

"Next time we see him, he'll have a bone through his nose."

The two men turned to face each other. "This is good material, we ought to be writing it down," Gutman said.

"Writing it down? We ought to be melting it and making jewelry. This stuff is gold!"

Instantly they seemed to forget me.

"So Adler is well?" I asked. "Not in the hospital or worse?"

"Don't you worry: Adler has never been better."

"Five hundred books his translator sold the first week."

"Now that he's been translated, he never needs to work again!"

The conversation lingered with me all week. At least once each hour of the working day, and even haunting my dreams, a word rang out in my consciousness, unbidden. Once upon a time, when this happened, the word was sure to be *Sasha*. My new obsession was a word far less lovely to me: *Translation!*

The idea of it now fascinated me. All my life I had encountered translation as a means by which the literature of others could be rendered in Yiddish for the Jewish rabble. Never had I considered that the opposite might also occur, or that I might prosper from it.

But what if it could? I kept the thought to myself as best I could. After all, who did I know that was gifted in such work? We all knew a handful of English words, certainly. But who knew better than a poet that knowing words is not enough? One must have a sense for transformation, for the process by which one thing becomes another, the way a sculptor can turn a block of stone into a statue that seems to live and breathe. But who in the shops or the café had such talent?

Despite my doubts, the notion would not leave me. Whenever in my wanderings I happened to find myself beyond the realm of the East Side, on streets and avenues in which Yiddish was an alien tongue, I allowed myself to consider that all those uncountable others might one day read my words. If it could happen for Adler, why not Malpesh?

Why not?

Why not!

The question, as ever, was how.

THE ANSWER CAME SOON ENOUGH. When Knobloch learned of Adler's departure, he was relieved to be rid of him. Like every other Yiddish periodical in the city, the *Naye Yidishe Tsukunft* had been losing readers. The *Forverts* had bet right: Jews were learning English and dropping their *mamaloshn* as fast as they could. The Yiddish market was not steaming toward a bright future, it was a sinking ship.

Knobloch Industries began taking on other printing projects to make ends meet. So long as he received payment up front, Knobloch held his nose and agreed to minuscule print runs of poets and memoirists he regarded as unpublishable hacks. "It's a short hop from there to wedding invitations," he moaned. "A short hop but a long fall." He felt his reputation as a tastemaker of the East Side crumbling beneath him. The editor of the *Forverts* no longer took his calls; Goodman now wouldn't buy him coffee, let alone agree to open his shop early as a favor. He became so dejected, he even began talking to me again.

"If you had started writing for me five years ago, maybe none of this would have happened," he said.

"You think I singlehandedly would have kept enough people reading Yiddish to keep the *Naye Yidishe Tsukunft* alive?"

"No," he said. "But if you had been writing for me, at least I would have you to blame."

297

One day Knobloch came into the shop in a jubilant mood. He'd just met with a client on Mott Street, he said, a client who might allow him to speak of numbers rarely associated with Yiddish except when counting the years in the Hebrew calendar.

"Guaranteed sale of five thousand units!" Knobloch boasted. "The fellow says he's been commissioned to do a book, and his backers would buy five thousand copies right off the bat."

"What is the book?" I asked.

"A translation."

"Of what?"

"Who cares!" Knobloch laughed as he turned to leave the shop floor. He'd had his fun rubbing his further successes in his workers' collective face, and no longer wished to be around us. He called over his shoulder as he went. "This isn't just news for me, you know. A print run like that will keep us in business another six months, maybe a year. Translation is big these days! Seems like all you need to do to make a set of words salable is flip them over into another tongue. Every one wants to read what they don't know how to read!"

"Where did you meet this translator?" I called after him. "How might I find him?"

"I met him at Goodman's. He's there most every day."

"What is his name?"

"A funny name," he shouted as he entered the stairwell. "Almost like he made it up."

"Well, what is it?" I asked.

But Knobloch was already gone.

I ran after him, into the stairwell. I looked down, then up, hearing his echoing steps but uncertain in which direction they were moving.

In desperation, I called out as loudly as I could, "Mr. Knobloch! The translator! What is he called?"

The name Knobloch called back at me echoed off the walls as if it would never end: "Hershl Shveig!"

THERE ARE SOME NAMES that haunt us, and some that we simply follow despite ourselves. Some names that we chase like a mirage, others that chase us like a shadow. All through my life the name Sasha Bimko had brought out the best in me. Only once had a name brought out the worst.

Hershl Shveig. I couldn't place it at first, but it did sound familiar. Perhaps the poets at Goodman's had spoken of him before? I could not be certain, as so many new writers emerged and faded away in those years. As the Old Home grew darker every day, they landed with a shrug and a look of relief on the East Side, or merely passed through from Warsaw or Vilna to God-knows-where. They came and went to places with names we who had ended our journey in New York had never spoken. There were poets who stayed just a week before they shipped off to tubercular sanatoriums in the Catskills or Colorado, others with family in Oklahoma, a few who went as far as California.

So it was entirely possible I had simply heard his name in passing at Goodman's. I returned to the café that night and every night, determined to meet this translator and achieve the success which with Adler's translation project, and now Knobloch's, seemed waiting for me.

It was perhaps a week or two later that I was sitting in my usual chair among the other sweatshop writers when, at a table nearby, I happened to overhear Gutman say to Glazman, "He is translating *that?*"

"Who is translating?" I asked.

"That fellow right over there," Gutman said.

Glazman shook his head. "That's one way to make a name for yourself, but what would his mama say?"

"You think a man like that has a mama?"

"What Jew doesn't have a mama?"

"That's just what I mean, 'What Jew?' I hear what he's working on, and I wonder."

Across the café, wearing a white suit with white shoes—how had I missed him?—a man sat behind a stack of books that looked as though he had dug them from a grave. They were enormous old tomes, dusty in the gleaming café light. I studied the face behind them, and saw something familiar in it. Had I known him in my previous life, another of my old school chums who somehow escaped to the Golden Land?

It couldn't be. And yet, why not? If Chaim and Sasha had come back into my life, why not him? Could it be that here, on the other side of the ocean, every Jew from the Old Home had been reimagined? That each of them—each of us—was no longer who he had been, and yet not fully someone new? There I was looking for a translator, and I came to realize that we were a translated people.

Any lingering doubt I had that this was indeed the same boy I had left stranded in the back of the *khapper*'s cart twenty years before left a moment later. Above the din of arguing poets and forks clinking on plates, a whistled melody rose up, just barely detectable. It was a religious tune, that much was clear from the first notes. Around the room, the poets of Goodman's looked left and right. *Who among us had kept his faith?* all seemed to wonder. We listened for any hint of irony in the whistling. There was none. We all prided ourselves on the distance we had come since the piety of youth. Was it possible there was yet a believer among us?

Gutman shouted, "Shut it, you Hasidic bluebird!"

Glazman said, "Get a load of the the pious piper!"

"The frumest flutist!"

"Save it for the synagogue, rabbi!"

But I could not help but pay attention. It was a haunting tune, similar to a hundred other Hasidic melodies. The sort of song that starts low and rises without warning to heights of tone and feeling. As much as it sounded like every other *nigun* I'd ever heard, something about it had particular resonance. I tried to tell myself that I had heard the tune in Kishinev, or in Odessa, or in steerage. Then came another shout, and there was no denying what I knew.

"Hershl Shveig, your name does not suit you!" Gutman roared. "For someone called 'silence,' you ring like an alarm!"

"Hershl Shveig?" I said. "That is Hershl Shveig?"

Following the stubborn piping of his whistled tune, I wandered through the tables until I was at his side. Sitting before an empty tea cup and a half-eaten sandwich, he was alone. A little man with the quick fingers of a tailor, he worked not with a needle but a pen. I stepped closer, close enough to peer over his shoulder, and saw that he was writing in Yiddish, then English, then Yiddish again, occasionally writing a word or two of what appeared to be—could it be?—Greek.

My breath quickened at the sight. He looked up with a start.

"Excuse me," I said. "Forgive the intrusion. Mr. Shveig, is it?"

He nodded.

"You are a translator?"

He nodded again.

"You translate from Yiddish, or to Yiddish?"

"I work in either direction, and from other languages as well."

"I can tell you are the envy of the café, despite the spirited critique of your whistling."

"Was I whistling? I often cannot tell. I merely let the spirit flow through me," he said. He leaned back and seemed pleased by this opportunity to take a break. He lit a cigarette and blew smoke between us. "Translating is not so different from carrying a tune, you know. It is nothing to envy anymore than we envy this teapot. I simply take words from the kettle and pour them in different cups. I didn't make them hot."

He poured more into his cup, and lifted it to me. "*Prost*, as they say. Or, as they also say, *sláinte. Na zdrowie.* Cheers."

"And *l'chaim* to you," I said, humbled by my options.

I started back to my seat, but I could not pull myself away. I turned fully around and marched back to his table, where I stood for several seconds before he noticed that I had returned.

"Forgive me. This is difficult to say"—I spoke quickly, embarrassed by the words—"but I believe we knew each other once."

He put his pen down.

"Oh?" he said, then reached into the inner pocket of his suit for a pair of metal-rimmed glasses, each lens no larger than a quarter. He squinted behind them, studying me.

"It will sound quite odd to you if you are not the man I think you are," I continued. "But . . . and again I beg your forgiveness for such a question. When you were a boy . . ." Out with it, I thought. Out. "Were you ever kidnapped by Christian *khappers* and transported along the road to Odessa?"

He stared at me blankly. I burned red as a flame.

"My sincere apologies," I said. "I don't know what I was thinking." I felt sweat drip down my face, into my collar, down to my chest. I was more shamed than warm, but nonetheless I said, "The heat. Yes, that's it. The heat. Forget I said anything, will you?"

I began once again to move back toward my seat, mortified to realize Glazman and Gutman had been watching the entire spectacle. I prepared myself for the worst of their ribbing, but then a voice called out behind me.

"You didn't tell me your name," Hershl Shveig said.

"My name is Malpesh," I replied.

"Ah, yes. Monkeypiss."

I swung around to face him, surprised to find a big grin on lips that a moment before had seemed immovable.

"It is you, then?"

"We're all made in God's image," he said. "Who is to say who is who?"

To this I had no response, and it was just as well.

"It is good to see you again, Malpesh. I have often wondered where you landed."

It all came back to me in a flash: our ride with the *khappers*, the bully who had tormented us both, my unexplainable attack on the only boy in the cart who had shown me a bit of kindness.

"I believe I owe you an apology," I said.

Shveig put down his pencil, picked up his sandwich, and went to work as if the task before him had not changed, chewing his bread as though it was made of words, translating it into the substance of his flesh.

"Apology? No," he said after he had swallowed. "It is nothing. Another world. Another life." He wiped his face with a napkin, took a sip of his tea. "I can see we both are not the boys we were. The ocean, it seems, is the greatest translator of all. What else could turn Jewish children into American men?"

There was something in this phrasing that gave me pause.

"Yes," I said. "But we are not changed entirely. We are still Jews, are we not?"

"We are what life makes us," Shveig said.

The Memoirs of Itsik Malpesh

kof

For days I stewed and pondered what this succession of occurrences might be leading me toward. If Adler could have such success with his thin proletarian verses, if Knobloch could revive his faltering business, each by proceeding down the path of translation, why not me?

Each evening after my shift, I walked the streets late into the night, until I was sure Sasha would be home from work, and only then did I make my way to Broome Street.

With much relief I saw that Mrs. Goldstein's door was closed. Ours was open, but there was no sign of Sasha when I looked inside. There was a light on in the kitchen.

"Where is my butcher's daughter?" I called.

"Just a minute," she answered. "Stay there. I am ... washing the floor."

"Washing the floor?" I said. "We don't pay Mrs. Goldstein so that you will keep her house clean."

I walked toward the kitchen, turned the corner, and then paused. Sasha was not washing anything. She was on her knees, opening a paper flour sack so large it had to be kept on the floor. I stayed where I was, not in the room, but peering in, and watched as Sasha pushed a jar—smaller than the one in the bedroom, but just as full—into the sack and kept pushing until her arm disappeared to the elbow. When she stood, her hand and wrist were entirely white, and the jar was nowhere to be seen. I backed away from the door just as she called out, "I'll be right there!"

A moment later she appeared in the sitting room. Her arm was clean. She said nothing of the jar, and since I believed I knew what it was—the money "for the baby," she had said—I decided to let her have her secret. I had bigger news to relate.

"I have met a man who may help us out of our financial troubles," I declared. I told her of Adler's good fortune. Then of Knobloch's. "Everyone is making a killing through translation! And now so will we."

Sasha smiled. "Perhaps if you focused your energies on learning the language, you could simply write your own poems in English, no translator necessary. And then perhaps you could get a better job as well."

There was a not-so-gentle rebuke in this. Sasha had begun working on her English within days of her arrival. She now knew the language far better than I did.

"If I could write in English, I'd just be another English writer. To be a Yiddish writer published in English, however. . . . Mark my words, that will be the key to someone's success. Why shouldn't it be me!"

"Just don't get so excited you miss your next shift," she said. "The jar for my mother is nearly full, and the situation in Odessa is not improving."

MISSING MY SHIFT was exactly what I had in mind. There was too much to do to prepare for my translation, and if all went well with the publication of my poems, we would soon have enough money not only to bring her mother over but for us all to live comfortably once she arrived.

I left home the next morning before dawn, with my valise of poems tucked under my arm. By then it was filled with hundreds of verses, collected through two decades.

How many should I choose for Shveig to translate? I wondered. And should I make my selection by theme, or would simply chronology suffice?

I went to the Automat to drink coffee and think it over while rereading long-forgotten rhymes written on the other side of the world. Much of it was embarrassing juvenilia, but nonetheless a useful reminder of the boy I had been. If there was a common thread to all of that earlier work, it seemed to me to be the theme of unlikely, often unintended escape: in the beginning there was my family's survival of the pogrom; next came my departure from Kishinev with a poem as my exit ticket; then my unexpected departure from starving Odessa. Had I slipped through fate's hands so many times, or was it the hand of fate that had saved me?

I was deep into my valise when Chaim appeared at my table. Turtle was by his side.

"It seems now that we are friends again, we will run into each other all over town," he said.

He pointed to the wall of windowed doors and slipped the boy his lock-picking spoon.

"I can't reach the top row," Chaim said. "Go empty them out while Itsik and I confer."

He saw my valise.

"Are you writing poems or skipping town?" he asked.

"Neither," I said. "I've been thinking of having my poems translated."

"Well, I'm honored you'd ask," Chaim said.

"Very kind of you, Chaim. But I had a professional in mind."

"A professional what?"

"A professional translator."

"Ach. That's not what you need. You need someone who understands the spirit of the language. No one understands the spirit of English better than Charlie Smooth. Watch, give me a poem. I'll show you some translation!"

306

He reached into my valise and grabbed the topmost sheet, my most recent poem, "In the morning she was a tiny fist."

"Okay, let's see here."

He took my pen and on the back of a napkin began to write and scribble, write and scribble, removing two words for every three he wrote. Five minutes later he sat back looking pleased with himself.

"Take a look at that," he said, sliding a napkin filled with hatch marks and English letters that I thought would be illegible even if I knew the language.

"Chaim, if I could read English, I'd try to translate it myself. How am I supposed to know if this is a good translation?"

"Take my word for it!"

"Turtle!" I called out. "Turtle, come here and read something for us."

"It's a translation of this—" Chaim said as he handed the boy my poem. "It says—"

I snatched it away.

"No, let's have him tell us what it says."

Turtle looked at the napkin, then at Charlie Smooth.

"Go on, read it," Chaim said. "We'll show him he's not the only poet from Kishinev!"

Turtle took a deep breath. "Okay, it says: 'After breakfast . . . the girl . . . punches . . . small . . . angels . . . and pilgrims . . . While the boy . . . '"

I looked at Turtle, then at Chaim, then back to Turtle.

"'While the boy' what?" I asked.

"I dunno. That's all there is."

"Chaim, that is the worst translation I have ever seen!"

"What, it's a free translation. You wanted literal, you should've said so."

"This is why I'm getting a professional. I need a salable product, not some patched-together nonsense."

"All right! All right! I thought I'd do you a favor. So who do you have in mind?"

"A man named Hershl Shveig."

Both Chaim and Turtle laughed out loud. "Shveig?"

"You know him?"

"The Christian?"

"Christian?" I asked. What was he talking about?

"Yes, yes. He's a convert! You don't know this? He is one of the gang from the Mott Street Settlement. They're constantly after my boys."

"After them for what?"

"For conversion!"

The broad strokes of Hershl Shveig's life began to come together in my mind. Of the dozen or so boys who had been stolen by the *khappers* on the road to Odessa twenty years before, he alone remained when I leapt from the cart. Had he stayed with them? Had he joined the Russian army? In one manner or another, he had somehow shed his earlocks and his Hasidic prayers along the way.

"What is that to me?" I asked. "He is able to provide a service, I would pay him for his work. It's just a business arrangement. No different than the one that brought us together, eh?"

"There's a difference. Take it from me: business with Christians leads to nothing good. Ask your father about that."

The mention of my father stung so that I looked away.

"I am sorry, Itsik. Perhaps I am just jealous. How many English lessons do I need to give you to prove I'm an expert?"

⤙⤚

LEAVING CHAIM AT THE AUTOMAT, I was soon overtaken by a surprising concern: I must warn Knobloch about Shveig, I thought. Surely he had been taken in by him as well. The thought of it: a Christian translator for a Yiddish press! I had no doubt it would mean Knobloch's ruin, and it fell to me to save him from it.

I ran nonstop to the Knobloch Building, then charged up to his office without even slowing as I passed Rachel's desk. I ran toward the Library of Broken Dreams, shouting as if we were a nation under siege and our borders had been breached.

"Hershl Shveig is a Christian!" I called out as I ran down the hallway of Sholems. "Hershl Shveig is a Christian!"

By the time I reached his office door, Knobloch was waiting, having poked his head out to discover the source of the commotion.

"Malpesh, what the hell are you yelling about?"

Breathlessly, I repeated my news.

"Of course Hershl Shveig is a Christian!" Knobloch said. "Otherwise, it would be pretty strange, him translating what he is translating."

He turned to walk back into his office, and I followed, still certain he was being fooled. Perhaps he didn't know the whole story, I thought. As it happened, that honor belonged to me.

"The translation was his idea, but I wish I had thought of it," Knobloch continued. "It's an absolutely brilliant business move, really forward-thinking. With things looking bad in Europe, even more Jews are going to want to get in over here. And you know what more Jews means? More missionaries who'll want Shveig's book."

I couldn't believe what I was hearing. "Mr. Knobloch, I'm confused," I admitted. "What exactly is Shveig's book?"

"Here you go. Hot off the presses."

He handed me a small blue volume that looked to me like nothing so much as a *sidur* from the Old Home.

"What is this?" I asked.

"It's gold," Knobloch said.

"You're printing prayer books?"

"Aha! It only looks like a regular prayer book, but open it up, read a bit."

I flipped through the pages, scanning the text. The words that jumped out at me were these: *Mary. Jesus. Nazareth. Bethlehem.* Then the least Jewish sentence I had ever read, repeated twice for good measure: *Crucify Him. Crucify Him.*

"A Christian book?" I asked.

"*The* Christian book," Knobloch said. "Shveig calls it *Der Bris Hadash.* Isn't that clever? *Bris,* for God's sake. This guy is a genius."

"You think people are going to buy five thousand copies of this?" I asked. "You think Jews are going to buy a single one? After we've spent two thousand years trying to keep it from being rammed down our throats?"

"Calm down, Malpesh. You've got it all wrong." Knobloch patted the air as he spoke, trying to soothe me like a wild beast. "Sure, there are a few intellectuals who will want to read this the same way they read Shakespeare or Guy de Maupassant in Yiddish. They want to know what's out there in the gentile world. But that's small change. The thing that you don't get, but Hershl Shveig does, is that the publishing business isn't just about sales. It's about *distribution.* On the one hand, you're right: most Jews won't be bothered with this. They won't even know it exists. But on the other hand: there's no end to Christians who will want to buy these things and pass them out by the truckload. And on the other hand again, I'll get the money no matter what nonsense the buyers believe. And on the fourth hand, what harm does it do?"

"But it's a betryal!"

"What betrayal? Betrayal of who?"

"Of Yiddish!"

Knobloch roared with laughter.

"Yiddish! Are you working on a comedy routine? You've been spending too much time with Gutman and Glazman. Tell me: How do you betray a language? And when you do, do its feelings get hurt? Only people can you betray, Itsik. You want I should call my sister in, and we'll ask her about that? Listen: I am being loyal to you and everyone who works for me by publishing this book. Soon as it's paid for, we can expand the *Naye Yidishe Tsukunft.* Maybe some of your poems will get published because I'm publishing this. You'll find your baby won't survive long with only your principles to eat."

As MUCH AS I HATED to admit it, Knobloch was right. I had not been mistaken when I identified translation as the key to reaching a larger audience with my work. And perhaps it was so, as Knobloch reminded me after I had calmed myself, that a certain amount of compromise was necessary in any business enterprise. Knobloch gave me Shveig's address and wished me the best of luck contracting him to undertake a collaboration.

It TURNED OUT that Hershl Shveig lived in a basement apartment of the Lutheran Church on Mott Street. I could see plainly that there was a light on in his window as I approached. As it was not yet too late in the evening, I decided I would simply knock and see what came of it.

He appeared at his door dressed, as ever, in a crisp white suit. He was the color of the purest goose down from his shoes to his shoulders.

"Mr. Shveig?"

"Mr. Malpesh!" he said, apparently surprised to see me. "To what do I owe the pleasure?"

"I would like to discuss a . . . matter of business with you."

He did not invite me in. Instead, he placed a matching white homburg on his head and directed me to a park bench across the street.

"I would like to propose a collaboration with you," I told him. "I have a number of poems, a great number of poems, really, all written in Yiddish, which I think would be well served if they appeared in English."

"I see. And you are prepared, I imagine, to do whatever is necessary to see such a translation come to light?"

"Yes, yes," I said with rising excitement. "I will give you all the poems you need."

"Yes, but beyond providing the original text . . . you have the resources required?"

"You will find me a tireless collaborator! There is no length to which I will not go in the service of my art!"

"*Money*, Malpesh. Do you have any money?"

"Money?"

Shveig shook his head. It had grown dark as we spoke, and with the streetlights now shining down upon us, his white suit seemed almost electric. As his hat moved from side to side in apparent exasperation at my obtuseness, I thought it resembled nothing so much as a searchlight, lancing its beam into the heavens.

After a moment of silence, he spoke as if he had been carefully considering his words.

"Mr. Malpesh, perhaps you and I do not understand each other. This is my livelihood we are speaking of. As much as I *enjoy* the process of translation, I do not translate for my *enjoyment*."

"Payment?" I asked.

"Payment!" he cheered. "I am glad we have finally broken through our language barrier."

I hadn't thought this through, I realized. Neither Adler nor Knobloch had made mention of payment.

"What sort of payment?"

"Do you have a sample of the work?"

I pulled a stack of pages from my valise and handed them to him. He glanced quickly over five, ten, fifteen of them, taking all of four seconds per poem.

"It will cost you a dollar a page."

"A dollar!"

"Good translation takes time. Time costs money. That is my rate. If you'd like to think it over, fine. But let me know soon. I have a number of projects I am considering."

Back at home that night, I found Sasha sleeping. Just as I was preparing to climb into bed beside her, I stopped. I retied my shoes, then, as quietly as thinking, I slid my hand under the bed. The jar weighed more than I'd expected it would.

I brought it out to the kitchen and counted a hundred dollars. Enough for one hundred pages. I looked at my stack of poems. It had grown to twice that at least. And then there would be the cost of having them printed.

I needed more.

I walked back into the bedroom, slid the empty jar into place under the bed, and sat for a moment, watching Sasha sleep. I watched her breath move in and out, the blanket rising and falling. Her belly had just reached the point of beginning to show. I could see she was pregnant even through the Bemkin Down blanket I had salvaged from Chaim's hideout below the bridge. Under that layer of feathers from the city that had seen our births, our child was growing.

Our child! Unimaginable even a year before, and now—soon—a reality.

Tiptoeing back to the kitchen, I found a knife, then I stooped down to open the sack of flour. I plunged the knife into the powder and stabbed again and again until I heard the soft clink of metal meeting glass. Only then did I reach my hand in and retrieve Sasha's hidden jar. I used the knife edge to pry open the lid, and then upturned it into my hand. Bills and coins fell to the surface of the flour with a soft hush, as quiet as leaves falling into snow.

If all went well, I would be able to earn the money back and return it before she noticed it was gone. I pushed the jar back into the flour, then left the apartment.

Ten minutes later I was tapping on Shveig's window.

"Mr. Malpesh? It's past midnight! What do you want?"

"How soon can you start?" I showed him the money.

He blew flour off the bills, and for a moment it seemed to fill the sky. "Right away," he said.

The Memoirs of Itsik Malpesh

resh

IT WAS THE NATURE OF OUR LIVES AT the time that days, sometimes nearly a full week, could pass before Sasha and I would both find ourselves at home together while awake. She worked the late shift, I continued to work my double time for Knobloch, and we would content ourselves with a sleepy embrace when one of us happened to find the other waiting, unconscious, in bed.

And so perhaps more time passed than should have before I was able to share with Sasha my good news. It was after my Tuesday shift on the garment floor that I headed home and found Sasha sitting in the kitchen. She sat with her head slumped back and a wet cloth draped over her eyes. When I saw her, I was immediately concerned.

"Don't you feel well, Sasha?" I asked.

"I'm pregnant," she said, which was proving to be a useful answer to almost any question.

"Well, I have news that might brighten your mood," I said. "I have been waiting to tell you until I could do so in person. I suppose some poets might prefer to leave a note, but I—"

"What is it, Isaac? Please just tell me and then be quiet for a while. I feel my head is going to split open."

"The translator I mentioned? The one who has done work for Knobloch? He has agreed to take on my poems."

Sasha sat forward, removing the towel from her eyes. She beamed with pride.

"That's wonderful news, Isaac! How much will you be paid? And when?"

"We'll need to be patient. Translation takes time, and costs, but it will be worth it—"

Sasha's smile dropped from her face.

"Costs?" she said. "Costs who?"

"It's a business venture, so there is always some risk. And the more the risk, the greater the gain! My father used to tell me, if you don't own the material, you won't own your idea. And of course I want to own the idea—"

"This isn't a factory, Isaac. It's a book of poems. So I ask you again, costs who? Costs what?"

"Costs me," I answered sheepishly.

"Costs us, you mean! Have you already paid this man? How much? Where did you get—"

She bolted by me, toward our bedroom. I caught her arm, pulled her back, and lodged myself in the bedroom door.

"I have a plan, Sasha," I said. "A plan!"

"A plan? We had a plan to bring my mother from Odessa! If you have touched a cent of that money, I'll—"

"Please, please. Calm yourself. It will all come right in the end. You should hear how Knobloch and Adler speak of their translation projects! This will be our salvation, I swear it!"

"Enough with salvation!" she shouted, as she pushed me into the door frame. Then, in one of the several uncanny moments of my life, Sasha managed to scream at me the very same angry command I had once heard from my father: "Show me the jar!"

I grabbed her wrists and twisted until her back was against the wall. When she fixed her gaze on me, and I saw anger flash in her eyes, I was about to release her arms. Before I could, she twisted free and hit me square in the jaw. After that, she studied my dazed face for a moment and seemed to determine that she didn't need to see the jar. She knew from my quivering lip that the jar was empty.

"What goes on here?" Mrs. Goldstein asked, peeking out of her room. "What goes?"

In the instant I turned away to answer—"Mind your own business, Mrs. Goldstein!"—Sasha slid out from between me and the wall. She ran toward the kitchen, then grabbed the flour sack off the floor.

"Sasha, no! I can explain!"

But she had stopped listening to me. She turned the flour sack upside down, painting the kitchen as white as the falling feathers of the day of my birth, as white as the snow of our first night together, as white as Hershl Shveig's immaculate suit. She tore through the sack and scraped at the pile, throwing fistfuls of flour everywhere. When she found the empty jar, she picked it up and smashed it on the floor.

"All of it?" she cried. "All of it gone? For a *translation?*"

Without another word, she shoved by me and moved toward the door.

I chased her into the hallway, then called after her, down the stairwell, "Where are you going?"

"To get our money back."

THAT NIGHT, ALONE ON OUR BED, I sat staring out the window and thinking of Sasha's mother. I remembered that on the evening I met her, the widow Bimko had been immovable in her grief, watching the city from above as if vigilance could bring back the dead. Finally I understood something of the loss she felt. I spread a blank page across a book and wrote a poem about that long-ago night in order to escape the night ahead.

Only when the poem was done did I wander into the corridor to ask Mrs. Goldstein if she had seen my Sasha.

"If you treated her better she would be home," Mrs. Goldstein replied.

"Thank you, Mrs. Goldstein," I said, cursing her silently. "If you see her, please tell her I am sick with worry."

As the hour grew later, and then the morning approached, I went out to look for her. I didn't know what else to do. I made great circles through the city, walking without thought of rest, always beginning and ending back at the apartment, where Mrs. Goldstein seemed to be keeping a vigil of her own.

"Have you seen her?" I asked after walking to Brooklyn and back.

"I hope she has left you for good!"

"Have you seen her?" I asked after a circuit of the Bowery.

"If she has any sense, she'll put you in jail!"

"Have you seen her?" I asked finally after a marathon hike to Harlem and home again.

"Yes," Mrs. Goldstein said.

"Yes?"

"She stopped by to tell you your next walk should be into the deep end of the ocean!"

"Did you really see her?" I asked.

"No, but that's what she would say if I did!"

IT WAS NOON the next day when I stopped by Chaim's toy shop. I pounded on the door and waited for the eye slot to open.

"I'm a landsman of Charlie Smooth," I told the doorman.

"How do I know you're not a cop? More and more cops keeping an eye on Charlie Smooth these days. So I need to ask you a few ques—"

"Turtle, just open the goddamn door."

Inside, Chaim was sitting by himself at a table in the back. The place was otherwise empty. He was looking over his accounting books with a bottle of schnapps at his side.

"Chaim, I need your help," I said.

"Now he needs my help! What, you need a rewrite of your translation?"

"I cannot find Sasha," I told him. "She went to see Hershl Shveig, and I have not seen her since."

"I told you not to trust that guy."

As much as it pained me, I admitted to Chaim that I was not sure it was entirely Shveig's fault. I told him everything: that I had stolen the money Sasha was saving to bring her mother to New York, that I had become enraged and violent with her when she found me out, that I was now unsure, yes, how much I could trust Hershl Shveig, and so I was concerned that I had allowed Sasha to wander into a lion's den.

"Well, what do you want to me to do about it?" Chaim asked.

"I want to know where they are," I said, "and, if anything has happened . . . I want Hershl Shveig to know that he cannot harm my family without consequence."

"Oh, I see. You think because your old friend Chaim runs a place like this, you can come to him with any dirty business you like, is that it?

"Do you see what I am doing here, Itsik? I'm doing the books. Making sure my income can cover my expenditures, and then some. You ever do this? You ever sit down and check your balance?"

"No, Chaim. I don't. But I don't see what this has to do with—"

"If I remember correctly, Itsik, this was a difference between us in the Old Home as well. I kept track of every penny coming and every page going out. You just spent what you had and stuffed your pages in a jar. But I got news for you, I've been keeping an eye on your accounts too."

"Chaim, please. Listen—"

"No, you listen. Here's the balance sheet." He looked down at his ledger as if he was reading, moving his pencil down the page.

"I try to teach you a few things when we were both *kheder* boys, and you tell your father I've robbed you. You attack Bemkin, and I end up running out of town with my dick in the breeze. I try to help you when you're fresh off the boat, you call me a thief and disappear without a thank-you.

"You think you are morally superior because you would never stoop to shortchanging the girl at the Automat—and then you go and steal from the mother of your child!

"You accuse me of hating who I am because I make an effort to learn the language of the country that is now my home, and then you go out and pay a Christian to make your poems palatable to his kind!

"I've done a lot in my life, Itsik. But my books are balanced, I assure you. I hurt no one who didn't have it coming, and I never owed anyone anything. Can you be so sure, Itsik? When you tally up your moral expenses, will you be in the red?"

He saw me staring at his notebook, trying to focus on anything but the truth of what he was saying.

"Nice ledger, huh? Hardback. Tight lines. Thick pages. The only kind I use. I buy them by the gross, got boxes of them in the back. As soon as you want to start keeping track of your debits and your credits, you let me know."

"Please, Chaim. I don't know what to do."

"Don't worry, Little Itsik. We'll look into it."

"Thank you. I owe you."

"Don't tell me," he said. He rapped his knuckles on the cover of his accounts book. "Get yourself a ledger and put it in ink."

He poured us both a drink.

"In the meantime, I'll ask around about your Hershl Shveig, and then I'll pay him a visit. Write his address down for me here. I suspect he has it coming. If there's one kind of man likely to have his moral accounting out of whack, it's a Christian. *L'chaim.*"

I LEFT CHAIM'S TOY SHOP feeling no better than when I entered. He was right. What sort of man was I to ask him to step in when I had not even attempted to right the situation myself?

It was a hot morning in the streets, and the smell choked me. Buckets of slop from the tenements with no toilet access sat out on the sidewalk. I hurried past the buckets, en route to the German church, to find Shveig for myself. The thought that I had dreamed of finding Sasha all those years simply to lose her in this way made every step a burden. When I reached the church, I stooped to peek into the basement window, then dropped to my hands and knees to get a better look.

Glancing this way and that down Mott Street, I saw that the street was empty. No one would see me if I went to his door. I would simply knock, inquire about Sasha, and be on my way.

That at least is what I told myself I intended. When I reached the bottom of the stairs that led to his entrance, I tried the doorknob, then knocked lightly. When there was no answer or any sign of movement within, I gave the door a solid kick, then another, then another. The latch wouldn't give, so I picked up a rock and bashed in a small window beside the door. Then I reached in and turned the lock.

Once inside, I satisfied myself that there was no one at home. Who did I think would be there? I dared not answer the question, though it formed over and over in my mind. The apartment was not at all what I expected: it was not as neatly put together as Shveig always seemed to be. Piles of Christian books crowded a small kitchen table. Behind them, there was an assortment of typewriters: one with a Hebrew keyboard, one with English, one with Russian, one with Greek.

Against the opposite wall, his bed was unmade, with dirty laundry slung across the headboard. Scattered on the bedside and spilling off in a ring around it, there were so many pages and envelopes it was a wonder I spotted it: my own folio of poems, scattered on the floor.

I gathered them up and left, leaving the door swinging open in the breeze.

BACK AT HOME, I read through my poems again. I had the sinking feeling that they were not all there. I had left my entire valise, after all, and the pile I'd recovered was disconcertingly thin. Fretting over this late into the night, I fell asleep with my face on my pages.

I woke to sunlight through the window, and the sound of footsteps.

Sasha looked pale as she stepped into the light. Her eyes were shot through with red and her cheeks chalked with salt. It seemed she had been crying.

"Where have you been?" I asked.

"You know where I have been. I went to see Hershl Shveig. To get our money back."

"You went two days ago."

"I have had a lot to think about since then."

"Two days of thinking? Have you been thinking in the company of Hershl Shveig?"

"No, I was only there one night."

"One night? How does it take a night to get your money back?" As soon as I formed the question, my tongue froze in my mouth. I sat stricken, afraid to ask any more.

"We talked," she said. "It was more of a negotiation."

"Negotiation?"

"He is a peculiar man, isn't he? I asked him to tell me what he believes."

"What he believes?"

"God," she said.

"And then?"

"And then I got our money back."

"Just like that, he gave it to you?"

"There is no just like that. There are always costs. There are always consequences. We needed that money, and I did what I had to do to get it back."

She let this ambiguous statement hang between us. To my shame and regret, I did not press her on what she meant. I was too focused on my agreement with Shveig, and what would now become of my work.

"And what about my translation?" I asked.

Her eyes filled with tears at the question.

"Is that what you care about? Is that what you are waiting up to ask me? To hell with you and your translation!" she cried. "And to hell with your poems!"

She shook her head, as if pitying me.

"For the longest time I thought you understood better than you let on, but you really don't know, do you?"

"Don't know what?"

"Your poems would be lies in any language."

"Lies?" I asked. "Lies? Call them shit, call them worthless, but lies?"

"You are blind to the circumstances of your birth, and you are blind to the consequences of your actions now! I have asked you several times, yet you seem to think the question is rhetorical: do you really believe that the birth of a child would stop pogromists in their tracks? Do you really believe that the raised fist of a four-year-old girl would do anything but draw her into their claws?"

"What are you saying?"

"I am saying this, Isaac: I was present at your birth. I know what happened."

"I know what happened too," I insisted.

"No, Isaac. No. You know what your parents told you. What you don't know is that the Christians kicked in the door of your mother's room, and they didn't stop until they were done."

"Didn't stop what?"

"How can a Jew be so oblivious to the world's cruelty? You wear your birth in the city of slaughter like a badge, and yet you think your family alone came safely through the storm?"

"Didn't stop what, Sasha? What didn't stop? How can you say this much but no more? Is all of this a ploy that I might stop asking questions about your evening with Hershl Shveig?"

"Enough! Enough. If you had given your family a moment's thought without the intention of making poetry of their suffering, I believe even you would have realized that your birth didn't protect your mother or any other woman or girl in that room."

Seeing my perplexed expression, she apparently saw the need to explain as if to a child.

"The door was forced open, Isaac. They rushed in and pulled you out by your neck. If there was a single miracle that day, it was only that you didn't die when they threw you to the floor."

How old is too old to have the foundations of one's life crumble? I was thirty-two years old. Sasha was thirty-five, as old as the century, and pregnant with our child. I was on the verge of becoming a father, but only then did I come to know the circumstances of my birth, my life.

"I have two early memories," Sasha said. " One is my father's botched slaughter of the cow. The other is the day of your birth. From childhood I have been haunted by it. By you. As much as you grew up with the belief that Sasha Bimko had something heroic to offer you, I grew up knowing that Itsik Malpesh was a name heavy with all the grief I have ever hoped to leave behind. I know this is difficult for you to understand, Isaac, but it is the truth. The day of your birth was the worst day of my life.

"That is all you need to know. I won't allow you to make a poem of the details."

* * *

I LEFT SASHA in the apartment, as agitated by her revelation about my birth as her reticence about what had happened with Hershl Shveig.

Other than the fact that it was spoken in a flash of anger, I had no reason to doubt the truth of her recollection of that awful Easter night in Kishinev. But on the other hand: she had been only four years old at the time. What could she possibly remember? Wasn't it more likely that her memories of a frightening event had been colored by the lifetime that followed?

None of these doubts did anything to answer my questions about Hershl Shveig. Was I to assume that in speaking of the long-ago crime that bound us together, she was describing another, one too close to be spoken of directly? Why else would she be so secretive about it? Shveig's name on Sasha's lips reminded me of nothing so much as the few times I had heard Chaim speak of Bemkin. The way three deaths had merged in Sasha's mind, three crimes now seemed to merge in mine. The crime that brought my birth; the crime that chased Chaim from Kishinev and caused him to hate a place he had once called home; and now the crime I supposed had occurred when Sasha went to collect our money. Was there something deeply rooted in Christians that they could not help but do harm to any Jews they met? And not just harm but the particular, peculiar harm of assaulting the will as much as the body? Was it Jewish will that most offended Christians? Did the will not to believe in their God so insult Christian reason that they felt they must assert control over some other hidden aspect of Jewish lives?

What had Shveig done? I asked myself this again and again as I neared Mott Street. When I reached his door, I saw that a scrap of wood now plugged the hole I had made days before. Only then did I pause to ask myself another, more pressing question: What must I do now?

I pounded on the door until the curtain behind the window moved and I heard Shveig's small voice ask, "Malpesh?"

324

"Yes, it's Malpesh. Open up."

Once inside, I was surprised by how much smaller the room seemed now that I stood beside another man. There was barely enough room for the two of us between the bed and the closest wall. I had no choice but to face Shveig from a distance so close that our toes nearly touched. Dressed as he was in matching white suit and shoes, he made every effort to avoid this. It seemed I had caught him just as he was heading out the door.

"I am late for my prayer meeting," he said. "But I suppose you have come about what your wife has done."

"She is not my wife," I admitted. "But in any case it is not what she has done. It is what you have done."

"Anything I did, I did for her own good."

"If you say another word about her—" I snapped. Unable to finish the sentence, I asked, "Where are my poems?"

"She is a tempestuous woman."

"Enough about Sasha! Where are my poems?"

"They are here."

He pulled my valise from under his bed. He held it at his side as if keeping a hostage. "But tell me, where does this leave our business together?"

"Business?"

"I know what this translation means to you. We needn't let this unpleasantness with your wife change things between us. Perhaps we could make some kind of arrangement?"

"Unpleasantness?" I nearly shouted the word, astounded by the wickedness of his understatement.

"I am sure you could persuade her. I would only need a little at a time. For this surely she would be willing, when you remind her how important this is to you."

"Persuade her? Persuade her to what?"

"If it would help, I will speak to her again and explain what she should expect if we proceed. Women often do not understand these

325

things as well as men. Of course, I would ask you to be there for this. Last time she and I tangled, I barely came out with my teeth."

I snatched my valise from his hand.

"I don't know what befell you in the *khappers'* cart all those years ago, but it made you a despicable man."

Shveig winced. "Despicable? I am only a humble scribbler like yourself. Perhaps I enjoy too much putting my pen in the inkwell when I cannot afford the ink. But is this despicable?"

"Enough!"

"Please, Malpesh. I may not be despicable, but I am desperate. I am low on funds until *Der Bris Hadash* is ready. I had wanted to present it to my brothers at our Sabbath gathering this Sunday. Then they will pay me, and I will pay Knobloch."

I was ashamed to realize that in his detachment from what he had done to Sasha, I saw something of myself. How could he talk of poems at a time like this? How could he be callused to the suffering his actions caused others? The answer came to me in a flash: he was no different than the Christians of Kishinev, no different than the men who kicked in my parents' door, the men who defiled everyone I ever loved as they pulled me into the world.

It was the desperation in his face at that moment that caused me to make my decision. That a man so indifferent could be vulnerable—suddenly it seemed to me an opportunity to make things right. Not just things between myself and Sasha, but between myself and the world. It was impossible of course to undo a crime committed so long ago, but vengeance knows no schedule.

"Your books are ready," I heard myself say.

Hershl Shveig's face brightened like an electric bulb.

"Are they?" he asked.

"I have seen them in Knobloch's office. I can take you there."

"That would be wonderful. You would do that for me, even after what happened with your Sasha?"

"I will take you because of what happened with her. Let's go."

We walked together down the autumn streets, quiet as any Friday afternoon as it turned into *shabbos* evening. The Knobloch Building was all but empty, just a skeleton crew on the typesetting floor finishing up the weekend edition of the *Naye Yidishe Tsukunft* and any other tight deadline projects Knobloch had lined up.

Up the stairs we climbed. We were nearly at the garment floor when I said, "I have been meaning to ask you. Unless my memory fails me, Hershl Shveig was a name given to you by another boy in the cart, the bully."

"Yes. After you left, I stayed with Dov and Wolf. They had heard me referred to by no other name. In time it became more my name than the name my parents had given me."

"What was that?"

"To be honest, I don't remember. But no matter. There is nothing left of that little Jew you met long ago. I learned a great deal in the year that followed. They were good to me. Well, Dov was. Wolf was not. The three of us tried to save other boys, as they saved me."

"You tried to kidnap them, you mean? As we were kidnapped?"

"I suppose some would also say Jonah the prophet was kidnapped. We are brought reluctantly to the service of God."

After that we climbed in silence, and in that silence I became aware that perhaps the body remembers better than the mind. With each step I thought of those other steps I climbed all those years ago in Kishinev, and I recalled how those steps had been guided by the steps taken by another. In the down factory, on my way to Mr. Bemkin's office, I had climbed inspired by Raskolnikov, who had approached his climatic moment with only his plan, and his ax, to guide him. Now I climbed empty-handed and with another, but I had never felt more alone in my life.

As I knew it would be when I suggested coming to the building, it was nearly time for late shift to begin.

"Have you ever seen the operations of the *Naye Yidishe Tsukunft*?" I asked.

"Why, no, I haven't," Shveig said.

"A little detour, then, but don't worry. It's on the way."

As we walked through, the top typesetters Roth and Nomberg were filling wheelbarrows with lead slugs, marching them across the floor and into the furnace chute. What did they make of me leading a man in a shining white suit through the alley of grease-black linotype machines? I never asked them, and about this night they never spoke a word.

I led Shveig through one door, then another, into the heart of the operation, the melting room. Protected from the noise of the typesetting floor by walls thick and strong enough to contain molten lead, we stood now in a hushed chamber.

"It is peaceful here," Shveig said. "Almost like a church."

"I wouldn't know about that," I told him.

"Maybe one day you will. You know, Mr. Malpesh, before things turned unpleasant with Sasha, she was very interested in hearing about what I believe. I was touched by her questions."

I could only stare at him. Filled with hatred and also a feeling I could not name, I saw him at that instant as himself and more than himself. He was one little man in a white suit, and also the mob that killed men, women, and children in Kishinev. He was the gang of goose-pluckers who had kicked in my family's door.

"If you wouldn't mind, I would like to pray with you," he said. "For you, and for Sasha, that you both find the happiness you deserve."

"You think you know what we deserve? And what is it that *you* deserve, Mr. Shveig?"

"I don't deserve a thing. What God desires for me is all I ask. And it seems God has desired that you and I should meet again, after all these years. Do you remember the word we had for such unlikely reunions in the Old Home? *Bashert?* I have since learned to call it *grace.*

"Come," he urged. "It is as easy as this." He dropped to his knees, his white suit on the dingy floor. "Join me," he coaxed, grinning. "I know it seems difficult for a Jew to kneel. But truly, it is as simple as falling . . . simpler, actually."

With that, he closed his eyes and began to pray.

"Lord Jesus," he said.

I did not not hear what followed, as it was drowned out by the furnace alarm, announcing that the fires were nearing the temperature for the melting of metal. Shveig opened his eyes in surprise at the sound, but when I nodded my head and said, "Go on, go on, just the noise of the factory," he shut his lids more tightly than before and continued his prayer.

"Thank you, Jesus," he said. "Thank you for allowing one of your chosen people to witness to another. Thank you for seeing fit to bring two Jews together, in your name, O Lord."

His head bobbed as he spoke, and he seemed to sway from side to side. Somewhere deep within him there was still a boy who had learned to pray standing up.

I turned and walked quickly from the melting room. The first door closed in its airtight frame without a sound. The second creaked as it met the latch. I drove the bolt home with a clang that reverberated like—yes, in my memory it sounds like only this—a church bell.

Perhaps that was the sound that woke Hershl Shveig from his prayers. Through the door I heard his plaintive voice, "Did you forget something, Malpesh?"

The siren wailed. Above the airtight door, the yellow No Entry sign flashed, and within the walls I heard the thick hush of hot metal moving down the pipes from the furnace, settling in a viscous puddle on the melting room floor.

A moment later, the cry went out for all setters of type to return to their stations.

"Blood in the veins! Blood in the veins! Let's make pages, boys!"

The sight of me on the floor seemed to indicate to the setters that

I was in fact working that night. As he had many times before, Roth called out to me, "Malpesh, what are we setting first?"

Without thinking, without needing to think, I answered, "A book of poems."

I walked among the typesetters, distributing pages that until that day I had thought told the story of my life.

"What's the title?" Nomberg asked.

"*Songs for the Butcher's Daughter*," I said.

"We got lead!" Roth called out. "Let's set some type!"

Soon the typesetting was done, and I printed my pages. Then I took them downstairs to the garment shop and stitched them by hand. By morning, I had one hundred slim copies.

As I held each one I trembled as if this book, this thin assembly of wood pulp and leather, was a piece of me that would carry my soul into the future.

Yet when I opened it, I found there was no hope hiding among all those printed letters. There was no pleasure in the white space that framed the verses with which I had marked my days. There was nothing anywhere that expressed what I had believed about my life. On every page, every line, every word, I read only *shveig . . . shveig . . . shveig . . .*

Silence.

TRANSLATOR'S NOTE

As perhaps should have been noted earlier, I am far from the first non-Jew to enter the world of Yiddish.

For the last three decades, the language and the literature it spawned have steadily gained traction as subjects of academic inquiry. In the process, ever greater numbers of scholars and researchers who have no ethnic or religious association with Yiddish have come to it. Among the most well known of this growing (though admittedly still quite small) population are, to name a few, the historian of the American left Professor Paul Buhle of Brown University; York University's Professor Tom Bird, an expert on Soviet Yiddish culture; and the Irish American playwright and performer Caraid O'Brien, whose translation of Sholem Asch's *God of Vengeance* opened in New York to considerable acclaim.

Most famously, former secretary of state Colin Powell is said to have spoken Yiddish since his teenage years, when he took a job at a Jewish-owned store in the Bronx and soon learned enough of the language to converse with his coworkers and customers. At the end of the first Gulf War, Powell is said to have visited Israel as chairman of the Joint Chiefs of Staff. Upon meeting Prime Minister Yitzhak Shamir, he spoke to him with near fluency. "*Men ken redn Yidish,*" he said. *One can always speak Yiddish.* The oddity of the son of Jamaican immigrants, a general no less, speaking *mamaloshn* was so newsworthy it appeared in media around the world.

Yet despite the apparent novelty of such stories, in truth there is really nothing new about non-Jews dabbling with this most distinctively Jewish tongue. Malpesh records Chaim saying, "You know they're teaching missionaries Yiddish to try to snag immigrants fresh off the boat?" By this he was referring not only to the converts such as Hershl Shveig, but to hundreds of others. The Moody Bible Institute in Chicago taught Yiddish to its Lower East Side missionaries for more than twenty years. And in the literature we see further precedent: the stories of Sholem Aleichem, the author once called the Yiddish Mark Twain, often feature the beloved character Tevye the Dairyman, later made famous by *Fiddler on the Roof*, in conversation with a Russian priest. When they speak, they do so in Yiddish, as below in dialogue from the film version of the story cycle *Tevye Der Milkhiger* (directed by Maurice Schwartz, 1939):

> Priest: I'll tell you some news. You know that your friend Mendl has a daughter?
> Tevye: You call that news? Mendl has a daughter. Some news! Mendl has, may the Lord have mercy on us, seven daughters! They keep growing. That's the way daughters are. They eat in the daytime and grow at night.
> Priest: Well, one of his daughters fell in love with Anton the forester's son. And she's marrying into our faith.
> Tevye: You keep yourself busy, father. You are catching fish in our muddy waters. As the Rabbis say, Where there are no men . . . you take what you can get.
> Priest: This is nothing to laugh about, Tevye. She is now in our domain.

Regardless of the context, it would seem that whenever a non-Jew and a Jew speak Yiddish, the stakes are high from the first word to the last. Lines of linguistic, ethnic, and religious identity have been crossed, and thus an expectation is created that other boundaries may be broken: families will be challenged, authority will be defied, sometimes blood will be spilled.

And so, my work here is not without precedent. However, as far as I know, I am the first Christian translator of a Yiddish writer to discover that his subject's previous Christian translator met an unfortunate end.

When we returned from our first incursion into the demolition site, Malpesh was agitated by the day's events, and most of all by his discovery of Clara's great-grandmother's letter. He urged me to sit down and read his notebooks while he studied the photocopy, which even for a native speaker seemed to require some work to read.

"*Zistn,*" he told me, for the first time since we met moving in and out of Yiddish. He shook as he spoke. "Sit and *leynt di notizbikher* while I decipher this letter."

"You want me to read your notebooks now?" I asked. "I thought we had to save the books? I thought it was urgent."

"After you have read the notebooks, you will know why you must now read the notebooks."

I did as I was told, making my way slowly through the yellowed pages, moving each hardback ledger from one pile, unread, to another on his kitchen table. Midway through the fourth notebook, marked with the letter *daled*, I looked up and watched Malpesh poring over Clara's grandmother's letter. He caught me staring.

"How far have you read?" he asked. "Have you yet met the *shoykhet's tochter?*"

"The butcher's daugher? Sasha Bimko?"

He held up the letter and shook it at me.

"*This* is Sasha Bimko!" he said. "Do you now understand?"

Spurred on by this connection, I continued to read his notebooks through the rest of the day and into the night, and then finally I dozed off while reading them. It must have been around 3:00 AM when my head dropped forward into the alley between the last notebook's pages.

Asleep there until dawn, smelling his ink, breathing his words, I dreamed there was no distance between Malpesh's story and my own. In the dream, which at times was more of a nightmare, I didn't know if I was Malpesh or if I was Hershl Shveig. I didn't know if I was Moshe Bimko, or if I was the cow he slaughtered, or if I was the mob that had slaughtered him.

The next morning I woke to find Malpesh tapping my shoe with his cane.

"You have finished?" he asked.

Had I dreamed what I'd read? Was it possible this little man was—did I understand this correctly in the text?—a murderer? Something in my expression, or in my behavior toward him—had I flinched at his touch?—must have communicated my questions.

Malpesh closed his eyes behind his glasses, then lowered himself into a chair beside me.

"I have never tried to explain, because no one has ever known the full story," he said. "Now that it is known, what is there to say?"

He took off his glasses, put them on the table between us. For the first time I saw his eyes unguarded by lenses; they were green-brown and looked as bright as I imagined they had been in Kishinev. Though the skin around them was spotted and gray, the eyes themselves caught light as the sun rose over the demolition zone just below the kitchen window.

"For many years I have considered causes, excuses," he said. "Isn't it so, that for too long we Jews have lived in the shadow of the cross? Isn't a convert a death threat to us all? So much blood in the name of their loving God! From time to time, how can we not strike back?

"You are a good Jewish boy, so tell me: Should one Christian answer for the sins of all?"

He stared at me as if his question were not rhetorical, sitting in silence with his hands clasped before him. I couldn't help thinking he looked like he had come to confession.

334

"But you didn't kill him because he was a Christian," I said.

At that he nodded, then put his glasses back on, looking less naked instantly.

"It would be easier to live with if I did," he said. "I think often of poor Hershl Shveig. And he makes me wonder also if a lifetime should be judged by the events of a single day.

"We can do right twenty-three out of twenty-four hours, and it is the twenty-fourth hour that will haunt us. To be a Jew is to know this, yes?"

Having read his confession, I decided finally that it was time to make one of my own.

"Mr. Malpesh," I said. "I need to tell you something. Perhaps it will upset you to learn this, but I am not a Jew. I was raised to be a Christian. A Roman Catholic."

Malpesh stared at me, reaching for his glasses to get a better look.

"Your parents, they were converts?"

"No. My parents were born Catholic. My whole family was born Catholic. We have always been Catholic." I said it with a mixture of pride, relief, and shame that was utterly new to me.

He stood up, then sat down again, then stood up and moved to the other side of the room.

"You are some kind of missionary?" he asked. "You have learned the Jewish language to convert Jews?"

"No," I said. "I learned the language to become something new."

He closed his eyes and took a long deep breath, which wheezed as it entered his lungs. In the space between us, dust hung as thick as a curtain. The slanting sunlight seemed to freeze solid in the apartment's dirty air.

"I understand," Malpesh said at last. "A lifetime it has taken, but I understand."

Without another word, he turned, walked toward the coatrack, and put on his cap.

"*Ikh muzt geyn tsu zamln di bikher,*" he said. *I must go to gather the books.*

"Wait," I called out after him. "*Mir viln geyn tsuzamen.*" *We will go together.*

335

The Memoirs of Itsik Malpesh

shin

"I AM SO SORRY, ISAAC. PLEASE FORGET THE awful things I said."

Sasha threw herself around my neck when I returned to the apartment. She did not notice the box of books I was carrying until I had dropped it to the floor. Several copies of my volume of poems fell open at our feet.

"What's this?" she asked. "Is this a book of your verses?"

"It is what it is," I said.

She picked one up from the floor and flipped through the pages. She smiled so warmly I thought I would die. "It's beautiful. I didn't know this was in the works. You spoke only of the translation . . ."

I barely heard her, so clouded was my head with what had just transpired.

"It's too late," I told her. "A book can't be unprinted. The past can't be undone."

"Why would you unprint it? Your life's work, and you talk of unprinting?"

"My life's work?" I repeated, almost laughing at the possibility that she was right. I had thought my life had been leading up to my reunion with her; that my pursuit, poetic and actual, of Sasha Bimko had been the defining quest of my days. Had I been wrong? Had all the events of my life truly happened solely to prepare for the murder—yes, yes, I will say the word—the murder of Hershl Shveig?

"Isaac, you look ill. Please sit down, and I will make you some tea."

Sasha led me to the kitchen and lowered me into a chair.

"Will you ever forgive me for what I said?" she asked. "Please. I think perhaps it would be better if you just forgot that such words ever came from my mouth."

I said nothing as she moved about the kitchen, boiling water, filling the teapot, placing a full glass and a spoon before me.

"That was one of the things I learned from my meeting with Mr. Shveig, that I should no longer dwell on the violence of the past. If I do not look to the future, the present will be consumed by the anger that should have been forgotten long ago."

As she spoke, I became more and more confused. "What exactly happened between you and Hershl Shveig?" I asked. "Didn't he—?"

I began to tremble. Resting on the tabletop, my hand shook so violently that my spoon jumped and clinked against my glass. Hot tea splashed out onto my hand.

"Isaac, be careful! You'll burn yourself," Sasha said as she rushed to my side with a towel.

When she leaned in to wipe my hand, I grabbed her wrist.

"I thought he forced you to—" I said.

She laughed, surprised.

"Force me? That silly little man? Hershl Shveig could not force a pigeon to poop!"

I put my hand to my mouth, then ran my fingers through my hair. I stood. I paced. I returned to my chair. To do nothing was to sit with the thought that he had done nothing.

"Sasha, please tell me," I said. "When you said you did what you had to do to get the money—"

"Isaac, what exactly are you asking?"

"I thought you and he . . . That he made you . . . To get the money . . ."

She shook her head, still laughing lightly, though now it sounded more annoyed than amused. "Do you believe I have no resources beyond my . . . knish? This is how you know me?"

"But then what happened? You were so upset . . ."

Sasha shrugged.

"It is not much of a story. As I said, when I went to his apartment, he wanted to share his beliefs with me, so he read for me much of his translation of the Christian Bible. I was trying to be kind, in hopes of persuading him of the necessity of giving our money back. But the more I listened to his Bible, the more agitated I became. Finally, I told him it was very interesting, and that having lived in Jerusalem I found Jesus speaking Yiddish to be a very good joke."

"A good joke?"

"That's just what he said. I told him that in Palestine, Yiddish is thought the language of only the worst kinds of Jews, and no one could think of a worse Jew than Jesus. He didn't like that much.

"Then I told him I would be taking our money back. He sheepishly proposed an alternative payment method. To which I proposed that if he didn't remove his hand from my knee and give me the money I was going to knock his teeth out with his typewriter."

"Sasha, I—"

"I didn't hurt him; I didn't need to. He believed I would have, and that was enough. And I would have. Up until the moment I had the money in my hand and I walked out the door, I held a typewriter above his head as if I was a caveman with a stone.

"I was feeling quite proud of myself for several blocks. But then I thought of the pitiful look of fright on Shveig's weaselly face. His nose twitched and his eyes closed tight and tears dripped from his eyelashes. Before I knew it, I was weeping, hating myself for what I had done, for what I was prepared to do.

"That sad little man. What sort of life must he have had to abandon every belief he was raised with? What kind of trauma causes a Jew to stop being a Jew? I could have killed him, I would have if he had offered the least resistance. But he already looked broken in his eyes.

"And so I cried all the way home; not just for him but for what I realized I am capable of. When I was nearly back to the apartment I just couldn't see you and tell you what I had done.

"That was my state when you saw me. And then I watched you walk out the door with barely an emotion on display. I knew you were going out to do something involving your poems. And I realized I both hated you and loved you for it.

"It was at that moment that I came to know what I believe," Sasha said. "My earliest memories are of violence. And I have long known I am capable of it myself. I can no longer stand to be around it. I cannot allow my child to be exposed to it. If my father was here today, I would tell him to stop his killing, find another profession. I want no part of it. No part of death, no part of violence, no part of anyone who lives his life that way.

"After you left last night, I felt so grateful to have found you. You were born of the same violence that has shaped me, and yet you are such a gentle soul. You believed that I had been hurt, and yet you did not seek revenge. You simply went out and made a book. You are a creator, Isaac. Not the destroyer I sometimes fear I am fated to be. And I love you for it. I need you for it. How do you turn pain into words? How do you transform the violence of our lives into something beautiful?"

She wrapped her arms around me again, and in that moment I believed that the events of the previous hours had been a nightmare. Sasha held me and spoke my name—my Hebrew name, my holy name—and for the duration of her embrace, I almost believed what she believed about me: that I had been able to turn the rage burning deep within me into harmless rhymes.

"Yes, Sasha," I cooed to her. "Yes, we are all right now."

I swore that our lives together would know no violence. And that our child's life would be unlike any life that had come before: peaceful, protected, immune to the hatreds that had made us who we were.

"Tell me we're safe now," she said.

"Yes, my Sasha. Yes. The butcher's daughter can leave her father's shed at last."

We lived with this illusion of safety for nearly a week. The *kheder* boy within me looks back on that time now as a kind of funhouse reflection of the six days of creation. That first day, as Sasha spoke more of her desire to share a life lived against violence, we separated the light and the darkness in our future. The second day, spent rolling in our bed without a care for what Mrs. Goldstein would say, was simply heaven. The third day, we went to Coney Island, baking on the dry land and bathing in the waters. On the fourth day, we created the moon and the stars from a perch atop our tenement roof. The fifth day, we rode a horse-drawn carriage in Central Park and pretended it was a droshky in Kishinev; the sixth day, rejoicing in the creation of humankind, I put my ear to Sasha's belly and listened to our child, now thumping with life.

And on the seventh day, while we rested, there was a knock at the door. Two police officers were waiting behind it. They spoke English, so I stood back to let Sasha ask what they wanted. Her eyes went dark as they explained.

She said, "They want to know if the name 'Charlie Smooth' means anything to you."

"Why do they want to know that?" I asked.

Sasha repeated the question and put her hand to her mouth as the officers replied.

"They say it is related to the disappearance of a Christian missionary."

The larger of the two officers opened his notebook, flipped

340

through the pages. I needed no translation when he said, "His name is—or was—Hershl Shveig."

Sasha said, "They say Mr. Shveig has been missing for a week. Since Friday night." She listened some more. "They say Charlie Smooth is a criminal they've had their eye on for years. They say they picked him up snooping around Shveig's apartment. They say Charlie Smooth claims you can vouch for him."

"Tell them I know nothing," I said.

As soon they were gone, Sasha turned on me with sadness in her eyes. It was the look not of a butcher's daughter, but a murderer's wife.

"Isaac, what have you done?"

The Memoirs of Itsik Malpesh

tof

It did not take her long to pack. She said she would return, that she only wanted to be with her mother for the birth of the baby, that perhaps I should follow when I had saved sufficient funds, that she would be back once she cleared her head, that she was sorry but, for now, she could see no other way.

When her time away stretched to months, I wanted desperately to go to her, to find her. But then came the war, yet another war, and I felt more separated from Sasha than I had ever felt before.

For a year in New York I waited for further word. None came. I sent letters to 24 Yaponchik Street in Odessa, in hopes they might be passed on by her mother, if her mother was still alive. If she was still alive.

Soon I decided she could not be. From both Europe and Russia, there was no news but death.

Somehow, life went on. For others, at least. As for myself, I found it difficult to leave the apartment. For days at a time I would be consumed by the thought, the absurd thought, that Sasha might suddenly return. For the first time in my life, I did not even have the solace of poetry. Whenever I lifted my pen to compose, I became so convulsed with panic that the nib tore through the page.

Knobloch came to me one day, complaining that the police still were making inquiries as to the last known whereabouts of Hershl Shveig. As a known business associate of the missing translator, Knobloch was questioned endlessly.

"Malpesh, I don't entirely know what you've gotten yourself involved in, but the police have been all over this place since you left," he told me. "They're constantly asking questions about you and Hershl Shveig, and about some character called Charlie Smooth. I'm reaching the conclusion of a business deal and I need for all this to come to an end. Now, if it were up to me, I'd simply send the cops to bark up your tree. But the truth is, my sister still cares about you, and she doesn't want to see harm come to you."

"Rachel?" I asked. I hadn't thought of my erstwhile intended—had she truly been that?—in years. At the moment Knobloch said her name, I could barely form a vision of her in my mind.

"Yes, Rachel. You tell me you don't remember her, I'll break open your ungrateful head."

"I remember," I said. "Of course, I remember."

"At her request, I have a proposition for you: We are leaving New York. She wants you to come with us."

"Leaving New York?" I couldn't believe it. Why would anyone leave New York?

"Knobloch Industries is going under," he said. "With Shveig missing, his backers want to pull out of our agreement. Now I'm stuck with five thousand copies of . . . What the hell is that thing called? *Der Bris Hadash*. God help me. Five thousand copies, and no one to pay for them! I'm going to throw the damn things out in the street. Whoever wants them can have them. I just need them out of my sight. I'll have to sell the linotypes to cover the loss."

"What about the *Naye Yidishe Tsukunft*?"

"It's dead. Looks like I misread the tea leaves. Turns out Yiddish is not the future for Jews in America."

"What is, then?" I asked.

"Real estate," he said.

343

He wasn't kidding. With the money he made on the sale of the Knobloch Building, he was able to buy an entire city block in Baltimore.

"It's in the Jewish Quarter of the city," he said, "but it won't be for long. Jews don't want to live over fish markets anymore. They're moving out. And you know who's moving in? Black folks. When the war ends, they're all going to come back with a little money in their pockets. They'll move out of the country and need a place to go. Naturally the city will want to keep them all together. That's where I will come in."

"Who would think a Jew would ever build a ghetto," I said.

"We should have such a ghetto! Three towers around a wide open court. There's even going to be a swimming pool!"

"Does a tenement become a castle if you call the gutter a moat?"

"I'm trying to help you here, Malpesh. Come with us, help us look after it. It will be a good life."

True to his plan, the Knobloch Towers were finished just in time for black soldiers to move in with their families when the war ended.

I gave up New York reluctantly, with the feeling of too much left undone, though in truth I had nothing to keep me there except so many loose ends my life resembled the fringes on a pious man's prayer shawl. Sasha I knew would never return, but I held out hope that I might yet see Chaim again. My last message from him came in the form of a package on my doorstep. It was a box full of hardback accounting ledgers, identical to the one he used to do the Toy Shop's books.

Last time you made me leave town, I urged you to keep up your reading. Now I think you should stick to writing instead. There's always an accounting, Little Itsik. Fill up these ledgers when you need to see where you stand.

—Chaim

Once again I never got to apologize. Never got to say good-bye. I don't know what became of him. But I have diligently filled these notebooks he gave me. It is the best I can do.

In Baltimore, I went to work collecting rent, painting walls, washing floors, fixing the furnaces when the pipes got clogged. From time to time, deep in the basement of those towers with the furnace raging and all manner of noise floating down from the apartments above, I imagined I had never left the goose down factory in Kishinev. And just as in those days, I had the solace of words. Knobloch brought down his entire Library of Broken Dreams. In the back rooms of his office, we installed what had been the largest Yiddish library on the East Side in the shadow of an East Baltimore housing project, just as all the Jews were moving away.

As Knobloch had said it would be, it was a good life. Rachel came down to be his secretary. One day she informed me she had been in the Knobloch Building the night Hershl Shveig disappeared. Never underestimate the knowledge of a secretary, or the cunning.

"I will never tell," she told me. Not long after, she became my wife. "You see, it is *bashert*," she said. The word cut me as if she were a *shoykhet* spoiling his kill.

I made no more attempts to write poetry, and neither did I have cause. Ours was a long marriage, happy enough, but it wasn't much of a story.

Of regrets regarding Rachel, I have only one: She wanted children, but I refused, insisting we were too old by then. She saw through me and came to hate me for it by the time she died.

From her hospital bed she accused me, "You are still thinking of Sasha Bimko, I can see it in your eyes! Is that why you never gave me a child? Is that why I die alone?"

"Not alone," I told her. "You are not alone. I am here."

"When has your company meant anything but loneliness?" she said. "We shared a bed for thirty years, but I lived by myself every day of it."

"No longer," I assured her, "and never again. I will see you soon in the hereafter." To lighten the mood I added, "I'll be the one who greets you with laughter."

Rachel looked away from me for what proved to be the final time.

"Even now he speaks words written for her."

KNOBLOCH AND I HAD LESS to say to each other after Rachel's death. Near the end, she had told him everything about Hershl Shveig's disappearance, and he came to hold me responsible for the closing of Knobloch Industries, the heyday of which had been the happiest period of his life.

After my retirement from his employ, my frequent visits to Knobloch's library became exercises in verbal self-defense. For a time I argued that a Yiddish daily would have met its end eventually, but he waved this off as if I had killed the language single-handedly.

From then on we divided on every issue. Most heatedly, he became a fervent Zionist; the idea of a Hebrew-speaking Jewish state only made me feel that even with a homeland, I was nowhere at home.

Often in moments of nostalgia for the East Side and the world we knew there, Knobloch's mood would grow dark and belligerent. Once he shouted at me, "It wasn't just the Nazis, it was poets like you! What good did all your scribbling do to keep our *mamaloshn* alive! The Germans and the poets! Together you killed Yiddish!"

Knobloch lost much of his sense as he grew older. It would have been kind to ignore his irrational rages. But as I grew older, I fear I became unkind.

"You're right, it wasn't the Nazis," I told him, "it was Israel! Berlin put Yiddish against the wall, but Tel Aviv pulled the trigger!"

By then we had known each other for—could it be?—fifty years. He knew that what I said could not be separated from the fact that I missed my wife and that missing my wife reminded me of other losses, losses of long ago. There always remained in my mind a possibility that Sasha and our child, wherever they were, had survived Hitler, Stalin, and all the rest, had survived and perhaps returned to Jerusalem after statehood was achieved. But of course I never heard a word from Jerusalem or anywhere else in that desert land. I hated the place for its language and its silence.

Knobloch knew all this, but he threw me out of his office anyway. And I was happy to go. He and I seemed to realize simultaneously we were to each other only reflections of ghosts.

I began doing my reading elsewhere. I had finally learned my English by then—working in a housing project was a great education—and so perhaps for the first time in my life I wandered freely around the city in which I lived. No regard for Jewish neighborhood or not, I walked and stopped wherever I chose. In a bar by Camden Yards I learned about baseball, and in my conversations with men whose names I rarely learned, men who welcomed me with beer-buying American charm despite the difference of our origins, I sometimes felt a bit of the passion I had felt through Yiddish, through poetry, but none of the pain.

Every afternoon I spent hours walking through this city that—by accident? by *bashert*?—had become my home.

My favorite walk took me to the Inner Harbor, to feed the birds that gathered there every season of the year—pigeons, ducks, seagulls, the occasional goose lost on its way to Florida. In those days they were calling old Jews who made a similar trip "snowbirds," and I counted myself among them, not because I traveled—my traveling days were long done by then—but because I felt I spoke the

347

language of the graceful, trash-eating creatures that swept down from the sky.

Some days at the water's edge I spoke to birds as if they were the ghosts of my past. They flew as erratically as my memories now did, flitting in and out of view as if to taunt me. More than once I caught myself calling them by name. A smooth mallard diving for fish I called Chaim. A gull circling high above I called Sasha. A great white goose, overdressed for the dirty water, I called Hershl Shveig.

On my more lucid days, I would simply throw crumbs into the wind while calling out to all of them at once, "Birds! I knew your cousins! I knew your cousins! We were landsmen in Kishinev! I am sorry for my father's machine!"

With every handful, I hoped these birds had not read that part of our scriptures that visits the sins of the fathers upon the sons.

So go an old man's days. I never bring food of any sort with me as I leave the house for the harbor, because I know there will be along the sidewalks of Lombard Street an abundance of cast-off delicacies. What do the gulls care? My pockets lined with plastic, I stoop to fill them, then I continue on to the sea.

When I reach the water's edge, I pull the plastic bags from my pockets and turn them inside out in the wind. Up goes the electric orange of cheese cracker crumbs, the yellow of fried potato bits, the red and silver of torn ketchup packets, the green of—what it is exactly I cannot be sure.

The birds fly in and peck like madmen, biting out each other's eyes as if they mistake them for candy corn. Fluffs of white feathers join the turning eddy above me, and then as suddenly as it began the bluster disappears, letting the garbage fall as if dropped from an unseen airplane shedding reminders of the city as it ascends from BWI.

At such moments, though I long ago gave up on verse, I cannot help but compose a rhyme or two:

> *Across the waves to the Inner Harbor,*
> *A cool sea breeze hits*
> *It fills the sky with dirty feathers,*
> *shopping bags, bird shit . . .*
>
> *All that is unwanted, tossed aside*
> *Tasted, rejected, forgotten*
> *Clogs the nose of passersby*
> *With the smell of a world gone rotten.*
>
> *And deep within this cloud of refuse,*
> *an old man gets a notion:*
> *If this is air, no thank you, God.*
> *I'd rather breathe the ocean.*

Like the streets I walk to get there, the harbor is an empty, dirty place. Yet I return each day. How can I not? The water before me stretches everywhere, even places now gone.

ON A WHIM during one of my walks last week, I decided to wander by Knobloch's office.

I found men boarding up the windows and spraying orange paint on the sidewalk.

"Excuse me," I said to a fellow in a white plastic hat. "What is going on here? Where is Knobloch?"

"Mr. Knobloch a friend of yours?"

"Yes," I said, without hesitation, realizing suddenly that it was true, and that he was the only friend I had.

"I'm sorry, sir. But Mr. Knobloch is dead."

"Dead? When?"

"Two months back. These buildings belong to the bank now. They were all condemned during the insurance inspection."

I peered in through a gap in the plywood covering the window. Through an open doorway at the back of the shop, I could see bookshelves lined with spines in a dozen colors.

"Is Knobloch's library still inside?"

"I can't speak to that," the man in the white hat said. "I'm just here to prep for the take down."

"Take down?"

"This whole block is scheduled for demo. Next week. Don't you read the papers?"

Only then did I notice that my neighborhood was suddenly a ghost town. Had I been walking in a daze? Around me, the only living beings were construction—no, *demolition*—workers.

For days, I wandered as if stunned. What had happened to all the families in the Knobloch Towers? And what about all those books! Would they be lost?

I walked to the harbor to consider what, if anything, might be done. My friends the birds flew low above me and seemed to hover, calling to me.

Caw! they said. *Caw!*

I looked for no meaning in this until a newspaper blew across my feet. I picked it up, happy for the distraction, and was surprised when it brought a smile to my face. It seemed to be titled the *Free Jewish Voice*—the very name of the paper that had so long ago published my first poem! Only on closer inspection did I notice that it was not the *Frei Yidishe Shtime* I had known in Kishinev. It was, in fact, *Jewish Voice of Baltimore,* and because it was mainly a vehicle for advertising, it was indeed free, this last word printed larger than all the rest.

Caw, the birds above me sang. *Caw! Caw!*

I looked around, this way and that. I saw a Chinese homeless man pushing a shopping cart, and a black lady out for a stroll with a young fellow I guessed to be her grandson. When I read the title of the paper again, I had a dangerously humorous thought, as old men often do. I laughed until I coughed and coughed until I choked, and the lady and her grandson looked up with concern.

I waved to let them know I would survive. And then I decided to share my humorous thought with them so that they would not think I was insane.

Holding up the paper for all to see, I said, "I thought *I* was the 'Jewish Voice of Baltimore,' but it turns out there is another!"

Caw, the birds laughed above us. *Caw! Caw! Caw!*

The lady and her grandson walked on and left me alone to flip through the articles. A synagogue in Pikesville had a weekly Yiddish reading group. Another in Eutah Place was holding auditions for something called a "Klezmer Choir." And then I read an article about an organization of young people who collect Yiddish books.

God knows what they do with them, I thought.

Caw, the birds said above me. *Caw! Caw! Caw!*

How the world opens up when you know a new language. My entire life I have listened to the cries of birds, and naturally I have translated them into sounds sensible in my native tongue. In Kishinev, I would sometimes believe the condemned geese of Bemkin Down called out *hon, hon, hon* with their honking, and in Yiddish this made perfect sense. "Rooster!" they would shout, "Rooster! Rooster! Rooster!" as if, on hearing them say *hon*, "rooster," the goose pluckers would suddenly think they were denuding the wrong bird.

What a surprise that day to realize the birds of the Inner Harbor were speaking to me not in Yiddish, like most birds I had known, but in English.

Caw, they said again.

"Call?" I asked the birds.

Caw!

351

I looked down at my lap, to the Jewish newspaper and its story of trucks driving around the country to save Yiddish books. Then I looked to the end of the article, and I saw a phone number.

Caw! Caw! Caw!

"Okay, then. I will call them," I said aloud. The thought came as suddenly as that. I was as surprised by it as the birds seemed to be. They flew in spirals above me now, like a galaxy rising above the waves. I shouted to each of them as if naming the stars in a constellation.

"Do you hear, Knobloch? I will call and save the books! Do you hear, Rachel? I will call and save the books! Do you hear, Chaim? Do you hear, Sasha? Do you hear, Hershl Shveig! I will call! I will call!"

Caw! Caw! Caw!

"Sir? Sir?"

When I turned toward the voice, the black lady's grandson was standing beside me, staring down.

"Are you all right, sir?"

I tore the paper and put the phone number in my pocket.

"I am," I said. "Thank you."

TRANSLATOR'S NOTE

His plan was simple. As soon as they knocked the first wall down, Malpesh would wander toward the building, playing the lost old man. He would raise a ruckus, shout for a missing dog, fake a heart attack, do whatever he needed so that work might cease long enough for me to get in and out of Knobloch's office five, ten, who knows how many times. Having spent hours watching from his kitchen window, he knew the work site to the last detail. He said there was a wheelbarrow not ten yards from the building. As I ran forward, I was to snatch it up and then start wheeling books out by the dozens. We wouldn't save all of them, but I guessed several hundred at least might find their way to the waiting shelves of the JCO's book warehouse.

Malpesh had at first looked as enthusiastic as a ninety-three-year-old man could while he laid out his strategy. Yet when we took up our position on the synagogue steps to catch our breath, he seemed lost in his thoughts.

"Mr. Malpesh, are you sure you want to do this?" I asked. "I can do this on my own. There's no reason for you to go in there."

His face remained expressionless, then he nodded to let me know he had heard.

"Thank you for your concern," he said, "but there is a reason."

He reached into the breast pocket of his shirt and produced a thick square of paper.

"Now that you have read my notebooks, is your ability with Yiddish script improved?" he asked.

"Not much, I'm afraid."

"I will help you with the words you don't know."

He handed me the paper. It was Clara's great-grandmother's letter—a letter written, I now realized, by Sasha Bimko for Itsik Malpesh.

With his own pen, Malpesh had darkened a few of the faded lines, filling in gaps in a letter written to him sixty years before, though he had not seen it until now.

This is what I read:

> My dear Isaac,
>
> I am long overdue in writing to you. I only hope you have it in your heart to forgive me for leaving, forgive me for my silence, forgive me most of all for preventing you from witnessing the birth of our child. She is a lovely girl, serious looking like her father.
>
> One year old already, the baby is getting so big. I have named her Minah, for your mother. For my presumption, I should also ask your forgiveness. We have heard from Kishinev that offering this name is now appropriate. I hope that you were notified. Perhaps it should have been me to do so, but I could not bear it. I have spoken to you too often of death.
>
> I write this letter now while on the train to Birobizhan, which perhaps you have heard Comrade Stalin has designated the Jewish autonomous region in the east. I'm told it is like Palestine without the violence, so perhaps there Minah and I will find peace.
>
> I do so desperately want you to know that we are well. I can only hope that you will know without being told, that something in your poetic sensitivity will know it the way one knows the meaning of a poem, without words.

Nonetheless I feel I must explain—to you, to myself, to Minah, who will perhaps read this one day—why it is that I will not send this letter.

You would find this foolish and irrational, but I left New York not for any of the reasons you might suppose. It was not disagreement but agreement that drove me away. For I have come to believe what you have long tried to convince me. That we truly are bashert. That our love simply was meant to be. Some would find endless contentment in this, but I find something else, because the ripples that led to and move away from our inevitable love speak to me of a reality I cannot stand.

Have you ever stopped to ask yourself, Isaac, if it is bashert that we be together, what that truly means? Think of the misfortune that set our lives in motion and determined that they would one day intersect. Was it bashert that my gentle father should die like an animal in a slaughtering shed? Was it bashert that your family should be attacked so savagely on the day of your birth? Was it bashert that my first intended, my poor zealous Nachum, should be killed in Jerusalem?

Was this long unfolding of catastrophe necessary to bring us together? I do not know what happened between you and Hershl Shveig, but I fear the worst. And the worst involves another senseless death that somehow had to occur for us to be and remain together.

I ask you, Do you believe that God watches over us as your father once watched over his goose-plucking machine? Do you believe that we are moved through life as though on wheels and belts to be plucked and killed for purposes beyond our understanding?

That is what bashert entails, and I do not accept a universe that functions with such appalling precision.

355

I will not send you this letter because I know if I do, you
will find me. And when you do, I would fall into your arms
as autumn leaves fall from the trees, naturally, inevitably,
with no choice but to do what they were made to do. But
in finding me, we would once again say yes to bashert.
We would once again be strapped to God's awful
machine.

To all of this I must say, no. To a God that would kill so
many merely to bring two people together, I say, no.

Please do not think me a fool. I am not so naive as to
believe that no one will ever die needlessly again because
of our separation. Yet I do know that in leaving you, I will
never again wonder if my happiness has been purchased at
an unbearable cost.

If one day our daughter finds you, I will be pleased. But
as for myself, I know that to struggle against the violence
of this world, I must make my life a reminder that there is
nothing destined, nothing bashert. *If I can turn from a love*
that seems inevitable, perhaps there is a chance that others
will turn from its opposite, the hate that seems to know no
reason and no end.

Please forgive me for my decision. And know that my
sole reason for it is this: My ability to choose is all that gives
me hope.

> *Always,*
> *Sasha*

When I finished the letter, Malpesh took it from my hands,
folded it, and put it back in his pocket.

"I no longer know the meaning of *bashert*," he said. "I do not
believe it is fate that has brought you here with this letter, and I do
not believe it is destiny that I lost a family a lifetime ago just so I
could save Knobloch's library now. A family for books! Was there

ever a worse trade?" He forced a hoarse laugh, then struggled for breath as it turned into a cough.

"So that's a no?" I asked. "You don't want to go through with this?"

"No, it is a yes. I've wasted too much time on destiny. Today, all I can do is try."

As far as we could tell from our lookout on the synagogue steps, the work in the demolition zone was being directed by a mustachioed fellow in a white hard hat.

"The foreman," Malpesh said. "Him, I met."

When we saw the man in charge disappear into a Portosan at the edge of the work site, we knew it was our chance. We moved across the road at a quick shuffle, Malpesh gripping my elbow with one hand and his cane with the other.

Judging by the size of the three apartment buildings, I guessed, and Malpesh's observations confirmed, that they were scheduled for some kind of explosive detonation. The two-story storefront that had been home to Knobloch's office, on the other hand, apparently wasn't worth the dynamite.

A ten-man crew armed with shovels and sledgehammers sat at the ready as a backhoe and a bulldozer began to bring the building down.

"Are you ready, Mr. Malpesh?" I asked.

"*Beser a gantser nar eyder a halber chochem,*" he said. *Better a complete fool than half a wise man.* Then he squeezed my shoulder and added, "*Gey gezunt.*" *Go with health.*

"Be careful yourself," I said.

With that, I charged, looking over my shoulder as I went to see Malpesh moving toward the work crew. He stepped slowly, deliberately. It wouldn't do to have him fall and break a hip before he caused his diversion.

I was within range of the building in seconds. With the wheel-barrow just where Malpesh had said it would be, I sprinted for-ward, grabbed it by the handles, and steered through a gauntlet of Bobcats, rock crushers, and pickup trucks. Then I made it past the backhoe and through the newly cut opening into Knobloch's library.

Glancing backward, I saw Malpesh lift his cane in the air, his mouth open wide in a shout drowned out by the whine of a circu-lar saw.

Inside, sunlight poured through a hole that seemed to have formed in the roof with the demolition crew's first assault. I began loading the wheelbarrow with the closest books at hand. I didn't sort through them, I didn't look at titles. Every book here was somebody's dream, Knobloch had said, and I tried to grab as many as I could.

Just then the wall behind me began to shake. The backhoe's bucket tore through the bricks and moved downward, carving a line from the wooden roof to the concrete floor. I had thought Malpesh would have been able to stop them by now, but maybe something had happened. Maybe he had fallen and broken his hip after all. Or maybe the workers had seen him but ignored him. Whatever was happening outside, it was doing nothing to prevent books and bricks from falling like hail around me.

From beyond what was left of the wall, I heard a great revving of engines and then the creak and scrape of metal treads. The fangs of the backhoe's bucket tore once again through the the north wall, and then the whole structure seemed to heave inward, as if Knob-loch's library had suddenly and violently sucked in its breath.

I turned the wheelbarrow over and curled up beneath it, lower-ing it like a turtle's shell. All around me, it sounded as if the world was coming apart at the seams. Metal ground on stone, glass and wood smashed onto the concrete, bits of crumbled brick shot off the backhoe's moving treads and whistled through the air. Under the wheelbarrow's metal dome—my shelter? my grave?—I pushed a book against each ear and begged for the noise to stop.

When finally it did, I climbed out and found myself no longer inside a former back room turned makeshift Yiddish library. In fact, I was inside nothing at all. It was difficult to tell with so much debris in the air, but I now seemed to be standing in a field. In the sky above me, the sun was blotted out by torn pages and pulverized brick.

A gloved hand grabbed my wrist and pulled me forward. I coughed and spat and couldn't see where we were going, but soon I saw a line of workers on either side of me. A white hard hat pushed its way through the others.

"Think I got time for this shit?" The foreman pointed one of his hands at me as if it were a six-shooter. With the other he swatted his clipboard against his thigh.

"Just what in the hell do you think you're doing on my demo site? Do you know you are trespassing on private property? Were you in there trying to get those goddamn Hebrew books?"

My reply came out as a whimper, "Yiddish."

"What?"

"The books weren't Hebrew. They were Yiddish."

"I don't care if they was Swahili! You coulda gotten killed!" He shook his head in amazement. "You wanted the books, why didn't you just ask?"

I said nothing. It honestly hadn't occurred to me.

"What, just because we wear hard hats, you think we don't have a love for literature?"

He looked to the crowd of workers, waving his hands until it parted like a sea. Then he called out as if to no one, into the gray air.

"Where's the other one? The geezer?"

Malpesh emerged from the smoke and wrapped his wire-thin arms around me.

"You ought to have more sense!" the foreman said as he stormed away toward his trailer. "Both you clowns get outta here before I call the cops."

"I'm sorry," Malpesh said to me.

"I'm sorry, too. I should've gotten at least a few books out of there—"

In fact, I had not saved a single one. Even as the dust in the air began to settle, scraps of pages flew all around us. Words and letters landed on my shoulders and in my hair. Slivers of paper clung to Malpesh's glasses as though he were the man of honor in a ticker-tape parade. He brushed what was left of Knobloch's library away, then examined the remains on his fingers.

"I am sorry not only for the books," he said. "I am sorry for everything."

We stood there for a moment, uncertain in the general mayhem of the demolition site which was the way home. Malpesh held my arm as if afraid we might become separated in the cloud of paper that now descended upon us. We didn't budge until the foreman was again behind me, shooing us away with his clipboard and shouting over the rumble of machines coming back to life.

"Jesus fucking Christ. Let's have *Tuesdays with Morrie* somewhere else, all right? I got buildings to take down here."

IT WAS AS THE KNOBLOCH TOWERS fell that day that Malpesh and I conceived of this translation. *Bashert* would be a tidy way to label such an unlikely series of events and their outcome, our collaboration, but after reading Sasha Bimko's letter, I cannot hear the word *bashert* now without beginning to count up all the major misfortunes that had to occur in order for the ending to a story to be happy in even a minor way.

Watching three buildings vanish while sitting with a man from, to use the photographer Roman Vishniak's famous phrase, a vanished world, I could not help but wonder if his story wasn't so inaccessible, after all; if the questions surrounding the life of a man who believed himself to be the last Yiddish poet in America might be relevant to anyone chasing love, losing love, or growing old with the fear of being forgotten.

More selfishly, I also wondered if by translating Malpesh, I might help right a wrong I had committed. I wondered, despite my lie of silence regarding who and what I was, if completing this translation might convince Clara Feld to give me another chance.

As we sat there that day, with great clouds of ash and the dust of pulverized concrete rising into the sky above Baltimore, having another chance was what I wanted more than anything in the world.

I met with Malpesh several times through the year that followed. As Isaac Bashevis Singer was with his translators, Malpesh was invaluable to the process of bringing his words into a new language. Throughout our collaboration, I endured all the expected frustrations of working with an elderly poet set in his ways. And yet there was real joy in it as well.

For much of that year, Malpesh remained unsure if he should, through me, initiate contact with Clara. He was pragmatic about it: After all, who was she really to him? Who was he to her?

"What would you do if one of your *Mayflower* ancestors knocked on your door tomorrow?" he asked me. Since learning that I was not a Jew, he had become convinced my forebears were New England bluebloods. He never believed it when I told him they got off the boat from their Old Home after he did.

"I would be to her family only a burden, I am sure," he said. "They would think I am looking for money. That I have medical bills to pay. That I want to move in with them in New Jersey."

All that aside, the truth was that he thought meeting Clara would kill him.

When finally he admitted to himself that he was sure to die soon anyway, he became eager to meet the descendants he had never known.

Clara took much more convincing—first that I was telling the truth about who Malpesh was, and then that it was a good idea. I had gone back to school by that point, and Clara had taken over my job at the Jewish Cultural Organization, which in the end was sorry to see me go.

By the time she agreed to meet him, both her Yiddish and her Hebrew were better than mine. (She has been a great help in preparing this manuscript, I should add, and has since forgiven me for my know-it-all tendencies early in our relationship.)

Clara's first encounter with her ninety-five-year-old great-grandfather was as bittersweet as you might imagine. Malpesh was by then living comfortably in the Baltimore Home for the Hebrew Aged (paid for in part by a generous translation grant I requested and received from the trustees of the Charles Smooth Family Foundation, without whose assistance this collaboration would not have been possible). His fellow *toyshovim*, inmates, as he called them, were a bit too pious for Malpesh, but among them he found a few Yiddish speakers and was, he said, happy enough.

About an hour into their visit, Clara suddenly excused herself and walked quickly into the hallway from his room. I followed, and found her crying.

"He's such a sweet old man," she said. "I don't know how to tell him."

"Tell him what?"

"My great-grandmother."

"What about her?"

"She's alive."

"No."

"*Emis*," she insisted. "It's true."

Clara told Malpesh before we left that day. Told him that Sasha

362

Bimko had spent the better part of the last two decades in a facility much like the one he now called home.

"In Jersey?" Malpesh asked.

"In Jerusalem," Clara said.

She told him Sasha Bimko was lucid and active, with a reputation for doing things her own way.

"In the family they used to say, 'She is a very *intelligent* woman,' which meant no one could get her to do what they wanted."

To all of this Malpesh listened intently and nodded when Clara finished. He patted her hand as she apologized for not coming to see him sooner, for not telling him about Sasha before anything else.

For his part, Malpesh appeared taken aback by the news, but insisted he was not surprised by it.

"I can think of no other reason why I should still be alive," he said.

EPILOGUE

SASHA BIMKO'S ONE-HUNDREDTH BIRTH-
day celebration represented about as broad a cross-section of contemporary Israeli culture as one can hope for these days. Crowded
into the community room of the Ezrat Avot Senior Center, just
beyond the walls of the Old City, with a view of the Mount of
Olives, the Dome of the Rock, and the surprising bulbous spires of
the Orthodox convent of Saint Mary Magdalene, some sixty well-
wishers sipped ginger ale from paper cups while conversing in a
half-dozen languages. It's not every day in East Jerusalem that one
sees black-hatted Hasidim, veiled Muslim women, and even a Russian nun or two joining in on a family reunion of American Jews.
But the guest of honor had apparently made as great an effort to
gather people to her heart as the father of her one child had made
to gather poems in his valise.

An easel at the front of the room stood crowded with thirty years
of press clippings. Three years after my college graduation, my Hebrew
was by then all but forgotten. I asked Clara to decipher the most recent
news item for me.

"It's a tribute," she said. "Just published today." She looked at the
byline. "Oh, I know this guy. He's like the Jimmy Breslin of Jerusalem.
I didn't know Ima Sasha was so famous!"

She read the article aloud for me, translating as she went:

OCTOBER 3, 1999 / 23 TISHRI, 5760.

With her history as both an early settler
of Mandate Palestine and among the first
Israelis to speak the phrase "Palestinian
rights," activist Sasha Bimko, born on this
day in 1899, straddles the heroic past and
the post-heroic future. Once a fighter for
Jewish land, she has for thirty years fought
on behalf of non-Jews who wish to live
peacefully, and with full rights, within the
borders of Israel. In the process, she has
made friends and enemies equal in their
fervor, with each faction sharing a passion for discussing the work of this singular woman, while holding vastly different
opinions of it. As peace talks continue this
week, we hope her spirit will be with the
leaders of both sides . . .

A voice behind us interrupted Clara's translation. "It reads like an
obituary, doesn't it?"

A little woman in a wheelchair was suddenly at our side. Sitting
rumpled in pink sweater and blue pants that stopped above her ankles,
she wore a smile that seemed to want to rise out of the chair. Behind
her, another woman, much younger, greeted us with a friendly nod.
She was one of several Filipino nurses pushing wheelchairs around the
room.

"Israeli journalists think elegy is the only form of effective prose.
I suppose they have had their practice, but when the time comes, I'd
prefer to be memorialized with a limerick or two."

She spoke English with an accent that seemed at once Yiddish,
Russian, and Israeli. Of course, it was all three.

"Is this my Clara?" she asked.

366

Clara stepped forward and kissed her gently on the top of the head.

"Hello, Ima Sasha," she said.

"I was just talking to your mother. I hear you have come with an admirer or two." She looked to Clara's side and, seeing me there, acted surprised. "Ah, and here he is! I take it you are the young man who found my Isaac?"

"Yes, ma'am."

"And where is he?"

"He is still in his room."

"Making himself handsome," Clara said.

"He will be down soon."

She nodded. "The family thanks you," she said, looking at me seriously for an instant before letting the smile return to her face. "One day when you are part of the family, you may thank yourself."

"Ima!" Clara said.

"An old woman may say whatever she likes! Haven't you heard? I go off my rocker from time to time. For this I want to ask your forgiveness in advance. I move in and out. One hundred is a strange age. We are susceptible to all the madness of a century's end, but we can endure none of the celebration. You watch: very shortly I will tune out as if dead. When this happens, my nurse is kind enough to wheel me to the side of the room. Better I should not be in the way. So before I disappear, let me tell you: I am very glad you are here."

With that her nurse wheeled her away, toward other guests. Two Haredi women wearing wigs and floor-length dresses stopped briefly at her chair and seemed to compliment her blouse. A young Arab couple approached shyly and simply said hello. Then a woman I first took for a Muslim in full *hijab* floated across the room and stood before the wheelchair like a shadow. Only when she stooped to speak to Sasha did I notice the cross dangling from her neck. An Orthodox nun from the convent down the hill.

Sasha smiled at the sight of her, reaching out to touch her face.

367

When the nun leaned into her touch and grinned at the contact, I wondered when the last time a physical connection had been offered to her so freely, so unself-consciously. The nun seemed to be telling a story when Sasha's eyes glazed over.

"*Ver zayt aykh?*" *Who are you?* she asked in an unexpected burst of Yiddish. A frantic tone had crept into her voice. She turned to look at the nurse. "*Veist ikh a monashke?*" *Do I know a nun?*

Apparently the Filipino nurse knew some Yiddish herself. She answered with full comprehension of the question.

"Miss Bimko, Mother Catherine is an old friend. She's here for your birthday." She moved her hands through the air, taking in the room. "*Everyone* is here for your birthday. You have so many friends."

Fear flashed through Sasha's eyes. She reached for the nurse's hand.

"All right, Miss Bimko. Let's go sit quietly for a while."

The nun nodded with understanding as the nurse wheeled Sasha to the side of the room. She stopped the chair beside a table dressed with flowers.

"I'll be right over here if you need me. You just rest a bit."

I watched her from a distance. Sitting without expression, her eyes closed every few minutes and stayed closed long enough that her nurse twice returned to reach down and touch her hand, a subtle check of her pulse.

Sitting by my side, Clara told me what more she knew of her family's story. As soon as her daughter was old enough, Sasha had sent her to America, where she began again the immigrant cycle as if she had not been conceived in New York. Sasha had never spoken of Itsik Malpesh to her daughter, and so the daughter never knew to look for him on the East Side or in East Baltimore, or anywhere else. Even as she married and had children, even as her children had children, one of them a girl called Clara, no one knew of Malpesh. Even when Minah Bimko died, not too young, but not too old, no one knew that her father still lived.

Sasha for her part left Russia in the 1950s to return to the vineyards she had known with Nachum Minkovsky in her youth. Upon arrival, she was dismayed to discover the violence she remembered had only become worse.

"Since then, her life has been about changing that," Clara told me. "Most of the family lives in the States, so we've tried to bring her over. But she would never leave. I haven't seen her since my grandmother's funeral."

The following year, when the worst violence the country had seen in a generation began, it was some small solace that Sasha wasn't there to see it. As the Second Intifada swept Israel, Jews killed Palestinians, Palestinians killed Jews. When the violence spread beyond Israel to include an upsurge of anti-Semitic attacks around the world, both sides managed to look at the suffering they had endured and summon up an archaic word to name it, a strange word that sounds the same in any language, perhaps because terror needs no translation: *pogrom.*

Clara was relieved her great-grandmother did not live to witness any of this, though of course she did not need our protection. Watching Sasha Bimko on the hundredth anniversary of her birth, I had no doubt that she knew enough of the past that nothing in the future could ever come as a surprise.

Sitting at our table perhaps fifteen feet away, I studied her as she moved in and out of consciousness, connecting this fading woman with the bright-eyed girl who had been the prime mover of a poet's life. With hair sparse enough that I could see the curve of her scalp, with arms so thin I could plainly discern the mechanics of how bone joined bone in her wrists, wearing a corsage that made the tiny woman appear to be hiding behind a pink-and-yellow shrub, there never was a muse more beautiful. She still wore the scar of Kishinev on her forehead, and it only made her more so.

I was watching her perhaps too closely, so closely, in fact, that I did not see Malpesh make his entrance. He was midway through the room when I noticed him. I jumped up to take his arm, to guide him to our table, but he knew where he was going. Wearing a blue tie and a gray tweed jacket, his hair combed back, slick just enough to hold, he walked deliberately, his cane clicking on the tile with every stride.

He called her name before he reached her, then called it again as he stood by her side. When she made no response, he simply pulled a folding chair beside her and began to talk.

He had only spoken a few words when the nurse appeared and said, "I'm sorry, sir. But Yiddish sometimes upsets her."

Malpesh nodded and switched to English without an instant of hesitation. I moved away to give them their privacy, and again I watched. He spoke at length and with obvious joy, a smile never leaving his face, his hands often rising and falling in illustration of what appeared to be a riveting tale. He had never spoken this language to her before, but it didn't seem to matter.

After twenty minutes or so, the party could wait no longer. The lights lowered. A cake floated through the crowd on a tray. Clara's mother lit a fire hazard's worth of candles and waved me in the direction of the reunited couple, bidding me to bring them closer, the long-estranged Adam and Eve to half the people in the room.

I walked toward them and was about to suggest to Malpesh that they move in to join the crowd of family and friends, all of whom were waiting in hushed anticipation.

Before I said a word, he was on his feet. He leaned his cane against the wall and left it there. Then he took Sasha's chair by the handles, and began to push.

Her eyes opened with the sudden movement of her wheels, and she turned slightly to see who had woken her.

"Isaac?" she asked.

"Yes, my love."

"Is it time to go home?"

"Not yet, my love."

Squinting toward a table glowing with candles, surrounded by silence in at least four languages, Malpesh gave his best guess as to what would happen next.

"I believe it is time to sing," he said.